HAVEN'S WARRIOR

MORGAN CHRISTENSEN

Also by

Morgan Christensen

The Matriarch Chronicles

Book One: The Maiden's Husband

Book Two: Haven's Warrior

Short Stories

The Healer's Wife

Praise for

The Maiden's Husband

"Some of the best worldbuilding I've read in a long time."
— Andrew Valenza, Author of *Empire of the Void*

"A strong social commentary about social norms and breaking gender barriers with fantastic worldbuilding."
— Ella M. Hayes, Author of *Witch's Brew*

"This story is one I think about every single day since I read it. ...Nearly every character in this book will pull on your heart strings or will tear your heart out completely. ... this story was incredible and I know I will be reading again in the future."
— Jade Nioma, Author of *Fate's Tether*

"Get the tissues ready! Truly love this book and need time to process..."
"This book was absolutely amazing!"
— Zaylann Flynn and Megan Turner, Authors of *To Be Damned: Arawn's Realm*

To the women throughout my life for demonstrating our power to me. Your guidance, strength, and perseverance are never forgotten.

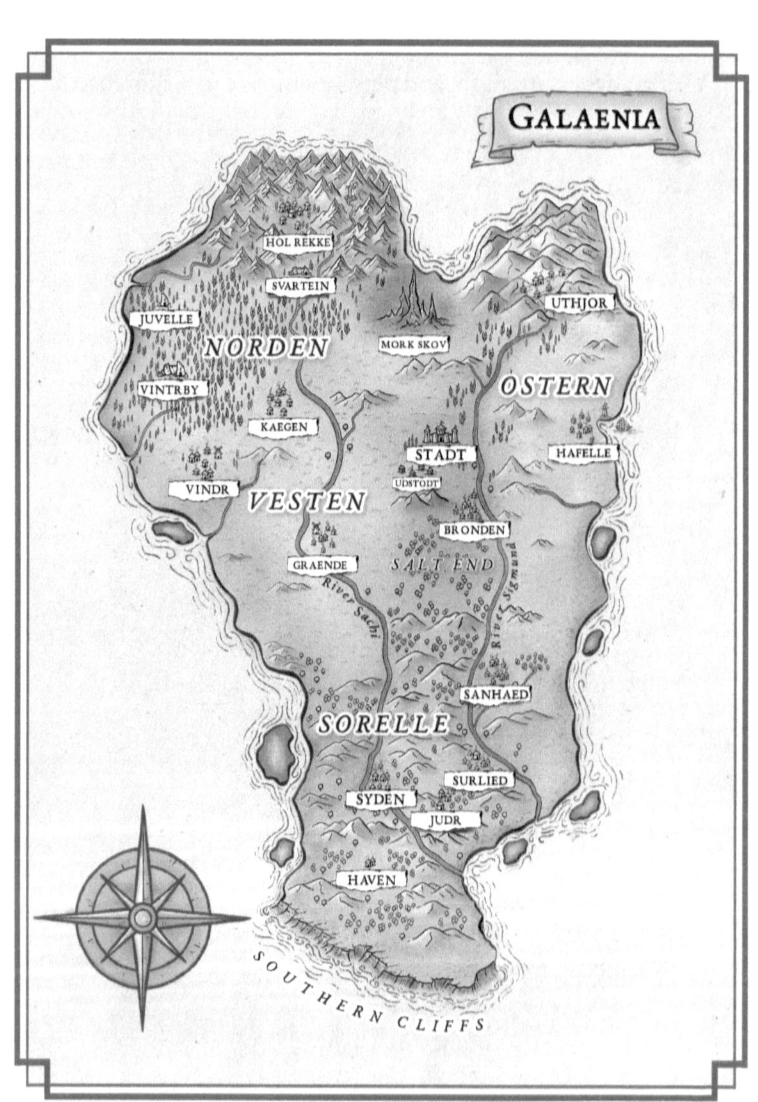

GALAENIA
HOL REKKE
SVARTEIN
JUVELLE
NORDEN
MORK SKOV
UTHJOR
VINTRBY
OSTERN
KAEGEN
STADT
HAFELLE
UDSTODT
VINDR
VESTEN
BRONDEN
GRAENDE
SALT END
River Sachi
River Sigmund
SANHAED
SORELLE
SURLIED
SYDEN
JUDR
HAVEN
SOUTHERN CLIFFS

CONTENT WARNING

Haven's Warrior is a dark epic fantasy with **adult language** and **mature content**. Harsh battles unfold with **blood and gore**, and despite the matriarchy's best efforts, **violence** remains an enduring reality. Galaenian law prohibits **sexual violence**, yet cruel acts still occur on page. The All-Mother weaves **death** into the fabric of life, encompassing all its forms, including **infant and child loss**, making it an integral part of the story.

Reader discretion is advised.

Previously

In book one of *The Matriarch Chronicles: The Maiden's Husband*, Raegna lost her mother to illness and was finally free to divorce the husband she'd been forced to marry—Bai. But when warrior men raided their village, Syden, Raegna kept Bai at her side as they had a common goal: protecting their daughter.

After swearing an oath as a priestess to lift Syden's fallen—including her dear friend, Pinar, and her daughters—Raegna guided her family to the next village, Judr, to spread word of the attack. Judr's Matriarch, Viona, was skeptical of the tale of men wielding blades. Raegna remained compliant to stay in the Matriarch's good graces. Meanwhile, she befriended the village healer, her warrior wife, the Matriarch's youngest sister, and the sister's quiet husband. She also found work for Bai in another woman's household. The tension between Raegna and Bai seemed to ease, though their past kept their hearts at a distance.

The peace Raegna had built for Matriarch Viona collapsed when Bai was wrongly accused of assaulting the woman he worked for. Ignoring Raegna's cries for mercy, the Matriarch ordered Bai to be flogged. But Raegna's testimony cast doubt on the accuser's claim. It struck a chord with Viona, who gathered a scouting party to see about Syden's destruction.

Unknown to them, Pinar's husband, Naleem, had survived the raid with his two sons and his brother, Hadwin. The warrior men had taken them captive, along with many Syden men, and brought them to Haven, a secret war camp run by the raiders and their leader, Thenalious. Days after their arrival, Thenalious offered Naleem a deal: serve in his household as caregiver to the sons born in Haven, and his family would be protected. Naleem agreed—on the condition that Hadwin was given the same role.

The brothers soon learned that Haven's cruelty ran deeper than raids and capture. Women were imprisoned and forced to birth the raiders' sons. When a girl was born, Naleem intervened before Thenalious' lover, Reynold, could kill her. Thenalious spared the girl, but pulled Naleem aside and demanded he swear allegiance and warm his bed. When Naleem refused, Thenalious and Reynold assaulted him and took his eldest son's life as payment for the newborn girl's. Naleem fought back, but Thenalious' wrath did not end there. As one final cruelty, he dragged Naleem from his surviving family and forced him to join an attack on Judr.

Back in Judr, the headless bodies of Matriarch Viona and her second sister appeared on horseback. Raegna sprang to action, helping the Matriarch's sister, her husband, and two nieces escape over Judr's walls. She aided Judr's Commander and warriors in defending the village and drove the raiders into retreat. But not before rescuing Naleem and facing Thenalious, unaware that he had killed her daughter before Bai's eyes.

Though Judr was victorious, many were lifted, including Raegna and Bai's daughter. The village was left without a Matriarch, and a trio of mourning parents turned messenger once again. Raegna and Naleem resolved to journey to Stadt to warn the Queen and rally her warriors and the Maidens. Despite her feelings, Raegna invited Bai to join them, though she knew she had every right to divorce him as she'd always wanted.

"We leave for Stadt," she said at once. "You ... You can come with. Or you can stay behind."

His voice rumbled like the thunder outside, distant and forlorn. "I'll come with."

Raegna coiled at the sound and the acknowledgment, the willingness. Yet some small part of her, deep within her, bloomed with relief ...

"Very well."

Prologue

Raegna

"Shield-Priestess! Shield-Priestess!" Incessant knocking pounded against the front door. Raegna dropped her fork, and it clattered against the table.

"Shield-Priestess Raegna! Are you there? Please, it's urgent!"

Naleem bristled across from her, his dreary brown eyes wider under tousled, darker brown, wavy hair. His ash skin paled. Like two bewildered children, he and Raegna turned to Banu and Jora. The old healer's gray hair shifted as she threw a cloth over her shoulder with a huff. Her wife, clad in armor, peered behind her as she marched to the door.

The hinges creaked when Banu opened the door and put a fist on her round hip. "You better have a good reason for interrupting breakfast. These poor people finally had peace from all this grief."

A young woman's voice squeaked from the threshold. "The Shield-Priestess was asked for. Is she here?"

Despite every muscle bidding her not to, Raegna stood from her chair and approached. "I'm here. What is it?"

The woman, barely in her twentieth year, took her in with doe eyes and small, parted lips. "Shield-Priestess. It's Lady Iida."

Iida. Raegna's heart slammed into her chest. "They've found her?"

The woman paused and fumbled with her fingers. "No. Well … actually … it's her husband, truly. He brought her back, but apparently, they were attacked during the invasion and …"

"Asmund is here?" Raegna stepped forward. "Where is he? Where is Iida?"

"They're in the temple." The woman pointed west. "He's asked only for you."

"Are they injured?" Banu piped up. "Why weren't they brought here?"

Raegna was already gathering her boots and shoving them on. A hard pit settled in her stomach, and her breath came short. Something wasn't right. But in recent days, her muddled head struggled to work through thoughts beyond the here and now. All that mattered was that her friends were in Judr and they asked for her help.

Banu and the woman's voices faded as Raegna strode for the door. Naleem watched her the entire way.

The floorboards thudded as Jora took a step to intervene. "Raegna—"

"I'll see them." Raegna trotted out and down the porch steps, giving the messenger woman a curt nod. "Thank you for telling me."

"Now, just wait a minute!" Banu called after her. "Didn't you hear what she just said, girl? Raegna!"

I heard what she said. My friends need me.

In Syden's massacre, Raegna didn't go back for Pinar. Truthfully, she couldn't after being knocked unconscious—but she didn't think about her friend when she and her own family fled. Never turned back for her.

Iida escaped over Judr's wall with a babe on the way and her husband and nieces in tow. And what did that cost Raegna?

Flashes of blood streaked through her memory like lightning in the dark. Raegna shook her head and kept on, the temple in sight.

Old rain hung thick in the air, with gray clouds rolling overhead. Saws and hammers echoed from reconstruction work in the distance. Footsteps crunched the gravel path behind her. The young woman panted at her heels. "Shield-Priestess—"

"I know where the temple is," Raegna told her without looking over her shoulder.

"Yes, but—"

Raegna halted, and her messenger nearly collided with her. A crowd had gathered before Gaea's temple, its domed wooden roof rising above them. People murmured to each other, craning to view the doors—a great difference from the air of four days ago, when every family in Judr had a loved one to lift.

Raegna's hand tightened around her sword hilt, and she wove through the gathering, losing her messenger and paying no mind to whispers and stares. At the top of the steps before the double doors, Matriarch Ase and a few warriors Raegna barely recognized waited. Each of them turned at the sight of her.

Matriarch Ase's thick, black hair was bound in a half-braid behind her head. Smaller braids clung from her temples and stretched back while the rest plumed above her shoulders. She raised her chin to Raegna's approach, her brown skin deeper under the gray clouds, her palm on her sword pommel. "Shield-Priestess."

The title marched over her tongue with more respect than Raegna could accept. She couldn't meet the brave Matriarch's eyes. "Iida is inside?"

Ase didn't falter, standing straight with the furs over her shoulders, giving her bulk. "Yes ... Her man carried her out of the woods this morning. He startled the patrols. Once he reached the temple, he asked for you."

With a nod, Raegna pushed forward. "Thank you. I'll see them now."

Before Ase could utter another word, Raegna entered the temple and let the doors shut behind her.

Morning brought light to the world within its walls, but the temple's interior lay still and dark. Smoke from the recent liftings stifled the air. Torches hung from sconces adjacent to the pew rows. Three priestesses congregated at a distance from the stone pyre at the head of the temple, their heads bowed, scarred palms held out as they faced the platform.

Raegna focused on what lay before her, and her limbs became iron as her heart folded in on itself.

Iida rested on the stone bed, unmoving. The old blood that covered her skirts wrenched Raegna's stomach, even from a distance. Dark hair that was once a vibrant brunette fell in tattered, dull locks. Over time, Iida's features had sunk, and her skin had turned gray.

Kneeling by her side with his back to Raegna was Asmund, ever attentive and loyal. His mouse-brown hair went in every direction, and his wide shoulders trembled. He placed an arm over another incredibly small, lifeless body.

Raegna's breath caught in her throat at the sight of the babe, sprawled on his belly against his mother's chest, eyes shut. Her gasp dragged Asmund's attention to her. A few scrapes and cuts dotted his light fawn skin. Purple and red bruises flecked his soft brow and cheekbones. Tears flushed his blue eyes, though he didn't seem to notice them.

"Priestess," he whispered. "You're here."

Raegna swallowed hard. "Of course. You sent for me. I'm so sorry, Asmund."

He took a shaking breath. "Will you lift them?"

Her throat pinched. She'd overseen enough liftings to last her a lifetime. "Yes. Yes, of course. We must act quickly."

A storm stirred in Raegna's core as she worked, collecting the driftwood and leftover wildflowers from the previous liftings. The flowers cracked and crumbled in her hands, but some held their shape as she placed them around Iida and her babe.

Asmund helped, adjusting driftwood here and there, the two of them moving in a mindless state before Raegna's fingers grazed the torch at one end of the altar.

As the wood scraped the pads of her fingers, she halted. Flames flickered above her hand and numbed her. Clenching her jaw and blinking to clear the fog in her mind, she pulled the torch out of its sconce and returned to Iida.

Asmund stood, rather lost, once he'd rearranged every bit of driftwood and every crumbling flower. The wood fell with faint clicks. The flowers shifted in his fingers with hushed cracks. He looked to Raegna for the next direction.

"Say your goodbyes before we send them off," she whispered. "You've done well for them."

A visible shudder coursed through him, and Asmund knelt beside his wife again, placing a hand over hers and their babe. He pressed his forehead to hers and rested there before settling a lingering kiss on her cheek. And then the babe's.

Asmund wobbled on his feet and let the tears stream down his face. Drawing a breath, Raegna swallowed and moved forward. She draped a sheet over Iida and the babe and lowered the flames to the driftwood.

"Go in peace, my friend," she said. "May Gaea receive you both in Heimelle, where you belong. You will be greatly missed."

The fire grew around the stone bed and reached Iida's body, consuming the sheet and the flesh beneath it. More smoke climbed the temple walls and traveled through the open dome in the ceiling. The priestesses in the congregation sang to see the souls off.

Having returned the torch to its place, Raegna joined Asmund's side and took his hand in hers.

***

Raegna guided Asmund with a hand pressed between his shoulder blades. Her sword hilt tapped her hip with every step, and she focused on it to bury the sharp throb in her chest. The crowd at the temple parted for them. No one spoke to them on their way through.

The Matriarch's house was no longer Asmund's own, and Raegna braced herself to explain Ase's rule. But when they veered from the great house's path, Asmund proceeded under Raegna's guidance without objection. Raegna's feet brought her in the direction she needed, and soon she helped Asmund up the healing house steps.

Inside, Banu pulled out a chair for him opposite Naleem. Neither man glanced at the other across the table. Raegna stepped back with Jora as Banu inspected Asmund for injuries. She turned his hands over, then cleaned his palms and knuckles. Blood trailed down the insides of his arms, though it did not originate from a cut.

Banu wiped away the grime, her expression hard. "We heard about everything, boy." Her brow rose when she looked into his hazy eyes. "Is there anywhere within you that aches? Any bleeding where there shouldn't be?"

Asmund shook his head, his gaze distant. A deep frown dragged Banu's mouth down before she sighed, cleaned his face, and tended to the bruising. Raegna noted the broken skin along his knuckles, coupled with bruises from the impact of punches. Whatever he'd done, he'd fought hard. But against swords and axes? And without skills of his own?

Banu had Raegna and Jora turn away when she examined Asmund's torso. Once he was covered, she rubbed a thumb over his cheek. "It'll be all right. If anything shows itself, tell me. For now, I'll fix you something to eat."

Asmund stared at the floor when she retreated, his hands limp in his lap. Raegna brushed her fingers over his shoulder, then joined Banu at the cauldron.

"Iida is—"

"I know, girl." Banu squeezed her wrist. Worn russet wrinkles softened with her expression as her warm brown eyes roamed over Raegna's face. "I'm glad you brought him here. We may be the only women he has to claim his care."

"He doesn't have a family?" Raegna asked, searching her memory for any mention of them when she spoke with Iida.

Jora walked up behind her. "His wife was all he had. Maybe you can offer to take him to Stadt with you. It might give you a little more credit than just Ase's sealed message. The former Matriarch's brother-in-law. Now a widower."

Raegna considered this and nodded. "If he wishes. I couldn't ask him to leave his homeland."

A sob stretched across the kitchen, and the women turned. Asmund curled in on himself, tears streaming down his cheeks. His arms wrapped his chest as he heaved and trembled at the table. Raegna stepped forward, but Naleem moved faster, draping a blanket over Asmund's shoulders.

As Asmund wept, Naleem pulled the blanket closer around him. "Shh. There now. It's all right."

"She's gone." Asmund's teeth clenched, and the blanket quaked over him. "I tried to … Our babe … I tried to keep him warm."

"You did well." Naleem knelt before him, rubbed his arm, and folded a hand over his. "Shh. You did well."

"I tried," Asmund repeated, his sobs growing heavier.

He doubled over, and Naleem embraced him, holding him still. A light in Naleem's eyes flickered. A deeper ash color returned to his face. When his hair fell over his brow, he brushed it back to see Asmund better. "Shh. It's all right. You did well for them."

The women looked on, frozen in place, staring at the men among the clutter of candles, book piles, and hanging herbs. Banu swallowed before returning to her work with more haste. Jora sighed and went to aid her wife with dinner, squeezing her arm before placing a gentle kiss on her cheek.

With a hand wrapped around her sword hilt, Raegna drew a shaking breath. A sheen of tears veiled her eyes, but she'd cried enough in these last four days. She would let the men weep. They should not have to endure this much pain. Those who dealt it would pay.

From her position in the kitchen, Raegna glanced into the healing room and marked her husband's form. The doorframe covered most of him, but his blond hair peeked from the corner of his pillow. Underneath, his arm folded to prop up his head. His back, once a warm beige, was exposed to the air as the healer wanted, crisscrossed with crimson gashes.

Raegna's grip tightened around her sword. The edges of the leather grip grated her palm. She yearned to reach him, her heart twinging. Adabelle's warmth flooded her. She would not want Raegna's wrath to persist and would not want her father denied the protection she would give the other men. He would join them in Stadt, and Raegna's sword would get him there.

PART I

Chapter I

Raegna

THE CRACKLING FIRE ECHOED past the orange-lit trees. Beyond them, pitch-black swallowed the forest. Raegna trained her eyes through the darkness, though the void stared back at her. She drew her knees to her chest, propping her sword against her thigh with the hilt in her opposite hand. Her skirts warmed her legs, and her chestnut hair buried her neck, curling below her shoulders.

Circling the fire, the men slept on furs. Naleem lay on his side across from her, and Asmund stretched on his back to her left. Raegna had her back to Bai, but knew he would be on his belly. The gashes from his flogging were healing into scars, but he kept the habit to avoid hurting himself further. Raegna watched as the flames stretched between them, then scanned the wood and listened for any threats. She'd long since learned Bai wasn't one.

Summer was steadily changing to fall, and the late hours came with cooler temperatures. The popping flames brought some relief as the smoke pricked her nostrils. Raegna pulled her sleeves over her white palms, one wool hem scratching along her priestess scar. An owl's hooting caught her attention, but an owl was harmless unless she and her friends were mice.

There would be less danger on the narrow roads to Stadt. Raegna chose them to avoid outlaws. Keeping watch would be more a comfort than a necessity, though none of them slept without someone on guard, with the terror of Haven's raiders at the forefront of their minds.

Dirt shuffled on the other side of the fire. Raegna turned to Naleem as he jolted, then lay back, still, with his eyes wide open.

Sitting up, Naleem scanned his surroundings. He marked the other men and met Raegna's gaze. Something terrifying rested on his gaunt face, the firelight hollowing the space beneath his brow and his stubbled cheeks. His muscles were taut, and it took him a few moments to return to himself with a heavy sigh.

Raegna shifted her weight, her hair falling from her shoulder. "You're safe."

Naleem looked over the ground. "I know. Am I the first awake?"

Raegna nodded. Then, on cue, Asmund's murmuring sounded. His head lolled to one side. His lips parted with the whimpers they knew well. Naleem rose and crept to him. He knelt and shook Asmund's shoulder.

"Asmund." He spoke as if to a child. "Asmund, wake up. It's all right. Wake up."

Their timid friend stirred, eyes still closed. Not quite out of his slumber, a sob broke from him. Naleem sat back and drew the furs closer to him. "Shh. Everything's all right."

He even brushed Asmund's mouse-brown hair from his forehead and remained beside him while he trembled. Raegna's heart sank, and her throat tightened. She wasn't sure what pained her more: imagining what horrible dream turned Asmund into a frightened boy, or Naleem's everlasting nurturing.

"Ada ..." Bai's voice carried from behind her. Raegna winced at the pain striking through her chest and peeked over her shoulder.

Bai twitched in his sleep with his brow knitted. His lip quivered, and tears escaped through his eyelids. "Ada, no."

He might as well have driven Raegna's knife through her. Most nights, he wept until someone jostled him, but he'd never said her name before.

Naleem moved to meet him, but Raegna stopped him and got to her feet. She didn't have a plan as she knelt a foot away from Bai. Prodding him with either end of her sword might not be the right thing to do. Raegna reached and merely pressed her fingertips into his arm. His muscles were tight beneath her touch.

"Bai. Hush, Bai." The soothing tone Naleem might have practiced was nowhere in her voice. "*Bai.*"

He gasped, gold eyes blurred with tears as he took her in. His irises and warm beige skin absorbed the orange of the fire, while his tears reflected the light. At once, Raegna retreated to her self-appointed post and let her gaze settle back on the flames. In her periphery, Bai didn't move, frozen on his stomach.

Naleem craned to see over the fire. "It was just a nightmare, Bai. It's all right."

Bai rolled onto his side, his back to them. Tears burned Raegna's eyes as she glared into the black forest. Broiling heat bubbled in her chest at such a speed that she took a sharp breath. Her nails dragged over the leather on the sword hilt.

Asmund quieted, and Naleem gave his attention to her. "Have you slept?"

Raegna thought of not answering, but Naleem didn't deserve her contempt. She shook her head.

"Try to sleep," he suggested. "I'll keep watch."

"I'll just wake in a few hours anyway," Raegna countered and placed her chin on her bicep to view him. "Like all of you."

Naleem gave her a faint, sad smile—a knowing, fatherly one. "You're our wagon driver. I prefer you to rest. Even for a few hours."

Raegna hesitated. Sleep meant nightmares, and all of them proved that. But her eyelids drooped at the very mention of it. The pile of furs beside her was so soft and inviting.

"I'll wake you at the first sign of danger," Naleem assured her. "Some ravenous squirrel or something you can protect us men from."

Asmund half-smiled beside him. Raegna dipped her head so they wouldn't see her quirked lips. She surrendered and lay down.

"All is well." Naleem went for his furs and dropped them over her. He placed himself between her and Asmund, bending a knee to his chest. "We'll get to Stadt, and those in our dreams will be avenged."

***

The late afternoon sunbeams shot through the forest canopy. The creaking of the old wagon's wheels used to be as irritating as a cat's yowling, but Raegna could tune it out, and the sound had become as troubleless as birdsong. Though even the birds had an agitating aspect to their voices. Atop the wagon, steering her horse, she could look up and pick out every sparrow and finch that darted through the tree branches.

Their tiny talons clung to the bark as the trees danced. Their rushing between boughs and trunks was like the tide's push and pull, but with a rhythm all their own. Fall breezes sent the changing leaves fluttering to the ground.

Bright oranges and dull reds and browns used to excite Raegna. Autumn meant the celebration of Leaf Fall Gift, and as a little girl, she would anticipate feasts and gift-giving. In recent years, the season was spent cheerfully searching for the perfect gift to make Adabelle's Leaf Fall more memorable.

Raegna constricted the reins in her grasp and held on to the memories, refusing to let them bring her sorrowful tears. She grounded herself with the thud of the horse's hooves and glanced at Naleem beside her. His gaze drifted along the colorful leaves above them. After escaping Haven, what went through his mind? What had he suffered? If she grieved over Pinar and her children, what could Naleem be going through?

Imagining never soothed her, so she turned her attention to the back of the wagon where their supplies bumped with the wheels. Among them sat Asmund, with his arms wrapped around his drawn knees, with only his slanted nose above them. Mouse-brown hair fell against his brow and temples while his eyes cast up at the sky, mirroring the blue above the autumn foliage.

Bai sat up with his back to all of them, blond strands lifted by the faint wind from his crown and past his nape. His plain shirt concealed his scars, but Raegna knew there to be red and pink crevices from his shoulders to the small of his back. Even from the driver's seat, she noted how his muscles tensed as he gripped the wagon edge and let his feet dangle over the end.

"Watch over him, girl," Banu had warned before they left. "My healing can only do so much. A man who has suffered such pain and violence needs a different tonic."

Yet Raegna was unsure if she could give it to him. Even if she could, Bai hardly spoke anymore, reverting to how he used to be—completely silent around her. Only now, he did not even give her worried glances or troubled frowns. No, now he would not look at anyone or anything in particular, still entranced in that dreary daze he had been in since Adabelle's death.

Raegna faced the road ahead. Her heart squeezed, and she blamed him once more, blamed him for everything.

Though the fact remained, he had tried to save Ada. How could he not? But in his condition, he'd been unable to, and it could be tearing him apart from within.

He'd had every opportunity; he was there. He was there to protect her. Adabelle could have been here with them now. He was there ...

And Raegna was not.

She winced when she bit her cheek. "Naleem."

Naleem jumped in his seat and turned to her. A fog dissipated behind his eyes. The spark emerged along with an attentive interest in the arch of his brow.

"Could you spread the map, please?" Raegna asked.

Nodding, Naleem twisted to reach their supply in the back of the wagon. He retrieved the map, rolled up and bound by leather ties. Freeing it, Naleem unrolled it for her. "Are we on the right road?"

Raegna scanned the route she chose in Judr. The choice was based on avoiding the main road for as much of their journey as possible and thus avoiding outlaws. But as soon as they drew close enough to Stadt, she would have to direct her horse toward it. Raegna traced the path that would fork, but there had been no forks on their road in days.

"We should be." She fixed her sight forward. "It shouldn't take another day."

Naleem frowned and rolled the map. "Food is low. If we don't reach Stadt soon, is there a village we can stop at?"

"The closest village to Stadt is Hafelle," Raegna explained. "That's a four-day ride north-east. Bronden is two days away, but we would be backtracking. If it came to it, we could hunt or set snares to keep on our path."

Naleem tied the leather around the map. "We can't waste a day. Hunting would slow us down."

But we are of no use to Sorelle if we starve. Raegna bit her tongue. "We could cut rations, then. But Stadt shouldn't be more than a day away."

Naleem remained silent with the rest of the men, not looking at her. "Gaea willing."

She had to be. They would not have gotten this far if She wasn't. As a priestess, Raegna was still green, but she had to believe that.

Morale dropped even as they neared the city. Deep within her, doubt seeded from the missing fork in their route. But they saw every landmark from here to Judr. They had to be going the right direction.

Raegna glanced at her cargo again. Asmund drew his shawl around him, resting his chin on his knees. Across from him, Bai readjusted and sat with one leg bent and the other folded beneath him. He kept his eyes down and allowed his back to be pressed against the wagon wall.

What a sad group they were, all of them headed toward Galaenia's great capital, a city none of them had seen before, and only for the darkest circumstances. What was sadder was that they may not make it. Raegna's doubt grew with the pang in her stomach, already prepared for her next ration. They could starve if they didn't stop, and they could not stop …

As Raegna's chest tightened, the thundering of horses' hooves boomed ahead. Each of them looked up over the path to find its source. Raegna's mare pricked her ears. The hooves became louder, and a team of two black horses turned a corner and cantered straight for them. They hauled a black carriage with a driver in dark violet.

Raegna waited for the driver to realize their wagon stood in her way. Instead, the driver brought her whip to the horses and urged them on, shouting a command to them. The horses picked up speed.

"Um" was all Naleem could manage to express his concern about being trampled.

Clicking her tongue, Raegna veered her mare to the side as the carriage was upon them. The black horses whinnied and bolted ahead, their feathered headdresses bouncing. They trotted down the path before the driver halted them and the carriage pitched forward.

Raegna and the men looked on as the driver grumbled curses, hopping out of her seat. She was a small and thin woman, bitterness and fury etched into her large eyes, with wrinkles like stained parchment. Clad in the deep violet dress, the skirt shortened for climbing carriages and saddles, she held her horsewhip above her head.

"What in Gaea's bloody name do you think you were doing sitting in the middle of the rotten road like that? Don't you know this is a private road?"

"I—This is a road to Stadt," Raegna said.

"Daft wench," the driver muttered. "This is a private road—on private, *royal* property. The main road is five miles west!"

Royal property? "My apologies. We're just looking for the gates to Stadt. If you could direct us, we would truly appreciate it."

"And have a pebble on the path confuse your direction and send you back here?" The driver sniffed, her nose turned up.

Then a settled female voice came from the carriage. "What is going on out here?"

A woman in an elegant dress emerged from the door and stepped to the ground. She stood tall—perhaps as tall as the men in the wagon—and had a long, strong face and narrowed eyes with lids that dipped over jaded, dark-brown irises. Her olive skin, which complemented the faded yellow and orange leaves around her, was framed by cascading braids of black hair. Her plump lips curled down as she raised a black eyebrow at her driver. Her dress fell about her in a deep violet like the driver's, though the fabric shined far more exquisitely and was far more beautiful than anything Raegna had ever seen before.

The driver turned to her and lowered her head. "Forgive me, Duchess Elmba. These common folk took up our entire path, spooking the horses."

Duchess. It could not be. The Duchess of Galaenia was second-in-command to the Queen, acting as an advisor. What were the odds that the Duchess herself would happen upon them on this road? Or that Raegna would take the wrong road ...

Duchess Elmba hardly acknowledged her driver as she beheld the hungry group of travelers in a wagon so pathetic compared to her sleek carriage. "What is your business on my road?"

Raegna struggled for words, or how to converse at all. She gaped like a fish before the Duchess, unable to believe how their luck had changed. Her mother's teachings resurfaced about making impressions and showing her worth as a lady above all else. Raegna straightened and lifted her chin.

"My Duchess, forgive us. We did not intend to trespass. I believed myself to be on a route to the main road. We are headed for Stadt. We have news of brutal attacks done to Sorelle by rebel men. See, I have a message from the new Matriarch Ase."

She dug into her pocket and retrieved it. "This bears the former Matriarch Viona's crest, though she was lost in an attack. The people of Judr elected Ase to take her place. We were sent because we have all been witnesses to these attacks and even the rebels' base itself. We wish to present this message to Her Majesty and avenge our fallen."

Duchess Elmba blinked slowly. "Bring it to me."

Raegna nodded and moved to drop down from the wagon, but the driver stepped in and snatched the parchment from her. Frowning, Raegna drew back and allowed her to deliver it to the Duchess.

Elmba's eyes fixed on Raegna's palm. "You are a priestess."

"Er, yes, my lady," Raegna stammered, displaying her scar. "I mean, Duchess. I—My husband and I were the last free survivors of Syden. I took it upon myself to lift the poor souls who perished. We could not leave them."

"Hm." Duchess Elmba flipped the envelope in her hand. "It is one of Sorelle's crests. Yet I would rather break the seal with Her Majesty ..."

It would reach the Queen. Raegna's heart lifted and an aura of relief and excitement rose from everyone on the wagon. The weeks of anguish, mourning, and worry would all be worth it. They would see their home and families avenged.

"I will have you stripped of your weapons," the Duchess said, "and one of your men will ride in my carriage."

This Duchess was quick to the point, but the things she may have seen or the risks she'd taken as a noblewoman surely made her that way. She wanted one of the men in her carriage for her security, but which one?

Raegna looked at the three in her wagon. They must have looked pathetic before the Duchess of Galaenia. Any unknowing eye might see them as a very mismatched family, or a lot of tramps and their madam on their way to start a brothel in Stadt. No wonder she noted Raegna's scarred hand, the mark of a priestess. Only Naleem and Asmund returned her gaze.

"Preferably your husband, priestess." The Duchess' thin, dark eyebrow arched. "You did say you survived with your husband. Is he among you?"

Before Raegna could think to answer, Bai raised his voice. "I'm here."

Duchess Elmba examined him in the wagon as many women in Judr had. Unlike those women, who measured him by physical appearance, the Duchess seemed to scrutinize his very soul, her dark eyes boring into his as he faced her. Bai stared back, his eyes uncaring, the color of gold coins. His blond hair fell over his forehead in a tousled mess and his sinewy shoulders set back. Raegna grimaced at his daring will, and shame tingled from her neck to her cheeks. Did he not know who this woman was?

"Very well," Duchess Elmba said. "Come, step off the wagon and sit with us. Then we may return to Stadt. Hilde, be sure he has no weapons."

"Yes, your grace." The driver, Hilde, squared her shoulders as she watched Bai stiffly climb out of the wagon. He waited in front of her, and she patted him down, lifting his shirt and running her hands down his legs. Bai glanced about at the birds flitting from branch to branch above them, lip pouted in boredom.

When Hilde declared him safe, she stepped aside so he could follow Duchess Elmba into her carriage. Before he did, the Duchess turned to Raegna once more. "He will return to you unharmed, priestess. And this"—she lifted the sealed parchment with Viona's crest—"will stay with me until we have an audience with Her Majesty."

Raegna nodded, for what else could she do? Duchess Elmba gestured for Bai to board her carriage with the door open wide for him. Inside, through dark curtains and cushions, sat the figure of another man, though Raegna could not depict details. Bai disappeared into the carriage, sitting across from him. Duchess Elmba followed, shutting the door behind her.

Praying Bai would make a better impression on them, Raegna surrendered her sword and knife to Hilde and let the driver search her. She scrunched Raegna's skirt along her legs, tugged at her sleeves and belt, and made her flush with an abrupt patting along each breast. Naleem and Asmund were searched before Hilde was satisfied, now she had a hunting bow, arrows, two knives, and Raegna's sword.

"I won't be taking you any farther down this road," she hissed at them. "I'll show you where the main road is, and you may see how daft you are."

Raegna scowled at her as she tossed their weapons onto the driver's seat beside her and took up the reins of the great black horses. This time, they started at a trot rather than the rushed canter, their hooves plodding along the dirt path. Raegna turned her mare at a pace behind them and prepared herself for this redirection, rolling her eyes.

The black carriage rocked as it meandered down the road—and it was hard to believe Bai sat alongside the Duchess of Galaenia herself. More surreal was that Matriarch Ase's message was in the Duchess' hands.

Raegna thanked Gaea for this chance. It had to be Her will alone that brought the Duchess to them. Though their journey was not over just yet.

Naleem tensed beside Raegna, watching the carriage with as much intent. "I would have rather seen it to the Queen ourselves."

"We will," Raegna assured. "The Duchess is second to the Queen. This is the best thing that could happen to us."

He snorted and did not relax. His unease was understandable, especially for Raegna, who'd brought such news to those above her status—and had been dismissed. The Duchess could wave them off just as easily as any Matriarch. But although Duchess Elmba had a similar authoritative aura about her as Matriarch Viona, something else in Raegna told her this was the right path toward vengeance. Straight to the Queen without having to jump over the obstacles of a hierarchy.

Hilde led them back the way they came until they reached a covert path through the brush and low branches. Pine needles scraped the carriage and wagon, scratching at Raegna's bare arms and tangling in strands of her hair. Soon the trail cleared of overgrowth and the branches retreated. Raegna's mare nickered with relief and shook twigs from her mane.

They followed the carriage before they came across the fork in the road. Hilde took the left, winding westward when Stadt was north. Raegna was sure it was, though she'd made a mistake by taking them too far, so who was she to say? At least the misguidance had brought them to the Duchess.

As the forest grew less dense, the trees' numbers decreasing the farther they went, other hoofbeats echoed on either side of them. Raegna searched the forest. A rider followed them at a distance, her brown horse catching the light with every step. The bright, spring-green blanket beneath its shining brown leather saddle fluttered as she adjusted her seat, the gold stirrups glinting with each sway of her legs. Metal armor clanked to the beat of the horse's hooves, and when the wind caught the rider's spring-green cape, it billowed behind her. Her silver helm caught the sun as she glanced up, and her braids tucked underneath shifted slightly with the movement.

Raegna's heart skipped. At first, she thought this woman might have been a Maiden, but the Maidens' colors were bright blue and black. This had to be a royal guard here to protect the Duchess. On the other side of the carriage, another guard rode a gray horse. The men noticed the riders, too, looking between them.

"Should we be worried?" Naleem asked.

"I don't believe so." Raegna kept her eyes on the road. "They are only here for her protection. I think they have been here this whole time."

"Then why was she worried about our weapons?" Naleem protested. "And taking Bai?"

"I'm sure she has her reasons. It's a dangerous world for someone like her to go, without taking precautions."

The guards gave them no particular attention and rode along, keeping their distance. But as the path grew wider, they edged closer. Raegna paid them no mind either, thinking that an escort for the end of their journey might prove immensely useful.

The road became a vast path of dirt and gravel dug out beneath the pines that towered over them. The guards flanked the carriage, and their horses' tails swished in Raegna's mare's face, but at least it kept the bugs away. The trees dwindled to just a few young firs as they traveled uphill, the horses lowering their heads with the effort to climb.

"This is your main road, priestess," Hilde called over her shoulder.

A distant hum greeted them as they breached the crest of the hill. Raegna and her rag-tag group could look out over the spread of land before them. Their jaws fell open.

Stadt stood miles ahead of them—great stone walls taller than redwoods containing an enormous expanse of towers, and buildings with rooftops and balconies that jutted above the wall's watchtowers. Before the gates sat wood structures and tents that made up the impoverished community, Udstodt.

The city stretched from east to west and disappeared northward with the faint silhouettes of elaborate castle towers. The Queen's palace, Vakkar Hold. Behind that lay the city's backdrop, the jagged mountain Mork Skov, colored in charcoal and a tint of deep green from the pine. A stark image to behold beyond the glittering city; one that placed a pit in Raegna's gut.

They'd made it.

Chapter 2

Hadwin

MUFFLED SCREAMS RANG THROUGH the darkness. Then a single cry echoed through Hadwin's bones, pulling him from sleep. A woman's scream that came with a pained, struggling shrill. Hadwin snapped his eyes open when a hand shook his shoulder.

"Had, wake up."

He stared at Naleem, who knelt over him as he lay on the fur rug. Despite everything that had happened to them, Naleem's eager face was devoid of all sorrow. Hadwin blinked up at him. "Naleem?"

"Shh." Naleem put a finger to his lips and nodded toward the flickering fireplace. "Let them sleep."

Hadwin tracked his gaze. Dakarai, Estrid, and Cadoc slumbered in a pile before the fire. Hadwin's heart skipped at the image of his eldest nephew and niece. Did he not witness their blood spilled? And how was Naleem with him?

The room was their home in Syden—the main room with a fireplace, a table, and a wide-open kitchen. All the children were alive and sleeping beside him. His brother stood before him. "Naleem ... What happened?"

Naleem chuckled. "It's all right. We'll show you before these little ones come to life. Come on." He pushed himself up and went for the bedroom.

Hadwin looked back at the children, his chest caving at the thought of leaving them. Would he ever see them again?

"Hadwin, come on."

Hadwin rose to his feet without his own bidding and followed Naleem to the candlelit bedroom. In the room blurred by haloed light, he stopped before the bed. Pinar rested with her back against pillows, cradling a swaddled babe, who cooed at her.

Pinar greeted Hadwin with a smile. "Hello, Hadwin. This is Nalani."

Hadwin fixed his sight on Pinar, taking in her soft features beneath pale white skin. Silver hair fluffed within a braid despite the exertion of the labor she'd endured. "Pinar. You're here ..."

Her smile grew, and Naleem sat next to her, kissing her cheek. "Come meet her," he said.

Though Hadwin had moved involuntarily before, now his muscles were stone. He opened his mouth to speak, but his jaw unhinged with the speed of thick honey.

Two shadows appeared on the other side of the bed, and an ax flew from their wake. Hadwin's heart raced but his body held firm. The ax's blade struck Naleem's shoulder, sending him to the ground in a spray of blood, speckling Pinar's cheek where he'd kissed her.

A figure appeared from one shadow, a large man with long, rust hair and bulking shoulders beneath a long beard. Reynold. He lifted a sword over the bed and drove it through Pinar's belly. Crimson burst over her lips before he snatched the babe, holding her in the air by her throat.

The children screamed in the other room, raising the hairs on the back of Hadwin's neck. Still he could not move. The second shadow revealed Thenalious, who held his hands behind his back, his chin raised with a neutral expression until a smirk twisted under his black, short-cropped beard.

Screams walled Hadwin in—with only that smug look within hazel eyes in his sight.

He woke up in a sweat, his heart still ramming into his chest. His arms and legs were lead.

The foreboding timber walls of the caregiver's room loomed above him, the bed across the way empty since Naleem had been taken away weeks ago.

Hadwin forced himself to take a deep breath. Cadoc curled into his side, snuggled against him. With a heavy arm, Hadwin reached and ruffled the boy's black hair. A faint blue light lined the bottom of the door. If they did not hurry, Else would start crying in the nursery next door. Then the entire house would erupt with angry men at the door.

Still shaking off the nightmare, Hadwin rose and gently shook his nephew. "Time to wake up, Cadoc."

The boy groaned when Hadwin picked him up and carried him out of the room.

He checked the hallway. Sometimes there were other early risers he did not wish to greet. With Cadoc's face buried in his shoulder, he crept from the bedroom to the nursery a few steps away, the floorboards squeaking under his feet. The door did not creak when he opened it slowly, careful not to disturb the slumbering little ones inside.

Rows of small beds lined the walls on both sides, and cradles stood tucked in the corner. Hadwin set Cadoc down on the floor on top of a wolf hide. The boy rubbed his eyes and yawned.

The morning light was not bright enough to breach the cradles, so the youngest of the nursery dozed. Hadwin hovered over Else's cradle, watching over her as she slept. So pink and new—her button nose wrinkled on her fleshy face before she went still. What a miracle she was to have survived this long in this cruel place so laughably called Haven. Being spared by her monstrous father was lucky enough, yet despite the terrors that surrounded her, she was alive.

Gaea must truly have something in store for you, Hadwin thought.

She at least gave him hope that they might all be freed. For now, they would remain here, and he would take her to her mother morning, noon, and night.

Hadwin scooped Else out of her cradle and held her, just as Pinar had showed him with his nieces and nephews so long ago.

The dull pain of her memory struck him, but he braced himself against it.

"Come along, Cadoc." Hadwin offered his nephew a hand and guided him back through the door.

Else did not stir as they shuffled downstairs through the hallways, past the huge dining hall, and out the great house doors. She curled against Hadwin's chest, perhaps cherishing the embrace of another human in her sleep. But Hadwin had no time to enjoy this as he briskly walked the path to the old horse barn on the southernmost end of Haven.

The sky hung pale blue over the orange and brown treetops and patchy tent arches, gray clouds fogging the dim light. A few birds broke into song in the trees. In the distance, a faint, stringy plume of smoke wafted from a stale fire just outside a cluster of tents. Someone must have done a poor job of putting it out before turning in for bed. Last night after supper, several groups of men had caroused around the campground in drunken stupors. But this morning, fewer bodies were strewn about than usual, sleeping wherever they'd fallen with their ale.

Hadwin kept details like this in mind, which could come in handy should he ever find the right moment to run.

He and Cadoc reached the brow of the hill before the old barn and beheld its tilted shape before descending toward it. An autumn breeze drifted past them, and Hadwin thought the barn might topple over with all of Haven's women inside. Some of the women might have been glad for that. The dark wood walls splintered and groaned as the seasons changed, and the growing cold stiffened what was left of its beams.

Hadwin pushed the door open and peeked in at the shivering bodies inside. The women rested in moldy straw with nothing but shriveled rags on their backs. Their hair stuck up in tangled messes or dangled in crazed waves about their shoulders. Some slept in piles, huddled together to keep warm. Others sat up, whispering and watching over their slumbering sisters, savoring the peaceful morning while they could. Their breath rose in steam.

Hadwin never surprised them when he entered their domain. He searched the room for Else's mother, Talia, who sat in a far corner alongside Farah, a woman Hadwin knew not to bother with questions or chatter.

"Good morning, m'ladies," Hadwin said in a whisper as he handed Else to her mother.

"Good morning, Hadwin." Talia took her babe, her pale daffodil hair falling about her shoulders, draping the dull gold in her skin. As she prepared to nurse, she glanced at Cadoc and gave him a warm smile. "And good morning to you, too, Cadoc."

The boy grinned and nodded.

Hadwin ruffled his hair and then noticed how Farah sat with her legs folded beneath her, while another young woman slept beside her, her head on Farah's lap. The woman's image took him off guard, causing a tiny gasp to catch in his throat. Unlike the other women, she appeared healthy, well-fed, and groomed. A common forest-green dress clung to her body as she lay on her side. Her honey hair fell in curls about her face and neck, framing the soft angles of her jawline and curved cheekbones. Faint brown freckles spotted her light sandy skin along her thin nose. She slept as if she were resting under her own mother's protection, her thick lashes barely flitting with her eyelids.

Hadwin struggled to find words again. She might have been the most beautiful woman he had ever seen.

"What are you staring at?" Farah hissed at him.

Hadwin flinched. "I'm sorry. I just ... Who is she?"

Farah scoffed and rolled her obsidian eyes at him, leaning over the girl with an arm wrapped around her small shoulders. Her rich, soil skin was a sharp contrast to the girl's warm tones.

"She has not told us her name yet." Talia shrugged as she nursed Else. "Poor thing has been frightened, and rightly so. She came from the recent raid and has been hiding in this corner ever since they threw her and a few others in here."

Of course, the men had returned from a raid weeks ago with only a trivial bounty, much smaller than what they'd stolen from Syden. "But why haven't I seen her before?" Hadwin asked.

"All she has done is weep and sleep under the hay," Talia explained. "She wouldn't even speak to us and has just started to come around, thanks to Farah."

Farah shook her head. "Just needed a little coaxing and gentle touch, is all. She's been through much."

Hadwin looked past her initial beauty, and Farah was right. The girl's eyelids had swollen from her tears, and circles banded under her eyes. There was a flush to her cheeks, red from her crying and dry from tear salt. Dark-brown eyebrows lifted upward in a permanent, worried, and anxious expression, even in sleep.

Hadwin was gripped with the urge to take her far from here and keep her safe somewhere in the woods. And he didn't know who she was.

"She'll grow comfortable with us," Talia assured him.

"And she doesn't need men gawking at her to do so," Farah snapped.

Hadwin averted his gaze. Beautiful as the new woman was, Farah was more fearsome. His shoulders slumped as heat rose from his chest to his neck. He was supposed to be a man these women could trust, not the same as the others, who slept in their tents outside, lusting for the company of a young woman like this one—the first Hadwin had been drawn to in a long time.

Once Talia had finished nursing Else, Hadwin would always let them spend as much time together as they could before he had to gather the babe, bid everyone a better day, and lead Cadoc back to the nursery.

The sleeping girl did not wake before he left. But even if she had, what would he have done? Perhaps frighten her with his presence, though the other women would assure her he meant no harm.

Was he truly considering how he might grasp the woman's attention—here, trapped in Haven? The days when that might have been possible were long gone. Haven made the old days feel like an absurd fairy tale. It was as if the camp was the only normal home he'd ever known; the only home in the entire world.

Everything else seemed so far away. Nonexistent, even. After two raids, why was Haven still intact and not destroyed by the Maidens already? Did the villages of Sorelle mean so little to Galaenia and her Queen?

The dull pain in Hadwin's chest returned, and he ground his teeth. Though the pain had eased, it never vanished, and perhaps never would. Grief, never so sharp since Pinar and his nieces were killed. Now the heartache was caused by the loss of Naleem, who did not return, even as a prisoner with the raiding party—that is, if Thenalious had forced him along at all. He might have been slaughtered.

Hadwin's eyes burned as his throat closed and his molars ached from the pressure of his jaw. There was no time to be consumed by mourning and nightmarish memories. He had to keep going. With his head higher, he cradled Else in one arm, took Cadoc's hand in his, and headed to the great house to endure the rest of the day.

Chapter 3

Raegna

A S THE CARRIAGE AND wagon clamored down the hillside, Udstodt appeared just before the city gates. Beneath the great stone walls stood dark wood buildings, which bustled with people. Passing tilting houses with thatched roofs, they entered the village outskirts. Pitched tents served as living arrangements, with small groups, some with children, guarding their few belongings as they watched the traveling party.

A distant hum became a crescendo of voices down the main road where the rickety houses grew denser.

"So this is Udstodt." Naleem gazed on either side of the wagon. "A little bigger than I imagined."

Raegna nodded, marking the unorganized placement of the tents and short buildings. "Stadt is a hard place to live if you don't have the coin."

Those with dreams and ambitions in the great city but nothing to show for it landed in Udstodt. The village structures piled on top of each other the farther the party rode—many of them residences for poor families, but more of them were shops, smithies, saddleries, inns, and taverns.

The entire population congregated on this market strip before the gates, with merchants hawking, women in plain common dresses darting about their business, and men in tattered shirts and pants herding crowded livestock or collecting goods for small households, sent by their wives if they had them. Beggars took up corners and alleys, their eyes following the Duchess' carriage as it passed.

Shadier characters eyed the party with scrutinizing gazes. Women who donned dark fabric cloaks over worn leather and steel at their belts. Criminals and bounty huntresses, perhaps, though none would bother the carriage with the two armored guards beside it.

Raegna and Naleem scanned all sides of their wagon. Asmund lifted his head over the wagon wall.

As Raegna looked about, a particular house stole her attention, and her brow furrowed. The building was more sound than most, with two stories and a wide porch. A dozen men leaned against the railing or sat posing on the porch steps, which might have been an ordinary scene had they laced their shirts. But all lounged with their chests exposed to the passersby, their sleeves lazily rolled up to their biceps, which they let flex over the rail. A sign hung above their heads, with words carved into it: *Desdemona's Brothel: Feasts, Pleasure, and Men.*

Raegna wrinkled her nose.

One man on the porch met Raegna's stare and smiled. "Good day, my lady! Long way from home, I see!"

The others caught on. "Surely you'll need a place to rest your head and a good man to warm the bed!"

Raegna flushed and averted her gaze. *Of all the shameful, horrible, brainless—*

"Oh, poor lady, she's shy," another blurted. "No need to be afraid of us. We'll take care of such a pretty girl like you!"

"Fuck off, you filthy piss-ends!" Bai shouted out the carriage window.

Raegna's eyes widened, and heat flooded her face. What exactly did he think he was doing, shouting vulgar language before the Duchess? Defending her honor? And why would he decide to do that? It did nothing but make the tramps laugh at him.

Asmund lowered back into the wagon. Naleem straightened beside her. "Don't pay them any mind."

"I cannot believe he did that," Raegna growled under her breath and urged the mare on.

When they reached the gates, her stomach somersaulted. After everything they suffered, Stadt lay just beyond the doors.

The gates groaned and creaked open to the Duchess' carriage. Raegna and Naleem's heads tilted back as they passed the old, wood gates that were as thick as a man was tall, and finally, Stadt surrounded them.

In an explosion of noise, the city engulfed them. It was much louder than any village marketplace. People hurried about on foot, on horseback, or by carriage or wagon. Common folk and nobles stuck to side paths closest to the towering buildings, while others clogged the cobblestone streets. The horses' hooves *clip-clopped*. People made way for the carriage with the guards about it. Other wagons, horses, and driven livestock nearly rammed against Raegna's humble wagon, which had been through enough as it was.

Too many things to take in at once. Bai may have had a closed carriage to muffle it all, but with the open wagon, Raegna winced at the voices calling, riders and drivers yelling, sheep and donkeys braying, metal ringing, food sizzling ...

The buildings rose stories high or remained grounded with large windows displaying lavish gowns, tunics, books, pastries, weaponry, and horse tack. A small flower shop nestled amid the hustle, reminding Raegna of Pinar's flower arrangements in Syden.

Modest taverns and inns offered sales for a night's stay and boarding for horses. Merchant tents flapped on the outskirts of Stadt, with everything from produce and fish to pottery and jewelry. One stood out as furs and leather hung from its beams. An old woman with jet-black hair lined with gray and russet skin as wrinkled and worn as the leather about her tent sat weaving a strange fabric from a stringy material.

Adjusting the goods they had to sell was a younger woman with the same black hair and light-brown skin, wearing a common dress. Her slender eyes found Raegna's stare, and she blinked before returning to her work.

They reminded her of Banu, all the way back in Judr, of Wa'Ni descent. People who roamed the northern mountains and Mork Skov without fear. Like the old healer, many lived south of the mountains within Galaenian villages. Even in Stadt.

"This place is incredible," Naleem said over the chaos. "I can't believe how many people there are, how big it is."

"Yes," Raegna agreed. "It is quite overwhelming."

Structures were built in stone with little soil or plant life. Stadt had an elegance, especially once they reached the heart of the city, which consisted of more nobles. Women escorted their men, wearing layered and beaded dresses, with the men in fine, colorful tunics, pants, and boots. The shops sold things Raegna herself could never hope to afford, with brightly colored fabrics and gold jewelry. Thick perfume wafted in the air and scratched her lungs. More carriages rolled by, and less common folk filled the streets. They passed grand estates with wide-open courtyards and buildings as tall as trees, topped with flying banners.

Raegna fixed her sight ahead, dizzy with the array of dress colors as aristocratic women walked or rode around them. These new streets had a different atmosphere—pleasant yet strictly business. She might have wondered why, but another wall loomed above them. An enormous drawbridge lay open, creating the only path across the deep moat that encircled the walls, where all the nobles crossed.

Raegna's breath left her lips as her shoulders fell and her brow lifted. "Gaea."

The drawbridge extended into a courtyard, perhaps bigger than Syden, paved in cobblestone and decorated with curving fountains that soaked statues of the goddesses. Trimmed rose bushes edged the paths, maintained by gardeners and their shears. Noblewomen strolled in twos or threes or with their gentlemen at their arms. More royal guards in the spring-green color marched by in various formations to attend their posts, and priestesses in their long maroon robes carried scrolls.

To the east, a quarter-mile away, stood a large stable. Behind it lay pastures teeming with horses and cattle. To the west, the rose bushes bloomed with the beginnings of a garden maze. The entrance was marked by an elaborate arch entangled with vines. Past that, a fountain gurgled with a statue figure Raegna could not make out.

Ahead of them, the Queen's palace, Vakkar Hold, dominated the courtyard. The great double doors were carved with images of Gaea above, overlooking Sachi and Sigmund standing hand in hand, surrounded by vines and animals. A doe posed beside Sachi, and a raven perched on Sigmund's shoulder. The castle towers almost touched the clouds, spring-green flags billowing on top of them, and banners hung from balconies that overlooked the courtyard.

The Duchess' carriage finally stopped. Raegna's mare halted with a snort, and stable girls came from different directions to tend to the horses. A group of four noblewomen hurried to the carriage, all in colorful layered dresses. Behind them, three gentlemen followed.

Hilde hopped down from her seat, pushing Raegna's sword and weapons aside to open the door. As Duchess Elmba emerged and stepped from her carriage, the noblewomen and gentlemen curtsied and bowed. "Your grace."

She ignored them and offered a hand to the other passenger. Raegna expected it to be Bai who'd take her hand and be rid of the carriage. Instead, another man took it and allowed her to assist him onto the cobblestones. He stood tall and poised with ink-black hair brushed about his forehead and deep-green eyes beneath long dark eyelashes. He wore a tunic and pants of dark blue lined with black. His physique could not be hidden, with broad shoulders, chest, and a slim waist and hips. With a squared chin, prominent yet soft cheekbones, and chiseled jawline, he had to be the most beautiful man Raegna had ever seen.

He did not notice her staring, and kept his eyes on the Duchess as he remained by her side. Then Bai climbed out in his dirty white shirt and dirt-ridden pants, his blond hair a tangled mess.

Raegna sighed hopelessly at him. Then she became all too aware of her appearance in nothing but a filthy, travel-worn dress under an old, wide belt. Her throat dried, but there was nothing she could do about it except hope she might make a better impression some other time.

The Duchess and her man turned to Raegna and Naleem in the wagon. Taking the crook of her man's arm in her hand, Duchess Elmba let a hint of a smirk tug at the corners of her mouth. "Is it all you could have imagined, priestess?"

"And more," Raegna admitted.

Duchess Elmba gave an amused huff. "Your husband is safely returned to you. An interesting young man you've pledged yourself to. Your weapons will be returned after we have decided what to do with you. Please, allow our hands to care for your horse and belongings as you shall be guests tonight before Her Majesty."

Raegna blinked as her chest expanded within. With the gorgeous courtyard around her, it was all too good to be true. She, Naleem, and Asmund hopped from the wagon and joined Bai before the Duchess, her man, and their attendants while the stable girls gathered horse reins. Raegna eyed Bai with a sideways glance, trying to figure out what he might have said to the Duchess to make her call him *interesting*—besides throwing curses at tramps. His face remained dull, despite the wonder around them, as if he would rather be somewhere else.

"Come." Duchess Elmba gestured to the palace. "Welcome to Vakkar Hold."

CHAPTER 4

HADWIN

THE BOYS RAN AND squealed before the great house porch, where Hadwin supervised on the steps. He cradled Else while the other babes sat around Cadoc, tilting their heads at his quiet peek-a-boo game. Blue skies stretched overhead and a chilled fall breeze pushed brown and orange leaves across Haven's paths. Hadwin rocked Else and—despite the terror weighing on his shoulders—he drew a deep breath to welcome fall's colors and brisk weather.

"No, Kili!" Audun's voice sprung up from around the corner, before the eight-year-old marched back into Hadwin's sight, the toddler, Kili, in tow. "Hadwin said no wandering."

Hadwin smiled at their approach. "Being a stowaway again, Kili?"

"He doesn't listen," Audun reported.

"He's only seen two winters." Hadwin adjusted Else into one arm. "He's still learning. Come, Kili. Sit with me."

The toddler hobbled into Hadwin's reach before he scooped him up and turned him sideways. Giggling, Kili wriggled, and Hadwin set him onto the porch before he could kick Else. "You're a good second caregiver, Audun. But you should play with the other boys. I'll keep an eye on him for now."

Audun shrugged. "Yes, Hadwin."

With that, he plodded off to join the others, swallowed in their game of chase. Hadwin kept Kili in his periphery as the boy explored the porch. Cadoc grew bored of peek-a-boo and watched the babes crawl and play with their wooden toys instead. His round, solemn gray eyes trailed the boys with a trance Hadwin didn't think a boy of five years could be capable of.

Hadwin nudged him. "You're a good little caregiver too."

The corners of the boy's mouth curled up. "When does Papa come back?"

Hadwin's breath caught in his throat as his heart split in half. "Cad. We talked about this, remember? Your papa might not come back. Just like Dakarai. Do you remember?"

Bringing up painful memories might not be the best idea, but Hadwin hoped it would stir his recollection of their conversations about lifting and meeting Gaea in Heimelle. The words always caused a dry, tight throat, but Cadoc needed to understand, somehow.

"Oh." Cadoc fiddled with a fold in his pants. "Not even for a little while?"

Hadwin sighed. "No ... Not how we'd like them to."

Cadoc retreated to his introspection, gazing at the other boys. Swallowing, Hadwin set his shoulders back to shake off the looming grief, just in time to catch Kili shoving himself between the porch rails. "Kili. Come away."

Hadwin guided him back when a scream broke out among the boys—and not the playful kind. Potential danger made him jolt, and he surveyed the commotion. One of the younger boys bawled on the ground, while Audun got into Ugo's face. Both boys glared at each other as fiercely as an eight- and nine-year-old could.

"Don't push, Ugo!" Audun snapped.

"Don't tell me what to do." Ugo promptly pushed him.

Another scrap. Else whimpered in Hadwin's arm as he rose to his feet. "Ugo."

The boy pointed at his victim, who still cried. "Fotr kept tripping me because he's slow."

"That doesn't give you the right to push him." Hadwin walked up to them with Else. He knelt before Fotr and dried his tears. "Apologize."

Ugo scrunched his nose. "I've heard my father say the weakest belong in the dirt."

Hadwin repressed a scowl. "Fotr isn't big enough to keep up yet. You should not push those smaller than you, or anyone for that matter. Apologize, now."

With a scoff, Ugo rolled his eyes and continued the game. Hadwin shoved the idea of wringing his neck aside and took Fotr's hand. "Come along. You can sit with Cadoc and me. Get your bearings and find your peace."

"I'll teach him," Audun grumbled.

"No, Audun. You will do nothing. All is well. Maybe start another game the younger ones can play."

Audun kicked a rock. "All right, Hadwin."

Fotr sniffled beside Hadwin when he sat with Else, earning a stare from Kili while the other babes cooed and played around them. Cadoc came to life and offered a lonely wooden man with scrapped fabric for clothing. "Do you want to play farm? The babes can be sheep. Kili can be something."

Kili perked to attention. "Woof!"

"Kili can be our dog," Cadoc affirmed. "Do you want to, Fotr?"

His tears dissipated and Fotr nodded, hugging the wooden man. Cadoc stood over the babes while Kili bounded about the porch. "Fotr, you can be a papa. I'll be the papa who watches the sheep."

Hadwin chuckled through the stone in his throat. "Good boy, Cad."

Audun's new group played stones while Ugo captained chase as the sun hung overhead. A raven glided over the clearing, flapping its wings to elevate itself. Hadwin watched the bird swoop, its image igniting a sense of solace for the first time in weeks—which left him the moment dark riding boots stomped to a halt on the porch step.

Hadwin held his breath and his muscles went rigid. Cadoc gasped and fled behind him. Fotr, Kili, and the babes peered up at Thenalious, the leader of Haven.

Thenalious merely glanced at the little ones with a knee bent and one foot on the step, dressed in a black shirt beneath a leather belt and dark-brown pants. His boots reached his calves and were weathered with dust and scratches. His hazel eyes followed Hadwin's recent gaze to the sky and found the black bird.

"The raven is Sigmund's." He leaned toward Fotr and Kili, gifting Hadwin a sideways glance. "They say he takes the form of a raven to watch over his children."

Hadwin drew Else closer to his chest and touched Cadoc behind him. With teeth clenched, fighting for steady breaths, all he could do was stare at the snake who had murdered his family. Cadoc buried his face into Hadwin's back, curling into him as if he could disappear. He knew all too well who this man was.

Fotr and Kili absorbed Thenalious without a clue, entranced by his friendly smirk. "The priestesses of the old world said he reports his findings to the All-Mother so she may guide those in need," he said.

Hadwin's lips pressed into a thin line.

"What truly happens is he flies to Mork Skov to report to Fan and be his eyes when the moon is not yellow. This way our lord may still rule and conquer, despite what woman and her Goddess have done to him." Thenalious looked Hadwin in the eye. "Or perhaps it's just a raven in search of rotting meat. Either way, you've no hope in it."

Hadwin lowered his gaze in reluctant submission.

"Let the older ones fight," Thenalious told him. "Reynold and I want them strong. Understood?"

Hadwin grimaced but nodded. "Yes."

Thenalious rose and started up the porch steps to the great house door. "You are fortunate to be just as good of a caregiver as your wretched brother. That is the only reason you and the boy live. Your second job is to remember that."

He stopped at the threshold before closing the door. "You will be just as easily ridden of as he was. Is that clear?"

Hadwin straightened and twisted his body to face Thenalious, chin high and daring to meet his eyes. One day, he would see this snake dead. "Like crystal."

Thenalious gave a quiet snort and went inside.

Hadwin pulled Cadoc as close as he could with Else in an arm. The boy whimpered into his chest with tears soaking into his shirt. "It's all right, Cad. I won't let him hurt you. I won't let anyone hurt you."

Cadoc did not raise his head until late afternoon when it was time to head inside for the youngest to rest. In the nursery, the little ones settled in beds or cradles and drifted off while the oldest played hushed card games or rested themselves.

Else still needed her mother, so Hadwin gathered her up and took Cadoc's hand. "Audun, you're in charge until we return. Keep it down for the babes now."

"Yes, Hadwin," Audun replied, already sitting to prepare a game of cards with Ugo and two other boys.

Things were usually in good shape when Audun was left as a caregiver. Besides, most of the rambunctious boys were fast asleep, and the only one who truly earned scolding was Ugo. They were fine on their own while Hadwin took Else and Cadoc on a trip to the old horse barn.

The later trips were always the most dreaded as Hadwin walked through the campground surrounded by the working men, who jeered, snorted, or spat as he passed. But he paid them no mind, not with Thenalious' words burning in his memory.

Hadwin made a good caregiver and was thus more useful alive. Though none of the children in that nursery were his, Thenalious must have cared enough to ensure they were looked after. How did he put it once before? They were Haven's future, and Hadwin knew they had more rights in this place than all of the men together.

Those boys were protected and revered. Unlike most of the caregivers assigned to them in the past, Hadwin made sure each had their meals, their time to play, and he regarded their safety. Previous caregivers had let babes die in their cradles, and boys would wander into the woods on winter nights, their bodies found by hunting parties, frozen or eaten.

At least, Hadwin considered, he and Thenalious had one smidgen of common ground.

Closer to the horse barn, Hadwin snapped out of his thoughts. They trekked downhill, and as they approached the door, he listened for any sounds of struggle or groans of pleasure. There had been too many times he happened upon one of the councilmen having their way with a woman, and it boiled his blood. Sometimes he wondered what would happen if he defended the women. Would he be killed—leaving Haven to find a lesser caregiver—or be punished by some other means?

By the time Hadwin came to a conclusion, the councilman would have finished and left the barn. Hadwin would wait outside, even if Else cried out of hunger. Then he would chastise himself and allow the women to recover before entering.

There was no sound but female chatter inside, so Hadwin sighed with relief and entered.

They all braced for whoever was to disturb them, but when they saw their friend, they relaxed, gathered in a group in the middle of the barn—even the girl with yellow hair who'd slept beside Farah that morning. She straightened with her eyes wide on Hadwin, her brows furrowed in a fearful expression. He blinked at her brown eyes, dark like caramel, her small nose speckled in dirt, almost like freckles above her parted pink lips.

"It's all right." Talia sat with her and Farah, laying a hand on her wrist. "This is Hadwin. He takes care of the children. You may have noticed he comes here every day to bring my Else to me. Come on, Hadwin, show her you're no harm."

With a gulp, he nodded and hobbled to her, kneeling before he handed Else to her mother. The yellow-haired girl watched him warily, but her muscles eased, her demeanor resolving into a sweet quiet. Hadwin found himself staring again and looked away.

"And this is Cadoc." Talia gestured to the boy. "He's Hadwin's nephew. He comes along as well to help. Don't you, little one?"

Cadoc nodded and gave the girl a curt wave.

She giggled. "Hello."

"Hadwin, this is Maura," Talia told him as she began to nurse.

If there was anything Hadwin remembered that his mother had taught him, it was that first impressions were important, especially before a pretty woman. "Hello, Maura."

Her eyes met his, and his palms slicked. "I—I'm from Sorelle too," he said. "Your sister village, Syden. The one that's, that's more west."

"Ah." Maura batted her eyelashes. "You were ... brought here too?"

"Yes." He balled his hands into fists. "My family was killed ... Cadoc and I are all that's left. But we manage. They have me take care of the children."

Maura tilted her head. "Do you like it?"

"Well, if it were anywhere but here, yes," Hadwin answered. "I love the boys. In Syden, I lived with my brother and his wife. I often helped care for their children, including Cadoc here. So it's almost like home that way."

"Well, that's very sweet."

His heart pumped blood that warmed his entire body like melted butter. All fears and anger toward Haven, Thenalious, and looming ravens vanished as she spoke to him. Her voice was light birdsong before evening became night.

Once introductions were made, Hadwin could find no more words to tell her. She turned her attention to the other women's talk.

Talia caught his gaze and gave him a sly smile with her eyebrows raised. He snorted a short laugh at her. Fancying herself a matchmaker. Whatever—she needed to have at least some fun in this place.

The boys would have supper in the dining hall soon, so Hadwin took Else back and went to leave with Cadoc. "I'll see you ladies tonight then."

Though he was sure Maura had forgotten him the moment their conversation had ended, as he crossed the threshold, she shouted, "Goodbye, Hadwin."

"Oh," he stammered. "Ah, until tonight, Maura."

***

As evening broke, the boys gobbled their supper before the dining hall filled with the men. Hadwin pushed his portion of salted root and pheasant about his plate, his stomach fluttering with moth wings. They were difficult to hide from Oberon, who sat with his two sons across the table.

Gael and Vihn were Oberon's two out of the dozen. Gael was the oldest at five years, like Cadoc, and Vihn would turn four in winter, Oberon had told Hadwin.

"The cold bit into your skin the night he was born," he reminisced perhaps a fortnight ago. "Vihn screamed at it and no one thought he would survive the season. Yet here he still is."

Though Hadwin despised every man in this wretched campground, he hated Oberon the least. This councilman, unlike the others, spent time with his sons whenever he could. He joined them for supper and bid them goodnight afterward with a kiss on each of their heads, like any doting father would. Such behavior seemed surreal here.

Oberon's service in procuring a lifting bed for Dakarai would never leave Hadwin's memory. But he couldn't use it to excuse the man's involvement in Haven.

What he had said that night before convincing Hadwin it was safe to lift his nephew—"I have my reasons for being here and Thenalious has his"—sent Hadwin's mind whirling. As Oberon played with his sons at the table, chatting and joking with Hadwin, it occurred to Hadwin that those reasons might have been the ease of a carefree family life. But every village in Galaenia could offer him that. So why choose Haven?

"Something is on your mind, Hadwin." Oberon raised an eyebrow at him. "Won't you tell me about it?"

Hadwin shook his head. "It's nothing."

"Well, you have been sighing all night," Oberon pressed, leaning back in his seat. A wry smile flashed white teeth beneath his black beard, which had grown within the autumn season. His rich, umber skin matched his sons', and all three of them had the same short, wide noses. Hadwin recognized that smile in Gael whenever he played tricks on the other boys. The eldest brother ate close to his father's side while Oberon held Vihn in his lap. "Tell me, who is the lucky lady you keep to yourself?"

Cheeks burning hot, Hadwin glared at him. "There is no lady."

"You're sure? I could have sworn I had seen such dopey eyes and distant thoughts on others who were madly in love. And you have it badly."

Hadwin straightened while his stomach did flips. "There is no one. And why would you care?"

Oberon gave a dismissive wave of a big hand. "You are a better caregiver than these children have had. And should you have feelings for the women you visit as often as any councilman, it could lead to your beheading, and I don't want that."

Hadwin took a breath and folded his arms over the table. "I suppose it's good you care a little."

"I'm hurt you wouldn't think that in the first place," Oberon teased. "So who is she?"

With a sigh, Hadwin met the councilman's gaze. "How am I to know you won't tell the rest of them and you are not my spy?"

"You would have to trust me." Oberon switched Vihn to his opposite knee and wrapped an arm around the boy's chest.

Some small part of Hadwin wanted to trust him. He knew he needed an ally and yearned for some camaraderie. Oberon had helped him this far with nothing to gain for himself and everything to lose. What would Thenalious and the others do if they knew he'd built a lifting bed for Dakarai and had allowed Hadwin out of imprisonment to lift him?

Hadwin dipped his head. "There is a girl from the recent raid. I just hope she'll be safe in that barn ..."

"Hm, which one? There were three more if I remember. Thenalious only allows so many from each raid."

"That's as much as you need to know," Hadwin muttered with his eyes narrowed.

Oberon shrugged. "Very well. Though if I knew, I would be able to claim her and keep her from the others for you. That is, if no one else already has."

"You *claim* them?" Hadwin's brow furrowed.

"Sometimes, when we prefer one woman to bear our children," Oberon explained nonchalantly as he held his son in his lap. "Some of us don't care, but the men know I do. Can you believe Reynold does too? Almost."

Hadwin shook his head with his nose wrinkled. "They are human beings like us. How would you feel about being claimed like they are?"

Oberon went silent. His confidence waned. Then, as quickly as it did, it returned, and his eyes met Hadwin's with a hint of mischief. "I'm just saying I could protect her if you told me who she was."

This could very well be a trick to compel Hadwin to trust him, see him as an ally before he went straight to Thenalious and the others, and use this information, use Maura against him. She was in enough danger as it was. Yet perhaps he could play the game. Wasn't that what Talia called him? Called them all? Pawns in Thenalious' game. Fan's game.

At the very least, Maura would be safe for a time, and again, Oberon did nothing for his own gain.

Hadwin's eyes darted about the tabletop. "You claimed Farah, didn't you?"

"Farah?"

Of course, he wouldn't bother to learn her name. "She's the black woman, and she's angry all the time. She's the one you claimed."

Oberon blinked, and his feet shuffled under the table. "I do prefer her over the others. And as far as I know, she has not been touched by anyone else in the Council, so her children are mine. I know they are, I see it in their faces."

"And no one else has touched her," Hadwin said.

"They know if they did I'd cut their balls off and feed them to the pigs," Oberon boasted before the children, receiving a chuckle from the older boys and a grimace from Hadwin. "She is safe, and your girl could be too if you tell me who she is. Just be sure you do not give her a child, though I would let you keep it if it were up to me. But it's not."

Hadwin's cheeks flushed. "Nothing like that will happen ... What do you get out of claiming her?"

"A happier, less lonely caregiver for my children and perhaps his own."

Hadwin's breath did not come easily after that statement. He had never thought about having his own children as he'd never been chosen as someone's husband. He certainly could not imagine bringing up a family here. "No. There will be no children for me ... and none for her if she does not wish it."

"Very noble."

"It would hardly be a family," Hadwin grunted. "Is this what you wanted from Haven, then? Taking advantage of a woman and her gift from Gaea just so you may have children who do not know who their mother is?"

"They don't need to." Oberon put an elbow over the table. "They have their fathers and a caregiver."

"Fathers that are never there for them," Hadwin argued. "Every child needs their mother."

The councilman recoiled, holding Vihn tighter. "I've been fine without mine."

Hadwin would beg to differ. He kept the thought to himself and sighed. It wasn't like his own was the example of motherhood. Maybe to Naleem, but not to Hadwin. A familiar ache throbbed in his chest that he hadn't had to deal with since Syden burned.

"They deserve good mothers," Hadwin muttered, for clearly he and Oberon didn't have such.

"The broads in that barn aren't fit," Oberon said, making Hadwin seethe. "Some of them didn't want their babes after they were born. We've had to force them to nurse before."

Hadwin's shoulders tensed as his stomach writhed. That wasn't the case for Talia. Why would the others be that way? He looked down the table at the little ones, who stuffed their faces. How could anyone turn them away? Especially as babes?

As Oberon plucked a scrap from Vihn's plate, the boy whined and chased his hand until Oberon popped it into his mouth. Hadwin's nose wrinkled, though the councilman offered the boy a new piece. The boys were among men who took advantage of the women. So of course some of the women wouldn't want anything to do with them.

Hadwin's jaw clenched; his appetite had vanished. "You can't imagine why, can you?"

Oberon pulled his attention from Vihn and narrowed his eyes on Hadwin. "It's the way of things."

It doesn't have to be. Hadwin let it go for now. He turned from the councilman and watched the boys eat. One day, each of them would take part in *the way of things*. It was enough to make Hadwin's heart cave. He had to get them out of Haven. Get the women out. Sitting around waiting for Maidens and warriors would take too long.

Chapter 5

Bai

A S THE CARRIAGE CREAKED along, bound for Stadt, Bai peered out the veiled windows. Nothing but trees looked back at him, passing in hordes along the brush and fallen trunks. Throughout the journey, he'd let himself fall into a trance, staring blindly between the dense trunks and wondering how the forest and life within it went on. The sharp pain would creep up the center of his chest, like an icicle forming over his sternum. He would shut it down with a hard blink and drive his focus to a mindless trance.

Months of that daily routine led to this. Bai sat in a velvet-covered carriage with the supposed Duchess of Galaenia and a man she introduced as her husband. Bai had forgotten his name already. By the look of his gleaming, slicked black hair, dark blue tunic beneath a wide brown belt, and shining black leather boots over brown pants, he was a spoiled nobleman with a wealthy wife to treat him well. Bai couldn't care less about the formalities they placed before him. All he wanted was what they could give him: an audience with the Queen. Then revenge.

"I've asked you what your work was in Syden." The Duchess's voice broke through his mindscape. It was a balanced, burning voice that matched her lethal beauty. Bai imagined she could use it to level a person.

Her heavy-lidded, dark-brown eyes alone could undo someone with a single glance.

He kept his sight out the window with their pompous figures in his periphery. "I worked in the fields."

"I see." The Duchess crossed her legs and rested her hands on one knee. Her husband sat up rigid, though relaxed, his hands folded in his lap. He gave her his attention when she spoke, green eyes fixed on her with a straight mouth above a chiseled chin. "Was there anything else your wife made you responsible for? Perhaps at nightfall?"

Bai met her gaze with a frown. "We are not tramps. Syden was destroyed and Judr was attacked. There was bloodshed and lives lost."

A slender eyebrow arched. "By these rebel men, I believe your wife said. That is truly extraordinary."

"I'd hardly call it that," Bai muttered. He got the gist. She did not believe them.

The Duchess leaned closer to him. "It seems to me a fallen priestess may be trying to set up her business in Stadt instead of starting in Udstodt like the rest of the madames."

"She brings news of attacks and a Matriarch's sealed message," Bai quipped. "I did not think nobles of Stadt would take suffering in Galaenia so lightly. Or perhaps this is a waste of our time."

Then she laughed. "Whatever has happened, it is safe to say she has her hands full with you. Though I would have thought her husband was the man who sat beside her. She must have you in the back of the wagon for a reason."

They both chuckled this time, but Bai turned back to the window. He doubted even Galaenia's highest power—or whatever this Duchess' status was. She and the rest of the noblewomen would be the same as

Matriarchs and common women. They would not believe, and more blood would be spilled for their pride and ignorance.

When the city came into view, Bai craned his neck. So unbelievably large, he wondered how Raegna could get lost on the main road, but he'd not been paying attention to the direction either. First, they plowed through the refugee village, Udstodt. Bai had heard of it once or twice: a pitiless place for thieves, rogues, and sad dreamers, though it appeared to be just a small village with a much larger main street cut into it that led to Stadt's gates.

He listened to the bustle and heard the tramps hawking to Raegna. Hearing their innuendos boiled his blood more than the Duchess' presumptions. Shouting a vulgar insult may not have been the best thing to do, especially before the Duchess and her husband. But it shut them up, and the Duchess smirked instead of scoffing in offense.

Stadt itself surrounded the carriage with sounds that burst through its windows. The chatter, shouting, braying, clanging, made him wince, but at least drowned out the buzzing in his mind. The sights were too much to take in, causing his head to spin, but he was not in Stadt for sightseeing.

Vakkar Hold was just as impressive, with a courtyard as big as half of Syden. The Duchess, her husband, and their entourage led them into the palace, which opened into a great hall where servants roamed, and long spring-green banners hung from the high ceiling. Along the stone walls hung velvet fabrics and portraits of royals and nobles, all posed with spouses, children, or pets. Despite his urgency to see the Queen, Bai gazed at the massive hall and its decor, as did the rest of his friends.

Asmund dipped his head at the overwhelming scale, but still walked as flawlessly as any of the gentlemen attending the Duchess' husband.

Perhaps that came from being a husband to a Matriarch's sister. Naleem gawked about, for like Bai, he had seen nothing like this being raised in Syden.

Then there was Raegna, who kept her head high, fidgeting with her skirts, and trying not to appear too impressed and amazed by her new surroundings. She did that in Judr too—her nose in the air to show off her family's pride, even in her circumstances. *Their* circumstances.

The cold pain crawled up his chest again. Bai averted his gaze from her.

All the while, the Duchess spoke to them over her shoulder. "I will bring this message to Her Majesty during our Council. I'm sure she will want to meet all of you. In the meantime, I will elect my servants to attend to you as you prepare to see the Queen."

Raegna nodded with her hands to her chest. "Oh. We would be ever grateful."

The Queen was so kind, yet lowly commoners could not see her in their own garb. Though the group came off as poor beggars compared to the rest of the nobles.

The Duchess guided them past two spiraling stone staircases that led up to more halls and rooms. When they stopped, Bai studied the large, intricate doors, each carved with interlocking designs, bearing iron knobs.

"Vera," the Duchess said to one of her ladies.

A woman with tawny hair pulled back in curls came forward from the ladies in the Duchess' attendance. "Yes, your grace."

"I am tired after our day and will rest before I see Her Majesty." Duchess Elmba started up the stairs with her husband and attendants in tow. "Will you find some suitable servants to tend to our guests?"

"Of course, your grace."

"Thank you, your grace," Raegna blurted up the stairs. "We look forward to seeing you and the Queen. And thank you for your wonderful hospitality!"

"We will call for you when we are ready, priestess." The Duchess sighed and disappeared with the rest of them upstairs.

Bai frowned. Was nothing too important, too urgent, and endangering to do anything about it?

At Vera's call, both female and male servants arrived. Six men and two women lined up before her. Vera gave each of them a stern face with her hands clasped before they bowed their heads.

"Our guests will see the Queen soon," she told them. "Show them to our baths and prepare suitable clothes. Those will be available in my chamber once I have acquired them."

"Yes, my lady," they all replied.

Vera turned to Raegna. "And please ask anything from them. They'll make your chambers for your rest. For now, enjoy the bathhouses."

"Thank you, my lady," Raegna replied as Vera went off to execute her plans.

A servant girl waved down the hall. "The baths are this way, priestess."

The mass of servants led the group further through the palace. The great hall thinned and broke into chambers the farther they went, and each grew dim with candlelight. Two chambers split before them, and the women servants ushered Raegna to the left. "This way, priestess. The men will prepare for their bath in the other room."

Raegna didn't follow and instead looked back at her men. Bai, Naleem, and Asmund stood firm even as their escorts started in the opposite direction. It was the first time Bai had beheld Raegna's rich brown eyes since Judr. They took in his and flickered with a longing that made his muscles tense. Separating their group sent a dagger through his heart, and a similar look stretched across all their faces.

A servant girl ushered Raegna closer. "It's all right. You will see each other afterward. May I ask which one is your husband?"

"Oh. Bai." Raegna gestured to him, her pleasantries waning.

"Very well." The servant girl gave a gentle smile. "Come along. You will see each other afterward, I assure you."

Raegna gave in, turning to follow the servants into the chamber before the door shut behind them. Bai and the others watched before trailing their servants into a room as big as a common house. Wall to wall was nothing but gray stone, strange cupboards and wood drawers. Small baskets were stacked in a corner.

Two servants gathered around Bai and two around both Naleem and Asmund. Bai drew back from them.

"If you would disrobe," one of them said, "we will bring you to the baths."

Bai snorted but did as they told him, pulling his shirt up and over his head to a small gasp from the servant behind him. Bai's throat tightened and he flushed. He hadn't seen his back, but he had touched the gouged scars and knew they were horrific. Keeping a stony face, he surrendered his shirt and slipped out of his pants. Together, the servants wrapped a towel around his waist. His skin crawled at the touch.

Naleem leaned away from his servants. "I'll do it all myself, thank you."

"But, sir, we can take your clothes—"

"I said I will do it *myself*," Naleem snapped at them, and they let him be, handing a towel over. They were probably used to harsh orders, but Bai hoped it instilled something in them. These were not hopeless beggars they were giving charity to. They were men on a mission, and this hospitality was nothing but an obstacle in their way.

Except for Asmund, who allowed the towel to be placed around him, and he folded his arms over his torso. He would be too timid to tell the servants off. With the three of them prepared, Bai's two servants led them through a door into a stone hall lit by torches. Old, tattered, spring-green banners lined the walls, frayed with age or even burned at the edges.

At the first entrance, they stopped and turned to Bai. "This will be your bath."

They opened the door, and inside was a dark hallway. Bai's brow furrowed, but he entered with a glance back at his friends. Naleem and Asmund stared back before the door shut on them. A shudder crawled over Bai, but he steeled himself and proceeded down the narrow hall.

It was a short walk that led to the bath, a large, square pool with water so clear that the cobblestones at the bottom warped from the surface. Each corner of the room held a torch, and sunlight made its way from two high, thin windows that stretched horizontally along the wall seams. The light and flames glittered across the pool. White silk draped in elegant curves from the rafters glowed with the bright ripples of the water.

This certainly was not his wooden tub in Syden, but it would do.

A door clicked open and shut across the room, and Bai froze. If they were sending Naleem and Asmund in, why could they not have done that with the first door?

Raegna came around the corner, about to slip her towel from her breasts as she studied the pool. Then her eyes caught Bai, and she yelped.

Raegna clamped the towel around her. "What are—what in Gaea's—what are you doing in here?"

He turned from her, his cheeks and ears burning over her loosened towel. "They put me in here."

"Gaea above, you frightened me." She whirled from him. "Ugh, they probably put us together because we're ... well, married."

Though they were husband and wife, this had to be the most flesh they'd seen on each other. Before they left Judr, she had released him as her husband, in a way. He could stay or he could follow her to Stadt, and he chose to follow her. Though it was not for her sake. Even though she released him in what he thought had been a quiet divorce, she still called them married. Or perhaps to outsiders, they were. That had always been the way between them.

Bai moved to the hall. "I'll leave then."

"No."

Fists tightened at his sides. He halted mid-stride and tilted his head to listen to whatever she had to say.

"Stay," she told him, her voice low. "They already believe us all to be strange, and we have told them time and again we are wife and husband. So ..."

Raegna looked at the pool and pointed to the side closest to her. "I will take this half, and you, that half."

Bai cut the halves in his mind. He still would have rather gone somewhere else, bathed in a pond or garden fountain instead, stark naked in front of all of Vakkar Hold. Instead, he kept his back to her. "You first."

Silence hung over the room except for the water that lapped over the sides. Her towel dropped to the floor, and he listened to the ripples, not daring to imagine her.

"There," she mumbled.

Bai glanced over his shoulder and spotted her in the water, her back to him and her bare white shoulders on the surface. She unbraided her long chestnut hair, and the locks flowed in the tiny waves. With a grunt, he removed his towel and stepped into the water, finding it cool against his skin.

He could not help but submerge himself. Bai pulled his feet up and floated with the still current on his face, coursing through his hair, pulling the dirt from him. He would remain underwater until he struggled for air.

Bai breached the top and shook the water from his hair. His heart opened and allowed a brief, airy joy within. Raegna's presence ripped through the opening, and the pain raked through without mercy. He flinched and stamped it out, the water rippling from his jolt. Reality returned, and Bai sank into the water, numbing himself into a trance again. The sooner he finished this bath and made himself a worthy image for the Queen and Duchess, the better.

"The water is nice," Raegna chirped, taking him off guard.

Did she truly mean to make small talk now? "Mm-hm."

Silence passed before she spoke again. "What did you think of the Duchess? Did she speak to you in the carriage?"

Worried I didn't make a good first impression, wife? "She is like other women. She didn't believe us. Perhaps still doesn't."

"I'm not sure if I would believe us either." She sighed. "But at least we are here. And it's not the Duchess we are trying to convince, but the Queen. She'll have the final say in things."

"Hm."

He thought their conversation might have been over, and he was willing to drop it, wade in the water a moment more, and be done. But Raegna kept going. "How is your back?"

Why was she doing this? He couldn't smother the pain forever, and she kept prodding at it. "Healing. I haven't seen it yet, but Naleem said there are a lot of scars."

"Does it hurt you anymore?"

"Sometimes."

She hesitated, but must have been fidgeting. The ripples she created stretched to his side of the pool. "I never ... I never got to say how sorry—how incredibly sorry I am for that."

"For what?"

"... For what happened to you."

His lips pressed into a thin line. Those terrifying memories in Turid's house hardly mattered anymore. "It wasn't your fault."

"You didn't deserve it, and I wish I could have slashed that wench myself, but ... I tried to stop them."

"You did." He exhaled. "I remember that. But I don't remember much else."

Her voice came out in a whisper. "Maybe that's a good thing."

The icicle settling on his sternum began to thaw. Raegna wasn't picking at the wound but lighting a fire in a place once barren and dusted with ash.

A giant stone wall stood between them, thicker and greater than the walls of Vakkar Hold. It had always been there, but it grew stronger, more impregnable, even as they tried to speak to each other. The stones gave way before, crumbling as they were forced to work together with one common ground that almost destroyed the wall to nothing but rubble. With that common ground taken from them, they fortified the wall once more.

Raegna's firelight went out when cold rushed in, and the ice clawed through Bai's heart. It took his breath. Blood and screams flooded his mind, and the trance wrestled to quiet it.

"Bai?"

"Hm?"

For a moment that stretched out like an eternity, he listened for her voice. He begged for the fire. When it finally came, it made him flinch. "... Nothing. I'm just glad your wounds are healing."

Tiny footsteps entered the room, and Bai looked over his shoulder. A young woman in a common beige dress with a small white apron appeared. Her dull black hair was pulled back and braided in a bun, but loose strands stuck out under a headband she'd fashioned on the crest of her head. Her long nose didn't seem to fit her small face. She greeted Raegna with a sweet smile.

"Priestess," she said. "I am Olena. I've been assigned to serve you on behalf of our Queen."

Raegna looked up at her. "Hello."

Olena kept her smile and nodded to Bai. "Serving men will be here soon to assist your husband. For now, I will take you to your chamber, and we can get you into your dress."

Bai looked away at once. The water sloshed as Raegna climbed out. A towel flapped, and the fabric shifted. Without another word, they padded out of the room.

Bai waded alone in the water. His core ached, and he grumbled under his breath. Hanging onto Raegna's words brought healing and pain both. They left with her, and Gaea knew if he would hear them again.

After what you've let happen, you don't deserve them. Bai winced and would have dipped beneath the water to hold his breath, stretch his lungs past their limit, if the servant men hadn't entered the room first.

They directed him out of the bath and dried him off. Bai jumped when they reached places too sensitive for his liking. When they approached him with a clean pair of pants, a long vest, and shirt, Bai shook his head at them. "I can do this on my own."

They must have remembered how Naleem barked at their friends because they complied and handed him the clothes. Once Bai had shoes laced over his feet, they led him out of the bathhouse and through the various chambers of Vakkar Hold. They didn't go far when they reached a spiral staircase in the hall and ascended.

Bai assumed it was either some tower they clambered up or one of the secret pathways he'd heard Vakkar Hold was said to contain. They went up until chamber doors appeared in wider hallways where servants and noble residents swept through. None paid Bai and his servants mind.

Finally, the servants stopped before a door, and one of them opened it. "Your chambers, sir."

Bai squirmed at the formality and entered. The room lay before him, larger than Raegna's house in Syden. To the left, a lavish bed adorned with plush silk pillows and crimson sheets stood beneath a dark wood frame. Curtains were drawn above it. Beyond the bed lay two velvet chairs before a large unlit fireplace. Between them, a small gold table waited for tea and treats. Bookshelves lined the back wall, with every other shelf filled end to end with book spines. Others held figures, pottery, and incense. A small window let in the orange sunset, filtering into the room with a gold hue.

Raegna sat before a vanity with Olena behind her, braiding her hair. Raegna's shoulders were bare, and a dress began just beneath them, clinging to her waist in maroon silk. Bai didn't have time to stare when Olena glanced back at him and the other men.

"Gentlemen, his garments are on the bed. Please make him presentable for the Queen's banquet tonight."

Banquet. The serving men guided Bai to the middle of the room and collected the clothes from the bed. One removed his vest before he could object. The other assisted him into a new silk vest that was black as pitch. They clipped it together in front of his torso, from chest to belly, and drew the string at his back in swift motions. Bai gasped when the vest cinched at his chest, then his belly. "Gaea, can't I breathe?"

The men were startled. The bravest among them spoke first. "It's a corset. It helps with your posture and physique."

"I care more about the air in my lungs," Bai grunted.

"Husband," Raegna warned from the vanity. Olena covered most of her, still tending to her hair. "Please try to tolerate it."

Easy for her to say. But Bai counted it as a means to an end and drew short breaths while the servants fitted more clothes on him. A deep-green tunic went over the corset, its hems embroidered with gold vines and leaves. Another pair of pants went over his existing ones, but not before a leather piece was strapped between his legs. Bai bit back a growl. At last, a belt finished the look, buckled around his waist with the loose end looped at the front.

With a thick substance, they slicked his hair back and split it so one side was thicker than the other. Feeling like a tacked horse, Bai stood with his arms stiff at his sides—the corset bones pressing his ribs and the scars on his back.

Olena finished with Raegna and turned to him. "Oh, what a dazzling husband to match you."

Raegna rose, and her skirt shifted. Bai's heart lurched, and he pressed his mouth shut so he didn't gawk. Woven in maroon fabric, the gown drew the eye with intricate lines of glittering black. The sleeves hung below her shoulders and dipped across the heart line that covered her breasts. The fabric moved with the deep dip of her waist to the strong curve of her hips, the skirt draping down to her feet. A long, black belt loosely tied to her waist complemented the maroon dress.

Thick chestnut locks went up in several braids that were pinned together in a circle at the back of her head. Still, there were enough loose curls to caress her bare shoulders. A garnet necklace on a gold chain clasped around Raegna's neck, with matching earrings dangling from her ears. Her face was paler, either from a powder Olena had put on her or from her nerves of having to face him in such attire. Shadows darkened her eyelids, bringing the dark-brown in her irises forth. Her red lips pursed as Olena placed a darker maroon shawl over her shoulders that hung down the length.

Bai averted his gaze, staring long enough. "You ... You do look well."

Raegna thumbed the garnet at her neck. "And your clothes suit you."

Olena clapped her hands together, making them both jump. "You can admire each other while we check in on your friends. I'll come back for you when we're ready to depart to the dining hall."

With that, she ushered the serving men out, and they were alone. Bai kept his eyes on the carpeted floor, but Raegna's image was stamped into his mind. He was worried he might learn what that damnable leather piece in his pants was for.

Raegna smoothed out her skirts before she raised her chin with a sigh. "We're not doing very well."

Bai allowed himself to look at her. "What do you mean?"

"We're supposed to be husband and wife," she explained. "For them to believe our story, we must make them believe we are real. We're a stranger party now than we were in Judr."

A quaint family from a quaint village was difficult for a Matriarch to believe. A priestess with three men who all looked like they hadn't bathed or eaten in days ... well, it was a wonder they'd gotten so far. Bai placed their luck on Matriarch Ase's sealed message. "All right. How do you propose we do that?"

Raegna frowned. "Neither of us will like it. But ... it is proper for a lady to take a man's arm to escort him. We need to be close to make it believable."

Bai fought a fidget. "If you insist."

"For Ada," she declared, taking him off guard.

His eyes bore into hers and the intense determination within them. The ice pain lanced through his heart as if she drove her sword through him, but her stare kept him upright. It stoked the fire she'd created earlier, thawing the ice. The suffocating clothes didn't matter, and neither did his discomfort at being so close to her.

Bai gave Raegna a nod. "For Ada."

Chapter 6

Hadwin

E LSE CHIRPED AT HER mother when Hadwin handed her over. The grin on Talia's face warmed his heart; the one joy they could all hold in Haven.

Farah and two other women leaned in and fawned over the babe while Talia prepared to nurse. Hadwin sat back to give them space, absent-mindedly playing with Cadoc's hair with the boy beside him. Casualness was his new guise with Maura so close. She was watching over Talia and Else before she turned and offered him a smile.

Hadwin averted a stare, but smiled back. What a balance this was. He never had to court anyone in Syden and never had the practice. This was some sort of game of skirting around each other, testing mutual feelings. Maura may not feel the same way, but Hadwin's heart throbbed when she stood and approached.

He jolted and startled Cadoc, who looked up at him with an upturned brow. Hadwin made room for her while readjusting Cadoc beside him. He brushed the boy's hair back with an apologetic smirk. One day, perhaps Cadoc would find himself in the same predicament. Gaea willing, somewhere far from Haven.

Maura sat beside them and folded her legs beneath her. "Hello, Hadwin."

He cleared his throat. "Hello, m' lady."

"I would like to speak with you alone tonight," she whispered. "Would you meet me?"

"Meet you? Here? I'm usually here ... Speak about what?" The words tumbled over his dry tongue.

Maura batted her eyes. "That's a secret. And here, but ..." She glanced over her shoulder at the other women. When she turned back to him, she lowered her voice. "There's a way out. Just into the woods. There, we can talk."

A way out. Hadwin buzzed as if bees swarmed within him. He gaped with his brow raised. "You know a way?"

Maura put a finger to her lips. "It's our secret. Will you meet me?"

"Yes," he hissed. "Why must it be a secret? What should I bring? What should I do?"

She giggled. "You're full of questions. I only want to speak alone for now. Just us."

A plan. She must have a plan. How could she when she'd arrived in Haven so recently? What did she know about a way out? Did she see something on the way in? What could she know that he'd missed?

Hadwin faltered. Alone. He must leave Cadoc behind, but he couldn't imagine that. Why couldn't Cadoc be at his side? Why must they be alone? He watched the other women break from Talia. All except Farah, who remained by her side. As if she could feel his gaze on her, Farah narrowed her eyes on him. Hadwin dipped his head.

If the other women knew about a plan, they would shoot it down. Before the men had left for Judr, Talia had warned him to do nothing. Play Thenalious' game. But perhaps now was the time to take matters into their hands. Hadwin could bring Else to her mother that night, leave

Cadoc in their care for a moment, and follow Maura ... but how could she get them into the woods?

"M' lady ... how will we be alone?"

"You let me worry about that," Maura answered with a smile.

Later, having tucked the boys in for bed, Hadwin led Cadoc to their room and allowed him to sleep for a few hours before they would embark into the night. He listened to the men dine downstairs and waited for the great house to go silent. Hours went by, and he thought to get some sleep, but grew restless as he imagined all the plots he and Maura might have.

As the kitchen boys clattered and clanged dishes downstairs, Hadwin waited longer so none might see him pass through the halls. He remembered from his first few days in Haven, when he was one of them, that they turned in for the night rather late. When he heard the last of them and even waited a little longer to be sure the entire house had settled in, he rose from the bed and woke Cadoc.

"Papa?" the boy mumbled as Hadwin shook his shoulder.

Hadwin held a sad sigh as he kissed Cadoc's head. "No, nephew. It's me. Come along, Else is hungry."

Cadoc did not wake but continued to sleep in Hadwin's arms as he carried him through the nursery, retrieved Else, and made his way downstairs.

Crickets chirped and stars twinkled above the trees in the clear night sky. Brisk cold sank into his skin. Hadwin hurried across the camp with Else and Cadoc in his arms as something swooped over them. A gasp left Hadwin's lips. He watched as an owl fluttered to the point of a pine and perched there. With large eyes, the bird studied him so closely that he thought it might have been sent by Thenalious or Fan himself.

Hadwin ducked behind the old barn door, Cadoc slipping from his grasp. At his arrival, the women leaped away but peered through the darkness until they recognized him.

"Hadwin?" Talia whispered.

"It's me," he panted.

"What are you doing here so late?" she asked. "One of them could have been here. What if you happened upon them?"

Before he could answer, letting Cadoc wake as he dropped from his arm, Maura stood over them. "I told him to come."

Talia's brow furrowed, wide eyes trailing her across the barn. "You?"

"Yes." Maura took Else in her arms and brought her to Talia. "I have things to discuss with him."

Heat simmered under Hadwin's cheeks, and his nape prickled. Maura wouldn't want the other women involved in an escape plan. They would convince them to cease their scheme and accept their lot. But her tone didn't fare well with them, either.

Talia matched it, and her voice clipped. "Discuss?"

"What are you planning, girl?" Farah hissed.

"Nothing," Maura told her. "Please, watch over the children. We will be back."

Hadwin squirmed at Farah's glare, but Maura ignored her, taking his hand and guiding him to the back wall. There she knelt and pried at a board. A space opened into the forest beyond Haven, and Hadwin gaped. *A way out.*

Before he could say anything, Maura tugged his hand before crawling out into the open. Hadwin's stomach flipped, and he glanced back at Talia and Farah. Talia's eyes remained wide, and Farah's brow arched.

"Don't do this," Talia begged. "No good will come from it."

Hadwin's gaze shifted to Cadoc. The boy stood beside them, rubbing his eyes. He would be safe with them for just a moment. "We'll be back."

They slipped into the night. Dark tree trunks towered over them in shadows, branches reaching out like a crone's bony fingers. Hadwin realized that perhaps his fear of the dark as a child had not truly left him. Haven was still so close with all its terrors.

Maura led them just a little farther from the old barn. The woods seemed to beckon them to slip into the trees and be done with Haven. Hadwin thought Maura might do just that, but she stopped in a clearing and looked about for anyone who followed.

"You came," she whispered.

"Oh, well, yes," he stammered. "I told you I would. I've been considering some tips and routines they do every day and night, so we might have a chance. See, I was thinking—"

"What do you mean? Routines for what?"

Hadwin cocked his head and raised his palms. "Escape. You might have a plan, and I've been here longer and outside the barn. If we worked together, we could leave this place. Even bring the other women and children with—if Gaea is on our side."

"Oh." Her eyes darted downward as a weak grin spread across her lips. "I did not intend to discuss that. I have no true plans for escape ... only that it would be fine with me."

His hands fell to his sides, and he lifted an eyebrow. "That's not what you wanted to talk about?"

Maura's grin twisted into a smirk as she shook her head. "No. I did ask the other women if they had ever considered it, but they told me to get the idea out of my head. That it's no use. If we try, we will be killed."

"I know how they feel," Hadwin admitted. "But we may have a chance if we are careful and work together."

To his surprise, she giggled, her hand over her mouth. "Oh, Hadwin. You are very sweet and brave. In time, we will have to speak of your plans. Though that is not what I asked you for."

His heart sank even as it fluttered for her. "Then ... what was it you wanted, m' lady?"

"You can call me Maura." Her hands folded in front of her, and she glanced at the dark ground. "Tell me this, Hadwin. Did you have a woman in your village?"

"Er, no." He gulped. "My mother never found me a wife. I lived with my brother and his wife because she was gracious enough to take me in."

"That is good." Although he did not know what she meant—that Pinar had taken him in was good, or that he did not have a woman. He hoped it was the latter. "I was betrothed to a young man, but Judr was attacked before we could be married," she said. "I did not know him well enough anyway ... but he did risk his life for me."

Hadwin frowned. "I'm sorry to hear that. I don't blame him for it. Sometimes I wish I had fought harder for my family as well, but then my brother's wife would have died in vain. She sacrificed herself for us."

"Then we have much more in common," she breathed. "Hadwin, I have a favor to ask of you, if you are willing."

"Anything, m' la—Ha, Maura."

"Hm." Her light-brown eyes brightened under the dim moonlight, and he absorbed every detail. "I have seen the other women suffer beneath the cruel men here. But you are not cruel. You're quite kind and caring."

"Ah, I don't seek praise for it." Hadwin rubbed the back of his neck, ears burning.

"But you deserve it," she insisted. "You are a beacon of hope in this domain of Fan. Or at least, you have become mine when I thought I would be lost. In more ways than one. Especially now that I know you mean to take us from this place. But … I am yet pure. A virgin. I always meant to keep it that way until I have found someone of my choosing, though I was unwillingly betrothed. I at least want it to be my choice and, clearly, these men hardly care for that.

"So I wish to lie with you. To give myself to someone good and gentle before I'm taken by some brute. I want my choice. But you must be willing as well."

Hadwin stared at her, all of his senses going numb. Long ago, he told himself he would never be with a woman, forever alone as a bachelor under his sister-in-law's roof. Thus, he would never indulge in intercourse with one either. No woman wanted him anyway. But Maura stood before him with sincerity in her eyes, and she held his gaze with such strength that the heat rising inside him might melt him.

"If you are unwilling"—she sighed—"I understand. You are certainly a stronger man than most."

"No, I—I mean, if that is what you wish," he stuttered. "If you want … me."

Her smile revealed straight, white teeth. "Yes. You, and for the first time to be of my choosing. Is that all right?"

"I had hoped mine would be … different. Then again, I had hoped my life would be different. Not imprisoned in a place like this."

"Me too," she agreed.

"But you are very beautiful," he told her, his voice rasping. "And I will not lie and say I have not thought of taking you away from here."

"Is that what you've truly been thinking?" She giggled, warming him more.

"Yes." He chuckled and ran a hand through his hair. "It's hopeless. I guess what I mean to say is that—yes, I am willing."

She nodded at his answer, considering for a moment in which he thought she was second-guessing herself. Instead, Maura lifted her chin and drew closer to him.

"Have you ever lain with a woman before?" she whispered, as if the trees did not need to hear.

He gulped again when she pushed herself up on the tips of her toes, nose-to-nose with him, but did not waver. "No. So I'm afraid I will not know what exactly to do."

Maura put her forehead to his. "Nor I. But I have been told it is natural. We will know what to do."

With that, she pressed herself against him, folding her arms behind his neck, and Hadwin froze up. He concocted the different ways he had seen other couples hold each other, but could not bring himself to copy any of them. Naleem often teased him about how to sweep a girl off her feet, but was it truly a joke? Did he mean it? How could he joke about such a thing? This was terrifying!

Then Maura kissed him. Her soft lips spread his mouth open, and his muscles relaxed as he gave in and placed his arms around her waist. Amid her kisses, his hands traveled to her hips, the small of her back, and her ass and thighs before he realized and stopped himself.

Maura laughed and pulled away. "It's all right. You may do as you wish. I will tell you if I need you to stop."

All Hadwin could do was nod, for no words came, as if she had taken them from him. Maura kissed him again. This time, he drew her in, pulling her close by her hips, and pushed his mouth against hers. He thought he had done too much, been too urgent. But she put her tongue past his lips and entangled her fingers in his hair. Hadwin had forgotten how long it had grown as she pulled on the shaggy locks.

He held her tighter, and Maura squeaked under the sudden pressure, perhaps at the show of strength she did not expect him to have—he did not expect to have. She had been right, though. His heart raced as if it might rip through his chest, his mind whirled like raging winds; his body almost did not feel like his own. He knew what he wanted without knowing, and explored her body through her skirt and the tight folds of her bodice.

"Untie it," Maura instructed, and kissed his neck.

Tingles shot down Hadwin's spine, and his fingers fumbled over the laces behind her. Untying it seemed impossible, so he pulled the laces loose. His fingertips brushed her bare back, and Maura hummed as she shuddered.

Maura pushed him forward—her own strength proved itself—until his back ran into the tree trunk, the bark scratching at him. Hadwin gasped at the sudden roughness after so much of her softness. But he could give no more attention to it as her fingers slid under his shirt, her nails running along his skin. They traced around his waist and then up his back as she kissed and sucked at his neck.

Hadwin groaned, knees buckling, and slid them down the tree trunk. He and Maura hit the ground with a thud, gasping.

"Are you all right?" Hadwin placed his palm on her cheek. Her hair tangled between his fingers.

Maura laughed breathlessly and took his face in both hands. "Are you?"

"I've never done anything like this before," Hadwin told her. "I did not expect things to go this quickly."

She laughed again. "You are still so sweet. It's as if Gaea sent you to me, for you are as innocent as I am. And yet not so innocent."

"Ha" was all he could manage before she kissed him again. Her hands returned to their work, lifting his shirt over his head before she tossed it to the ground beside them.

The cold autumn air nipped at Hadwin's skin, and the bark raked deeper. He didn't care about those things as he sat before a woman without his shirt, like a tramp in a brothel. Unable to remember any time in his life he had been shirtless before a woman—except, he supposed, birth—he froze up again. Maura did not seem fazed. Her hands glided from his shoulders, over his chest, and down to his belly.

"I've always been afraid of marrying a very hairy man," she said, baffling him. "You have hair, but it is finer. I like that better."

"Oh. Good."

With another giggle, Maura reached for the hem of his pants and then stopped. "We should be equals here."

Before Hadwin could ask what she meant, Maura took her skirt in her fists. She pulled it up farther and farther until her dress was over her head and joined his shirt.

Hadwin thought his racing heart had stopped completely. Maura stood on her knees over him, naked, with her skin reflecting the dim, blue light. She was not as thin as the other women in the barn, but her ribs showed below her breasts, which his eyes could not part from. Her small hips dipped away from her waist before her thighs touched beneath her womanhood, unbearably arousing.

Seconds passed when Maura parted her lips, perhaps to speak, but Hadwin gripped her waist and pulled her to him. The coolness of her skin against his hardened him. As they kissed, he clutched her, unsure where to go. Maura loosened the pants and worked them over his legs and feet. Hadwin kicked them away and lost them in the forest ground. Maura straddled and lowered herself over him, letting him enter her.

"Oh." She rolled her hips in a whimper. At the heat of her, the space he filled within her, Hadwin stifled low groans and gasps. She was so small, he thought he had to be hurting her, but she controlled her movements as he heard women did in their lovemaking. This was her moment as much as it was his. With a new light and heartening emotion blooming inside him, Hadwin let her do as she wished, holding her as close as he'd wanted the minute he'd seen her.

Maura braced herself against him, curling around him and riding him until her legs shook and her body weakened. "Oh, Hadwin."

"Are you all right?" His voice and breath came more regularly than he thought, though quiet. But he had to be sure of her.

"Yes," Maura squeaked, and her body melded to his, her warmth protecting him in the brisk fall night. "Yes."

Hadwin kissed her neck and her shoulder, still hard within her. She gave a weak laugh as if she read his thoughts and whispered to him, "Your turn."

Instinct flaring, Hadwin grunted and drew a breath to steady himself. He took her in his arms and put her on her back over the pine needles. Maura whimpered and wrapped her legs around him as he thrust inside her. Gritting his teeth, Hadwin fought to control his voice as he grunted and panted, the pleasure building. His heart rammed so hard within his chest that she must have felt it against hers. His vision blurred, and he dropped his head beside Maura's, her yelps and cries right in his ear. She cried out in her pleasure, her body giving way beneath his. Her legs quaked and loosened around him.

Then Hadwin burst and shouted, clinging to her. His cheek brushed against hers as they both heaved for air. The cold iced his lungs until breathing became painful, and he slipped away from her. Lightheaded, he pushed himself up and looked down at her.

Maura's hair flowed about her head in wild arrangements, with pine needles catching the locks. Her breasts rose up and down as she caught her breath and stared back at him, a grin spreading across her face. Drowsy and full of satisfaction, her eyes drooped but held his gaze.

Hadwin drank in the sight of her underneath him and could not catch his breath, despite himself. He laughed until they were laughing at each other, and he rolled onto his side with a heavy sigh.

"Oh, Hadwin," Maura cooed as she stroked his face and hair. "Thank you."

"Thank *you*," he repeated in a whisper.

She smiled at him and stroked his bicep, shoulder, and chest. Hadwin basked in her touch, Haven and the world disappearing around them like a distant, foggy memory. With his eyes heavy, he couldn't stay awake. The entire night of waiting for Haven to sleep crept back up to him, the exhaustion doubled by the intoxicating pleasure.

"You truly are a man like no other, Hadwin," Maura whispered. "My breasts have been bare before you all this time, and you have not touched them."

"I told you I would not exactly know what to do," he whispered back with a foolish grin.

"Let's see then." She took his hand in hers and guided it to her chest, his palm pressed against her breast. His hand took up its entirety and held it, soft and yet firm. A huff of air escaped Maura's lips as she urged him to squeeze and play, her hand over his.

In the pitch-black of the forest, they giggled and kissed. Crickets chirped in the brush all around them, and the same owl that frightened Hadwin earlier hooted in the distance, but he paid it no heed. Worries and terrors did not plague his heart as they had for so long. On this night, the only other thing that existed was Maura before him. Her beauty and body.

Chapter 7

Raegna

For Ada.

Raegna absorbed Bai's determination through those gold eyes and knew their mission was the same. He looked like a completely different man in noble clothes. How had Olena put it? *Dazzling.*

Raegna scolded herself. She thought the same because she only ever saw him in common clothes, usually filth-ridden and grimy. Her head spun to see him as a proper man, that corset setting his shoulders back and broadening his chest beneath the long tunic.

Olena opened the door and smiled. "It's time. Your friends are waiting in the hallway."

Raegna and Bai peered at each other, rigid and waiting for the other's next move. She put a hand around the crook of his arm and clung as close as her body would allow. The tunic rubbed her skin, the deep-green fabric bound by gold stitching. Despite their proximity, Bai raised his chin and let Raegna guide him out with Olena.

Naleem and Asmund waited outside their chamber next door and blinked at their friends. Raegna halted Bai at the sight of them in nobler attire. Naleem donned dark gray pants with high black boots like Bai's, but his tunic was of a gray-blue color. Dark stitches wove over the hems and breast pocket. His black hair had been pulled in a half-braid over his scalp and ended in a small tail.

Asmund stood in a sapphire blue that brought out his eyes. The flashiness did not suit his underlying, timid personality, but he was dashing. With his mouse-brown hair brushed away from his eyes, Raegna could see why Iida had chosen him as her husband. He fidgeted under the attention.

"You both look well," Raegna commented. "I hardly would have recognized you."

"Nor us you." Naleem tugged at his collar. "Though I hate these clothes and the layers we have to wear."

Bai grunted in agreement, so close the deep rumbling in his chest reverberated against Raegna's arm, and she tensed. No skin showed beneath the men's clothing, save for their faces and hands. Everything was laced tightly over what Raegna knew were wired muscles. Even their necks were concealed by a high collar.

"It is customary for men to dress this way," Olena explained. "For chastity and so no other woman but his wife may see him."

Raegna grimaced, having seen as much of Bai in the bath as she ever had.

"Whatever it takes to see the Queen," he blurted. "Shall we go, then?"

Olena curtsied and led them down the hall to the next staircase. Other nobles migrated in their direction. Noblewomen paraded past in dresses like Raegna's with men latched to their sides, and every couple matched with vibrant or muted colors. The men stood straight-backed with their corset vests beneath their tunics. At least Raegna and Bai blended in even with Naleem and Asmund in tow.

Hallways expanded into rooms as the palace flourished before them. Each room had portraits, iron chandeliers, and mythical artistry, with historical figures and heroes portrayed in sculptures. Olena stopped before a threshold of double doors where nobles passed in and out. They led to a foyer where another set of doors opened to a crowd standing over shining tiles.

"This is the dining hall," Olena explained. "Allow the herald to announce you and help yourselves to food and drink. The Queen should arrive soon, and then supper will be served."

"Thank you, Olena." Raegna took the lead inside.

The dining hall spread out before them in a clamor of voices, clanking drinks and silverware, and the ambient flutes and drums played by musicians in the back corner. Spring-green banners hung from the high rafters. The nobles stood elbow to elbow. To the side walls, long tables held platters of fruits, sweets, and small appetizers of roasted roots, fried fowl bits, and sandwiched ham. Servants walked about with these platters and goblets of wine.

Raegna's mouth watered at the sight of it all, and beside her, the three men drooled like dogs. Drawing a breath of sweet, incensed air, Raegna pressed forward.

The herald stood in her simple spring-green dress, grasping her staff that towered over her small stature. She announced the nobles as they entered. An older woman in purple, adorned in silver brooches and beads, who had to be in her forties, stuck her nose in the air as she approached the herald. She guided a rather handsome young man in paler purple clothing. Raegna guessed him to be her son, but he kept quite close to her.

"Lady Abela," the heraldess called out, "of Feh Hall, Jera Hall, and Ostern. And her gentleman, Dagfinn."

Her gentleman. Not her son.

"We just walk past?" Naleem asked.

"Seems so." Raegna strode forward as Abela and Dagfinn joined the crowd. The herald eyed their approach before placing her staff in front of them. Raegna faced her. "Is this not the way?"

"You are the Queen's guests, I hear," the heraldess said.

"Yes."

"How shall I announce you?" she asked, taking her staff away from their path. "What are your names?"

Raegna faltered. None of them had titles to speak of, and their names would not hold any significance to these people. She recalled Ase's message, settling with a plan to remain consistent, and explained their names to the heraldess while Bai and Naleem fidgeted to get going.

Finally, the heraldess took a breath and raised her voice. "Shield-Priestess Raegna of Syden, Sorelle, and her husband, Bai. Former Matriarch Viona's brother-by-law, gentleman Asmund of Judr, Sorelle. And the gentleman Naleem of Syden, Sorelle."

All eyes turned to the four of them. The vast sea made Raegna's stomach flip, though she had faced more dangerous crowds before. A hand encased hers, and her quaking ceased with a jolt. Stone-faced, Bai looked over the nobles without heed to their newborn whispers and stood straight like the other gentlemen. But was his touch for her comfort or their guise?

In any case, Raegna refused to bolt from his hand. They needed to appear normal in the royal court's eyes. A commoner priestess, her husband, and two widowers could not be an average sight in Vakkar Hold.

Half of the nobles returned to their chatter as the next attendants were announced. Others gave sideways glances and more hushed whispers as the four mingled with them.

"What now?" Naleem asked.

"Act natural." Raegna leaned closer to Bai as bodies enclosed around them. "Treat yourselves to food and drink. You deserve that much."

On cue, a servant woman held a platter of fried something to them. Each of them took one and gobbled it up.

Asmund's nose wrinkled. "Fish."

"Better than nothing," Bai said.

"Ambassador Kunto," the herald announced next, "of Awevi and her companions."

The court turned its attention to the new attendants. A woman with glowing dark-brown skin that was almost like ebony held her head high, dressed in a bright-colored sash that wrapped about her with black symbols dotting the yellow, orange, and red fabric. Her black, coiled hair was cut short. Behind her stood more women with deep brown skin wearing similar bright garb, their hair cut to different lengths. Though the court eyed them with a hint of disdain, the women joined them as if they did not notice—or chose not to.

"Awevi," Naleem repeated. "They've come a long way."

Raegna tracked the women amid the crowd. "The herald said the one in the lead is an ambassador. They must be here to present themselves to Her Majesty."

"What for?"

"Trade perhaps? Galaenia has tried for many years to stay in Awevi's good graces after years of estrangement and even war. It has always been a more prominent issue in Ostern over the last decade or so."

"Do you think they'll take precedence over us?" Bai wondered aloud.

Raegna's heart sank as she looked away from the foreigners and their regal stature. "I don't know."

Surely, she comforted herself, the Queen would take care of domestic matters before foreign affairs. The relationship between Galaenia and Awevi had been peaceful for many years, as far as she understood. Perhaps the ambassador was here for small, tedious matters.

"Duchess Elmba," the herald called, then, breaking Raegna's thoughts, "and her husband, the Duke Ioan. Their children, young gentleman Edric, and Lady Signi, and Lady Vig."

The court hummed with approval as the Duchess appeared with her beautiful husband before they bowed. Raegna and her men did the same.

Duchess Elmba wore an extravagant pale lavender dress with white stitching down the bodice and around the hems. Bound in a high net of pearls and braids, her black hair contrasted with the bright colors. Her husband had a tunic and pants to match, though with duller lavender. The fabric did not suit his green eyes and fine, chiseled features, but he outshined every man in the room. Raegna's heart fluttered as he walked, but she controlled her breath and chastised herself as she clung to Bai.

The two girls stood side by side with straight black hair and long, elegant faces, like their mother. They wore matching lavender dresses as well, and judging by their similarities and age of perhaps nine or ten, they must have been twins. The boy was older than them, the spitting image of his father, though his green eyes were brighter and more innocent. He had to be going on fourteen or fifteen.

"I wonder how one even gets to be the Duchess or Duke," Bai grumbled as he plucked another appetizer from a passing platter.

"Bloodlines," Raegna said, happy to put her attention elsewhere. "Like the Queen, the Duchess' title follows her lineage, though it is trickier and harder to keep. Or so I've heard. A Duchess can still upset the Queen or the High Council if she is not careful and be removed from her office and court. It has happened before. Though I don't imagine Elmba is one to ruin herself that way."

"No," Bai agreed between bites. "I imagine not."

"Will the Queen be here soon?" Naleem asked.

Raegna placed a hand on his arm. "I am sure she will be. Olena said so. We will see her, Naleem."

"And not a moment too soon," Bai grumbled.

As the night progressed, more stragglers entered the banquet room in twos or in large families, like the Duchess'. Friends greeted each other, praised the good food, drank their wine, and gossiped. As the Queen's guest, Raegna thought she would feel a bit more welcomed, but the four huddled together and snatched food off platters whenever they could. With time waning, they grew on edge. Even Asmund brewed in his silent way.

A blowing horn sounded, and the court musicians ceased. At the other end of the room, new great doors opened before a short staircase where a woman stood in a gold dress beneath a billowing red cloak, and a man in a matching red tunic and white pants stood before the crowd. A new herald announced, "Her Majesty, Queen Kjerstin of Galaenia, daughter of Queen Sassa. And her husband, King Jerrick. Long live the Queen!"

"Long live the Queen!" the court repeated.

Queen Kjerstin lifted her voice. "Hail All-Mother Gaea."

Their voices came louder this time. "Hail All-Mother Gaea!"

Raegna stared in awe at the Queen of Galaenia and her beauty. Her gold dress flowed from the plump curvature of the bodice, with two bronze brooches on either side holding the crimson cloak over her shoulders. Scarlet beads and rubies stretched between the brooches across her breasts. The dress roamed over her waist and hips, with a wide brown leather belt hugging her belly. A gold crown sat on her brow, its points the silhouettes of stars and diamonds. Beneath it, her orange–brown hair fell in waves, prettily streaming over her shoulders and down her back. Her round face held no blemishes or marks but a light pink tinge, fair eyes and brows, and a straight Galaenian nose.

King Jerrick was an underwhelming sight only because Raegna imagined the King of Galaenia to be as devilishly handsome as Duke Ioan. He certainly was not unpleasant, with sweeping black hair and warm sepia skin, but had small, drooping eyes. His nose was longer and more crooked, but he had a nice smile that made his brown eyes sparkle. Beneath the bulk of his clothes, one would guess there would be a small, thin frame of a man, almost as if he were sickly.

Queen Kjerstin regarded her husband with more love in her eyes than Raegna had ever seen on a woman before. Except maybe when Pinar would look at Naleem. Or Iida at Asmund. She must have chosen this man herself or somehow gotten lucky with a political marriage. At least she seemed happy with her King.

Queen Kjerstin lifted a hand and gestured to another room. "Come. Dine with me. I hear there is much to talk about."

The courtiers laughed as they drifted to the next room. The four followed, unsure of what would happen next. How were they to have an audience with the Queen with all of these people in the way?

In the second room, three long tables were arranged in a geometric U with the Queen and King's throne-like chairs at its end. They took their seats as the crowd gathered and dispersed down either side of the tables. The Duchess, her Duke, and their children sat beside the Queen. On the far side, Ambassador Kunto and her companions settled next to the King and rather close to the Queen, a position Raegna would have preferred.

She assumed her little group would have to join the rest of the court, watching Lady Abela and her gentleman take seats beside the Awevi women. But when Raegna led the men down the tables to choose the far seats, a servant woman stopped them.

"Forgive me, Shield-Priestess," she said. "But your assigned seats are beside the Duchess."

"What?"

"Come. I will show you."

Back they went and took their places on the other side of the Duchess' family, with Raegna sitting at the end of the table. To her left sat the young daughters, then the boy, and then the Duke and Duchess, the Queen, and her King. Across the table, Raegna could look directly at Ambassador Kunto, who nodded to Queen Kjerstin.

"We must thank you for your royal hospitality, Your Majesty." The woman's voice came from her chest in a deep Awevi accent that lulled in an ancient melody. "Vakkar Hold remains beautiful. As well as Stadt and Ostern."

"It is always our pleasure to have you here, Ambassador," Queen Kjerstin replied, her voice light and sweet, curt and clipped like a common Galaenian. "Whatever we can do to make you feel more comfortable. How long do you intend to stay?"

"My Empress has already summoned us back," Ambassador Kunto answered. "We will leave before winter. As beautiful as Galaenia is, we do not anticipate its cold winters."

Queen Kjerstin laughed. "Neither do we."

Dinner was served on silver platters: seven roasted pigs, five dozen pheasants, more baked and candied roots, carrots, and beans. Alongside them were steaming honey bread, puddings, and tart berry sauces. Servants poured wine by the pitcher. The banquet proved to be a greater feast than any Solstice, Leaf Fall, or Winter Mull festival Raegna had ever indulged in. She attempted to keep her poise with a straight back and careful bites, but she shoveled her plate's contents into her mouth together, carrots mixing with candied root over her tongue. Raegna hardly cared except to get it in. Her men were worse.

Bai tore through four pheasant legs like a starving stray dog. Naleem wolfed his portion of the roast pig, and though he still kept his head low, Asmund inhaled baked root and honey bread. Several moments passed before they noticed eyes on them, widened in masked disgust. Raegna swallowed and wiped the corners of her mouth with a cloth as her mother had taught her.

"The food is good, then?" A smirk played on Queen Kjerstin's lips. Her bright blue eyes shined beneath torchlight.

Raegna hiccuped in her surprise. "Oh yes. It is truly wonderful, Your Majesty. We too thank you very much for your generosity. Vakkar Hold is beautiful."

"Thank you, Shield-Priestess. I've read the Matriarch's message of the attacks on Sorelle with a heavy heart. Though it is distressful, I certainly cannot offer the Maidens or royal warriors for village civil war."

All four of their heads jerked up. "What?"

"Well, I grieve for Syden's loss, but it simply isn't done." Queen Kjerstin folded her hands, treading carefully with her words. "In the Dark Days, we ravaged war on each other for certain rights of men, but those days are done. I might encourage your Matriarch to gather more forces of her own if there are unruly men in her village."

They stared dumbfounded at her until Bai said, "What letter did you read?"

Her Majesty stifled a small scoff. "The one I was given, from the new Matriarch Ase."

"With all due respect, Your Majesty," Naleem spoke up, "the attacks were not done by men of Syden. They were rebels with a base in Sorelle's hills. They attacked both Syden and Judr. This isn't about unruly men, but dangerous and organized armies enraged by hatred and Fan's evil."

Kjerstin frowned. "I don't understand. The message spoke of men who attacked, but I assumed this was a village's internal issue."

"It is far more likely," Duchess Elmba interjected.

Raegna's hands balled into fists, bunching the fabric of her skirt. "But it is not so. Your Majesty, it's much worse than that. They have killed warriors, women, their children, and men who fought like Sigmund to protect them. My family and I barely made it out of Syden alive. Naleem, his brother, and his sons were taken captive, along with other men who survived as recruits for their society. A patriarchy."

Laughter broke out over the tables. Even Duchess Elmba and her Duke hid their chuckles. Again, they did not believe them, just as Viona and Femke did not believe them. And where were they now? Raegna's blood boiled until she bubbled over and got to her feet, her chair scraping behind her.

"If you do not believe me, go to Sorelle and see for yourself! I will not be seen as a fool. They killed my daughter in cold blood. In a time of great loss, we've come to you and our Queen for help, and you all mock us!"

The laughter vanished, replaced by stares above frowns or gaping mouths. The only courtiers Raegna regretted surprising were the Duchess' twin daughters beside her, leaning back from her outburst with wide eyes and raised brows. Raegna's throat and chest coiled, and she flinched at Bai's touch. He squeezed her arm and held her startled gaze, the gold in his irises glinting like coins. Raegna held on to them, her body uncoiling as she sank back into her seat.

"Indeed." Queen Kjerstin stared down the tables with her chin high. "You should all be ashamed. These people come to us for our help. Attacks on Sorelle are not a laughing matter. I apologize, Shield-Priestess Raegna, for our behavior. And forgive me for the great misunderstanding. You must tell us more about these rebels."

"Your Majesty." Lady Abela wiped tears from her eyes in her laughter. "Can we truly believe a group of men can defeat an entire village of women? In my opinion, both Syden and Judr should have controlled their men or better armed themselves."

Kjerstin closed her eyes to the claim. "We will not make such accusations until we have heard Raegna's story. Let her speak." She turned to Raegna, her brow raised. "Go on."

Raegna's heart pounded. When she glanced at her men, they offered encouraging nods. The court would not listen to them. They were just men. Raegna was a woman and had earned the Queen's ear.

With as much detail as she could manage, Raegna explained the night the Haven men invaded. She told the court about the screams and how she looked out her window and beheld women slaughtered outside her door and on the street. She told them how she and her family escaped to the hills, and even when she wanted to ride back, how Bai had hit her over the head.

"It was the only thing he could think of to protect me," she told them in a flurry of words, as some women bristled at the retelling. To sell it as a wife and husband's love, she gave Bai a brief look. The tiny muscles in his eyelids tightened. The words weren't a lie.

Raegna clarified that the souls of the people who died in Syden were lifted by her blood oath to Gaea, and how she took her family to Judr and met Matriarch Viona.

"They did not believe us either," she admitted. "Matriarch Viona said she would send a party to look into it. After several days, when they finally did, the Matriarch and her sister returned ... beheaded on horseback. The men followed them and attacked Judr. That was when we found Naleem again, but those devils still hold his family captive. Asmund also lost his family, the Matriarch's sister. My husband and I ... We lost our daughter."

Each man lowered their head, and Bai tensed beside her. Raegna almost allowed her hand over his, but could not bring herself to do it or meet his eyes again.

Tears glistened in Queen Kjerstin's eyes, reflecting the firelight. A sob threatened the back of Raegna's throat, and her hands trembled over her skirt. She could have crumbled to the floor and wept for the mere look on Kjerstin's face. Someone heard her.

"If it pleases you, Your Majesty," Ambassador Kunto's lulling voice broke the silence, "I will tell my Queen of this. We too value the control of men in some factions more than others. I am sure she would like to send some of her forces to put these *khalas* in their place."

Kjerstin composed herself with a sharp breath and raised her chin. "There will be no need for it, Ambassador, but I thank you. I will not stand for these murderers. Any attack on my people is an attack on me. I would like to send Maidens in to destroy them." She looked across the tables. "What do you think, Commander Gittan?"

All eyes darted to a tall woman with a long, angular face and light tawny skin. Her blonde hair flowed in waves over her broad, muscular shoulders, with half of it done in braids, the rest was a waterfall over the cliffs of her chest and breasts. She wore a dress with dull red fabric and black fur trimming the hems. An emblem hung from her neck, round like a shield, with the same blue and black colors as Maiden banners.

Raegna's energy surged from her mournful tales.

The woman wore a Maiden's emblem, and the Queen had called her Commander. Raegna's frame quaked. She'd dreamed of this moment since she was a child. She was feasting with the Commander of the Maidens!

Commander Gittan chewed her food, an eyebrow raised in acknowledgment of her Queen. She swallowed before saying, "These men sound like Fan-spawn." Her deep voice came from her nose and held a stronger Galaenian accent than most, lilting on occasion. "They're cowards to be attacking innocents, and I will gladly go with my Maidens and show them who they're dealing with."

"Could not have said it better myself," Kjerstin agreed with a firm nod.

"What we would need is more information about them." Commander Gittan turned for a better view of Raegna and her group. "One of you men was held at their base?"

"I was, um, Commander," Naleem stammered. "They call their camp *Haven*. There must be at least two hundred of them living there. Runaways or captives from previous raids. They are led by a man named Thenalious. He has councilmen under him, and below them are the regulars. Haven functions like a small village with livestock and goods. They make weapons and plan to attack Your Majesty when they are strong enough. They take men from villages and sire sons from the women they imprison."

The court shifted with murmurs echoing over the food platters and wine goblets.

Gittan propped an elbow on the table with a loose fist under her chin. "This *Haven* is in Sorelle's hills?"

"Yes. About a day's ride from our villages, or at least from Judr," Naleem added. "They are brutal fighters, and besides the women and children, there are men there who do not fight with them. My brother is one of them, with my son."

Forehead creased in concentration, Gittan scanned the table as if it held a map of Galaenia and not their elegant dinner. "Very well, gentle-man—Naleem, is it? You will be my counsel as we strategize our plans for this Haven. Your knowledge will be extremely beneficial."

Naleem blinked in disbelief but nodded to the Commander. Raegna corrected her pouted lip as heat burned her cheeks. Envy would have to be put aside. Naleem's trials and pain would help his family out of Haven, and the Commander of the Maidens was so willing to take his counsel, it seemed like a match made in Heimelle.

A fork scraped a plate, piercing the whispers. Duchess Elmba's black eyebrows arched, and her thin lips pursed. "Perhaps we should also take this to the High Council. Nothing like this has ever occurred in Galaenia's history. A male rebellion? Much is unknown, and this is a high risk to our Maidens, our warriors, and our finances."

"We are perfectly stable to embark on this mission, Duchess," Queen Kjerstin said, staring straight ahead. "And we have strong, courageous women in our defenses."

"But such decisions in uncertain situations will not bode well with the Council, Your Majesty," Elmba countered as she lifted her goblet to her lips.

"I am sure my Queen will offer warriors," Ambassador Kunto reminded them.

Kjerstin laid a palm on the table. "With respect, I am Queen of this land, and I must decline, Ambassador." Kjerstin looked at Elmba then. "But we will discuss it with the High Council as soon as possible. Lady Abela, request an audience with them by tonight."

"Of course, Your Majesty." Lady Abela raised her goblet. "A wise choice."

Queen Kjerstin ignored her and turned to Raegna and the others with gentle eyes. "In the meantime, gentleman Naleem, you will aid Commander Gittan in the matter of strategy. The rest of you will take refuge here in Vakkar Hold for as long as you wish. For life, if you desire. You have my thanks for journeying to Stadt from Sorelle for your fallen. You only deserve more."

Raegna gasped. Live in Vakkar Hold? "You—Your Majesty, we could not impose—"

"Nonsense." Kjerstin chuckled with a wave of her hand. "You are all welcome here. I am sure our royal temple of Gaea needs brave priestesses such as yourself, Raegna. Your husband may stay with you. Naleem will aid Gittan, and Asmund, I see you are deserving of court life, what with being a Matriarch's brother-by-law."

Asmund shrank down in his seat.

"I think," Bai spoke up, his eyes on the Queen, "that we would also like to help in the destruction of Haven. If we can be of any help, we would gladly do so."

"I'm sure you would," Kjerstin agreed. "Commander?"

"We will have to see." Gittan looked at Raegna and made her freeze in place. "I wonder if they don't call you Shield-Priestess for just anything. It's not typically in a priestess' interest to take up a sword."

"But I have done just that," Raegna told her with her chin high.

Commander Gittan laughed. "I like that. We must discuss the matter of location and, of course, consult the High Council, *Duchess*. Then I will let you know. But our Queen is right that you deserve our luxuries and rest now. Thank Gaea for you four."

"Yes, thank Gaea." Kjerstin raised her goblet in the air for the entire room to see. "Praise All-Mother Gaea!"

"Praise All-Mother Gaea!" the court rang out.

Yes, praise Gaea, Raegna thought, for it was She who guided and protected the group over their journey. A misguidance down the wrong path brought them to the Duchess' carriage, and nothing could have been planned more perfectly. The Queen had heard them out, but there was a long way to go yet. They would have to convince the High Council, who might deny their story, and the Queen's word could not overrule the Council.

Raegna shoved that to the side and allowed herself this one victory. Her men were smiling for once in several weeks. Bai returned her gaze, his crooked smile making a small dimple on his left cheek, and his gold eyes catching the flames. Raegna huffed in amusement and smiled back.

For Ada.

Chapter 8

Hadwin

Hadwin breathed in a deep sigh. In the dim forest, a single bird sang in the branches above. In a state between sleep and consciousness, he found himself curled around Maura, his chest pressed against her shoulder blades and the tip of his nose touching the back of her neck. He drifted back to sleep.

He woke again to the sound of her breath, the feeling of her chest rising and falling beneath his arm, and she rolled to meet him.

Maura's blonde hair curled in tangles and brushed against her freckled cheeks. Her eyes fell half-closed as she took him in with a blissful smile. "Good morning."

"Good morning," he murmured.

With a breeze floating along his hips, waist, and bare shoulders, Hadwin realized the two of them lay naked on the forest floor, and he recollected the night before. "Ah."

Maura chuckled and cupped his face. "Sweet Hadwin."

Propping himself up on an elbow, he kissed her. Her warm lips contrasted with the cool morning. Then Hadwin jolted as his memory slammed him like a horse's kick. "Cadoc."

"What?" Maura retreated with a furrowed brow.

"Cadoc and Else," he said. "They are still in the—Oh, Gaea, damn it all!"

Hadwin leaped to his feet and stumbled over the ground in search of his clothes. Maura sat up and rubbed her eyes. "Hadwin, it's all right. We'll get back in time. It's barely light out."

"The councilmen might have noticed I was gone." Hadwin pulled his shirt over his head. "And I meant to get back to Cadoc and Else earlier, but we must have fallen asleep and—Gaea, help me. I'm such an idiot!"

Maura plucked her dress from the ground and held it to her breast. "An idiot to be out here with me?"

He turned to her just as he was slipping into his pants. "No. That's not true. I'm sorry, but I have to get back to them and then to the nursery before anyone notices we're gone."

"For all your talk of escape, I didn't think you feared them so much," she admitted with a half-smile. Her dress hung from her shoulders once more. "I'm sure the children are all right."

"Maura, you must know they are dangerous men." Hadwin tied the string of his pants. "That's the reason I want to escape. When the other women tell us to do nothing, to play our role, I know they mean it. They've witnessed things. Horrible and unimaginable things. I hate being Thenalious' tool or plaything, but I cannot risk the children's safety."

She absorbed his words as she looked on with sad, doe-like eyes. "But we can leave now. Gather your nephew and go. It's all out there."

Maura gestured to the open forest. Hadwin's brow furrowed, and he watched the trees. The pines and leaves rattled as a fall wind coursed between them. Birdsong continued through the branches. They could run. They could go down the hillsides until they reached a road and a village.

But Else would be left behind in a world like Helved. Talia, Farah, and the other women, the other boys, though they were oblivious, would still be trapped in suffering. Freedom lay before him in those trees, but Hadwin did not have the heart to take it.

Hadwin offered his hand. "We'll find another way. I promise."

Maura's lip pouted, but she took his hand and followed him back to the old barn.

They ducked through the broken board in the wall, checking first to see if any of the councilmen had made a visit. There were none. All the women slumbered in the hay, save for Farah and Talia, who'd woken to feed Else. Cadoc slept with his head in Farah's lap, and Hadwin's chest bloomed with relief.

The two women glared at the couple as they snuck back inside.

"What on Gaea's good earth were you two *thinking*?" Farah spat. "Thought you could sneak off like love-struck children? Fucking all through the night? Fan's cock, I'm sure all of Sorelle *heard* you!"

Hadwin's cheeks burned. "W—What?"

"It's not exactly your business," Maura protested, giving Farah a cold sideways glance.

Farah's eyes seared like fire, and she opened her mouth to throw more curses, but Talia spoke first. "Neither of you gave any explanation as to what was going on. One of them could have been here to—Well, if you want to be together, I beg you to reconsider such an affair, but I cannot stop you. Instead, I will make it known—we wish for you two to be more careful. Hadwin, lower-ranking men have been here before and have had their manhood cut off for it, or worse. And Maura, the women they took have been killed or ... cleaned out for a man's seed or child. We could not bear it if that happened to either of you."

Hadwin lowered his head, and his shoulders curled in. "Yes, of course, Talia."

"Never mind everything that could happen to *you*, you foolish man," Farah added. "What would become of your nephew here? What do you think he would do without you? Do you think they would spare him?"

Hadwin looked to Cadoc, who stirred at the voices that filled the room. He'd left him alone, at the prospect of organizing an escape, but still. It should have remained simply planning, and it hadn't.

Ragged claws sank into Hadwin's chest. He'd left Cadoc alone. After losing Naleem and Dakarai, he promised himself he would protect Cadoc in this world of Fan. Already, he'd failed him.

"No, they wouldn't," he said. "I'm sorry. It won't happen again."

Maura tensed beside him.

Talia took Else from her breast. "Please take them back to the nursery. We'll see you later."

He gave a short nod and left the old barn with Else in his arms, hand in hand with a sleepy Cadoc. As he turned to shut the door behind him, he stole a glance at Maura, who watched him go. Frowning, she stood in the middle of the barn, preparing to be scolded by Farah some more.

Farah and Talia were right. Last night had been too great a risk. To continue living in such a fantasy would prove dangerous. Hadwin would have to leave Maura be and focus on keeping his head low before enacting any escape plans.

Shutting the door without another word to her, he guided Cadoc through Haven and back to the nursery.

The camp's crisscrossing roads came alive with the men starting their morning duties as always. The sun's rays peeked over the treetops, and light clouds streaked the purple sky above them. This was typically the time Hadwin would leave the nursery to take Else to her mother, but the men around him didn't seem to care about that. They sneered or shoved past as they always did.

The great house bustled with the kitchen boys preparing the Council's breakfast. The dining table was set in the hall as Hadwin walked to the back room and up the stairs. Otherwise, the house remained quiet and still. Hadwin hoped he could make it to the nursery without arousing any suspicion.

When he came upon the door, he found it open and silent. Hadwin's heart seized. He pulled Cadoc behind him and slowly approached.

Inside, all the boys slept in their beds. None of them stirred, despite the light that filtered through the window's curtains. Hadwin's eyes roamed the entire room until they fell upon the cradles in the corner—where the beast stood.

Towering over Else's empty cradle was Reynold, bulking shoulders draped in a furry, black wolf's skin that doubled his size. His unkempt beard hung from his thick, set jaw. Rust-colored hair fell in loose locks and braids past his shoulders, taking in the light like his pale pink skin. The beast turned to the caregiver, stone-faced. His amber eyes settled on Hadwin like an anvil, crushing his body.

"You're early," he rumbled, sending a jolt up Hadwin's spine.

"She was crying," he spluttered. "She started crying earlier than usual."

"Hm. We didn't hear it."

Hadwin swallowed. "I try to be quick about it."

Reynold stepped forward and loomed over Hadwin, a head above him. Though his entire body quaked beneath the beast's size, Hadwin remained stiff and straight. He brought Else closer to his chest and braced in front of Cadoc. The poor boy trembled behind his legs. Hadwin's thoughts swam. Did Reynold know he'd snuck off with Maura somehow? What was he going to do with him now?

The beast let the intimidation linger before his voice rumbled deep within his chest. "The only reason the brat still lives is because Thenalious wanted to bed your bitch-brother. Now that he has, I see no reason why we let it live."

What? The air fled from Hadwin's lungs as if he had fallen flat on his back. Thenalious had ... to Naleem ...

"Where is my brother?" Hadwin demanded, the words pouring out of him before he could stop them.

"Dead in Helved."

Hadwin's heart plummeted to his gut. "No."

"As you should be," Reynold growled. "But we keep you because you're a decent nanny. So long as you don't cause trouble. There is still no good reason for the brat to live."

Hadwin gritted his teeth. "She's your daughter."

"It is a mistake and a curse." He took another step forward, and Hadwin stumbled back. "I should have smashed its head in when I had the chance. Now let's be done with it."

Reynold clamped his huge hand around Hadwin's arm to wrench Else free, but Hadwin held fast and twisted away. He shoved his shoulder into the beast's chest with all his might. Pain shot through his shoulder blade and down his back, but Hadwin knocked Reynold off his feet to crash against the opposite wall. The force of it shook the room, and the boys woke with a start in their beds. Cadoc dropped behind Hadwin, erupting into sobs. The babes cried in their cradles, and Else wailed with them.

"Stay away from her!" Hadwin shouted over them. "You agreed to keep her here because we promised to raise her the way you all want her to be! Under the rule of men. Isn't that what you wanted?"

Reynold stepped away from the wall and glared at him. "You little wretch."

"Go ahead," Hadwin snarled. "Threaten me, call me what you want. But if you want her, you'll have to kill me. And I'm a decent nanny, aren't I?"

"I hardly care for that."

"Oberon and the others care for their sons," Hadwin barked. "They would give you and Thenalious a rise if anything happened to me. Maybe they could bring the two of you down!"

Reynold's fist collided with Hadwin's face, and he fell, Else tumbling with him. Where and how she landed, he wasn't sure. She wasn't in his arms anymore, though he could hear her sobbing on the floor. He couldn't search for her in his daze as Reynold gripped him by the throat and slammed him against the door frame.

The boys screamed, some of them shouting. "Hadwin!"

Hadwin clawed at Reynold's hands as they enclosed his throat, cutting off air. Choking, he scratched and kicked, but his strength diminished. Blood pulsed in his ears, and his limbs were going numb.

"I should tear your throat out for that," Reynold grumbled. "You only live because we let you. Give me one more reason to suspect you are conspiring against us, I *will* strip your hide off your back." His grip tightened around Hadwin's neck. "Now watch the brat die."

Another fist thrust into Hadwin's belly, and Reynold released him to collapse onto the floor in a fit of coughs, gasping for air. "No."

Reynold stalked toward Else on the floor, and lifted a boot over her. Before he could crush her, Audun leaped between them. The boy shielded his baby half-sister before their father, four times his size, his breath coming ragged and shaking. Tears glittered in his large eyes. Reynold stared down at him.

"Get out of the way," he snarled.

Audun shook his head.

Hadwin propped himself on an elbow and watched, praying Gaea would spare the siblings. The beast stopped and didn't even push the boy out of the way. He didn't budge and only stared as if Audun had some power over him.

Yes. Of course he had.

The sons of the Council were the future of Haven. Caregivers who neglected them were severely punished. Those who sought to harm them would surely be killed, even their own fathers. Whether Audun knew all of this or not was up for debate. It was more certain that he threw himself into danger simply to protect Else.

Audun remained still and stared Reynold down with the same amber eyes.

Only then did Reynold retreat and step back. He started for the door but halted before Hadwin as he fought to rise off the floor. Then Reynold's boot came down on Hadwin's hand, crushing his fingers. Hadwin cried out, and the boys yelped.

Reynold twisted his boot. "One more slipup, and you'll join your brother."

With that, he lifted his foot and left, slamming the door behind him. Hadwin grunted and pushed himself to sit against the wall. He held his throbbing hand to his torso and turned to Audun. "Is she all right?"

Audun flinched as if he had snapped from a trance. Blinking, he looked over his shoulder at Else as she wailed, wrapped in a blanket on the ground.

"Pick her up like I've taught you," Hadwin instructed gently.

Cadoc wrapped his arms around his bicep and cried into his shoulder. Trembling, Audun nodded and retrieved Else from behind him while the other boys whimpered or left their beds to tend to Hadwin.

Sitting up, he braced his hand as the boys surrounded him with small hugs. Audun brought Else to him and set her in his lap.

"Thank you, Audun," Hadwin said. "She seems all right."

"Are you all right, Hadwin?" Audun asked.

Every boy lifted their gaze, awaiting an answer. After meeting their eyes, Hadwin gave a weak grin and nodded. "Yes, I'm all right. I promise. I'm sorry you were all frightened."

They hugged him tighter or plopped themselves down close to him. The poor things should never have had to witness this, and Hadwin had let it happen. If only he'd left the woods before dawn or had left Maura in the middle of the night, his absence would not have been noticed. Now Reynold and Thenalious would be ever more suspicious of him, which put him, Cadoc, Else, Maura, the other women, and even the boys in danger. All because of him.

Hadwin pulled Cadoc and the other boys closer, all of them hovering over Else as she whimpered in his lap.

"I'm sorry, little ones. I'm so sorry."

Chapter 9

Naleem

S ILK AND FEATHER PILLOWS unnerved Naleem's senses as he stirred to life. Meeting the Queen of Galaenia and the Commander of the Maidens last night should have led to the best sleep of his life. Instead, Naleem tossed and turned beneath the silk.

Asmund slept in the second bed, lying on his belly and snug under the sheets. Exhausted by their first day in Stadt and Vakkar Hold, he was gone from the world before Naleem even reached his bed. He deserved peace after their journey—and after losing his wife and babe in Judr. Naleem's heart twisted for him, partial to the strange, timid young man who experienced the same terrors he had. They were connected that way.

The sheets ruffled as Naleem slipped out of bed and searched for decent clothes. He couldn't meet with Commander Gittan in his nightshirt.

A knock came at the door before it clicked open. Asmund jolted awake and raised himself onto his elbows. Naleem turned as two servant boys entered, balancing silver platters of food in their arms. They could not have been older than thirteen. Each split to the nightstands and rested the platters there.

Naleem offered them a smile. "Good morning."

The boy at his nightstand blinked before he bowed. "Good morning, sir. Breakfast."

As lovely as breakfast in bed was, Naleem stifled a frown at this servitude. Especially as it came from children. "Thank you."

"Of course, sir."

Asmund watched the other boy set his platter down before the two of them left the room and shut the door behind them. Then he sat up and investigated the food.

"It smells good." Naleem continued his search for clothes in the wardrobe.

At the Duchess' instruction, servants had filled it with garments, but Naleem did not think any would suit him. Many were rather flashy, brightly colored, and sparkling. Others were duller, but still too much. All he knew how to wear were pants, shirts, and boots, so he picked what he could, donning a white shirt under a black vest and dark-brown pants and boots not quite fit for riding or work.

He returned to Asmund with his hands at his sides, his palms open. "What do you think? Proper enough to meet the Commander of the Maidens?"

Asmund took a bite of a biscuit from his breakfast and chewed thoughtfully before nodding.

"Hungry, eh?" Naleem chuckled. "I guess it would be better not to go on an empty stomach."

They ate breakfast together: sausages with biscuits and spiced cream. Naleem gobbled it up, thankful for real food again. He considered everything he would tell the Commander, though that meant reliving Haven. He had to try for Hadwin and Cadoc.

Naleem drew a breath, expanding the tightness in his chest. The pain of missing them was too much for him to eat any more. They might be starving while he lived in luxury. He put his breakfast aside and stood. "I'm going to find the Commander now. Do you want to come with?"

Asmund stared with bewildered eyes, his light-brown eyebrows raised. He nodded and got out of bed. "Have to get dressed."

At least he was now speaking in complete sentences. "Take your time," Naleem said. "There are hardly any comfortable clothes in there."

Asmund donned a white shirt as well, cinched in by a deep blue corset vest that hugged his angular frame from wide chest to thin waist. The black pants and boots were similar to Naleem's, not fit for work of any kind.

"Far more fashionable than me," Naleem said. "I'm sure the snobs out there will appreciate your taste better."

Asmund fidgeted, his shoulders pitching forward to slouch, though the tight corset would not permit it. "I like yours better."

"Perhaps later we can request different clothes." Naleem headed for the door. "For now, let's go find these Maidens."

Outside their chamber, the hallways buzzed with activity. Scattered nobles passed while servants rushed by with fabrics, platters, and brooms. Sweating and pulling weeds in a field seemed more appealing than this. At least when Naleem worked in Syden, he worked for himself and his family and served no one but Galaenia and those he loved. But these servants earned coin for their families, too, he supposed.

The two men merged with the routines of the palace, dodging passersby and navigating the hallways. Naleem tried to map the palace as they'd come in the day before, entering from the courtyard and traveling through halls and double doors. But the bathhouses were underground and being led through stone tunnels threw off Naleem's plot of the place. He remembered the dining hall and followed that route. Surely someone there could tell him where the Maidens were.

The double doors stood open as they had the night before, so Naleem and Asmund entered. A much smaller crowd milled about, socializing with drinks in hand as servants offered platters. Women wore regal dresses, and their men clung close to their sides or ventured to chat with each other.

A larger group gathered at a table in the middle of the room. In a lavish, blue-green tunic, black pants, and boots sat the King with his grooms surrounding him. A few rings glittered on his fingers, though not as many as on his counterparts. Woven beneath his swept-back black hair was a gold band that crested the top of his forehead.

The man across from him was puzzled over a board game they were playing, with a couple more gentlemen at his side. King Jerrick seemed rather smug, watching his opponent's next move with mischief in his eyes.

No one would know the palace grounds better than His Majesty. While the other nobles in the room turned their noses up at the sight of Naleem and Asmund, the King seemed the most approachable, with a soft face and playful smile. He might be more like his Queen—open and sympathetic.

Naleem's body begged him to find someone else as he approached the King—who leaned in his chair with an unbothered confidence and similar hair and broad shoulders to the man who plagued his nightmares.

Biting the inside of his cheek, Naleem pushed forward, Asmund at his heels. When Jerrick turned to him with a face devoid of cunning, manipulation or wrath, Naleem's nerves quieted. He picked out differing features from Thenalious, like sepia skin that drank the morning light from the high windows, drooping dark-brown eyes, and a longer nose.

"Er, Your Majesty." Naleem dipped in a curt bow. That was how one approached royalty, wasn't it? In the corner of his eye, Asmund copied him.

King Jerrick gave a warm smile. "Good morning. You two are our guests from Sorelle, aren't you?"

"Yes."

The other men examined them from head to toe now that they were up close. If they could inspect them like show dogs, they might.

"Well, should you be with Commander Gittan?" Jerrick asked. "I'm sure she's waiting for you."

"Ah, yes. That's what I came to ask. That is, if you know where the Maidens are."

"Of course." Jerrick stood and faced the others. "Gentlemen, if you don't mind."

He reached to take his piece from the board and tapped it over several circular tiles in a rapid pattern before resting it on the other side. His opponent groaned while others praised him. As the King took his leave, the gentlemen stood to bow before returning to their games.

"Come." King Jerrick gestured out of the room. "The Maidens have a training ground near the stables."

The King's grooms trailed them as they navigated out of the hall. They were all young men, about Hadwin's age—at least twenty-four. Asmund would have fit in among them had he been better dressed. King Jerrick had to be a few years older, like Naleem. Not that such age differences mattered in friendships, but why would such a young bunch be in this

King's company? Perhaps he looked older than he was, with a few lines etching his features.

"I am sorry to hear about what happened in Sorelle," Jerrick said as they reached the entry hall. "It breaks all our hearts to learn about such a tragedy. Her Majesty has made it her utmost priority to end these attacks and save our imprisoned sisters and brothers."

"Thank you." Racking nerves could not bring Naleem to say much else, or allow him to believe he could have eloquent conversations with the King of Galaenia. Nothing from farming had taught him how to.

The courtyard opened before them, and sunlight poured in, accompanied by hooves on cobblestones, women barking orders, and the clanging of steel against steel. More servants and stable girls went about their duties than the day before, Naleem had taken the time to note them. Gardeners trimmed the hedges of the rose gardens to the west, settling themselves on towering ladders to reach the tops of the shrubbery, and their wide-brimmed hats kept the sun off their heads and shoulders.

Young horsewomen paraded here and there as the King and his entourage walked past the stables. They pushed barrels of hay, led horses, or carried water buckets. Their skirts stopped above their ankles, and their tattered high boots could be seen underneath, coated in dust. Most of them had braided their hair back to keep it away from their faces as they worked.

"Strange," Naleem murmured.

King Jerrick chuckled. "What is?"

"Forgive me, but no men are working in your stables. Or tending the gardens. Where are they?"

"Well … at home with their children, I suppose," Jerrick guessed. "We've never had men working in the courtyard unless a servant was sent for something."

"In the villages, we work," Naleem told him. "Most of us, anyway. I thought there would be more men doing the hard labor."

"Ah, well, that might be because a village must contribute to its realm and its country," Jerrick said. "Twice as much work would need to be done. We only need our gardens to look beautiful and our horses taken care of. Neither is an easy task, but they are not as grueling as growing crops to feed Galaenia."

"What about the servant men inside the palace?"

"They are required to wait upon the noblemen," Jerrick explained. "Servant girls could not do that. And just as a share of the field is given to your wife when you work, their wives or mothers are paid in coin for their service."

"It would be too much coin to have even more men in the stables and gardens," Naleem thought aloud. "They don't give us any in Syden. That is strictly crops."

"There is a budget in place," Jerrick admitted with a sigh. "All of that Her Majesty, the Duchess, and the secretaries deal with. Ah, here we are."

They came upon a dusty area in front of a small stone building. One side opened to an armory. The other had wooden double doors that hung open, though Naleem could not make out what was inside. But the Maidens caught his attention, sparring with swords and shields and kicking up dust in front of the armory.

Four pairs clashed their swords or rammed their shields with short cries and grunts. Naleem had seen village warriors spar, but they weren't as agile or tactical as the Maidens. Each woman became a blur of motion in her leather armor, weaving and twisting as she battled. Through the dust, Naleem found the Commander bracing her shield against a Maiden a head taller than her. Her opponent gave a deep cry as her sword connected with Gittan's shield. The blade hit it with a hard thud, and Gittan shoved it away and made her blow. Her opponent dodged as the blade barely missed her thigh.

"Quite the spectacle they are," King Jerrick commented. "The fierce Maidens of Galaenia, known for their loyalty to their country and people. It's always good to see them in action."

His words barely registered in Naleem's mind as he studied the Commander's movements. Her yellow hair flashed in its low, twisted braid—enough locks below it to imitate a horse's tail. With keen eyes, she anticipated each of her opponent's blows and countered them. She found an opening and drove her shield against the other Maiden's chest, placing her foot just behind her heel and knocking her off balance.

A yelp escaped her opponent's lips as she fell flat on her back. Commander Gittan brought her blade to her throat and smiled before pulling the sword away.

"Excellent job." She offered a hand to lift the other Maiden to her feet.

"Never quite as good as you, Commander." The Maiden rose and glanced at the King and his company. "I do believe we have visitors."

Gittan turned, and her striking, sunlit brown eyes met Naleem's. He looked away, silently wishing he had put more thought into dressing like the rest of the noblemen. She and the Maidens would surely think of him as a dull southern commoner.

"Your Majesty." Gittan approached with her head bowed. "You've brought me our guests, I see."

"Indeed." King Jerrick gave a short wave. "No need for pleasantries. We'll let all of you discuss these heinous attacks. Good day, you two."

Naleem and Asmund bowed as the King and his grooms departed. "Thank you, Your Majesty. Good day to you, too!"

The grooms filed behind him and set a fair pace across the courtyard.

"Even his grace has much to do," Gittan told them. "Always having to set an example for the other men. Well, for every man in Galaenia." She offered Naleem a smile. "So, let us get started. I'll show you how we'll plan our strategy."

They left the sparring Maidens through the double doors of the stone building. Inside, rows of long tables stretched out, where women in dresses or armor leaned over Galaenian maps pinned down by pawns and stones.

"Many of our meetings happen here if not before the Queen or High Council," Gittan explained as they passed the tables, everyone too engrossed in their discussions to pay them any mind. "Currently, Hafelle's port is our main concern. Awevi ships have been spotted trespassing Galaenian shores without invitation or means for trade. That is why Awevi's ambassador is visiting us. In addition, there is the matter of the Wa'Ni populations in the north. We continuously work with Norden and the Matriarch of Hol Rekke to take care of such hostiles."

"You are all certainly busy." Naleem peered at each map and the various pawns the Maidens used to mark different parties.

"Yes. All of this must be done to protect Galaenia." Gittan stopped at a door at the back of the building. She slipped a key from her belt and unlocked it.

A single table sat inside with a blue and black flag of the Maidens as its backdrop. Two vertical windows let sunlight in. A tapestry of Maidens on horseback in battle hung to one side of the room with another large map of Galaenia on the other. On either side of the map hung a sword and ax, neither marred by battle, but sharp and gleaming.

Naleem and Asmund stopped in front of the map and gazed at the etchings of mountains, plains, and rivers that coursed through the rendering of their homeland. Each region and village was marked by its name: Ostern, with its five villages—big and small—in the east beside the ocean; Norden to the north, with its lone village of Hol Rekke tucked away by the mountain range; Vesten and its three settlements scattered about the western plains; and their own district of Sorelle, with Syden and Judr pressed into the southern hills. Naleem traced the route from Judr to the mark of Stadt.

"We came a long way," he murmured.

Below the tapestry stood a cabinet topped with unlit candles—the wicks blackened and the wax frozen in melted beads—and piles of maps and parchment. Gittan dug through them. "I've prepared nearly every current map of Sorelle and its hills for us."

"If you light the candles near all those papers, you'll surely have a fire," Naleem teased.

A small smile played over her lips. "You sound like my mother. She always chided me when I studied geography like this. I could not help but get started after the banquet. Don't worry, I've never had a fire ... yet."

Naleem dipped his head and fidgeted with his sleeve. "Well, thank you. I—We truly appreciate what you are doing for us. What you all are doing for us."

"Of course." The papers rattled as Gittan laid them across the table. She pointed to a small patch of a blank valley on the first map. "Here is Syden, where Matriarch Alv ruled."

Her finger traced just a few inches southeast. "This is Matriarch Viona's village, Judr. Or now Matriarch Ase's village. Those hills closest to the southern cliffs are full of wilderness. That is where you believe these traitors have their base?"

"They blinded us," Naleem explained, examining the land. "But they took us uphill, and nothing but forest surrounded Haven. They used the trees and forest debris to make a gate to conceal them."

"It may not look it," Gittan told him, "but that land is vast and can be dense. Tracking them will be difficult, especially if they are clever and do not want to be seen. Where there is a village, there is always a river or stream. That is why the villages of Sorelle reside along River Sachi. But I imagine they do not wish to be near either Syden or Judr, and you traveled upward ..."

Her eyes flitted across the parchment just as they had over the dining table at the banquet. Naleem's blood pulsed through his veins as he watched her, tilting his head at her concentration. Intelligent women always impressed him, no matter their field. His mother's was coin, finances, and even the social order of the village. Pinar's was weaving and wildflowers, and though that might be simpler than most professions, Naleem admired her passion for those things.

Gittan had many talents, what with being the Commander of the Maidens, but her focus on the landmarks—with her eyes narrowed and a dimple under her chin when her lips pursed—made Naleem lightheaded. She flipped through more maps before revealing a larger depiction of the hills. "Ah. A few streams from the snowmelt. Do you remember a stream near the base?"

Naleem blinked, collecting himself. "Apologies. We crossed River Sachi on the way up. They had a bridge made from the trees. That was all the water I can remember. They wouldn't let us venture far to find out otherwise."

"That's all right." Gittan straightened, planting her palms on her hips. "We've sent word to Matriarch Ase as Judr will serve as our base. That is, if the High Council approves of the mission."

"But they will, won't they?" Naleem asked. "They have to."

Her shoulders slumped before she hooked a thumb into her belt, resting a wrist over her sword pommel above her waist. "The High Council is a group of traditional old crones who keep to the laws of the matriarchy our ancestors created. Though that *should* mean they would heed your message and take action against these men ... they are also very comfortable with their positions and preserve their coin more than their people's well-being."

"The Duchess did not want the mission paid for." Asmund's deep voice infiltrated the quiet beat.

Gittan cleared her throat. "Yes. This mission would take several warriors that Vakkar Hold and Stadt cannot afford to risk. Our very best are keeping the peace in Hafelle's ports with Awevi ships on the horizon, or holding the mountain borders in Norden from the Wa'Ni. Mercenaries would be the best option, but we'd have to dip into Galaenia's treasury. The Council is already unnerved with Her Majesty's funding for the impoverished who fill up Stadt's streets. It does the people good, but their coin is falling from their hands, and for that, they don't favor her."

Naleem faced her. "So even if I tell you everything, even if we speak to them, there's a possibility they won't do anything?"

"Unfortunately."

"But the Queen is the ruler of Galaenia! Doesn't her decision overrule theirs?"

"To preserve the voices of the people, the High Council was created to eradicate total dictatorship by the monarchy. If their decision is unanimous against this mission, it will be illegal."

A hard lump formed in Naleem's throat. Gritting his teeth to swallow it, he slammed his fist against the table, pounding into the wilderness that held Haven. "So we've still come all this way for nothing! My brother, my son, will die in their hands if they haven't already, after all we've done."

A silence hung over the room as heavy as the old tapestry. Asmund lowered his head. Naleem remained rigid in his anger until Gittan folded her hand over his fist.

"It won't be legal," she told him in a hushed tone, "but I didn't say we would not try."

Blinking back warm tears, he looked at her and met her brown eyes full of determination and assurance. She squeezed his hand beneath hers. "I am still a Maiden, and the oath I took to protect Galaenia and its people overrules any Queen or Council. I've sworn my life to you then, and I promise you now, I will do whatever it takes to destroy these traitors and bring your family back to you. You have my word as a Maiden."

A brief terror had snaked up Naleem's arm at her touch, but her words soothed it. As much as he yearned to accept them, to believe her, there had been too much hurt in his life as of late. Letting her in, trusting her or anyone else, proved difficult.

Despite her broad physique, her strength, and her reassurance, her rugged features beneath the framing strands of blonde hair reminded him of Pinar. They eased him enough to allow her touch. Naleem nodded and turned from her before a tear rolled down his cheek.

Gittan's hand slipped away. "I'm sorry I upset you. That wasn't my intention. We will meet with the Council, and if they deny us, then we just won't have royal warriors or Galaenia's treasury. I may have to pull a few strings and my own coin. Call on a friend or two. This will be done one way or another. But neither of you can tell anyone else. Understood?"

Naleem brushed the tear away with the back of his hand. "Bai and Raegna. They are the ones who are here with us. They need to know."

"Well, all right. But after that, no one else shall hear of it." She leaned over the table again. "And please be careful when you do tell them. The palace walls have eyes and ears."

Chapter 10

Bai

"**P**APA!"

Bai crawled across the ground that was slick with blood. The thick crimson oozed between his fingers, and he slipped and fell into it. He cringed and his face itched as the spatters caked on his skin.

"Papa!"

Bai opened his mouth to return the call, but a wave of white pain pulled the air out of his lungs. With a gargled grunt, he curled, and the blood from his back soaked his skin, rolling down his sides. Pitch-black walls towered over him, and he could not be sure if his eyes were open or closed. Nothing existed except his pain, the blood, and Adabelle—somewhere.

"Papa!"

"I'm—" Bai yelped as claws raked down his back. "I'm—I'm coming!"

A deep, resonant laughter shook the damp ground, rattling his bones. The claws dug into his skin, and heavier blood streams poured over his shoulders. Bai screamed through gritted teeth.

Hot breath warmed the back of his neck. Fangs grazed his skull as the creature seized his head in its jaws. A clawed hand reached for his chin and jerked his head up. His gut dropped, and he whimpered. Adabelle stood before him, the gash over her throat spread from ear to ear. A red waterfall flowed down her dress. She shrieked with her eyes wide and her gaping mouth dripping with blood.

Held in place, Bai screamed until he woke.

He jolted upright, his shout carrying across the chamber. Raegna gasped, and the sheets shifted over the bed. "Bai? Gaea, what is it?"

Bai panted in the pile of blankets and pillows that were his makeshift bed on the floor. His fists closed around them as his muscles trembled. "I—I'm fine."

The bed creaked as Raegna crawled and peered over the edge at him. Chestnut hair hung past her chin as she balanced on her hands and knees. Bai turned from her when tears burned his eyes.

Raegna's voice came softly this time. "It's all right. You're safe. Nothing's wrong."

Bai thought sunlight might find Helved before Raegna ever tried to comfort him. Yet, she swung her legs over the foot of the bed and sat, perhaps deciding whether she wanted to draw closer. Her feet dangled in his periphery.

"I'm sorry." Bai heaved a breath and wrapped his arms around himself. "I'm sorry. I didn't, didn't mean to wake you."

"It's fine." Raegna adjusted her nightgown skirt to cover her shins and ankles. "Was it a nightmare?"

Before a tear could escape, he brushed his eyes with the heel of his hand and gave her a swift nod.

"Well, um, would you want to talk about it?"

This time, Bai shook his head. "No. It's nothing."

Talking about Adabelle would only make things worse between them. To tell Raegna that he was having nightmares about their daughter every night, what would she say? Surely, she would get furious or upset somehow. How dare he mourn for their daughter—no, *her* daughter—and scream in the night for her? Was he not there when she was killed? Could he not have done more to protect her?

All things she was bound to say. All of them true.

But Raegna spoke of her last night and had made their mission clear. *For Ada.*

Bai bit his lip hard as he sucked in air and stamped down the dull ache between his ribs. Before Raegna could say another word, a knock sounded on the door.

"Yes?" she called out.

Olena's voice came from behind the door. "Shield-Priestess Raegna, you've been invited to the Maiden's grounds with your other men, Naleem and Asmund. The Commander is eager to meet you all and review what you know about Sorelle's attacks."

Raegna's shoulders raised. "Oh. Yes, of course. If you could, tell them we are on our way!"

"Yes, Shield-Priestess." Footsteps scurried behind the door, and Olena was gone.

Bai watched as Raegna slipped off the bed and hurried in her frilly, white nightgown, circling him and his pile of pillows and blankets. She threw open the wardrobes at the back of the room, her hair in bed-made tangles sticking out in odd directions. Bai dropped his eyes from the gown's white fabric—and how it draped over her wide curves.

Just another thing to fight with. These frequent involuntary thoughts had started before they left Judr, before he was flogged. Raegna was nothing more to Bai than the woman he was forced to marry. The mother of his child and the woman who owned him. In all their years together, the word *ugly* could never be used on her.

She pressed a knuckle to her chin and searched the wardrobe for suitable attire. When her brown eyes caught the sunlight and her face lifted when she made her choice, Bai's pain-stricken heart fluttered.

"Try to wear something casual, but not too casual," she said, pulling out a dull red dress with a cream stripe running down the middle. The skirt was embroidered with woven designs that stretched into two elegant does meeting beneath the dress's ruddy brown leather belt. "The Maidens will be sparring, so don't wear anything that shouldn't get dirty."

Bai grunted as he got to his feet. "Yes, wife."

Perhaps it wasn't infatuation, but bewilderment. Raegna never acted so giddy about anything, not in front of Bai, and certainly not in recent days. This light she emitted and allowed him to see was foreign to him.

"Here." Snapping him from his thoughts, Raegna handed him a bundle of fabric. "This belt and this shirt underneath. These pants and a pair of boots to keep it simple."

The wide belt hung over Bai's waist, complementing the deep-green shirt with its pale-yellow stitching along the collar and sleeve hems. The dark-brown pants and boots were similar to something he would wear in Syden, but fine enough for Vakkar Hold.

Raegna led the way at a pace that surpassed Bai's long stride. He had to jog a couple of times to keep up. They passed hustling servants and sniveling nobles who barely gave them a passing glance. Bai grimaced at their upturned noses. They walked from the hard stone floor of their chamber tower to the carpeted first floor.

"Do you know where the Maiden's grounds are?" Bai asked, trying to mask his panting.

"Just north of the stables," Raegna answered, her eyes fixed ahead. "On the eastern side of the palace."

"How do you know that? We couldn't have seen it on the way in."

Missing a step, Raegna glanced over her shoulder at him. "Oh, I just ... know. I read it somewhere."

"Huh." Bai concentrated on the red carpet as they passed the double doors to the courtyard. "You know a lot about Vakkar Hold, don't you? Even other countries."

Raegna turned eastward, toward the stables. "What makes you say that?"

"Well, you know almost everything about how court life works, about the Awevi, a people we've never seen before in Syden—"

"There have been Awevi merchants in Syden before," Raegna told him with a wave. "The relationship between our countries is always changing. It's in a woman's best interest to know the goings on in her land and others."

"So you've gotten all this from reading?" Bai jogged a few paces. "Out of books?"

"Books and hearsay. Yes."

"I didn't think books would be that interesting."

"Some aren't. I had a book about the Maidens and their history when I was a girl. That is how I know where their training grounds are. My mother forced me to read Galaenian chronicles, which I found immensely boring."

"Galaenian chronicles." Bai looked at her and ignored the path before them, with a few servants and stable girls trickling by. "What's in that book?"

Raegna shrugged with a pouted lip. "Text on those who came before us. The explorer Galia who found this land. The skirmishes with the Wa'Ni, the civil unrest and wars between our people, which led to the Dark Days, and the establishment of what Galaenia is today."

"And you know all of it?"

"What I care to remember, anyway."

"Would you tell it to me?"

Raegna frowned. "Tell you about the chronicles?"

"Yes. I'd like to see the books, too."

Then she came to a halt. "Bai. It really isn't a man's place to learn these things. I'm not sure if I should allow it."

"Who says it isn't our place? I'm Galaenian, too, aren't I? Is it not in my best interest to know about the Awevi and our history? About the old wars and how we came to be?"

Raegna pressed her lips into a thin line, her brow a flat plane. "It just isn't done. I'm not even sure telling you about these things was the best idea."

"Then I'll just pester you with questions whenever I have them," Bai said with his head high.

Raegna rolled her eyes. "If you must." She gasped and picked up her pace once more. "There it is."

Bai promised himself he would not let the subject fall so easily later, and followed her gaze straight ahead.

For the most elite warriors in all Galaenia, the Maidens had a simple arena and surprisingly modest quarters. The armory looked just like any other, though a little larger, with weapons perched tightly alongside each other across its walls. A wooden building just smaller than a great house stood beside it, and women in leather armor or noble gowns milled in and out of its double doors.

Before both buildings, two groups of women reenacted a small skirmish, sparring with swords and shields. Spectating were Naleem and Asmund, with Commander Gittan standing beside Naleem, pointing and noting the sword skills aloud.

"Naleem?" Raegna squeaked, dragging her feet.

The three turned, and Naleem gave them a grin. "Good morning, you two. We wanted you to see the Maidens. Gittan was telling us about the different strategies they use."

Bai was more impressed that Naleem seemed in a decent mood today. Perhaps they all were, finally rested and prepared to move on to the next part of their mission, taking out Haven.

"Oh." Raegna approached, and Bai followed. "You've discussed Haven's location, then?"

"Indeed." Gittan answered this time. "And without Naleem, I am not sure how we could find it. We suspect the base is in the hills, of course. More importantly, just over the River Sachi and not before it. That is a great start that gives us plenty of information to present to the High Council."

Trying to absorb her every word, Bai could not help but study the Commander up close. Sitting at the banquet table last night did not do her any justice. Her voice came deeper than any woman's he'd ever heard, and she stood as tall as he and the other men. A straight nose stretched beneath light-brown eyes that sparkled with her wide smile. Muscles coursed beneath fair beige skin under her armor. She reflected the perfect example of a Galaenian warrior, especially a Maiden with her yellow hair pulled back in braids and her leather armor broadening her chest and shoulders.

"Oh, well, that is good news." Raegna glanced at the sparring Maidens as if she had just noticed them. "Ah, simulation like the battle at Hafelle's ports."

"Something like that." Gittan shrugged as Raegna and Bai stood on the other side of her. "Though a little closer to home, without different fighting styles. Though I wish we could have a stand-in Awevi or, even better, a Kaliqsi to test my girls."

"Kaliqsi?" Naleem repeated.

"Yes, people of Kaliq," Gittan answered. "The country is east of us, with Awevi below them. Born warriors, they are. Every woman and man there knows how to fight."

Bai perked to attention. "Truly?"

Gittan nodded. "Fighting a completely different style is one thing, but to have your opponent use a different style and be a man is quite another. Not that it makes it any more difficult, but it would give us the experience. The battle of Hafelle's ports was more like a small skirmish. Tensions just got high between traders, but Galaenians still won the peace. My mother just entered the ranks at the time."

"Your mother was a Maiden?" Raegna gasped.

"Commander before I was." Gittan slipped her thumbs through her belt and shifted her weight. "Long ago." Her eyes lit up at the sparring, and she touched Naleem's shoulder. "Ah, see there? Bryda used her smaller size to worm between Arne's shield and sword. Just goes to show that brute strength is not all you need on the battlefield."

They all watched the small woman, Bryda, find an opening. She knocked Arne's sword from her hand and rammed her chest with her shield. Arne grunted and counterattacked, bringing her shield up into Bryda's shoulder.

Bai had seen women fight before, but never surveyed them this way. In other lands, men also fought. How could they? Were their women not as fearful to put blades in their hands? As he watched the Maidens, examining every move, every swing of a sword or raised shield, Bai imagined himself beside them. If only he knew those skills, too. Would that have changed everything?

"Gaea, you are all so incredible." Raegna sighed. "I, well, I've admired that for so long. Ever since I was a girl."

"As many girls do, Shield-Priestess." Gittan chuckled. "Though we are no different from any other warrior, except our loyalty is to no Queen, Matriarch, or coin-filled purse. Only to Galaenia and its people."

"Still admirable."

Bai looked down at her. A certain solace washed over Raegna's face as she took in every sword swipe. She'd commended them since she was a girl. Before Bai could even ask, she'd known where the Maidens' arena stood within the palace walls. The way she watched them and spoke to Gittan in the most respectful way she could—so much so, she stuttered if she got the slightest words or phrases wrong—differed from how she would speak to any other woman.

As if a wave rose and crashed into him, Bai understood. The disdain toward their marriage in the first place, how her mother scorned her for wanting to "gallivant" and "get herself killed on horseback." Raegna wanted to be a *Maiden*.

While Bai flipped the idea over in his head, Gittan continued their conversation. "Perhaps we could see your skills with a sword, *Shield*-Priestess."

Raegna flushed. "Oh, I um, it's nothing like this. Merely basic defense, should my family need protection."

"Would you like further lessons?" Gittan asked.

Raegna's brow raised. "L—Lessons? Truly? No, I couldn't."

"You could if you wanted to." Gittan started for the armory. "It is my understanding you would all like to help find and destroy this *Haven*. If you are to do that, I want to ensure you can handle yourself in battle. No offense, but I suppose your skills of basic defense are not quite sufficient, though you have survived two attacks."

"With luck," Raegna muttered before quickly adding, "And Gaea's will."

Gittan waved for them to follow her. "Let's get started in sharpening your skills, then."

In the armory, to Raegna's evident disappointment, Gittan retrieved a couple of wooden swords. She tossed one to Raegna, who fumbled but caught it, grasping the hilt with both hands. As Gittan pulled Raegna forward to face her, Bai looked on with envy.

"Everyone wants to start with a real blade," the Commander said, "but these wooden ones are just as good. They are made to emulate the weight of a real sword, so you can practice your balance as you fight. Now, Shield-Priestess, I wouldn't hold it with two hands. Your other arm will be bracing a shield."

Gittan turned back to the armory and slipped two shields off the wall. Both had the blue and black stripes of the Maidens. Then she showed Raegna how to hold hers.

"Very good. Already starting to look like a true warrior."

Raegna's shoulders fell as she blushed. "Forgive me, but I feel more like a child."

"When we begin, you'll appreciate being hit with wood rather than steel." Gittan positioned herself in a stance with her shield in front of her chest and her sword up at an angle. "Now, try to make a blow."

Raegna rushed forward, raising her wooden blade. Gittan rammed her shield into Raegna's chest. Raegna gasped, falling flat on her ass. She rolled onto her back, sucking the air into her lungs.

Naleem and Asmund winced. Bai's hand fled to his mouth to hold back a snort of laughter. Gittan stepped forward and moved as if to swipe her blade across Raegna's throat, but she stopped just before her neck.

"You left an opening bigger than the two Rivers are wide," she said. "I don't suggest doing that again."

As soon as she brought her sword away, Raegna panted and got to her feet. "What do you suggest?"

Gittan assumed her stance once more. "See that my shield is close to me, and my sword is here, though not extended in any way. This would be defense, Shield-Priestess."

"So your vitals are protected," Bai commented.

"Essentially," Gittan admitted. "In stories, the heroes raise their swords and make giant sweeps with their blades. But if I do that, I am exposed, and you can easily sneak in and gut me. Or slam me with your shield and take me out on the ground."

Raegna frowned.

"Master this stance first."

The men watched as Raegna mirrored the Commander, who adjusted her here and there until she was satisfied. She instructed Raegna to be at ease then copy the stance again and again. Finally, she began basic sparring where they both assumed the stance. Gittan shoved forward with a close blow from her sword, which Raegna parried with her shield.

"Good," the Commander said. "Close quarters for now. Watch me."

They tapped each other's blades and collided their shields, adding more and more strength with each blow. Gittan's eyes brightened. "Keep it up, Shield-Priestess. I won't go easy on you anymore."

Raegna looked winded, but she kept a steady pace, dodging, blocking, twisting. Bai and the others followed their movements with anticipation.

"I don't think I've ever seen any warrior fight like this," Naleem said without taking his eyes off the match. "Have you?"

"Not in Syden anyway," Bai mumbled, far too distracted by the clash of shields. "And to think in other lands, they would let us fight beside them."

An amused huff escaped Naleem's nose. "In another life, I did not think we would need to."

That was just it. If any of the men in Sorelle had been warriors like their women were, would they have stood a better chance against the invaders? Certainly, the warriors of Judr fared better in battle than Syden's. The warriors were quite capable. But how different would the outcome have been? Would so many have died or been captured? Would Adabelle still be here?

She would have been overjoyed to see Vakkar Hold and all the pretty things it offered. There would be stars in her eyes at the sight of her mother sparring with the Commander of the Maidens. All that could be ... it was too painful.

Even if Bai knew how to wield a sword, he was wounded from the flogging and did not have the strength to hold his own weight. But if men could fight like warriors and be held to the same standard as women, he might not have been punished like a criminal in the first place. Not without trial. He would have been more able.

Nothing could change the outcome of those dreadful attacks. However, as Bai absorbed every piece of advice the Commander gave, he thought additional swords might help their cause at hand.

Gittan and Raegna ceased their sparring, heaving for air. The Commander straightened, squaring her strong shoulders, and rounded Raegna as she turned to the men. "As you gentlemen can see, any woman can make a warrior as fine as a Maiden. Skills are sharpened with training. A heart need only be set in the right place."

"Could we try?" Bai blurted.

Every pair of eyes turned to him in astonishment. He caught Raegna's expression, her eyebrows arched in disbelief.

"You?" Gittan looked between the three of them. "All of you?"

"Um—" Naleem started while Asmund's eyes grew wide.

Bai swallowed. "It's just that if we are going to help defeat Haven, would it not be crucial for us to know how to fight too?"

Gittan blinked with her eyes cast down. "Well …"

"It is not a man's place to imply such things, husband," Raegna scolded. "Especially before a Maiden."

For a moment that stretched like decades, Bai held her gaze. Weeks ago, he would have submitted to her authority, avoiding conflict and the prospect of her wrath. Things were different between them now. They would play the part of wife and husband before the royal court, but their act could never obscure the memory of the time she released him from her. When she'd given him the choice to stay or go. Besides, this was too important to allow Raegna to brush aside his words.

"Our odds would be greater with more blades and skilled warriors," he said without taking his eyes off her.

Raegna glared and opened her mouth to speak.

"It typically isn't done." Gittan rubbed the back of her neck. "But I have heard of some men allowed knives, at least. And did you three hunt with a bow in your villages?"

Asmund nodded.

Naleem shrugged. "Sometimes. We fished mostly. My wife would buy meat from the butcher—"

"I've hunted with a bow before," Bai said in a rush. "Raegna allowed me to have a knife when we fled the first attack. A sword would be no different—"

"And that is just it, Bai. We were under attack. You were carrying our daughter. You had to have a weapon."

"And I killed the bastard that tried to stop you," he countered. "You admitted you might be dead if I hadn't killed him. Imagine if we all could fight like you two. Like the Kaliqsi over the sea."

"Kaliq is a very dangerous place because of it," Raegna said. "Men with weapons only cause war as they have before. What do you think we're fighting against?"

"Men with weapons ..." Gittan started. "That might not be a bad idea."

Raegna whirled to her. "Pardon?"

"When we find this Haven, it might benefit us to have a man or two on the inside." Gittan paced before Bai and the other men. "And if they are to fit in and protect themselves, they would need some skills with a sword or ... if it would make a certain priestess wife more comfortable, an ax. Men use axes for many things, don't they?"

Bai's heart raced. "You would have us fight from within?"

"At the very least you could let us in on the routines and goings on," Gittan said. "Should anything go south, should they suspect you, you ought to know how to defend yourselves."

"You honestly believe that would be wise?" Raegna stammered.

"What better way to infiltrate the place?" Gittan asked. "Obviously, Naleem could not be the one to do it. They would recognize him." She stood before Bai and Asmund with a smirk. "Perhaps a couple of young men of Syden returned from a hunt and found their village had been attacked."

Bai bounced on the balls of his feet. "And we could learn with an ax and a knife and a bow—"

"I can't fight," Asmund murmured.

"We can teach you," Gittan assured him. "You have a very quiet personality. You don't attract attention. Out of all of you, I believe you would make the perfect spy within Haven's walls."

Asmund fidgeted in place. "I can't. I couldn't ... They've seen me too. They killed ... I can't fight."

"I'll go," Bai insisted. "I can learn. I'll fight, and I can be quiet and blend in."

Gittan laughed. "I'm sure you could. You could also learn from your friend here and hold your tongue now and then. But a man with a mind and mouth like yours could convince them you would want to be free and defend their cause."

"Except they've seen him too," Raegna interrupted. "After ... Adabelle."

Bai rolled his eyes. "Just two out of however many hundred there are."

"Only two?" Naleem asked.

Perhaps Naleem could assure them of the insignificance. "There was a big one," Bai said. "I couldn't get a good look at him. The one that—that took Ada was tall but had black hair. Lighter brown eyes. Vile as a snake."

That ought to be good enough. Bai turned to Naleem to better see his reaction, expecting a puzzling expression. Instead, the blood drained from his face as if he had seen one of Fan's demons. "The big one … did he have reddish hair?"

"Yes. And a red beard. The snake had a shorter beard. Black too."

"Does that sound familiar?" Gittan asked Naleem.

Naleem drew wavering breaths. "The big one is Reynold. The other is Thenalious, the leader of Haven. The one that took your daughter and my son. The one responsible for all of this." He turned to Raegna. "When you found me, he was the one you fought in the wagon. The one that pierced your shoulder."

Then both of the men would be Bai's targets. An intense heat broiled in his chest. He and Raegna exchanged a glance. Her irises went black, and a muscle in her jaw peaked as she clenched it. White knuckles clamped around her wooden sword.

Gittan shook her head. "Perhaps you are too close to the situation."

"I've been too close since the day they took my home," Bai growled. "And then the only family I had left. We've been successful enough to reach Stadt, haven't we? I can fight and keep my head down to live among them before the time is right to kill them all."

Gittan sighed. "I suppose I will not hear the end of it if we do not at least try. However, we might as well follow some Galaenian laws. You will need your wife's permission to wield a weapon. So how about it, Shield-Priestess? Do you trust your husband with a blade?"

All eyes turned to Raegna. She stood with her sword pointed at the ground and her shield flat against her side. With a grimace, she cast her black eyes down. Bai never thought she would struggle with this concept so much. When they fled for their lives, she allowed him to be armed. Now, when they would avenge their daughter's life, she hesitated.

Raegna's gaze lifted and met his. Bearing her stare, he pleaded with her silently.

I will make this right. I won't fail again.

Finally, Raegna released a heavy sigh and grunted. "Very well. I see no better plan or option. You may teach him."

Bai gave a slight nod of thanks. If Raegna noticed it, she did nothing in return.

"I'll do my best," Gittan said, rounding on Bai. "In doing so, I may teach him the discipline every warrior ought to learn. Woman or man. That might do him some good." She turned to Asmund. "Then give you some confidence and courage."

"No, he has plenty of courage," Raegna said. "I've seen it. He's more than capable, and it will show in time."

Asmund's lips parted when he stared at her, brow raised, before dipping his head again. Bai glanced between them. Asmund had been Iida's husband, the young woman Raegna grew fond of in Judr. Had he proved himself to her while the two women spent their time together? Bai couldn't be sure if she had ever given another man a compliment like that.

"No doubt," Gittan agreed. "There is a fire in those eyes beneath his cowering. You are all fighters for coming this far. I suggest training late in the night or before dawn. Others may not take kindly to this idea."

"Whatever it takes," Bai affirmed.

Raegna let out a hopeless breath.

Chapter II

Hadwin

The older boys played a game of stones while the babes slept. Hadwin sat in the chair by the door, holding his wrapped hand to his chest. He thought of calling for Haven's only healer, a frightening warlock of an old man, but to request mending after Reynold's assault seemed like a death wish. His hand swelled, but he could move his fingers with a dull throb. It might not require a healer, anyway.

Audun governed the game between himself, Ugo, and Gael. Cadoc and Vihn watched with a few others, everyone waiting for their turn in a tournament they'd organized. One Ugo had been determined to overrule, but Audun had put him in his place. Then Hadwin when he'd argued. Peace finally appeared until a knock came on the nursery door.

Oberon opened it at a slight angle, peering in before his sons could see him. Hadwin frowned at him, uninterested in seeing any councilmen, but Oberon ushered him with a head tilt.

Dragging a breath through his nose, Hadwin stood. "Stay here, boys. I'll be right back. Audun's in charge."

"All right, Hadwin," a few of them answered.

Feet scraped the floor behind him, and Hadwin turned to Cadoc, who scampered up to him. Hadwin's throat closed, and he ruffled the boy's dark-brown hair. "Stay here, nephew."

Cadoc's face fell, and his lower lip hung. The door and Oberon be damned. Hadwin turned and knelt before Cadoc. "I will be quick. Oberon just wants to speak. I shouldn't have left you last night. That was wrong, and it won't happen again. It won't happen now. Will you wait for me?"

The boy's eyes glistened, but he nodded. Hadwin kissed his forehead before he rose. "Go sit with Audun. He'll keep you company while I'm away."

At the sound of his name, Audun pulled his attention from the game. He watched Cadoc shuffle back before the younger boy plopped himself beside him. "Watch how Gael rolls the stones, Cadoc."

Hadwin's chest ached as he took them all in and turned for the door.

In the hall, Oberon stood with his hands on his hips. "What have you done?"

Hadwin glanced down both directions of the hall, especially toward the far end that faced the nursery where Thenalious' double doors loomed. Before he could answer, Oberon waved a hand. "They're all out on a hunt. Reynold needed to blow off steam."

"What do you think I've done?"

"I'm not sure. But at breakfast, Thenalious was rather smug, and Reynold never stopped glowering. They spoke of you and how you *weren't* in the nursery this morning."

Hadwin swallowed hard. "I took Else to her mother."

"Earlier than that," Oberon snapped. "We're not fools. They know when you leave with her and Cadoc, just like you know when we eat and sleep. You're drawing attention to yourself."

"It won't happen again," Hadwin assured.

Oberon's eyes sharpened. "You've done it, then. Warmed your cock between a particular pair of legs, am I right? Trust me, they haven't given you any punishment like the one that deserves."

Hadwin's jaw ached with his teeth clenched. "I fail to see how I'm the one deserving of punishment around here."

"Your defiance only reveals you." Oberon shook his head. "I thought you were smarter than that. Go have your way together and be back when you're done. Not spend the entire night like newlywed virgins."

Hadwin dropped his gaze.

"Fan alive, I'm right about that too."

"Just shut up!" Hadwin hissed. "I've put enough people in danger, and I feel immense shame for it. He would have killed Else if Audun hadn't stood up to him. If he had ... I don't think I could show myself to Talia."

Oberon's brow raised at the mention of Audun's bravery. Then he sighed. "Enjoy yourself if you want, but do it sparingly and quickly. I want a happy caregiver, not a dead one."

"Then you ought to help us leave this place."

"What did I just say?"

Hadwin made sure the hall was empty before he spoke again. "You should know the best way out. I had the opportunity to leave with Maura, but Cadoc and Else weren't with me. And I would rather bring the other women and even the boys—"

"Shut up," Oberon growled. "Do you hear yourself? Thenalious would send dogs after you. He'd gather a whole hunting party! They would make a day of it and hunt you for the stupid boar you are."

Hadwin's hands balled into fists at his sides. A flying rage nearly drove them into the door, but he drew a breath. "So we are to suffer here for the rest of our lives. My nephew will grow up to be a caregiver as well. The boys will turn into brutes like the rest of you, and those women will die in that forsaken barn. Else will be raised beneath us if she isn't killed first."

Oberon's wide chest rose and fell, while his eyes darted over the floor. "Listen, caregiver, I know you're in Helved now. I know you've been through much. But there's no way out of it on your own. Especially if you drag the women and children with you. Even if I try to help, if we fail, they will kill me and my sons. You must know what's at stake."

Dakarai's blood splattered in the hallway in Hadwin's memory. Naleem's anguished scream echoed before he sighed in defeat. "Yes."

Oberon shifted his weight. "Just keep your head low for a while longer. Stay out of Thenalious' and Reynold's way. You ought to do that, anyway."

He dismissed Hadwin back into the nursery, and Hadwin leaned against the shut door. Cadoc ran up to him and hugged his legs. Tears burned the backs of Hadwin's eyes, and he knelt, enveloping the boy in a bigger embrace. He held him tight, squeezing as if he could press the fear out of him. Cadoc couldn't hug his father after he had left and never returned, and Hadwin had not considered him when he'd left him with the women last night.

"I'll come back," Hadwin whispered in his ear before the other boys peered to see what might be wrong. "I'll always come back."

I'm sorry you're trapped here. There had to be another way. If not a way to leave all at once, perhaps there was something else Hadwin could web together. In some smaller way he could keep his head low so Thenalious wouldn't suspect a thing.

Whatever it was, something had to be done. Cadoc couldn't grow up in Haven. He would know the rest of Galaenia to be his home.

Chapter 12

Raegna

R AEGNA RAISED HER CANDLE, suppressing a scowl. She and Bai crept downstairs, the light flickering against Vakkar Hold's halls. As they made their way down the spiraling steps toward the entry hall, Raegna didn't know what was worse: the fact that Bai would learn how to wield an ax or how he practically skipped like a child behind her.

"Do you think Gittan will teach us more than just the basics?" he whispered. "I want to spar like a warrior by the time we're done today."

Raegna chewed the inside of her cheek. "I'm sure Gittan will teach us what she deems necessary. She is the Commander of the Maidens."

"I know. I just hope that we'll learn everything soon enough to take our skills to Haven. Asmund and I will need every move and trick before we even look upon the place."

"Nothing has been confirmed about Haven yet," Raegna hissed back at him. "You heard Naleem. Gittan made it clear Her Majesty will take the matter to the High Council before anything is decided."

"Yes, but Gittan also made it clear that whether the old crones would agree to send Maidens or not, we would go anyway," Bai countered. "It's her oath to protect Galaenia."

Raegna rolled her eyes. "The point is to keep that part confidential. And you ought not to call them *old crones*. The High Council exists for the good of the people. They are wise and hold on to tradition for a reason."

"So long as tradition doesn't keep us from tearing that Thenalious to pieces, I hardly care."

A hard pit formed between Raegna's ribs. Her disdain bared its fangs at the memory of the man she'd battled in Judr. His wicked eyes were most prevalent, and so was Naleem's fear. The man had killed her daughter. She only wished she had known so she could have sliced more than just his leg. Raegna's shoulder twinged where he had pierced her. Her heart ached as Adabelle's blood flashed in her mind.

Yes. He will die regardless.

Sconces held weak flames in the courtyard, lighting the cobblestone paths. Dawn would break in a couple of hours. The night swallowed the land in darkness. Raegna and Bai clung to Vakkar Hold's shadows to stay out of sight. Her Majesty's warriors kept watch from towers and patrolled the yards. Their green and white uniforms were easy to spot in the dark. Their clanking armor gave them away from a few paces.

As instructed, Raegna and Bai scurried to the back of the Maiden's quarters to a door Gittan had pointed out the day before. Raegna blew out the candle and knocked three times. After a few whispers and scuttling behind the door, it creaked open, and Asmund stood at the threshold.

Raegna offered him a gentle smile. "Thank you, my friend."

Bai nodded to him as they entered. They found Gittan and Naleem pushing long tables to each side of the room. Yesterday, the same room had been filled with Maidens discussing plans over maps. Raegna's heart had fluttered at their work, which Gittan swept aside to empty the floor space. Parchment and pawns rattled as Naleem and the Commander pushed the last table.

"Won't that ruin the work they've put into strategizing?" Raegna asked.

Gittan dusted her hands. "Not at all. We'll put everything back as it was, and they'll never know the difference. We needed time in here without a crowd. There are some Maidens who wouldn't approve of this."

"You're sure this is enough room for training?" Naleem asked.

"Plenty! Now let's get a feel for our weapons, shall we?"

Bai perked to attention while Asmund dipped his head. Gittan disappeared into a room to return with two wooden axes and a wooden sword. Raegna frowned; she was again without steel. Bai's shoulders sank, but his eyes did not leave the wooden weapons.

"One for you," Gittan said, handing Bai the first ax. Then the other to Asmund. "One for you. And a sword for you, Shield-Priestess."

Raegna took the wooden hilt and played with its weight in her palm. "We will get to use real ones eventually, won't we?"

"Certainly." Gittan rotated her wooden sword in her hand. "But I want us all to get used to weight and balance before I give you something with an edge and one of you accidentally slices someone's arm off. Not to mention your own."

"But I've handled a sword before," Raegna protested.

"If I may speak plainly. The longer you complain about it, the longer it takes for training to begin. Now, I want Asmund and Bai up first."

Bai squared his shoulders and moved to the middle of the room. Asmund fell in behind him, holding his ax as if it might come to life and attack him. Raegna and Naleem stood back and observed.

"I'd offer you both a shield," Gittan started, "but entering Haven armed like warriors may not bode well with their lot. So first you'll both learn some defense with your axes alone. A man is typically given an ax to cut wood for the home and hearth. You will learn to avenge your home and hearth and perhaps be the first men to train like Maidens."

Bai knocked the flat of the blade against his thigh. Asmund fidgeted under the Commander's gaze.

"Let's begin with a proper stance."

Gittan instructed them on how to stand with their weapons similarly to how she'd taught Raegna. Bai easily assumed the position while Asmund teetered on his feet. Gittan straightened him out, lifting his chin and readjusting his arms and posture. Then she turned to Bai.

"Relax," she told him. "The art of combat is not all brute strength."

Bai's shoulders settled. "Will we learn combat today?"

"What do you think we're doing?" Gittan pushed his shoulders down. "Practicing your initial stance is crucial. Learning to balance that weapon properly is essential. There's more to this than just swinging swords and batting shields. Now, as you were, and get into position again."

Raegna looked on, only a little smug that Bai did not get his wish. Though she understood the frustration. Becoming a skilled warrior took time, and becoming a Maiden took twice as long. Learning self-defense with an ax would be simpler but would still require time. Especially for someone as determined as Bai or as timid as Asmund.

By the end of their first morning, the two men had mastered their stances with their legs spread apart, gripping their axes at the ready. Raegna even got to spar with Gittan a little, the Commander using Bai's ax to demonstrate a few slow moves they would try within the next few days. At least Raegna could spar and understand what not to do when facing an opponent with an ax.

Sunlight alerted them through the windows and they returned the tables to their places.

"You all show promise, I'll give you that," Gittan said. "The sun will rise soon and there was one more thing I wanted to discuss."

"What is it?" Raegna asked.

Gittan leaned against a table. "The Council has accepted Her Majesty's request for an audience. They have been given a brief reason. The agenda is to attend the Council's court today, and I've been told to ask if you would attend, Shield-Priestess."

Raegna nodded. "Of course."

"Just her?" Bai intervened. "What about Naleem? He was in Haven."

"Unfortunately, men are not permitted within the High Council's court," Gittan said. "Raegna is the only woman witness to the attacks. After talking with Naleem, I will relay every detail of Haven myself."

"How do you think it will go?" Raegna asked.

Gittan crossed her arms with a shrug. "Smoothly, Gaea willing. Wear something modest, perhaps priestess robes. You'll ride alongside me, and I'll explain everything on the way." She looked at each of the men. "You three will stay behind."

Bai snorted. Naleem raised his chin. "Whatever it takes. We have plans to find Haven, regardless. Right?"

Gittan nodded to him. "I've pulled together a few mercenaries we favor and have told them to stay close, should we need them. We won't know until the end of the day. I'll send for you when we are ready to depart, Shield-Priestess. For now, all of you get some rest. You did well today."

Raegna and Bai returned to their chamber, softly shutting the door behind them. While Raegna sat herself on the edge of the bed to be off her feet, Bai flopped face-down over his pile of blankets on the floor. The thick fabric crowded around him.

Raegna leaned to peer at him with a raised eyebrow. "Still fuming over the fact you can't go?"

The blankets muffled his voice. "Can you blame me?"

"No. I'm sure you're as passionate about this mission as I am. If not more."

Bai lifted himself onto his elbows. "I'll go back myself if I have to."

Raegna's shoulders hunched and she knocked a heel against the bed's edge. "I know you would. But here we have allies and a plan, one way or another. Let's just hope the Council allows the Maidens and Her Majesty's warriors to go forth."

Bai rolled his eyes and planted his face into the blankets again.

***

Later that morning, Raegna dressed herself in a maroon priestess robe sent from the royal temple. She tied the thick brown belt bordered by gold stitching around her waist. Her single braid did not travel as far as most priestesses grew their hair, but it was a start.

Bai watched her tidy herself, sitting cross-legged over his makeshift bed. "You know, watching you cut yourself open was one thing. You look rather official now."

"What exactly are you implying, husband?" she asked, far more playful than she meant.

Bai smirked, and a few blond strands fell to his forehead. "I mean to say I thought you were a righteous idiot back then. I was wrong. It was brave, and you deserve this."

Raegna turned to him, and an amused huff left her nose. "A righteous idiot? I suppose I've called you many things through all of this. I deserve your name-calling as well."

"Well, in truth, I deserve every strike, name, and foul word you have for me." Bai lowered his head, playing with a thread on a pillow seam. "And we could never be even."

She hesitated as she smoothed out her skirts. What did he mean he deserved all that? All of it?

Raegna treated him terribly because of what they were put through, finding someone else to blame besides her mother. Bai was an easy target. The one who had physically pinned her to the bed so long ago. But her mother had the knife pointed at his back. It took seven years and his life being threatened to realize that. *It wasn't Bai. Not Bai.*

"Bai—"

"Shield-Priestess Raegna!" Olena called from the other side of the door. "Commander Gittan told me to summon you. The congregation is ready to depart for the High Council's court."

Raegna sighed. "I'll be right there!"

Bai stood and gave her a faint smile. "I suppose I should see you off."

They walked together down the halls toward the courtyard. Raegna took the crook of his arm to escort him like a proper wife, her breath short and her heart jerking. Bai played his part with a stony expression, but his chin tilted down and his gold eyes held a gloom. Somehow, she had to assure him she placed no blame on him—at least, not like she used to. The words themselves would be impossible to express. A stone wall stood between them, and it was difficult to speak through it.

The courtyard was filled with horses and their riders. Stable girls hurried along the cobblestones to prepare every steed. Two grand carriages stood in the middle of the commotion; one of them Raegna recognized as Duchess Elmba's dark carriage, and the other was a lighter wood carriage decorated with Queen Kjerstin's spring-green and white colors.

Gittan, Naleem, and Asmund stood beside a couple of horses among the many others. As they approached, Raegna gaped at her mare that had survived Syden and Judr with them. The chestnut shook her mane, the shiny black bridle around her face clinking. A new saddle had been placed over her back. She had come a long way from being a village farm horse.

Raegna stroked the mare's nose. "Don't you look pretty?"

"She cleans up nicely, doesn't she?" Gittan said. Her horse nudged her with its nose, a gray mare with a white mane and tail. Gittan patted her neck. "You're very pretty too, Siggy. Let's get into the saddle. This procession is about ready to leave."

Before she mounted, Gittan took Naleem's hand firmly in hers. Raegna peeked with a sideways glance as his fingers wrapped around Gittan's.

"I swear to recount every detail," she told him. "We will see a victory by the end of this."

"I trust you," Naleem whispered before their hands slipped from each other.

Raegna and Bai exchanged a look. Had he seen that too? They'd speculate later. For now, Raegna supposed she ought to give her husband a farewell.

"I'll be back," she told him.

Bai nodded to her. "I'll be here."

Raegna mounted her mare. As soon as she and Gittan sat in their saddles, commands stretched throughout the riding party full of warriors and Maidens to protect the Queen, Duchess, and attending noblewomen. Gittan guided Raegna and her mare behind Queen Kjerstin's carriage, and they followed through the gates, leaving Bai, Naleem, and Asmund behind them.

Raegna glanced back at her men before the gates closed. Her chest ached to leave them, just as it had when the servants took them to Vakkar Hold's baths. Her eyes locked on Bai's, his gold irises absorbing the sunlight.

"Don't worry," Gittan assured her as the gates closed. "We're just going to see the Council, not going to war. You'll see him tonight."

Leaving him was never this hard. Never hard at all. Raegna took in Gittan's words and drew a breath that strained her lungs. Bai remained in her mind, stoic angles with determined eyes. The wall stood between them, but he didn't deserve her hatred. It wasn't set between the stones anymore.

For Ada.

And for you.

Chapter 13

Hadwin

THE FOREST LEAVES TRANSFORMED into bright red and orange. Even during daylight, the air grew crisp and cold. Servants brought the boys' winter wardrobes to the nursery, so they wore shirts, pants, shoes, coats, and little boots.

Days went on with business as usual. Hadwin rose early to bring Else to her mother, Cadoc toted alongside him. Then he returned to the nursery and had the boys dress for breakfast and whatever daily activity he planned. By afternoon, they ate their lunch, rested, woke for supper, and stayed in the nursery until bed. All the while, Hadwin kept his head low and did not meet any councilman's gaze, not even Oberon if he could help it.

Oberon visited his sons whenever he could find the time. He remained polite enough to give Hadwin small talk. "It's good to have relief from this summer heat. But you should let the boys play in the leaves and enjoy themselves outside before winter. They'll be holed up in the nursery as much as possible."

"Of course." Hadwin focused on the babes, who grew at an alarming rate, even Else. He wondered how much longer it would be before she didn't have to see her mother anymore. "Do you celebrate anything in Haven? Like Leaf Fall Gift?"

Oberon shook his head. "The only thing we still celebrate is Fan's Eye, but in a very different way."

"I can imagine."

"You'll see," Oberon said. "Then we might as well celebrate Winter Mull in a way. Being cooped up for the winter can lead to many things."

Hadwin lifted his head. "What do you do with the women? It's too cold for them to stay in that old shack."

Oberon shrugged. "They're given blankets, and we'll board the old place up more. But ... there is a reason we have to find more women at every raid."

Hadwin glowered.

"I know you're upset about it, but it's the way of things here." Oberon leaned back in his chair, holding Vihn in his lap. "If we want, we could bring our claimed women to our chamber, but that's only if you want to pup her."

Hadwin grimaced and focused on the babes again. Most of his concern these days went to Maura and the other women in the old barn. The fall air was enough to make them sick in their condition, and these monsters expected them to fend for themselves in winter?

"If you want," Oberon added, "I can bring your girl to my chamber. That's what you're worried about, isn't it?"

"I worry for all of them because they are human beings like me," Hadwin hissed.

"I can only bring her and my woman inside," Oberon said, as if he didn't hear him. "I can't do anything for the others. And if you wanted, you could take her to a real bed, but only when Thenalious and the others go hunting or something."

It wouldn't be our *bed.* The very thought of being with Maura again sent shivers through Hadwin's body. To keep her warm during their own Winter Mull in this place, even for a few moments ...

The days continued like this. Hadwin assured himself that at least Maura and Farah could be kept in Oberon's chamber, but what could he do for the others?

Escape before winter set in.

Hadwin fought over the idea every day. While he kept his head low, he devised a plan to snatch a map of Galaenia and a knife that would be easy to conceal. It didn't have to be a dagger or hunting knife. He could sneak a steak knife from the kitchen. He remembered where the kitchen boys stored them. There was just the matter of the map.

When he took Else to her mother, he chatted with Talia and Farah before turning to Maura. Cadoc leaned against him and dozed.

Hadwin lowered his voice before Maura. "I believe the maps are kept in Thenalious' chamber, and some might be in Wyn's. But Thenalious and Reynold are in charge of strategy and raids."

Maura shook her head. "I want us to do everything in our power to be rid of this place, but that might be too risky. Couldn't we head through the woods, find a river, and follow it to a village instead? I know we both heard the River Sachi on our way here. If we follow it west, we'll find Graende. If we went east, Surlied is closer."

"We would be more sure with a map," Hadwin insisted. "We could also pinpoint just where Haven is if we're successful, and find help for the others."

"Is that the plan, then? Going on our own and coming back for them?"

Hadwin glanced at the other women to be sure they weren't listening. They were all engaged in their own conversations, though Farah glanced over her shoulder at the two of them now and again.

"There are too many to flee at once," Hadwin whispered. "Some probably wouldn't make the journey. I couldn't gather all the boys quietly either. I can't decide what to do about Else. She still needs Talia … but we can at least get the map and have a better chance."

"If anyone would believe you." Maura sighed. "Well, if you are to risk your life for parchment … will you visit me tonight? Much later when they are all asleep."

Hadwin's heart sank and skipped a beat at once. "I can't leave Cadoc. I shouldn't leave Else either."

"This time we'll cut it short and make sure you're back before you're noticed," she said. "Please. We don't know what is to come of this. I want to feel you again and pretend we aren't in danger."

Maura leaned so close the tips of their noses touched. Everything within Hadwin screamed yes, that he could leave Cadoc behind in their room for just one night. But the thought of Reynold or Thenalious slinking into the nursery or his room where Cadoc lay alone …

"I can't," he sighed. "But Oberon told me that when winter comes, you and Farah can stay in his chamber. You'll be closer, and maybe then … we can figure something out."

Disappointment washed over Maura's face, but she nodded. "At least winter won't be so horrible."

But winter could be spent in a bed of their own if Hadwin was quick about it.

One morning, he slipped into the kitchen, where the servants prepared breakfast for the councilmen. With their tasks at hand, they paid him no mind. Hadwin made his way to a drawer where the knives lay waiting for him to select just one.

"Caregiver," a familiar, scratchy voice snapped at him.

Hadwin winced and turned to the head kitchen boy, who'd woken him from a dead sleep for a day of serving Haven so long ago. Though it surprised Hadwin to realize it was only that past summer.

"What are you doing in here?" the young man demanded, earning the attention of every servant in the room. "Shouldn't you be upstairs?"

"I ... the boys fight over their toys too often," he said with a short laugh. "I thought I could carve their names into the wood toys so they might not argue so much."

The head kitchen boy raised an eyebrow. "Very well. But next time, just ask for one to be sent to you. You shouldn't leave them alone when it's just you. Thenalious gave the last caregivers good lashings for their negligence."

Hadwin nodded. "Of course. Apologies."

He tucked the knife in his belt under his shirt. The next matter resided in Thenalious' chamber, and the hardest part was deciding the best time of day to sneak in and snatch a map.

The only time Hadwin could be sure Thenalious' chamber lay empty was once the dinner horn blared. He checked every night that each councilman was accounted for in the dining hall, leaving the boys for just a few moments before creeping downstairs to eye the hall's tables. Every night, Thenalious jested with his fellow men, Reynold sitting close to his side.

After check-ins, and gathering the courage to venture down the hallway to the doors far across from the nursery, Hadwin chose a night. He left Audun and even Ugo and Cadoc in charge while he was away. The boys didn't question it, though Cadoc expressed a little concern.

"You'll come back, Uncle Hadwin?" he asked.

"Yes, nephew," he assured him. "Now stay here."

Hadwin confirmed that Thenalious and Reynold remained in the dining hall. When he spotted them feasting with the others, a smirk pulled at a corner of Hadwin's mouth, and he ascended back upstairs.

His bones rattled as he approached the double doors, venturing down the hallway lit by torchlight. Naleem had come down that same direction before, beaten, bruised, and perhaps tortured. Hadwin was never sure. The terrible memories didn't make the task any easier, but he pressed forward.

The doors creaked open no matter how carefully he pushed them. Hadwin found it strange that they were unlocked, but didn't speculate for too long. Nor did he marvel at the inside of the chamber. This had to be done quickly.

First, Hadwin went to the trunk at the end of the giant bed. The head of a grizzly watched him lift the trunk open and rifle through its hunter's things, its hide stretched across the bed. The old trunk contained parchment and scrolls along with a few knives and jewels, but no maps.

Hadwin tried the closet, which had been filled to the brim with coats and furred cloaks. Even councilmen must have had their wardrobes rotated for the winter. Hadwin pushed through them, searched beneath them, and finally reached for a shelf above them. His fingers grazed the edge of a paper, which stung him. He hissed at the pain, but took the rolled parchment and spread it apart.

Nothing in his life taught him how to read a map, but it was one of Galaenia. He could make out the two Rivers. Great mountains were etched in the north, and the plains spread beneath them. Hills decorated Sorelle and marked the familiar makeup of home. Hadwin's heart drummed in his chest. He rolled the map up and headed for the door without another moment to spare.

He thought up an excuse, should anyone find him lost in the hallway. Gael and Vihn would have been asking for their father, and he went searching for Oberon. The fact that it was dinner time would have slipped his mind. He was so exhausted from his work. The time passes so quickly.

Hadwin opened the door and stopped dead in his tracks.

Thenalious stumbled before him, bracing himself against the doorframe when his hand did not find the knob as Hadwin opened it. Hadwin stifled a yelp and stared at the councilman. His heart leaped into his throat as if it might escape his gaping mouth.

Thenalious collected himself and studied him before glaring.

"What exactly brings you here, *caregiver*?" He straightened, but staggered. He had to be drunk from the ale downstairs.

Hadwin reminded himself of his knife tucked close to his hip. "I—I was looking for Oberon—"

"Well, this isn't his chamber," Thenalious growled. "And I suspect you're a thieving liar. What are you holding?"

The words came more like a demand than a question. Hadwin didn't move, glaring back at him before Thenalious raised his fist and smashed it into the side of his head.

Hadwin shouted and fell to the floor. The map rippled open and lay flat on the floorboards. Thenalious stood over it and chuckled. "What did you think you could do with this? Surely you don't know how to read it."

Hadwin recovered from the blow and sat up, though his face swelled. He would feel it tomorrow if he survived this.

"Would you have brought it to your whore friends in the cow pen?" Thenalious jested. "We all know you're fond of—"

Thenalious stiffened and his hazel eyes lit up. Hadwin didn't notice, but in his fall, his shirt had folded up. The knife's blade glinted in the low light.

"You little rat." Thenalious threw a kick into Hadwin's gut and sent him across the floor. Hadwin gagged for air. Thenalious pinned him and pulled the knife from his hip. The edge licked his skin, and Hadwin winced.

"What's this for, then?" Thenalious sneered. "Better yet, who is it for? Did you think you were safer with it?"

Thenalious kept the blade pointed down at him. Hadwin trembled beneath him. A sob crawled up his throat.

A grin spread across Thenalious' face. "Don't worry, caregiver. I won't kill you. I need you to raise my love's sons. You're lucky you're so good at it. But we can't let you think you can just get away with this, can we?"

Tears burned Hadwin's eyes. Thenalious raised the knife and ran the blade through Hadwin's thigh. A scream tore from his throat, and another as Thenalious ripped the knife back out.

"We thought Reynold would have frightened you enough." Blood dripped from the blade and over Thenalious' hand. "I suppose you're a lot like your wretched brother in that regard. A bit difficult to break. But not unbreakable."

Naleem.

"Where is my brother!" Hadwin snarled through his tears. "Where is he? What did you do!"

A wild stare sparked in Thenalious' eyes, and he slashed the knife down. The blade cut the bridge of Hadwin's nose. Had he not flinched back, he might have lost both his eyes. Blood blurred his vision and he screamed in terror.

Thenalious held the blade under Hadwin's chin. "I bent him over and made him my bitch if you truly want to know. Then Reynold did. When he fought, we all did. Every man who raided Judr made him theirs. Every last one."

Hadwin couldn't fight back the sob that left him then. "No."

Thenalious dragged the knife down his chest almost like a hunter would gut his kill, but did not let it sink in deep enough. Hadwin yelled.

"I ought to do the same to you." Thenalious leaned over him and put his lips to his ear. "But you're not quite as pretty, are you? I wonder sometimes if you were brothers at all. Did your mother fuck too many men?"

Hadwin shouted and jolted to fight back. Thenalious shoved the knife into his hip and a silent scream spread Hadwin's mouth wide open. He cried out when the blade left him again.

"Your precious brother rots in Fan's realm with the rest of your pathetic family," Thenalious told him. "Of course, that might not be such a bad thing. He's partaken in so much fucking, he might like a place in Fan's own bed."

Anguish washed over Hadwin all at once. His strength seeped away from him with his blood. Every shaking breath pulled his fresh wound open.

"Anything else you wish to know while we're talking, caregiver?" Thenalious asked. "There are a few things I would ask you. It isn't Oberon who wants to claim that blonde wench, is it? He's very particular about his women, and you've been very fond of them and him. Why is that?"

The door opened and Thenalious drove the knife into Hadwin's shoulder at the same time. Another scream poured from him and echoed down the empty hallway. Two familiar giant boots stood at the threshold.

"I hardly care where you put your cock," Thenalious growled, "but when that cow produces a child, no matter the sex, I will bash its head in myself. Is that clear?"

When Hadwin choked on a sob, Thenalious twisted the knife into his shoulder. "You'll answer me."

Hadwin sobbed through his teeth. "Yes."

"Yes to what, caregiver?"

"I ... under—I under-s-stand ..."

Thenalious released the knife and let it sink into Hadwin's shoulder. He stood and revealed Reynold at the door, who watched the scene stone-faced.

"You're lucky I don't kill that nephew of yours." Thenalious turned to Reynold. "Summon Oberon. Unless you wish to fuck him."

Reynold shook his head, hiding a smug smile. "Too much of a bloody mess you've made. Some other time, perhaps."

"No. You'll have him now or never."

Reynold sighed and headed down the hallway. "Never then."

Hadwin lay on the floor and prayed he wouldn't bleed out. Part of him wanted to die and go to Helved to search for Naleem, Pinar, and their children. The other part begged to stay alive for Cadoc.

Oberon followed Reynold in and hesitated at the sight of Hadwin on the floor.

Thenalious stepped over him. "Take your caregiver and get him out of my sight. From now on, he's your responsibility. If anything happens again, it will fall on you as well."

"Yes, my lord." Oberon met neither pair of eyes while he gathered Hadwin up and hauled him out of the room.

Hadwin struggled alongside him down the hallway. They reached his room, where Oberon placed him on the bed and called for a servant.

"Get a healer now." He cut Hadwin's shirt, carefully maneuvering around the knife that still protruded from his shoulder.

Blood filled Hadwin's mouth and dripped over the corner. Tears washed the blood from his eyes. "I can't die ..."

"You're not going to," Oberon told him. "Don't talk. A healer will be here soon."

"Cadoc ..."

"I'll watch over them until you're taken care of. Now shut up and focus on staying awake. You have to stay awake."

For several agonizing minutes, Hadwin fought for consciousness until a healer arrived—an old man with beads braided into his silver hair and long, gnarled fingers. He couldn't be a healer, not truly. The only men who practiced anything remotely medical were Fan-worshippers and warlocks. Hadwin flinched away from him.

"Deal with it, caregiver." Oberon faced the old man. "He is to survive and be well enough to look after the children again. Make sure of that."

"Yes, my lord," the old man assured and got to work.

Hadwin gripped the sheets with his good arm and growled on screams when he could manage it. He could only drink ale for the pain as the old man peeled the knife from his shoulder, dressed his wounds, and stitched him back up. All the while, he murmured quiet chants, and he smeared some of Hadwin's blood on his face.

Hadwin did as he was told and dealt with it. He prayed for Cadoc's safety and the safety of the rest of their family, wherever they might be, whatever world they traveled through. He would remain in this version of Helved and do Fan's bidding, as everyone warned him to do.

CHAPTER 14

RAEGNA

THE CARRIAGES ROLLED OVER the drawbridge into the main square, surrounded by little shops and houses. People milled about the street and in and out of shops but made a path for the carriages and their attendees with humble bows. Raegna struggled to take in the sights as she rode alongside Gittan behind the Queen's carriage. Weapons clinked from warrior belts and spring-green round shields hung from their backs, making a loose shield wall between Raegna's horse and the Queen's carriage.

Gittan's mare tossed her head, and when she nipped her horse, it disrupted Raegna's admiration. Regaining control, Raegna wrapped her legs around her mare's belly as she jerked with a whinny. Gittan reined her gray mare in. "Oh, quit that, you jealous nag."

"Jealous?" Raegna repeated. "What for?"

"Perhaps for how pretty she is," Gittan guessed. "That's why most of us women are jealous of each other. And I'll let you in on something. Stallions pull the Queen's carriages, the finest and most well-tempered beasts in Galaenia. Siggy here is aware of that, and your mare is fair competition."

Raegna gazed down at the Commander's horse. "But you're a Maiden's horse. How can you be jealous?"

"Much like their riders, Maiden mares cannot breed. It keeps them in better shape into old age since the scars of foaling haven't ruined them … Lucky, village mare."

Raegna tilted her head, wondering if they were talking about horses anymore. But Gittan let the subject drop.

The deeper they traveled through the streets, the more dense Stadt grew. The more diverse as well, when Raegna noted Awevi traders and even a small party of Kaliqsi women, their hair concealed and wrapped in fabric. They watched the carriages and inclined their heads when the Galaenians bowed.

"Quite different from Sorelle, isn't it?" Gittan said. "You southerners are a bit cooped up with your own kin and no one else."

"Plenty have migrated south," Raegna said. "But they're just as Galaenian as we are. The men were very surprised to see the ambassador and her company."

"I don't doubt it." The Commander paused for a moment, glancing at the saddle horn. "Shield-Priestess. Do you … Do you know Naleem well?"

Raegna's eyes widened before she could hide her expression. Perhaps there was something to Gittan's farewell to him. "In truth, his wife was a very good friend of mine."

"Pinar." The name left Gittan's lips so casually, Raegna could not fathom the fact that she knew it, even if Naleem had clearly told her.

Raegna's throat closed and she swallowed to speak again. "Yes. They were quite the pair. She treated him very well, and they had four children."

"He told me," Gittan explained. "They sound like darling things. It's a true shame only one is alive in that Haven."

As far as they knew. On top of her tightening throat, a pressure settled behind Raegna's eyes. Pinar's last child was imprisoned in such a dark place, and poor Naleem had lost his family, enduring whatever torture Haven gifted him. Raegna could never forget the look on his face in the wagon she found him in, how he cowered and trembled. Pinar would weep for him and her young son, not to mention Hadwin.

"I'm sorry," Gittan spoke up. "I've stirred sad memories for you, too. I only wish to help, and I've told him I will bring his family back to him safely."

"That's a difficult promise to keep," Raegna muttered.

"I understand. But I hate to see such a man suffer. Or any of you suffer. I'm going to ask the Council to have us search for the place by winter, before snowfall. We can leave just after Leaf Fall Gift when everyone else is drunk from the festivities. We'll celebrate like normal, then be gone by morning. It will be the same if they disapprove of the journey."

Raegna straightened in her saddle, more sure of the plan than before.

The High Council's court towered over the rest of Stadt, dwarfing even the wealthiest inn, but not as large as Vakkar Hold. It wasn't as spectacular either, save for its size. More like a fortress, its square shape was only interrupted by the double doors Her Majesty's procession halted before. Silhouettes of women meandered along the highest balconies and a few warriors kept their posts in the two watchtowers in front.

No men or children accompanied the women in the courtyard. These women walked in and out of the court building, carrying scrolls or bundled parchment.

"Not a man in sight," Raegna reported.

"I did not lie," Gittan told her as they dismounted. "I fought tooth and nail to convince Her Majesty to at least allow Naleem in. She said it was best to keep the Council's traditions. She's right in most things. Now, let's hurry to get beside her. That way we get the best seats, and those old, deaf hags can hear you."

Raegna stifled a chuckle and shook her head. So much for keeping tradition and being respectful. The Council's servants tended to the horses and led them away to rest. Raegna gave her mare a good pet before leaving her. She followed Gittan to Queen Kjerstin, who had just stepped out of her carriage.

Kjerstin flashed a smile at them. "Commander. And Shield-Priestess. Your robe suits you. Have you seen the temple yet?"

"Not yet, your grace," Raegna admitted.

"Well, there's so much to be done as of late," Kjerstin said. "Let's see the Council. Not a moment to lose."

"Yes." Duchess Elmba exited her carriage. "It would be a shame to waste time over this matter."

Gittan rolled her eyes and placed an arm around Raegna to guide her forward. She whispered into her ear, "Ignore her."

Raegna focused her attention on the court building instead. She wrapped her head around the idea that the Queen of Galaenia walked beside her.

Queen Kjerstin folded her hands before her skirts and stepped over the cobblestone to the double doors. Her rose-gold gown fitted her curving figure beautifully, and her copper hair had been done in a braided bun, the rest of the locks spilling over her shoulders and down her back. Skin like sun rays glowed in the midmorning. Gittan's armor clicked with her movements and her braids clung to the sides of her head. Raegna fancied them as a strange trio heading into the building: the Queen, a Maiden, and a priestess with a sword.

No. A Shield-Priestess. Regardless, Raegna's mother was stirring in the wind to see them from Heimelle.

A hall wound in a circle, revealing the building's cylindrical structure. Small studies decorated with elaborate desks and bookshelves packed with volumes took up every room along the hall. Raegna followed Gittan and the group of warriors tailing the Queen and the Duchess around the hallway until they reached two large wooden double doors. Sachi and her firstborn daughter, Ailbhe, were carved into the wood as if protecting what lay behind the doorway. Not even Sigmund was allowed within the walls.

The doors opened as the group approached, and Raegna gaped at the giant room with a ceiling that stretched high above them. Tapestries of Gaea and Sachi hung on the walls along with other heroines and warriors of the sagas. Stone pews curved with the circle of the room to envelop a table of six seats. Sconces held fires that lit each pew and the table of six.

Gittan had been right. Each of the seats below the pews was occupied by elderly women far older than Raegna had ever seen a common woman become. These women appeared to have witnessed the Dark Days themselves or even the founding of Galaenia. Raegna wouldn't be surprised if they'd sailed in on the ships from Laefold.

Gittan took Raegna's arm and led her to the pew directly behind the Queen and the Duchess. The councilwomen peered at the royalty with narrowed, tired eyes. Several warriors and Maidens assumed their posts and guarded their mistresses before their table and the doors.

The first councilwoman to speak sat in the middle of them all. Her voice came out like she gargled dry sand. "It pleases us to see Your Majesty still so beautiful and healthy. We beg to know why you have called us so urgently. Have we finally got an heir on the way?"

Raegna raised an eyebrow and watched the back of Queen Kjerstin's head. Not that it gave any sign of her initial reaction.

"Head Council Inge, I've explained before," Kjerstin started, "my husband and I will worry about having children ourselves without any outside input."

"We are concerned about the well-being of Galaenia's future and its royal family," the woman beside Inge said in a raspy voice. "No Queen has gone this long without an heir. We're beginning to wonder—"

"This meeting is not about my future children," Kjerstin interrupted.

Raegna blinked at her.

"Women of the Council," the Queen started again, "it has come to our attention that the villages of Sorelle have been attacked and even destroyed by a savage group of rebel men."

"Men?" the second woman croaked.

"Yes. Witnesses of these attacks have traveled from Judr to tell us their tales. These men have a secret base hidden within Sorelle's hills. They are armed and have been reported to be holding fellow women hostage. We've come here to propose a full investigation and destruction of this community and the evil inside it."

The councilwomen did not mumble a word to each other, much less look at each other. Head Councilwoman Inge said, "Are these *witnesses* among you?"

"Most of them were men," Queen Kjerstin explained. "Their lives were spared for being just that. The only female witness among us is our courageous Shield-Priestess Raegna, named by Judr's new Matriarch Ase."

Kjerstin turned to Raegna and gestured for her to stand. Raegna gulped and jittered as she got to her feet. She bowed to the Council, unsure of what else to do.

"She made herself a priestess when her village, Syden, was destroyed, and lifted all the fallen," Kjerstin told them. "She escaped with her family to warn Judr, though the former Matriarch Viona did not heed her. Viona has since been lifted after the attack on Judr, and its people elected Matriarch Ase. Her crest decorated the message of Judr's attack to prove these terrible stories are true."

Every councilwoman's eyes roved over Raegna, picking her apart. Her lip stiffened and she kept her chin up.

"Priestess," Inge spat, "show us your scar, which you must have inflicted on yourself."

Raegna gulped and raised her hand, her palm facing them. The scar would be there, a dark pink striping down her hand. "I—I was ordained in Judr's temple when I arrived."

"At what time did you feel it right to lift your village?" Inge asked.

Raegna's brow furrowed and she retracted her hand. "Late summer, my lady."

"Explain to us, then, so that we might be clear, the exact nature of these attacks."

Taking a breath, Raegna mustered her courage. *For Ada. For Pinar, her children, Naleem, and Hadwin. For Iida, Asmund, and their son.*

For Bai. His gold eyes pierced through her memory of the dining hall, full of admiration for speaking against the nobles who laughed at their story. She would make him proud here as well.

"It is as Her Majesty said," Raegna began. "These men killed my people, destroyed Syden, and we were the only family to survive. I made my oath to Gaea so She would lift all those who lost their lives. I still pray they live with Her in Heimelle. My family and I journeyed to Judr to warn them of what happened to our home so they may not experience the same fate. Unfortunately, they did not respond fast enough and scouted Syden too late. The men returned and attempted to take Judr, but despite their weaknesses, the women of Judr defended themselves to victory.

"By Gaea's will, I stand before you today with a daughter lost and a husband and heart torn for her. If you do not believe me, there is a man taken from Syden who has been inside the raiders' Haven, or so they call it. Perhaps if you want to listen to his story—"

"It is rather convenient," the second councilwoman spoke up, "that you have survived *two* attacks by these *savage* rebels and you have a witness who has been to their base."

Raegna's mouth hung open. "I—I assure you, it is the truth."

"If I may speak plainly," Gittan put forth, "I have discussed the base with the witness myself. He has endured many terrors, and his tale deserves to be told."

"But you haven't been permitted to speak, Commander," the same councilwoman said. "You'll all understand that these reports sound like history excerpts from the Dark Days—men wielding blades and fighting in arms. I would expect such from the wild plains of Vesten, but quiet Sorelle?"

"These are indeed incredible stories," Inge said with a nod.

Raegna shook her head. "No, you must understand. Matriarch Ase sent the message with her crest, and Viona is dead. If you went to Syden now, you would find it in ashes. If you would permit men within these walls, my friends would tell you what they have suffered."

"Friends indeed." Inge sniffed. "Is it possible that quiet Sorelle let their men go unchecked?"

"She is very fond of the three that accompanied her, your graces," Duchess Elmba said, her voice cutting through the room like a dagger.

Every councilwoman turned to her. "Three?"

"The next *truth* is I found this Shield-Priestess in a meek wagon on my private road near the city walls," Elmba explained. "Among her poor provisions were three men of about the same age, and only one she claimed as her husband. A rather unruly and foul-mouthed beast he is, at that."

Raegna groaned inwardly. Bai's actions within the Duchess' carriage were bound to bite them back at some point.

"They are survivors of a travesty," Queen Kjerstin added. "Of course, they appeared to be a strange bunch."

The Council went quiet, but did not look to one another for guidance or any further opinion. Inge asked, "What say you on the matter, Duchess?"

"The only opinion that would matter belongs to your graces," Elmba told them. "But if you'll let me, I say there are more important matters to attend to in these times. For instance, the Awcvi ambassador visited us before the cold bothered her, and she and our Queen discussed a trade agreement I found rather expensive, to say the least. Not to mention the fear the people of Norden have of the *vildr* and how Kaliqsi sneak within our city right under our noses. Udstodt grows larger, and our city grows poorer. Many of our people have immediate struggles for work and food, and we're told to risk our resources for tales from a priestess and her small band of bachelors?"

"Naleem and Asmund are grieving widowers," Raegna argued. "Bai *is* my husband. These are not tales—they are the truth."

"Your graces," Queen Kjerstin spoke up. "The Shield-Priestess had asked for help before, and the consequences of those who did not listen are immeasurable. I beseech you to agree to have a few Maidens and warriors investigate Syden's well-being and report to us before the snowfall."

"Why, when Maidens are needed in Norden to defend our borders?" a councilwoman at the end of the table said. "From the sounds of this expensive trade agreement, we will need Maidens and extra warriors on the shores of Ostern to prevent any skirmishes with the Awevi. And you would have more chase down a village of men?"

"Warriors can be hard to come by these days when so many young women choose to raise families instead," another added.

"A small search party, then," Kjerstin negotiated. "Just to see if the village is standing."

"An inquiry will be sent to this new Matriarch Ase about the situation and the condition of Sorelle's villages," Head Councilwoman Inge said. "When we hear back from her, we will review our inventory of warriors and Maidens and perhaps see if any other villages are harmed. In the meantime, I suggest we delegate certain Maidens to Hafelle in Ostern to supervise the trading ports."

"A message to the Matriarch could take another season," Kjerstin argued.

"Your grace, I believe it is in your best interest to step down from the throne, so to speak, and focus on the conception of an heir. Let us and Duchess Elmba oversee things while you put your husband to good use. The future of the Crown and your mother's lineage depends on you, and you cannot meddle in every matter in Galaenia or heed every call for help. Are we clear on that matter?"

Queen Kjerstin's lips pressed into a thin line, and she glowered at the councilwomen before letting her gaze drop to the floor. "Galaenia will have an heir yet."

"Gaea willing, a princess," Inge put in. "We would request a full report on this Awevi trade agreement, then we will decide how many Maidens and warriors will be needed. We will draft this inquiry to Matriarch Ase and continue from there. Would this compromise be satisfactory?"

Raegna opened her mouth to say something else, but Gittan took her hand. The two of them exchanged a look before Gittan guided her back down into her seat. Fists clenched over her skirts, Raegna gritted her teeth.

"Yes," Kjerstin said. "That will do."

"It is an honor and pleasure, as always, Your Majesty. Good day to you all."

With that, each of the old women stood and slipped away from their table to exit the room. When the Queen turned to leave, every warrior and Maiden stood at attention. Everyone followed her out and through the court building.

Raegna cast her eyes down with her heart sinking. Even the highest forces in the land would not listen. When they walked outside and found their horses waiting for them, Raegna watched Queen Kjerstin climb into her carriage, and the driver shut the door behind her.

"Don't worry, Shield-Priestess," Gittan assured her as they mounted their mares. "You will still see your village avenged."

"Perhaps," Raegna uttered. "But not for another season."

"No, I've made a promise to a man as a Maiden. And if the Council prefers to draft an inquiry, that is fine. We will be the ones to take it to Sorelle."

When the procession arrived back at Vakkar Hold, stable girls and servants awaited the horses and their riders. Though she dreaded telling Bai and the others how the meeting had gone, Raegna steeled herself and found the three almost exactly as they'd left them. Naleem stood between Bai and Asmund.

Gittan and Raegna rode to them and halted their horses. Naleem stepped forward, a tentative expression on his face. "Well? How did it go?"

"I'll give them this," Gittan started, "they did not deny that something could be done. They will send a message to Matriarch Ase, asking about the events, and they want to wait to hear back from her."

Naleem frowned, and his shoulders fell.

"That could take until spring," Bai said. "That's too long."

Gittan shrugged. "It was a compromise the Queen had to agree to. However, though I was *not permitted to speak*, I will implore Her Majesty to allow us to be her messengers. I'm sure she wouldn't mind that."

"Us?" Asmund's voice broke out first.

Gittan nodded. "The plan still stands. We must get you boys into shape. You too, Shield-Priestess. This will all be sorted before Leaf Fall."

Bai looked at Raegna. After the day's disappointment, she returned his gaze from beneath her brow. His gold stare meant he would press her about the details later, but he must have understood her exhaustion not to bother her right then. Raegna's intentions to make him proud before the High Council had not been fulfilled, and she dreaded telling him anything.

"For now," Gittan went on, "look upset and cheated. No one can know, and they must believe that if any of us leave, it is because we're taking the inquiry to Judr. Enjoy the festivities while you can before we embark."

Leaf Fall Gift was just around the corner, and by Gittan's plans, that meant their journey to Haven would be soon. Disappointment was an easy guise when the High Council would not believe their story, just as Matriarch Viona and her sister had not. Raegna took the crook of Bai's arm to escort him back to their chamber. She leaned on him a little, spent from the ride and the meeting.

"Were they truly just as ignorant?" Bai asked her softly.

"I'll tell you everything later," she said. "I just want to rest."

He nodded. "We'll see Haven for ourselves soon."

"Yes. We will."

Chapter 15

Naleem

"**D**on't lose focus, man," Gittan snapped at Bai. "Sharpen your eyes like you sharpen that tongue."

Naleem leaned against a table and watched the two of them spar. Raegna and Asmund practiced different moves Gittan showed them. She wanted them to be reenacted steadily. Meanwhile, Bai was losing his patience, and Gittan had to be growing equally frustrated with him.

"You call this combat?" Gittan growled. "I've trained children stronger than this."

Bai stormed at her, maneuvering his ax to hook her sword. Gittan twisted, parried, and shoved him back with her shield.

"I hope you're not sparing your strength because I am a woman," she said. "That's quite insulting to a Maiden."

"Then you don't hold back, either!" Bai heaved.

"Very well."

Gittan tossed her shield to the side. It landed beside Naleem and wobbled before lying flat on the floor. Her sword collided with Bai's ax several times, and they shuffled around each other, adjusting their weight and dodging blows. Raegna and Asmund stopped their sparring to get out of the way. The three of them looked on while Bai and Gittan battled.

Though Bai continuously attempted to hook Gittan's blade and rid her of it, she escaped his lock and kept attacking. Bai snarled and swiped his ax with more force.

"Bai, that's not wood anymore," Raegna scolded. "Do not hurt her or yourself!"

"Oh, let him blow off some steam, Shield-Priestess." Gittan wrenched her sword from underneath his ax once more. "A man needs an outlet for his natural rage."

She whirled and rammed her elbow into his chest. Bai choked and stumbled backward while the others winced.

"See what happens when you let your anger get the better of you?" Gittan swept his feet from under him.

Bai toppled to the floor, flat on his back. Raegna gasped. Naleem worried about the scars on his back, but if they pained him, Bai didn't show it.

"You need to grasp some patience and focus on your opponent," Gittan said. "Not just wave your weapon around in the same movements. That makes you predictable, and then I would kill you."

She stooped and offered Bai her hand. He took it but would not meet her eyes.

Gittan gave him a wry smile. "It's nothing to be ashamed of. You're all learning. But that's enough for now. I want you all to rest before the palace goes mad for Leaf Fall Gift. Asmund, I want you to continue practicing those basic techniques if you can. Raegna, when you spar, tighten up those openings. Bai, meditate. If you were a woman training to be a Maiden, I'd take you somewhere in the woods and make you sit in silence myself."

"Maybe back in our chamber," Raegna suggested.

Gittan shrugged. "Whatever you can do."

Once the Maidens' tables and maps had been set back in their places again, three of them departed. Naleem hung back with Gittan, arranging pawns over a map.

"You might have to be a little careful," he told her. "Bai has these scars from being flogged in Judr. I think even Raegna got frightened when he landed like that."

Gittan collected their weapons. "I understand. But do you suppose those men in Haven will be just as careful?"

Naleem grimaced. "No ..."

"He's tough as stone," Gittan said. "Especially if what you say is true, though I won't press for details. You've all been through much. For now, you ought to enjoy yourselves and the festivities Her Majesty has planned."

"Well, it's a little difficult," he admitted, casting his eyes down. "This would be my first Leaf Fall ... alone."

She put the weapons away and turned to him. "You're not completely alone. There is lots of company to be had in Vakkar Hold. Your own friends."

Naleem fiddled with his fingers and then the sleeve of his shirt. "Our Matriarch would hold a feast the night before, and Pinar, Hadwin, and I assigned a child to each of us before our youngest daughter was born. We'd take them home early, have a little feast of our own, and go to bed. In the morning, we would give each of the children their gifts and then to each other. Then we'd walk through the woods together, look at the leaves, make piles, and play in them."

Gittan smiled. "Those are lovely traditions. You will have them again. I've promised you that."

"Hm. You shouldn't make promises you can't keep. For all we know, the moment they returned from attacking Judr, they killed them. My son and brother may not be waiting for me, after all."

"That's enough." Gittan took his hand in hers. "They're your family. Would you not sense that something was wrong or that they were both gone?"

Though her touch startled him—not because he feared the touch itself, but because she was a Maiden and was forbidden to treat him this way—Naleem did not shy away from it. He searched within himself and sighed. "No, not like that. Clearly, they're in danger, but ... I just don't want to get my hopes up."

"Rest assured something will be done, and we will try." She squeezed his hand before letting it go. Naleem wished she hadn't. "If you don't mind, you won't have to enjoy the holiday alone. I could escort you to the banquets."

He raised an eyebrow. "Are you allowed to do that?"

"I can escort and dance with men." Gittan chuckled. "I just can't marry them or bed them. We could manage that, couldn't we?"

Naleem laughed. "Of course. I just thought Maidens couldn't do anything with men. If you escorted me, wouldn't everyone be suspicious of something?"

Gittan shook her head. "An escort differs from courting. It's much more like how a mother or sister would take you to the banquet."

"Ah. Well, then I don't mind. I look forward to it."

A smile spread across her face. "Come. We'll practice and I'll *escort* you to your chamber."

They walked back to the palace, keeping a lazy pace beside each other. Gittan explained the traditions and routines of Leaf Fall Gift in Vakkar

Hold. Much like his Matriarch, Queen Kjerstin held a banquet the night before and the night of. A breakfast would be offered on Leaf Fall morning, but every noble family was free to do as they wished. Her Majesty often went for a ride or hunting with her husband.

"What do you do?" Naleem asked as they crossed the threshold into the palace. The servants hadn't appeared yet to begin the day's chores. Dawn still clung to Vakkar Hold's walls.

"Sometimes I'll join her," Gittan explained. "They also hold little tournaments and events for warriors, Maidens, and nobles. I used to do that when I was younger. But I'd rather save my strength for our journey."

"I'll bet you were amazing."

Gittan flushed. "Well, I wouldn't say that. I mean, I am Commander for a reason, but back then, I would sometimes trip over my own feet or couldn't rein in a horse during a joust. Once I became a Maiden, I got in trouble for accepting the favors of young men. I suppose after that, it became less fun."

"Hm. Is that not included in the procedures of an escort?" Naleem asked.

Gittan chuckled. "No, it is not."

"That's too bad. You would have my favor and luck when we see you off to Haven."

As soon as the words left his mouth, Naleem stiffened. Perhaps it pushed things too far. It might even be too soon for him. He had only lost Pinar this summer, but after everything that had happened, summer seemed like a lifetime ago.

He opened his mouth to apologize, but Gittan was already smiling. "I'm glad. It'll be our secret then."

Naleem chastised himself as they ascended the stairs. Would he give up the memories of Pinar so easily? Was his first love and the mother of his children meant to be forgotten and replaced with the Commander of the Maidens? While his heart collapsed in on itself, they approached the chamber door and stopped.

"I'll let you take it from here." Gittan nodded to him. "Get some rest. Good day, Naleem."

"Good day," he said, exhaling.

Inside, Asmund had already curled into bed and had fallen asleep while he still could. Naleem lay down to do the same but found sleep hard to accomplish. His heart ached for Pinar and their children. Then ached for Hadwin. Though the others were learning to fight and would go off to face Haven, he would stay behind. Useless and hopeless, he lay there and worried.

When the sun rose, Asmund stretched and sat up, rubbing his eyes. He glanced at Naleem and gave a quick, shy smile.

Naleem returned it. "Asmund. Do you mind if I ask you a difficult question?"

The younger man looked at him with eyebrows raised. Naleem waited for him to answer, but found Asmund was waiting for the question.

"Do ... Do you think you could love again after losing your wife?"

Asmund's gaze fell away from him, and he folded his legs underneath him. He remained silent, thinking, before he looked at Naleem again. "Is this about Gittan?"

Whenever he spoke, Asmund's voice came out so much deeper than Naleem ever expected. He sighed. "I just—Is it so obvious?"

Asmund shrugged. "I think it depends on you. I don't think she would mind waiting on you if you needed more time. That is, if she felt the same way. The only problem is that she's a Maiden."

"Right."

"And I don't know your wife." Asmund fidgeted in place. "But ... I know mine would not want me to be miserable. Or fearful. She would want me to find courage and happiness wherever I can."

Naleem smiled and sat up. "I'm sure she would. Mine would as well."

At least they had that much in common and could confide in each other during small, shared moments. Relief flooded through Naleem as he remembered Pinar. She would want the same, though he couldn't find happiness without Hadwin and Cadoc, or without closing a door on Haven forever. There was still so much time until that would be possible.

Naleem's friends had to travel across Galaenia without him, and he would stay behind, praying they would come back alive.

Chapter 16

Bai

Vakkar Hold bustled with the preparations for Leaf Fall Gift. All his life, Bai had grown used to hanging branches of colored leaves from rafters, eating a good meal, and hearing the story of Sachi and Sigmund's first child, Ailbhe. The birth of humanity. But the nobility took the festivities to a new height.

The stone walls and royal portraits had been transformed into a fall forest. Servants strewed bright leaves about the hallways. When children ran to crunch them under their feet, they received harsh scoldings from adults. The entire palace was filled with the scent of cakes and pies baking in the kitchens. Samples were brought to the chambers for breakfast, a small taste of what would come.

Raegna chewed on a disk-shaped cake topped with white cream and blinked at the display card on its plate. "Cinnamon–pumpkin cake. Not bad."

Bai balanced an assortment of desserts in his hands and added the cinnamon–pumpkin to his hoard, taking a bite. "Not at all."

Raegna rolled her eyes with a smirk and took her sword to the middle of the room. Bai settled on the bed and forced himself to relax with his treats on his chest, lying on his back. He took a bite, but the sweet flavor was lost on his tongue. He closed his eyes and took a breath as the silk sheets and down pillows muffled the pain of his old wounds.

He couldn't meditate: too much stirred in his mind. The urgency to go to Haven and prove all the ignorant windbags wrong. To find Thenalious and rip him to shreds. Bai supposed this was the anger Gittan had warned him not to let fester. But if it wasn't anger, then it was sorrow.

Defeated, Bai sat up and ate another cake. Raegna had pushed the chairs aside for more room, and with enough space, she wielded her sword to perfect tighter movements. When her eyes found his, she paused.

"I thought you might have fallen asleep," she half-joked.

He shook his head and sampled more cake. "No. Meditating is difficult."

Raegna let the tip of her sword touch the floor. "Not even with sweets? Don't be too hard on yourself. You're an excellent fighter. You just need the focus to become a better one."

Bai wasn't sure where this assurance and comfort was coming from, but he accepted it with a forced smile and devoured the rest of his desserts. She resumed her stance and sparred with an invisible opponent.

Bai leaned back, forcing his eyes on his food and away from her form. The way Raegna's brow furrowed in her concentration, her lip pouting, reminded him of Adabelle when she grew frustrated. The dull ache pulsed between his ribs.

He looked down at the floor. "You're not a bad fighter yourself."

Raegna wrinkled her nose at him, but a smile grazed her face. Bai returned it, no matter how strange it felt. She moved to begin another imaginary battle, but stopped and lowered her sword. "Perhaps since we both agree we are more skilled than we were, we could allow ourselves a break. It is Leaf Fall tomorrow, after all. We shouldn't miss the opportunity to enjoy it in Vakkar Hold."

Bai's mouth twisted. "Seems like it'll just be more elaborate, is all. Besides, Leaf Fall hasn't been an especially cheerful holiday for me in many years."

He didn't mean to sound so pitiful. Raegna's eyes cast down. "Well … in Syden, Ada and I always went to the market, and I bought her a gift and let her pick another. Then she would pick something for me. And then one year, she refused to leave until we found a gift for you. Heh, do you remember that?"

Bracing himself for the heartache, Bai heaved a sigh. "It was a fishing rod. I'm sure you only agreed to something practical."

Raegna nodded. "And you snuck her treats they gave you men in the fields for working the holiday. I did notice that, by the way."

"How could you not?" An amused huff left his nose. "Her face was covered with sugar and frosting when she finished them. I tried to clean her off."

They both laughed before silence took over again. Bai might have slipped into the sorrow had Raegna not spoken again. "I meant to say that we could explore the square outside the gates or other parts of the city for the holiday," she said. "I have some coin. We can keep some traditions alive."

"We? Like the two of us?"

Raegna's cheeks flushed, and she looked away, tossing her braid. "I mean, we could invite Naleem and Asmund. Maybe Gittan, if she isn't busy. That is, if you want?"

"You do mean the two of us, then?"

"Only if you want."

Bai looked at her and raised an eyebrow. "Careful, wife. Or I might think you're courting me, like Gittan is with Naleem."

Raegna whirled on him. "So, there *is* something between them?"

"Obviously." Bai chuckled. "If you'll have me at your side, Shield-Priestess, I would go with you into the city. Whatever you wish."

"I would wish you never to call me that again," she admitted. "Coming from everyone else, it's fine."

"Hm. Yes, wife."

"Much better, husband."

They dressed for their outing, and Raegna chose Bai's clothes. An orange long shirt that stopped mid-thigh over brown pants. Black boots covered the pants' hems. A wide brown leather belt hugged his waist, the material woven in braids with etched runes through the center. He wrapped a brown shawl over his shoulders and pinned it with a less flashy bronze brooch at his chest.

Raegna could not decide what to wear, torn between a red and a gold dress.

"The red one," Bai suggested. "Red suits you."

"Then you could wear this red shirt to match."

"Let's not push this affair too far."

However, he regretted choosing the red dress. The collar—if one could call it a collar—dipped down just above her breasts with only a thin gold bind to clasp either side of the bodice together. The middle hugged her waist with a looping red belt, and the skirts spilled over the curve of her hips. The color brought out the red hue in her hair, which had grown down to the middle of her back. Her brown eyes regarded him when she wrapped a cloak over her shoulders.

The two of them walked through the marvelous fall decor in Vakkar Hold, across the courtyard, and out the main gates, which were left open for the festivities. Several wagons of food, equipment, and kitchenware paraded in and out of the courtyard.

In the square, many people scurried to order gifts and trappings for dinner. Most of the shops sold clothes and jewelry. Bai tilted his head at a shop that stood out from the rest. Old leather books were displayed in the windows instead of pretty jewels and fabric.

"Can we look in there?" he asked.

Raegna frowned. "What for?"

"Isn't it a bookshop?"

"Yes, but I don't need books," she said. "There are books back at the palace. And I know what you want, Bai. You'll not have a book."

He supposed Gaea could not allow his wife to be kind in all things. Though he did half expect her to give in at this point. Raegna's sudden softness seemed limited to nice words and festive outings.

With everything being too expensive in the square, they meandered deeper into the city, where riders on horseback passed and old wagons creaked. Merchants in their booths hawked and attempted to stop Raegna with whatever they had to sell.

"Pretty beads for your jewelry box, my lady? We have glass ones straight from Ostern!"

"Wool cloaks and dresses from Hol Rekke, Norden. They'll keep you warm through winter!"

"Would my lady like leather from the hides in Vesten? We also have exotic binds for your husband to spice up your bed-play this Winter Mull."

Raegna and Bai turned beet red and hurried away from that merchant.

They browsed different shops that carried things their friends or friends long gone might have liked. In a quaint dress shop, Bai caught Raegna sliding her fingers across gowns for little girls.

"Found something?" he asked.

"This green one would look darling on her."

Bai glanced at the dress—small and modest, with a large skirt. It was the same green as the tunic he wore when they'd arrived. He nodded.

Raegna went on. "I could have stitched some gold thread in. She would have matched you. She would have loved that."

Pain struck Bai's sternum like lightning, sudden and knee-buckling. He stood firm as Raegna withdrew her hand and stared at the little dress with tears in her eyes. At first, he didn't know what to do. Leave her like that and wait until she felt better, perhaps? But she never would—he knew that well enough.

Bai put a light hand on her arm, and Raegna turned to him. She arched a dark eyebrow, the way she did in her sleep. Tears glistened in her eyes. He tilted his head to the shop door. She nodded, and they left. The green dress stayed behind.

They stepped out onto the street as the sun dipped lower in the sky. Around them, shops began to close for the holiday.

"I'm sorry we couldn't find anything," Raegna said.

"It's all right. There's still dinner and dancing tonight. Stadt just doesn't suit our tastes."

"Hm. Are we silly southerners out of our element?"

"No, we're too good, even for the great city and the royal palace." Bai smiled at her to lighten the air. Raegna copied him.

At the clinking of metal on metal, the two of them lifted their heads toward a large blacksmith's shop. The woman wore a thick apron over her dress as she hammered orange metal into the shape of a sword. Her fire lit up the street while the other booths and shops went dark for the night.

Raegna furrowed her brow and started toward her. Bai bounded behind, catching up to her as they approached the blacksmith.

"Excuse me, my lady," Raegna called over the metal clang.

The blacksmith, a woman with black hair braided into a bun and grime coating her brown skin, looked up at them.

"Do you have enough time for requests?" Raegna asked when she said nothing.

The blacksmith stood and sank the piece into a bucket. It hissed and steam rose around her. "What kind of requests?"

Raegna glanced at Bai. "An ax."

Bai gave her an incredulous look, but she ignored him. The blacksmith raised her eyebrows. "Of course. When would you like it done?"

"I can pay extra for it to be done by tomorrow night."

The blacksmith snorted. "My lady, do you know what tomorrow is?"

"I'd be happy to pay extra. As much as you need."

"Ten in silver," the blacksmith told her. "You're lucky I've had all requests finished this afternoon. I may have yours done sooner."

"Raegna, that's nearly all you have," Bai hissed.

She ignored him and stepped forward to pay half. "And one more thing."

Raegna unsheathed her knife from her belt—Bai recognized it from their escape in Syden—and handed the hilt to the blacksmith. "I could not afford a ring for my husband when we married. Could you make one from this?"

Bai blinked. Truly, he'd never gotten a ring, because neither of them had agreed to the marriage. Even if Raegna could have afforded one. The blacksmith inspected the knife, turning it over in her hand. "I can. Seems a shame to melt a decent blade, though."

"It has a story," Raegna told her. "Could it also be done by tomorrow? We're traveling soon."

The blacksmith grimaced to hide a scowl. "Next year, I suggest planning gifts for your husband ahead of time. Six more in silver will cover it. I'll need to size him."

As Raegna paid her more, Bai stepped forward, glowering at her for spending so much. Raegna rolled her eyes. "It's not like we found anything else, anyway. A thank you might have done you some good."

Ah, there she is. "Of course. Thank you, wife."

Chapter 17

Hadwin

ADWIN LAY IN HIS bed with Cadoc sprawled beside him. All he could do was muss his nephew's hair and stare at the ceiling to distract himself from his pain. Though day by day, it subsided. Sunlight beamed under the door, and Hadwin winced at his stitched shoulder when he twisted to see it.

Hadwin's heart sank when shadows of several little feet passed. Audun's voice was clear through the door. "Where is Hadwin?"

"He's resting and unwell," Oberon answered. Their voices ventured down the hall. "He'll be all right. Let's get you all to breakfast."

"But Hadwin should take us," Ugo argued.

"Come along."

Hadwin sighed, missing them, too. His fingers combed through Cadoc's hair and he listened to the sounds of Haven through the walls. The familiar shouts tore over the camp. Metal rang from sparring and the hammering in the forge. Hadwin closed his eyes and tried to rest while he could, but besides the pain, his guilt and shame gnawed at him from within.

He'd only meant to get a map to use should he escape. The damn thing had almost cost him his life and Cadoc's.

You're lucky I don't kill that nephew of yours. Thenalious' threat plagued Hadwin's thoughts. One more slipup and Cadoc would be gone, and it would be Hadwin's doing. All he wanted was a chance.

On top of the threat was the news of Naleem. *I bent him over and made him my bitch ... Then Reynold did. Every man who raided Judr made him theirs. Every last one.*

Hadwin's gut flipped as he stared at the ceiling, his hand curling over Cadoc's scalp. Thenalious could be trying to frighten him, telling him lies to make him furious and miserable. To egg him on and hurt him more. Reynold had already said Naleem was dead, left unlifted somewhere in the woods.

Tears sprang to Hadwin's eyes, and he swallowed hard. He'd nearly thrown Cadoc's life away—after everything. For a damn chance with a piece of parchment.

The door opened and the old warlock entered, carrying a tray in trembling hands, his pale ash skin stretched thin over purple veins. "Good morning, caregiver."

His faint, scratched voice came as slow as he walked. The old man set the tray on the stand beside Hadwin's bed. Cadoc stirred at the noise but continued to doze. The warlock stood over them, surveying Hadwin with tired eyes lined with wrinkles. "Feeling better?"

Hadwin frowned. "Better than yesterday."

The old man's shaking fingers rested on Hadwin's forehead before they trailed down his face and stopped at his chin. Such was an ancient gesture between men, but its origins were beyond Hadwin's knowledge. He perceived it as a way to clear another's mind and ward off Fan's evil. But this old-timer followed the Evil One's footsteps, so it could not be all that comforting. Hadwin squirmed under his touch.

"Guilt-ridden," the warlock reported. "For the boy. As you should be."

Hadwin shot him a look. "Stay out of my head, Fan-spawn."

The warlock chuckled. "It doesn't take magic to sense that, young one. Mine is not of Fan. I hold to Sigmund. I use his essence through myself and you. It pulses in your blood."

"Sigmund doesn't give his power like that."

"If he didn't, you would not still be here." The old man sat on the edge of the bed, avoiding Cadoc. "He moves through all men. Even under Thenalious' rule."

Hadwin narrowed his eyes. "Even in Thenalious?"

"No. That is a darkness too great. The Evil One has his claws deep in his sides. Now, let old Drengr see to those stitches."

Drengr. Hadwin had never thought to learn the warlock's name.

Before Hadwin could move to wake Cadoc, Drengr traced the boy's arm, and his eyes snapped open. Yawning, Cadoc sat up and slipped out of bed.

"Thank you, little one." Drengr removed the blanket and inspected Hadwin's torso, the bandages wrapped where he had left them.

"Don't use your magic on my nephew," Hadwin grumbled. "Fan's or otherwise."

"As you wish." Drengr offered a hand. "Sit up so I can change the bandages."

Hadwin took his hand and growled as he hoisted himself up with Drengr's help. Cadoc looked on with worried eyes, but Drengr waved at him. "On the tray is breakfast. Get some strength and help yourself, little one."

Cadoc looked at Hadwin first and didn't move until he'd nodded. The boy went to the tray and brought a biscuit to his mouth. Drengr smiled at him as he unwrapped the bandage from Hadwin's shoulder. "Good boy. Your uncle can eat once I'm finished with him."

Despite the pain, Hadwin's stomach rumbled. Cadoc hopped onto the opposite bed, munching away as he made himself comfortable. Dipping his head, Hadwin eyed the warlock. Drengr's wrinkled brow knitted as he concentrated. His trembling hands were deft in their work, pulling and unwinding.

"Did you learn magic in Haven?" Hadwin murmured.

"I have known Sigmund's ways since I was a little younger than you," Drengr answered without breaking focus. "He is a part of all men. As Sachi is a part of all women. They speak to those who are special to them."

Hadwin mulled over his words, and a new shame arose from pondering these things. "How do they speak?"

"You know the answer to that," Drengr said. "Priestesses tell you in the temple still, don't they? Sachi may come in the form of a doe. Sigmund flies as a raven."

"Those are animals," Hadwin told him. "There's no telling if that's truly Sachi or Sigmund. How do they *speak*?"

"Animals speak just as well as we do." Drengr freed Hadwin's shoulder. "Like other people across the seas, they just speak a different language. But the goddess and god sometimes appear in dreams. Many in our history testify to seeing them and hearing their voices, as well."

Hadwin had never seen Sigmund, and those who did were often labeled as lunatics. And yet ... "I've seen a raven fly over camp. Just one."

Drengr prepared the fresh bandages. "Our father always guards Haven."

Hadwin blinked. "Why would he guard it? You can't possibly believe he would stand for this place."

"Oh, he doesn't." Shaking hands worked around Hadwin again. "He guards this place from Fan."

"I don't understand."

"A few years ago, the Evil One showed himself in different forms," Drengr explained. "One, I believe, is Thenalious. Like Sigmund, Fan can move through men if they choose his path. This is why we hold to Sigmund, so the Evil One cannot conquer us as he cursed it. Sigmund wards off Fan from sinking his claws even deeper."

"Why can't Sigmund snap his fingers and take out Thenalious?" Hadwin asked.

"Sigmund cannot change what pleases the All-Mother. What pleases Jorde and all that it creates."

Hadwin's mind whirled. "This can't be Gaea's doing."

"Gaea has no power here."

"She's the *All-Mother*," Hadwin grunted. "But I don't know why I argue with your lot. This is all Haven's nonsense."

Drengr finished dressing Hadwin's shoulder and moved to the bandages around his waist, securing the stitches above his hip. "Thenalious, like you, is still a product of love between a daughter of Sachi and a son of Sigmund. He, like you, is a son of Sigmund. Our father cannot kill his own."

"Even if Thenalious has killed others?"

"Even then. Even when Sigmund walked on Jorde as we do, he could only do so much." Drengr removed the bandages. "But he can warn his other sons. Guide them and hope they take the path. Sachi does the same with her daughters."

"Haven nonsense," Hadwin grumbled.

"I would admit it if I didn't mention Sachi. Speaking her name would have me killed, but she needs to be heard by you and others in camp. I will not demean the mother of our sisters. The wife of our father. The raven flies, and I am telling you all this, dealing with your questions. Is that not proof enough for you?"

Hadwin frowned but looked away as the old warlock worked. "Why do you stay in Haven if you believe in Sachi, too?"

Drengr went quiet as he tied off the bandages. "Sigmund called me here long ago. When Haven was peaceful, I thought it was so I could practice my healing without fear of the matriarchy. Now I believe it is to be a beacon to men like you. Sigmund may not be able to change what is done, but he is wise and can see beyond us. He must have known of Thenalious' rule and put me here to counteract it. To help him guard Haven."

"But Sigmund is powerful. Why doesn't he just stop this?"

"I told you he can't bend the All-Mother's will."

"But this can't be Gaea—"

The door opened, and Hadwin's stomach dropped when Thenalious walked in, hazel eyes roaming over him. Cadoc fled to Hadwin's side, climbing behind him on the bed. Hadwin winced when the boy grazed his wounds.

"Healing up, caregiver?" Thenalious' smirk played under his beard. "Drengr, how does he fare?"

"The gashes are healing well, my lord," Drengr told him. "Another week and he may resume some duties, provided the older children can aid him."

"I'd prefer the older ones to train soon," Thenalious said. "Reynold's oldest, especially. But it can't be helped. I'll see if I can find another caregiver before winter. Perhaps one who knows his place."

"Of course, my lord."

"Leaf Fall is tomorrow, Drengr," Thenalious went on. "Ward off the goddesses and make a sacrifice to Fan. I'll provide one for you."

"Yes, my lord. Much thanks. Hail to the gods."

Thenalious turned and shut the door behind him. At last, Hadwin could breathe. He gave the old warlock a sideways glance. "You're a pretender. Either you're lying to me or you're lying to him."

"It's good that you learned not to place your trust in others so willingly," Drengr said. "Perhaps this last lesson has taught you pretending is survival. Honor has its place, but it's not in Haven."

"I suppose you'll tell me this is Sigmund speaking and not Drengr?"

The old man met Hadwin's gaze, making him jump in place. Wrinkles etched around small eyes with irises the color of obsidian. Hadwin's heart lurched.

"You ought to play the caregiver." Drengr's voice did not waver. "To pretend is to protect your nephew. Pretending is survival."

With that, Drengr finished his work, and Hadwin's injuries were covered with fresh bandages. As he rose, the old man tapped on the tray beside the bed. "Eat up and grow your strength. The quicker you are back to work, the less likely Thenalious will settle you with an imbecile."

Cadoc emerged from behind Hadwin, gobbling his biscuit once again. Hadwin watched Drengr carefully as he chose his biscuit and sausage, then the old warlock gathered his things and went for the door. He turned and smiled at Hadwin. "And happy Leaf Fall."

Hadwin fought to breathe when the warlock shut the door behind him, leaving him and Cadoc alone again. Drengr's eyes were a faded blue and not obsidian. Outside, a raven called, and fluttering wings brushed the great house walls.

Chapter 18

Raegna

Once Olena had pinned the last braid to the back of Raegna's head, she gave her a satisfied smile in the mirror. "There you are, Shield-Priestess. Very pretty."

A doubtful huff escaped Raegna's nose—though she admired how her chestnut curls framed her face before the braided bun. "Thank you, Olena. Will you do anything for Leaf Fall tomorrow?"

"Well, I was going to ask you if you needed me for anything," the servant girl said. "Otherwise, I will finish some chores early and then see my family in the lower part of the city. We'll exchange gifts and have dinner. I'm very excited because my eldest sister had her babe and we'll all get to see it."

"That is lovely," Raegna said, smiling. "I don't think I'll need you, though you've been incredibly helpful. Happy Leaf Fall, then."

Olena curtsied. "Happy Leaf Fall, Shield-Priestess."

She turned and left the room, passing Bai and the servant, who was fastening Bai's collar beneath his chin. All the while, Bai frowned and fidgeted.

Dressing up for their first banquet in the palace had been one thing. All four of them still looked run through the mud compared to the rest of the court. However, this servant took it upon himself to cut an inch or two of Bai's shaggy blond hair and turned him into a gentleman. Though layers of clothes had been added, a black vest ribbed with metal bound his torso, making his chest appear broader and his waist and hips slimmer. The servant laced this vest up in the back.

Raegna stood in a scarlet dress that left her shoulders bare. She lifted a long maroon shawl stitched with runes and designs that stretched at the fabric corners. A heart line dipped over her breasts and stopped at the leather belt beneath. The heavy skirts reached the floor, and the fabric glittered with the gold strands woven with the red. Raegna caught Bai stealing a look at her, something he'd been doing more often lately. Part of her thought she ought to say something about it, but another wanted to let it be. She pulled the shawl tighter.

The servant boy finally stepped from Bai, gave a short bow, and left the room. Bai was a vision in green again, with gold and furs for the brisk weather. He yanked at his collar. "I can't wait until I don't have to look this ridiculous again."

Raegna rolled her eyes. "You don't look ridiculous. This might be the most dashing I've ever seen you."

Bai fidgeted a little less. "And Olena is right. You do look … pretty."

His voice grew faint as he said it, and though Raegna did not mean to, she soaked it in with a hot flush crawling up her neck. How long had he been thinking these things? Was it similar to how she thought of him, caught up in the luxuries of Vakkar Hold? Were their thoughts genuine? Why did she care?

Raegna shook her head at herself. "Let's go. I'm starving."

As they left their chamber, they found Gittan waiting in a dark blue dress outside Naleem and Asmund's room. A yellow shawl draped from her shoulders, pinned by a round brooch on her right. Yellow hems finished the skirt on the floor, decorated with dark-brown curves and forest trees. "Hello, you two. I was just waiting on Naleem. I'll be escorting him this evening."

Bai and Raegna gave each other a knowing look as the chamber door opened and Naleem stepped out. His deep purple tunic fell to mid-thigh, cinched at the waist with a wide brown leather belt, and he wore boots strapped over dark-brown pants. He smiled at Gittan before he took notice of Bai and Raegna.

"Oh, hello. You both look well."

"I hope so," Raegna said. "We've trudged around Stadt looking for gifts. You look rather handsome as well, Naleem."

"I meant to say the same thing," Gittan said.

Naleem fiddled with his sleeve. "I only hope I put all this on correctly."

Then Asmund stood at the doorway in more casual clothes than anything befitting a Leaf Fall Gift banquet in Vakkar Hold. "Have fun."

"You're not coming?" Raegna asked.

Asmund shook his head.

She faced him. "But you ought to. You can't spend Leaf Fall by yourself. Come with us and at least have something to eat."

"That's what I told him," Naleem added. "And you won't be a bother, Asmund. We're all here together. We should be together for this holiday."

When Asmund hesitated, leaning against the door frame, Bai spoke up. "I don't think they'll stop insisting if you say no again."

"... All right."

Naleem helped him into something more suitable. Asmund emerged in a brown shirt of the same style as Naleem's and a black belt buckled above his hips. The difference was made by the ruddy orange shawl they wrapped over his shoulders and pinned so one half fell over his left side.

The five meandered to the ballroom, where the heraldess announced everyone in attendance.

Peering at Naleem and Gittan, the heraldess raised a suspicious eyebrow. "Commander Gittan and gentleman Naleem."

Gittan took the crook of Naleem's arm as she guided him down the steps and into the ballroom. Raegna didn't have time to see them as they went, nor could she note the other courtiers who gazed at them.

The room had been decorated to imitate the fall forests with leaves strewn about the edges, tree branches adorning the rafters, and small aspen trunks holding shelves of pastries and sweets. Music played from one corner as a band thrummed lyres, beat on drums—and a flute echoed across the room. The singer began her melody, something cheerful and festive.

"Shield-Priestess Raegna and her husband, gentleman Bai," the heraldess announced as they passed. "And gentleman Asmund."

Bai gazed at the decor. "They know how to celebrate Leaf Fall."

They joined Naleem and Gittan in the crowd as the Commander conversed with a woman Raegna had not seen before. Small and slight, this woman wore a dark gray dress, and her brunette hair spilled over her shoulders and down her back. Her black eyes regarded Gittan with respect, a scar etched into her gold-tinged skin through her left eyebrow.

"And everyone is gathered?" Gittan asked her.

"Just outside Udstodt, Commander," the woman answered. "All is ready."

Gittan grinned and kept her voice low. "Shield-Priestess, men, this is Thekla. A mercenary I've hired to organize our journey for tomorrow."

Raegna nodded to her. "Your work is appreciated. Any help is precious to us."

Thekla smirked. "Gittan and I are old friends. After hearing your tale, I refused the coin she offered. The others, however ... they are a rugged bunch. A few purses add to the incentive."

"We'll have to thank them too," Raegna said.

A spark lit in Thekla's black irises. "Your image alone is thanks enough, Shield-Priestess." She started toward the double doors. "I can't stay long. I'm not exactly invited. Happy Leaf Fall, Gittan. Shield-Priestess."

Thekla's shoulder brushed hers, her fingers fiddling with Raegna's. Raegna struggled to catch her breath. Gittan stifled a laugh, and Bai's brow furrowed as he turned to watch Thekla go.

"You'll have to excuse her." Gittan chuckled. "Thekla can be quite fond of other women."

"What sort of old friends were you, then?" Naleem teased.

"Oh, I'm far too brutish for her taste," Gittan assured him. "Shall we enter the dining hall?"

Raegna cleared her throat, her cheeks on fire. Bai closed in, leaning toward her ear. "I'm not sure if she realized your arm is around mine."

Despite herself, Raegna's mouth quirked. "I don't think she cared."

"We may have to pretend a little harder." Then he jolted and shook his head. "Never mind. That was forward."

Raegna's skirt swished against his legs as she drew into him, so close his calves brushed hers and their strides matched. "Not a bad idea, though."

Bai stiffened in her grasp, muscles tightening under her fingers. In turn, Raegna fought a squirm and focused on her steps.

Dinner was announced, and they joined the rest of the courtiers in the dining hall.

Each person in attendance took their seat. The Queen and her King sat at the head of the table with Duchess Elmba, the Duke, and their children on the right side of them. No foreign ambassadors were staying at Vakkar Hold, so Lady Abela and her companion sat to their left. Raegna, Bai, and Asmund sat opposite her, with Gittan and Naleem across from them.

Platters of ham and turkey legs were served with stews, roasted vegetables, and candied roots. Now well-fed, Bai and Asmund ate like proper gentlemen—and not ravaged common men who had been on the road. All of them blended in. Raegna glanced across the table at Naleem and Gittan, who got on like a fine courting couple.

"What do you think of them?" Raegna asked Asmund and Bai. "Do you think it'll be all right?"

"Naleem likes her," Asmund murmured. "Though I think he's worried about betraying his wife."

Bai glanced at them before taking another bite. "They were close."

Raegna nodded, a pain striking her chest as she remembered Pinar. "She wouldn't feel betrayed, though. She would want his happiness."

"That's what I told him," Asmund said between bites.

"Hm. I don't think I've heard you talk this much," Bai commented. "It's good to hear your voice."

Asmund dipped his head and chewed more slowly.

"It is," Raegna agreed. "You're not in Judr anymore, Asmund. And you know, Iida would want your happiness as well."

"I know, priestess."

They enjoyed cakes and pudding desserts before being ushered into the ballroom again. The music continued with happy beats and pretty melodies. Couples began dancing, twirling with the beat of the drums.

At first, the three lost Naleem and Gittan, then spotted them on the dance floor among the other couples.

"So much for sticking together," Bai said.

Raegna smacked his shoulder. "Be kind. This is the first time I've seen him happy since ... probably Syden."

"That's true."

They stood against the wall while servants offered them drinks. Raegna allowed herself to indulge in the wine. Even Bai and Asmund had a few glasses. Perhaps the wine loosened her mind while she watched the others dance. A chandelier decorated in fall leaves glittered enough to make her head swim, and an awkwardness settled in her.

"Bai. Would you like to dance?"

He glanced at her, gold eyes widening. "Dance?"

"That's what I said."

Bai looked out over the other couples and pulled at his sleeve. "I don't ... I don't dance."

"Why not? It can be fun. I used to when I was younger, when Matriarch Alv had Leaf Fall and Winter Mull celebrations. Didn't you?"

"No." Bai dipped his head, matching Asmund beside him. "I never did that."

Raegna faltered but took the crook of his arm and squeezed. "It might help."

He looked down at her, muscles tighter than they had been before dinner. Another glance at the crowd, and he gulped. "I don't know how."

"That's all right." Raegna guided him away. "I'll teach you. You can learn to fight, you can learn to dance. Asmund, should we find you a dance partner?"

Asmund startled at his name. "Oh, no. You go. I can stay."

"You're sure?" Raegna asked.

He nodded. "I'll save the wine for you."

Raegna held back a frown but set her glass on the windowsill beside him. "If you insist. We'll be back. Come along, husband."

Bai dragged his feet behind her. "Is it too late to revoke those marriage vows?"

"Shut up." Raegna stopped them at the edge of the dance floor, scolding herself in her disbelief. If she went back in time to tell herself she would be dancing with Bai in Vakkar Hold, she would have accused herself of being a trick from Fan.

Raegna faced him, and Bai quaked in her wake, his face paling. His eyes darted around the room before they landed on her. Raegna tilted her head. "Are you nervous?"

"No. I've never been more tranquil."

That brought an unexpected smile to her face. Raegna took his hand, her stomach flipping. "It's very easy. I promise."

She guided his other hand to her waist, and lightning stroked her spine. Raegna drew a breath to remain calm for him. Bai had enough jitters for both of them. His hand was so light on her hip, she touched his knuckles to be sure it was there.

Raegna placed a palm on his shoulder. Beneath his tunic, the delicate corset bones curved over what she knew to be hard muscle.

"See?" Raegna gulped, a pit in her throat. "Easy."

Bai's chest rose against hers. "Easy ..."

Drums pounded into a new song. Raegna steeled herself and surveyed Bai, who assessed their position, limbs light everywhere they touched her. She moved his chin with gentle guidance. "Look at me."

Bai stared at her with big gold eyes that glistened.

Raegna bit the inside of her cheek and took the first step. "Follow my lead. Just like this."

The music itself seemed far away, muffled down a long tunnel. Raegna conjured the steps from her memory, slowly instructing Bai before speeding up the rhythm. Fortunately, Bai was a fast learner, matching her steps until they moved with grace alongside the other couples. His touch was still light as air, and her head swam.

"Time for a spin," she murmured. "Ready?"

Bai gave her a small smile. At least his confidence was growing. Raegna released him, lifted his hand, and spun beneath it. His fingers grazed hers as she turned, and he caught her again when she came full circle.

Raegna resumed the steps. "Not so bad, eh? I knew you could do it."

"Yes." Bai's shoulders bobbed as his mouth twisted with a hidden smirk. "I suppose I should listen to you more often, wife."

Raegna raised her chin. "Like a good husband should."

He huffed in amusement, and they twirled with the others.

The drums pounded in Raegna's ears. They spun and jumped when the dance bid them to, and she found herself bracing against Bai for support, and pulled away. That was the only time she felt his touch holding her firm. When she regained her balance, his hands seemed to disappear again.

"Don't get sick on me," Bai warned her. "You've only had a few glasses tonight."

"Well, all this spinning," she breathed.

"Not to mention the surreality of us," he murmured. "I know."

A beat of silence passed between them as Raegna fought to steady herself.

Bai spoke first. "We do this for Ada. Continuing to tolerate each other, I mean."

"More than tolerate, lately," she admitted.

"You're not so bad when you're not berating me," he told her. "Or striking me. Glaring at me. But then I don't blame you."

There it was again. "Bai. Please know ... I don't blame you, either."

Bai came to a halt, and they both stood in the middle of the dance floor while the others waltzed around them. He stared down at her, his eyes dulled. "You don't mean that."

"I do."

"You mean to spare my feelings, maybe," he said. "I'm not exactly sure why, all of a sudden. I appreciate that, but you don't mean it. You can't."

"I can and I do. I don't blame you. Not for anything, and I mean it."

He pulled away from her. A few dancers glimpsed their way as Bai stumbled and shook his head. "You can't."

Then he turned and left her there. Raegna gaped, watching him disappear into the crowd before she snapped back to herself. "Bai!"

She strode through groups and knocked against other shoulders to find him. Somehow, he seemed to have evaporated into thin air. The bright fall colors blurred as she whirled to spot him among the others—even to find Asmund, Naleem, or Gittan and ask if they'd seen him leave, and where he'd headed.

Had she been too forward, then? Did he want them to walk on the crumbling rubble of the wall that stood between them forever? Was that to be their life? Things would be different after they marched to Haven. They might not survive, and she couldn't leave the debris in front of them and not do anything about it for the rest of the time they had left.

"Shield-Priestess," a warm voice said, interrupting her thoughts.

Raegna jolted and turned. She lost her breath when her eyes met the deep green of the Duke's.

Duke Ioan stood a head and a half taller than her. His edged cheekbones and jawline were even more stunning up close. His inky hair had been slicked back, but a few strands fell over his forehead. Silver glinted in the strands above his ears.

"Are you all right?" he asked.

"Fine," Raegna squeaked. "I've—I've just lost my husband."

Though the word *husband* came like gravel over her tongue.

"The blond one, right?" The Duke gave her a reassuring smile. "I'm sure he's around, partaking in the banquet with others who came with you."

"Yes, perhaps." Raegna's panic had been replaced with a new kind as her heart drummed faster than the music.

"I am glad I caught you." A servant passed with a tray holding glasses of wine. Duke Ioan took two and handed one to Raegna. "I wanted to tell you I admire your bravery through all you've endured."

Raegna's mouth twisted, and she glowered up at him. "Forgive me, your grace. But I recall you laughing along with the others at our first banquet here."

"A patriarchy in Sorelle was at first a laughable thing to imagine," he said. "Especially for Judr. But I am the one who should be begging for your forgiveness. After hearing your story, well, it's enough to break any heart."

"Any except your wife's," Raegna quipped, thinking of Duchess Elmba during the High Council's meeting. "But I suppose you have my forgiveness. I wouldn't have believed us either. I need to find my husband, though."

"Unfortunately, I have not seen him," the Duke admitted. "But the other fairer man you came with is alone on the balcony."

He pointed across the room where glass doors opened to the starry night sky. Perhaps Bai had passed Asmund or had told him where he would be. Raegna nodded and then curtsied. "Thank you, your grace. Happy Leaf Fall."

"Happy Leaf Fall, Shield-Priestess."

Raegna took a deep drink of her wine before pacing across the ballroom to Asmund.

Past the glass doors, a few couples gazed from the balcony at the stars and the lights of Stadt. Asmund folded his arms over the stone edge. Raegna approached, and he turned to face her. He gave a small smile before he noted Bai's absence with a tilt of his head.

"You wouldn't have happened to see him around, would you?" Raegna asked.

Asmund shook his head. "Did something happen?"

"No," she lied. "I've just lost sight of him. Maybe he's gone to bed. What are you doing out here?"

Asmund shrugged. "Looking at the stars. Though they are a little faint because of the city."

Raegna followed his gaze and joined him. The sky drew a blank in some spots, but the stars twinkled all the same. In Sorelle, they would look different—brighter, and spread out across a canvas of black. Raegna looked Asmund over once more, his cool blue irises soaking in the starlight.

"Asmund," she started, "are you all right?"

He glanced at her with his brow raised.

"Much has happened," Raegna explained. "Much more is happening. Tomorrow we'll face Haven. Naleem is somewhere with Gittan, and I need to find Bai. Will you be all right?"

Asmund's shoulders bobbed. "Don't worry. The stars are more of a comfort than you know."

Perhaps he saw Iida and their son in them. Or he sought Gaea's presence in them. Whatever it was, he seemed more confident than Raegna had ever seen him. She took his hand and squeezed it. "I'll find Bai in our chamber, I'm sure. If you need anything, my friend, please let me know. We'll avenge our people together."

"We will."

***

Before going up to her chamber, Raegna ordered a pitcher of wine to be sent ahead of her. It would take a few more glasses to muster the courage for what she knew she must do tonight. Lifting her skirts, Raegna trudged up the stairs and left the sounds of the banquet behind. Asmund went up some time ago, and she told him she would rather stay and look at the stars a little longer. Gaea knew where Naleem and Gittan had stolen off to.

Raegna braced at the door before entering. Much to her relief, Bai sat before the fire, sulking. He didn't turn when the door opened and shut, his outline etched by the firelight, sharpening the angles in his features. Blond hair soaked in the orange glow. The pitcher had already arrived, sitting on the table beside him, and he balanced a goblet in one hand.

So it would be tonight.

Raegna steeled herself and took the seat beside him. She poured herself a glass and took a ladylike sip.

"Have you been up here long?" she asked.

Bai didn't look at her.

"Well, I have a mind to tell you, *husband*, that you have no right to tell me what I can and cannot feel or say. I'll do those things as I wish."

A stifled, manic chuckle left his throat. He covered his mouth to hold it back and pulled his goblet closer to keep it from spilling.

"This isn't a laughing matter," Raegna told him.

"It's just that I can't believe I've missed that about you." He laughed. "I miss when you hated me. When you wouldn't look at me. I miss it."

When his voice trailed off, her heart sank. "How could you? We're speaking to each other. Isn't that what you wanted back in Syden?"

"I wanted to stay with Ada." His voice caught and he brought the wine to his lips. "That's all I wanted."

Raegna sighed and took another drink. "I know."

"It doesn't matter now, does it?"

"It does."

Both of them stared into the fireplace. The flames blackened the wood within and embers snaked up the chimney. The fire reminded Raegna of her daughter's lifting, and she shivered despite its warmth. "I truly don't blame you. Truly."

Bai's jaw set before he downed his goblet and poured more into it. "Do as you wish, then."

Raegna swallowed and raised her chin. "A long time ago, you asked forgiveness for it. I've given you that forgiveness and you won't take it."

"Because it's so horrid you won't even say what *it* is," he growled.

Raegna took a drink. "My mother forced us. She forced us to bed so she could keep me in line and safeguard her bloodline."

"But I had a choice." Bai's voice rumbled like distant thunder. Their inevitable storm was incoming. "To have my throat sliced or to take you. And I should have let her kill me."

"No, you should not have—"

"Then you would not have had to endure it. Adabelle would have never been born, and she would have never suffered or been as frightened as she was!"

Bai's voice rose with every word before it crumbled into a choked sob. Raegna looked on as his rain cloud downpoured, and stones tumbled as his walls caved. Bai's shoulders shook and he pushed his goblet onto the table before attempting to hide his cries.

Hot tears burned Raegna's eyes. "I don't blame you for that, either. I did, truly I did. But I know you must have tried. How could you not—"

"It didn't matter," he sobbed.

"For Gaea's sake, Bai. You were near death the night before with a flogging you didn't deserve. If anything, I should have never left you two alone. Whose fault is it then?"

Another sob escaped him, and he shook his head. "You helped Asmund and Iida."

"And look where that got them!" she snapped. "Just when I thought I had gained a new friend, she's snatched away from me. Even when I did help her, she was dead. Then I found my daughter dead. I left her. I couldn't say goodbye."

Her cries racked her, and Raegna wrapped her arms around herself, clanking her goblet on the table. Bai sniffled and wiped his eyes with the heel of his hand.

"What happened then?" Raegna managed. "Tell me what happened to her."

Bai straightened and swayed in his chair. "There were ... there were a few men who came into the house. They put Banu and Jora on the ground, and I tried to hide us in the back room. I didn't want to put her through a window. It was too dangerous outside. So I thought I might try to pull the floorboards up and hide her underneath. Let them do what they wanted with me ... but I wasn't—I wasn't strong enough for the boards to even budge, so then they broke in.

"I tried to protect her and fought, but they pushed me on my back, and it hurt so bad I couldn't see. That Thenalious took her ... He held her up. I begged ... but he took his blade to her—"

Raegna covered her mouth to muffle a sob. She folded her legs to her chest and curled into the chair, longing to hold her babe. The emptiness made her arms throb with every heartbeat.

"I'm so sorry, Raegna," Bai whispered to her.

"Was that when she died?" Raegna blurted through her sobs. "Did he have her when she died?"

"No. No, he—well, gave her back to me. I tried to stop it, to stop the bleeding. I—No, she died with me. I tried to stop it, but I knew, and told her I loved her and that she was safe. Then she ..."

Raegna fought with several breaths to control her weeping. "At least she had you. She had her papa."

"What good that did her."

"Shut up. It was not your fault, Bai. She was lucky to have you and not have lost you the night before. If you must be angry, put your blame on that wretch who killed her. He'll feel our wrath like Fan felt Gaea's."

Bai went quiet. As Raegna wiped her tears, she noted how his eyes glowed with the flames, like the richest gold, tears glittering in them. Perhaps there was no fury like a mother's, but could it be compared to a true father? Even Sigmund's cries for a child lost could be heard throughout Jorde before he obliterated Mork Skov into the barren, wicked mountain it was.

"Thank you for telling me," Raegna said finally. "I needed it."

Once he wiped his eyes with his sleeve, Bai picked up his goblet again and drank deep.

Raegna did the same. "And if nothing else, I don't regret her. I don't blame you now, but I'll not lie and say I was never angry with you or resented you. But I never regretted her."

"I don't either," he said. "I was speaking out of grief. I regret what I did to you, and that's all. I'd give anything to have her back, Raegna."

"I know. I would too."

He drank again, laughing a little. "I remember when you first caught us playing. Gaea, I thought you would slay me on the spot. Why didn't you do anything?"

"Truly, I didn't know what to do." Raegna sniffled and wiped under her eyelids. "My mother always taught me that men are beneath us, but I never learned her way of punishing one. Even if I did, I'm not sure if I would have been brave enough to face you back then."

"What changed? You would snap at me when I spoke and hit me in the forest."

"Well, you became so damn infuriating." She gave him a weak smile. "And you hit me first."

"Only to keep you from being more of a righteous idiot."

They laughed at each other, wiping old tears away. The walls crumbled further. The stones at their feet. They swapped little stories, asking one another what went through their heads in each. The wine subdued the strangeness of it all and made the painful memories more tolerable.

"What did you think of her when she was born?" Raegna asked when a pause interrupted their chatter. "Back then, I couldn't begin to read what went on in your mind. Nor did I care to."

"Hmph." Bai settled back in his chair, his once sharp eyes dazed. Sobriety slipped away from him by the moment and his head tilted in funny ways. "Honestly, she was a bloody mess when the midwife held her. I've never seen a woman give birth, so I was busy trying not to look too revolted."

"I appreciate that." Raegna's mouth quirked as she recalled his tight expression back then.

"But then she cried, and it was as if something snapped into place and everything in me stood at attention. You know when dogs hear something, and they prepare to protect ... But that must sound stupid."

"No, I know what you mean." Raegna shifted her weight in her chair. "When I held her in my arms ... I didn't know what exactly to do, but only that I would do something."

"Yes. Of course, I had to bring her to you, and I knew she did not belong to me, not like she belonged to you. She was so small and so precious, I couldn't stay away. You named her Adabelle, and I thought it was perfect. The first thing we must have agreed on."

"She was very beautiful. Our beautiful babe."

When silence washed over them again, they drank and braced against the pain. Tears still welled in Raegna's eyes. She let them spill over before wiping them away. Something sprang to life in her mind that raked the inside of her chest. The wine loosened her enough to reveal it. Their walls were already crumbling.

"Do you—do you think we could do it again?" she whispered.

"Do what?"

"… Have a child."

Bai's glazed eyes looked her over before he laughed again. "Now I know you've had too much to drink. Isn't it enough that we look at each other nowadays?"

"It might … might make it easier."

Bai swayed and leaned against the armrest of his chair. "You can't bring her back, Raegna."

"No. I could never hope to. And I could never replace her, not ever. But we could begin again. Have a better start than we did. It could be our choice."

His head lolled to the other side. "Well, it would be your choice, wife. You know we men crave sex like nothing else, anyways."

Raegna let her head roll as she stared at the dark ceiling flickering with firelight. "But you were hurt too. Twice over."

At first, his eyes bore into her before he shrugged lazily. "This wine has not been altered, so you don't mean to hurt me. And I suppose it would help our endeavor to appear happily married."

Raegna's heart twinged at the truth of how Turid had taken advantage of him. All this time, she'd never wondered how it happened. They'd lost so much since then. "So it must be your choice, too."

"… Only if you wish."

Raegna chewed on her lip. They could do it. Some semblance of what *was* could be again, but better with the two of them on good terms and safe within Vakkar Hold. Maybe in the city—if they couldn't stay in the palace much longer. If they survived Haven, what would become of them afterward? Though motherhood hadn't been her choice, Raegna had taken it in stride with time. It had turned her into a warrior in her own right. It was all she'd had to undo her mother's control—by not seeking to control Ada. To instead protect and love her.

Bai deserved to be happy again, not withered and torn by grief. Their grief would not subside if Haven were gone, nor would it with another child, but they could try again and find new happiness.

Adabelle would want their happiness.

Raegna hauled herself to her feet, the walls drifting around her. "I do."

Bai glanced up at her, relaxed yet on guard all at once. His eyes did not reveal his true self, the sharpness long vanished. He trembled in the chair when she approached him before he jolted and shook his head.

"Not here," he whispered.

"No." Raegna staggered when she took another step. "The bed."

Bai nodded and rose to reach the bed. How they came upon it, Raegna was not sure. One moment they sat before the fire; the next, they stood at the foot of the bed. She took Bai's hand and guided him to face her.

"Lie down," she instructed.

Bai obeyed, stretching out on his back with his arms at his sides. He pressed his palms against the sheets. Raegna hesitated, looking him over from above. His tousled blond hair fell over his brow. Wine had softened his hollow and crooked features. His lips parted with small, quaking breaths. Mind buzzing like a hive of bees, Raegna braced herself against the bedpost, and Bai's image rippled in her vision. This wasn't like before. Nothing like it. He lay beneath her, and she would have control, and her mother could not humiliate them.

"Don't," Bai murmured. "Don't, Raegna. Not if you don't want to. You have to be sure."

She clung to the bedpost. "Are you sure?"

He faltered and closed his eyes tight before opening them again. His breaths quaked. "I want whatever makes you happy. Always. Whatever makes you happy."

Raegna didn't remember what she said in return. An agreement of some sort. She didn't remember unbuckling his belt or untying the laces of his pants, though the copious layers beneath were quite infuriatingly memorable. She lost track of how much she pulled away and did not remember finding him hard.

Everything blurred with the memory of the dull burn between her legs. Raegna gripped the post in one hand, balancing across Bai's hips, and thrust against him. She wouldn't remember every detail except that his fists bunched the sheets with white knuckles, and he refused to touch her. Bai turned his head to the side and shut his eyes, his face strained. He couldn't fight back the pleasure as he grunted and groaned beneath her. She would remember him crying out, his back and neck arching, and how his seed spilled into her.

Please, Gaea. "Please, Gaea."

Chapter 19

Naleem

I N THE BALLROOM, DANCING and surrounded by other bodies, the court hardly needed fires to keep themselves warm. But outside in the courtyard, the brisk air stole Naleem's breath away. Gittan led him through Vakkar Hold, and he shivered beneath the layers he had been wrapped in.

Gittan didn't seem to mind, even in her dress. A breeze tossed her loose braids about her face and rippled her shawl as she took his hand. "Did anyone show you the rose gardens yet?"

Naleem shook his head. "I've only seen the palace and your training yard so far."

She gave him a bright smile and guided him to the west side of the courtyard. The cobblestones stopped before a gravel path and a wall that loomed over them, its stones woven with dark green leaves and vines. A few rosebuds nestled among them. Sconces held torchlight before the arched entrance to the gardens.

Within, rose bushes stretched up the walls of a maze. Naleem followed the Commander over grassy paths that passed hidden gazebos and benches. He chuckled when he thought she might stop, but then she did a double-take and pulled him down another path.

"Where are you taking me?" he laughed.

"The gardens are much prettier in daylight," she told him, ignoring his question. "Though there is beauty to be seen at night."

"It is beautiful." Naleem admired the biggest rose blooms that made their appearance even through the darkness.

Gittan brought them to a stone gazebo where torches lit every pillar. Vines entangled over the angled roof, and each pillar had been carved with stories from scripture, most about Sachi and Sigmund. As he examined each one, Naleem searched for the one representing Leaf Fall Gift.

"Sigmund's creation and vows." He ran his fingers along the stone. The image of the goddess and god facing each other hand in hand had been carved in with the details of a woodland summer.

The next pillar had the two lying together beside a hearth. Wherever the hearth had been placed, Naleem knew from stories it would be cold outside of it. "The first Winter Mull."

Other pillars depicted Sigmund protecting Sachi from Fan's demons, Sachi healing him afterward, and the two building their home together, the foundation of their future village. Naleem stopped at a pillar where Sachi held a babe in her arms, and both figures looked down at the child with faint smiles on their stone faces. A fall forest surrounded them, with a doe beside them and a raven in the treetops.

"Leaf Fall Gift," Naleem said. "The birth of Ailbhe. The birth of humanity."

"Hm. Do you think the goddesses and gods are real?" Gittan hummed.

Naleem blinked at her. "Of course they're real. How couldn't they be?"

Gittan smiled with a shrug. "I was never one to pay attention during ceremonies or listen patiently to scripture stories. And you know how the mind wanders. Other cultures have other deities, so who knows which one of us is right?"

"They're real. They have to be. Priestesses have seen Sachi; other women have seen Sachi, and she has guided them before. And there was always a single raven perched somewhere when I needed some cheering up or guidance. Well, almost always." Naleem let his hand rest on Ailbhe swaddled in a bundle in Sachi's arms. "Though I'd be lying if I said I didn't feel a little betrayed by them."

"I'm sorry," Gittan said. "I've soured this whole thing. I truly wanted to bring you here to give you a proper farewell. Not the kind I would give you tomorrow before we depart."

Naleem turned to her, his heart sinking. Tomorrow they would ride out with a band of secret mercenaries to take Haven themselves. Meanwhile, he was to sit alone in Vakkar Hold and wait for their return. If they returned ... That's what Gittan was prepared for.

Instead of feeding into the gloom, Naleem gave her a weak smile and sat on the bench. "What sort of farewell would you not be able to give me?"

Gittan raised her chin and joined him. "One where I promise you I'll bring your son and brother back to you."

"You've already daringly made that promise. You shouldn't. You don't know what will happen."

"I'm admittedly a little more confident in our plan than I was before," she said. "Both of your friends need to practice courage and restraint along our journey, but I think they have it in them. With the Shield-Priestess at our side, we'll take these heathens by surprise. That I can promise."

With nothing else to say, Naleem sighed. The thought of Haven being sacked by true Galaenian warriors, the look on Thenalious' face, was pleasurable enough, but far more unlikely than what Gittan made the goddesses seem to be.

"I will promise to do everything in my power," she said. "How's that?"

He nodded. "More attainable."

Gittan inched closer to him. "Whenever I would go to battle, I always had my mother to say goodbye to, should I fall. She would tell me I was far too capable and strong not to come back, and that even though she was the mother of a Maiden, she would die before I would. She was right in the end. Now I'm headed to a very uncertain battle. One even my old veteran mother might be wary of. And so, should the worst happen—"

"You're coming back," Naleem interrupted. "You will come back."

"Naleem—"

"I can't be foolish and assure myself for certain that Hadwin and Cadoc will be unharmed, though I still hope," he interjected. "But you must come back. You—You're the first happiness I've had in what feels like two lifetimes."

Gittan gave a warm chuckle and cupped his cheek in her hand. "Oh, Naleem. I've never had to give a man a proper farewell like they do in the sagas." She brushed a stray lock of hair from his temple. "But I hope this will suffice."

Gittan leaned in and pressed her lips against his, kissing him. Or perhaps attempting to, for all she did was keep her lips on his and hold them there. Despite the fact that she was a Maiden, it never occurred to him that she was just that: a Maiden. She always walked and talked too confidently, held him in such high regard, and spoke so soothingly—part of him imagined she had at least been with one other man before. This kiss told otherwise.

An amused huff escaped his nose and he began a proper kiss, tilting his head. He opened her mouth with his but didn't push further, so as not to startle her. Gittan went rigid beside him, her hand freezing at his cheek.

Naleem gripped the edge of the bench while his heart raced, and he struggled to grasp the fact that he was kissing the Commander of the Maidens in the royal rose gardens at Vakkar Hold the night before Leaf Fall. Her warm mouth carried the hint of the sweet wine from the banquet. He wanted to pull her close, use her warmth in the chilly night, but a few thoughts brought him to a halt. He pulled away, mindful of her inexperience and wanting to be sure she wasn't uncomfortable.

Gittan sucked in a breath once they separated and looked at him with her cheeks flushed. Her hand still on his face, she stroked his cheekbone. A small part of him screamed at the touch, but he kept his eyes on her and let it happen.

"Well," she started, "how about that?"

Naleem laughed, remaining so close to her their noses touched. "Was that your first?"

"Was it obvious?"

"Well, you are a Maiden."

"Right."

He stroked the back of her hand. "Is this part of the escort?"

Through her blushing, Gittan beamed and nestled her forehead against his. "Not exactly. But there's no one in attendance at *this* gathering. No one except us and the flames and the stars."

"I wonder how that was your first kiss if you talk like that," he whispered.

"If I talk some more, could I have another one?"

They smiled and leaned in for another kiss. As Gittan melted into it, Naleem braced to hold her and rested a hand on her waist, the way he had when they were dancing. Only now, he could dig his fingers a little deeper and hold her a little tighter. Her hand dipped down to caress his jaw and neck; the other found his waist and belly.

Naleem nearly froze, but he fought through it, opening her mouth once more and daring himself to slip his tongue inside. Gittan grunted in surprise but didn't resist. She pressed closer, and her hand felt for his thigh and crept up. Too close.

Naleem jolted, gasping. "Stop."

Gittan hadn't heard him, moving in when he retreated. Naleem raised an arm and pushed her back. "Stop. I said, stop!"

She snapped out of her daze and gawked at him. "What is it? Did I—did I do something?"

"No ..." Naleem settled. "No. It's not you. It's nothing you did. It was fine. I just—I'm just not ready."

Her face fell, and she straightened. "Is it Pinar?"

Naleem winced as his heart tore in half. "No. But it ought to be."

"I understand if it is. I heard you were close, and I wouldn't want to come between that. You have every right to turn me away if you still love her and would rather honor her."

"I would honor her," he said. "But it isn't her. It would be easier if it were just her. But even if she were still here, if she were the one going to battle tomorrow, I don't think ... I couldn't."

Gittan stared at him before her eyes fell to the ground. "And you're sure it was nothing I've done?"

"I'm sure. It's just … Haven. Haven is a very dark place, and it leaves its darkness within you." His voice caught with the last few words, and he shut his eyes tight, fighting to rid himself of all the terror and memories of absolute humiliation, sneering faces, and calloused hands.

With that, Gittan gave a solemn nod, and he was grateful that she didn't press for any more details. "May I escort you back to your chamber, then?"

Naleem nodded, and she helped him to his feet. The palace did not grow quiet upon their return. Gittan avoided the ballroom and headed straight upstairs to the bedchamber. In the dim candlelight, Naleem continued to reassure himself of his safety, and he replayed some of Gittan's words in his head. Especially how she respected and regarded Pinar. Far more than he ever had.

Guilt shredded through him, but he soothed himself of that, too. *Pinar would not want you to be miserable forever.*

When they reached the chamber, they faced each other again.

"I suppose this is goodnight," Gittan said.

"Until tomorrow. I'm sorry I've spoiled your farewell."

"You didn't spoil anything," she told him. "We'll focus on tomorrow. Be sure to act like you're enjoying yourself."

Naleem gave her a nod. "If you can't take my favor as a Maiden, could you take this for luck?"

Once he'd glanced down both sides of the hallway, he kissed her cheek. Gittan's eyes fluttered, and she blushed again. "I suppose I can. But I'll do everything in my power. Go to bed now. Happy Leaf Fall, Naleem."

"Happy Leaf Fall, Commander."

As she trailed down the hallway, Naleem watched her go, then slipped into the chamber and shut the door behind him. Leaning against it, he heaved a sigh and took a moment to recount the night's events.

Asmund's head rose from his sheets in the dark room. His blue eyes almost glowed in the pitch-black.

"Hello," Naleem managed.

Asmund inclined his head. "Did you have fun?"

"As much as I could. And you?"

"Maybe less so," Asmund admitted with a shrug.

Naleem took off his tunic and a few layers of clothing, down to a shirt and pants, to collapse on the bed. "Well, tomorrow will be better. I hope. You should get some rest."

In silence, the two of them curled into bed. Naleem fiddled with the raven pendant and left his eyes open, though they drooped now and then. Typically, if he fought sleep, it would bring him nightmares, so he tried not to worry so much. But his heart ached for Hadwin and Cadoc, and it ached for Pinar and their lost children. More so now, it ached for Gittan and her comfort and company. If nothing else could be returned to him, he prayed Gaea would at least let her come back safely.

Naleem had only just drifted off when rhythmic groans broke through the walls. Furrowing his brow, he forced his eyes open.

There wasn't any doubt the noises came from Bai and Raegna's chamber next door. As they grew louder, Naleem recognized their voices, and his ears burned. Bai growled, but Raegna snarled louder before they yelped and groaned some more.

What Naleem knew about the two of them came only from what Bai had chosen to tell him and Hadwin long ago in the fields of Syden—and he didn't know they were capable of that kind of passion.

Naleem glanced across the room and found Asmund was also kept awake by the noise, his face flushed. With another sigh, Naleem whispered, "Happy Leaf Fall, Asmund."

"... Happy Leaf Fall."

Part II

Chapter 20

Bai

B AI STIRRED AWAKE FROM the most peaceful sleep he'd had in weeks. The crisp fall air greeted him through the open window, and faint blue sunlight beamed into the chamber. Before he could get his bearings, footsteps clamored on the other side of the bed, and something heavy dropped over the sheets.

Bai startled and twisted just before maroon skirts dashed out of the room, and the door slammed shut. In the empty space on the bed where Raegna should have been lay an ax with a polished blade, its haft extending over the edge of the bed. The beard curved just under the head, with a silver edge glinting in the low light. Orange leaves were tied to the top of the haft by twine, decorating the weapon like a Leaf Fall Gift.

Blinking, Bai sat up and inspected it. Then he stopped, finding his pants were missing. Every layer of pants was missing. The damnable corset lay at the foot of the bed, the laces ripped about. He wore only an undershirt that hung off his shoulders. Bai gathered the sheets around him and peered at the floor. The several layers rested about where his makeshift bed of blankets would normally be.

What happened? Though all the clues told him what, Bai sat in shock, realizing Raegna had dropped the ax and fled the room.

Had they ...? But why would they? They just spoke of Adabelle, but then his memory got fuzzy. They must have talked through the night ... half-dressed? In bed?

Bai shuddered and looked over the ax again. The blade was cool as he let his finger drag along the edge. Raegna must have picked it up from the forge. The hasty drop reminded him of the first supper she'd given him after their marriage: a pack of jerky she threw at him before fleeing. Back when she couldn't look at him.

Something had happened ... Did their drinking go too far? Had he done something wrong?

Bai's heart sank into his gut. There was no time to ponder it. The party destined for Haven would leave soon, before anyone in Vakkar Hold could notice. He shoved into a pair of pants, put on another shirt, and tied on riding boots. He packed the leather armor specially made for him by an armorer Gittan had said was discreet. All the while, his head spun for an inkling of a memory. When none came, his stomach knotted further.

What had he done?

Bai picked the ax off the bed and faltered at the small box beneath it. Parchment was tied around it with a yellow-gold leaf secured by the stem within the bow. Bai rested the ax against the bedframe and took up the box. Reluctant to ruin the presentation, he tore the parchment away without destroying the leaf. He slipped the lid off the box and found a wide wedding band inside.

The grit of the iron was familiar. The same metal that had been fashioned into the blade Bai and Raegna had carried through Sorelle and to Stadt. The same blade she'd shoved into his hand when Syden was attacked. Bai plucked the ring and set the box down. Letters were etched on the inside while runes stretched around the circumference, but he could not read them. Bai ran his thumb along them. Did he still deserve this? Or was it all part of the plan to pretend for the rest of the world? For Adabelle?

Growling to himself, Bai slipped the band onto his left ring finger. He snatched his ax and went for the door, leaving the box, its parchment, and the yellow-gold leaf on the bed.

***

Vakkar Hold's courtyard carried hushed tones with the harsh clopping of horse hooves. Bai's breath left him in a light steam as he walked to the gates to join the party. Four horses stood at the ready, with Gittan, Asmund, and Naleem beside them. Bai trained his sight on Raegna—dressed in leather armor over maroon priestess robes—as she tied furs to the back of her mare's saddle. She glanced at his approach but did not look him in the eye as she joined the others.

Bai faltered. He knew that look from thousands of glances over their eight years bound together. She hated him again.

What had he done?

A hard stone welling in his throat, Bai pressed forward and stopped between Naleem and Asmund, avoiding Raegna entirely. The others served as a good distraction as Naleem nudged him. "Thought you would be the first out here. Too much wine last night?"

Too much. Bai shrugged.

"That ax suits you," Gittan piped in. "Now that we're all here, we'll say our goodbyes and mount up."

Every eye turned to Naleem, and he looked between them with a forced smile. "You will all come back. You must come back."

"We will." Raegna stepped in for a hug. He pulled her close and squeezed before they released each other. "All will be well, Naleem. You just rest here."

Naleem sighed. "I'll try."

Bai tried for a smile, but the corners of his lips only pulled back. He embraced Naleem too, locking his arms behind him. "Don't worry, my friend. We'll bring them back."

Naleem held Bai's shoulders tighter. Bai's sinking heart twinged for his friend. Days in Syden's fields flashed in his memory, sweltering in the heat or harvesting. Fishing days, too, casting reels into the river alongside Naleem and Hadwin. The brothers seemed inseparable back then, yet they lay on opposite ends of Galaenia from each other. Bai had to help bring them together once more.

Then Naleem turned to Asmund. "You have more courage than you think. Don't waste it out there, all right?"

Asmund nodded and they embraced, though he seemed a little unused to the concept. Gittan came forward and took Naleem's hand, squeezing it. "Try to rest. We will do everything in our power to bring them safely to you."

"I know you will." Naleem's fingers curled around hers before they let go.

The four mounted their horses, and Gittan motioned for the gates to open. As they rode through, Bai glanced back at Naleem in the courtyard. The gates began to close, and Naleem shrank behind them. Bai gave an encouraging smile and hefted his ax.

As the gates shut, Naleem raised a fist in return.

***

They traveled through the quiet of Stadt to Udstodt, where Thekla met them on the outskirts. Bai bristled at her approach on a dusty, dark-brown horse. Instead of a dress, she wore leather armor and carried a sword, a bow, and a quiver full of arrows. Two daggers were sheathed at her hip. He'd forgotten about her and what she'd said to Raegna last night, but he resolved that he had no right to let the agitation continue.

Gittan did not look at her. "The others are posted farther, I expect."

"We can't risk spies seeing us gather in numbers so close to the city," Thekla told her. "They're in the woods."

"You ought to ride off, then. The likes of you with a Maiden will encourage talk."

Thekla shrugged. "There's hardly anyone out here, anyway. They're all in bed with tramps and sick with drink. I can be a beggar if the Commander will offer me a job and coin. I can protect your priestess."

"You're shameless, Thekla," Gittan scolded with a smile. "She's a married woman."

"Pity." Thekla nodded to Raegna on the other side of the Commander. "But I suppose with a sword like that, you can protect yourself."

Raegna nodded, flanking Gittan's horse. Thekla looked back at Bai and Asmund, who rode behind them. "And you're worried about me drawing attention. That man has a mean-looking ax."

Bai kept his eyes ahead, his ax heavy as it hung from the saddle.

"Along with the Shield-Priestess, they are your new pupils," Gittan explained. "I want them to have sparred every woman in our party before we reach Sorelle."

"My mother will be stirring in the wind watching me train men to fight," Thekla grumbled.

Gittan chuckled. "I'm sure mine already has a few words ready for me in Heimelle."

"Mine certainly does," Raegna piped in.

Gittan and Thekla laughed, though Raegna did not. Bai watched the back of her head, her chestnut hair flowing down her back with a half-braid in the middle. She was well enough to make jokes with the other women. Part of her was still intact, and that was reassuring. She wouldn't look his way even as they entered the woods and found the hidden camp of warriors taking down tents and packing their saddles. Over two hundred women scattered the camp, giving orders and strutting in every direction to begin their journey.

Thekla held her chin high. "Your army, Commander. More will join us on the way. Swords from Ostern, Vesten, and Norden come to avenge their sister, Sorelle."

"Sell-swords," Gittan grunted. "But I'm sure they're honorable, all the same."

"There are no better women in Galaenia than those who fight for coin." Thekla rested her hand on her chest. "If I do say so myself. They'll all have their reservations about training men, however."

"They'll learn it's necessary for the mission." Gittan kicked her heels in the stirrups. "We'll ride on to the edge of Salt End, and I'll explain everything when we camp."

"Of course, Commander." Thekla inclined with a theatrical bow in the saddle. "Ride well, Shield-Priestess!"

Raegna granted her a nod back. "And you, sell-sword."

Thekla's laugh echoed behind them. The forest ahead bloomed with light from the east. Bai rode behind Raegna, glancing at her now and then but letting his gaze wander about the woods. They would reach Salt End by sunset, and it wouldn't be soon enough.

Gittan and Raegna spoke of plans ahead of him, their words lost to the rising birdsong and rustling tree branches. Vibrant orange and red leaves floated around them and piled along the road. Bai kept a hard stare on the horizon, which disappeared with a cluster of trees or a rising dune. It would take a few weeks to reach Sorelle, and over two hundred warriors would slow them down, especially if Gittan wanted them to mentor Raegna, Asmund, and Bai.

The training would be good, though. It would teach him how to stand up to Thenalious and tear his throat open with this new ax blade.

Raegna chuckled at some joke Gittan made. The sound tugged at Bai's heart, then squeezed in a painful grip. Halfway through the first day of their journey, she still did not look at him. Not even a glance. She chose to ride alongside Gittan and focus on the conversation with her. Something had happened last night, and Bai knew he had no right to feel hurt by her evasion. But the hurt came nonetheless.

A lump formed in his throat as he turned from her and fiddled with the horse's reins instead. Last night, he'd told her he missed not speaking to each other and the days when she'd despised him. He didn't mean it. Especially not now—he was missing her eyes.

"What's wrong?" a deep voice murmured, tearing through his thoughts.

Bai looked at Asmund riding beside him. The usually shy and quiet man tilted his head at him, though he never met his eyes. They kept darting around his face, down to the ground, and up again.

"Nothing," Bai answered. "I'm just ready to fight."

Asmund nodded and let his gaze settle on the horn of his saddle, where his hands wrapped around to keep steady. Even that sparked guilt in Bai. He and Asmund would go into Haven together. They ought to make better friends to work as a team.

"You're getting better at it," he tried. "Fighting, I mean."

Once again, Asmund's expression glossed with worry as his eyes flitted over Bai. "Oh. Thank you."

"Do you think you're ready for Haven?"

"I ... Truly, no."

"At least you're honest," Bai said with a small smirk.

"... But I am ready to have this all done," Asmund spoke up. "I want to put everything to rest if we can. And I don't want anyone else to get hurt, not anymore. I'm ready for all of this to be over."

That had been perhaps the most he had spoken to him or anyone. It seemed so long ago that Raegna had brought Asmund into Judr's healing house, shaking and full of tears. Throughout their journey, he had been nothing but the frightened mouse, ducking behind his little hole in the wall at the slightest hint of danger or silently watching everyone from the background. Now here he was, armed and riding to fight the cat.

"You've come a long way," Bai thought aloud. "At this rate, I'd say you're ready for anything, which will be good. We don't exactly know what they'll do to us when we show up."

Asmund gulped. "No."

The sunlight in the west drew long shadows beneath their mounts when they reached Salt End. A couple of hours after the four had settled into their first camp, Thekla and the army appeared over the crest of a dune. After them, two more groups rode out of the sunset—the first strays to join the bought army.

Bai and Asmund helped pitch their tent, while Raegna tended to the horses. Every woman around them stared at Bai's ax strapped to his back and Asmund's at his belt. The two of them blended in well with the women, except that they were men. Bai ignored them until Gittan and Thekla called everyone to the middle of the camp.

Gittan rested her hands on her hips, surveying every woman in attendance with a keen gaze. Thekla stood behind her with a gleam in her dark eyes. Bai, Raegna, and Asmund shoved in alongside their peers, though Raegna stood opposite Asmund, and Bai tried not to notice.

"I want to thank everyone for their organization and cooperation," Gittan shouted over the crowd. "You'd nearly pass for a Matriarch's army, if not the Queen's. We're set on our path to Judr, Sorelle. We will reach it within a few weeks and perhaps by the first snowfall. From there, we need to move quickly and circle the approximate location of this rebel base, Haven. Quickly, because I want us gone before the snow keeps us in Sorelle.

"From our post around Haven, within Sorelle's wilderness, we will send in two men to pose as rebels themselves." With that, Gittan beckoned Bai and Asmund forward.

Bai rolled his shoulders and obeyed, and Asmund fell in behind him, ducking his head. Gittan gestured to them once they reached her. "As you can see, I've begun training these two in combat. I understand this may be absurd to some of you, but I believe these two are our only chance of infiltrating Haven. It will be better if they know how to defend themselves should anything go wrong or they be caught in battle. On this journey, they will be treated as proper warriors. Green warriors, but warriors. Their training will proceed over the course of our trek, so should you volunteer to help, it would be appreciated. Regardless, we will make women of these two yet."

A few chuckles reverberated through the gathering. Bai kept his head high, not sure if he'd ever seen so many warriors at once. Still, his eyes picked Raegna out of the lot of them, and he averted his gaze. He couldn't know what she was thinking from that single glance, but he hoped she was assured. No matter what had happened between them, their mission was still his focus. Bai straightened as the warriors were dismissed—Raegna among them—praying she knew his true intentions.

For Ada.

Chapter 21

Raegna

Snow fluttered to the ground, and flakes rested in the mare's mane. Raegna stroked them off and offered grain. The mare took it, her velvety lips brushing over Raegna's glove. The grain crunched between her massive teeth.

"Good girl," Raegna said with a smile, which vanished with the clang of steel behind her. She peeked over her shoulder at the day's sparring lesson.

A quarter of the army circled Bai and Thekla, engaged in their battle. Thekla moved with precision, and Bai matched it, watching her and countering. His frustration and impatience from the early training days had all but vanished. From her distance, Raegna noted the keen focus in those gold eyes.

The other women noted different things, laughing with each other or cooing like green girls. Raegna rolled her eyes with a scoff.

"Take him off his feet, Thekla!" someone shouted.

"Show her what I taught you, Bai!" another instructed.

They all prided themselves on any ounce of his attention. A sticky brew bubbled within Raegna's chest and her jaw set with her lips pressed together. Training had been so much easier when most of them had shaken their heads at the prospect of arming the men. These days, Bai and Asmund were celebrities among them.

Raegna pivoted and allowed herself a slightly better view. The warriors' attention on Bai didn't bother her as much as watching him. In his training, he became graceful yet forceful, a blaze of flames he controlled with the temperament of a lethal warrior. Whatever simmered within Raegna seared her heart as if it would peel within her.

A foggy memory billowed like storm clouds behind her eyes. Bai's strong hands that hefted the ax were the same hands that had clutched the bedsheets, white-knuckled and straining. The broad chest that bore armor was the same that had heaved beneath her. The steady hips and long legs were the same she had clamped—

The mare nibbled on Raegna's sleeve, begging for more grain. Raegna gasped at the touch and spun. "Oh. Be patient."

"Shield-Priestess." Gittan appeared at her side, sending the heat that flushed Raegna's cheeks higher. "I'm glad someone remembered we leave for Judr today. Are they at it again? They trained last night."

"It's not just me," Raegna admitted. "Asmund is packing the rest of our things."

Gittan clicked her tongue. "I'll put an end to this. Don't be intimidated by their numbers. Bai is still your husband to rein in."

Raegna ground her teeth as she fed her mare the last of the grain. She dusted her gloves and rubbed the horse's neck. There would be no more reining Bai. Enough of that had been done to him, and he certainly didn't need more from her. Raegna watched Gittan break up the match just as Thekla gained more ground. The warriors groaned at the Maiden's chiding.

When Bai strode to the horses, resting his ax in the holster at his belt, Raegna turned from him. Bai stopped at his horse, which she'd already saddled for the journey. In her periphery, he gave a sideways glance. "Thank you."

"Don't mention it." Raegna took her mare's reins and led her away. The beast snorted and her great hooves thudded over the cool, lush ground. Such exchanges were their reality again. Raegna preferred to keep it that way. Bai deserved as much, but not for the same reasons as before.

Before it was to protect herself and her dignity. Now Raegna meant to safeguard him—and his dignity. Like the time her mother had forced them, Raegna had forced him—had taken advantage of the moment for her own gain. He'd agreed, but had he been in his right mind? She certainly hadn't.

Leaving him alone had seemed the best option. At first, Raegna hadn't been able to meet his eyes. But she'd noticed the forged ring around his finger, and no one could miss that ax. He carried her gifts, but did they matter? Bai barely looked at her, and the gifts had been part of the rouse. She wouldn't let them lift her spirits, and she spared him her company.

But in the few weeks of traveling, a new development had twisted Raegna's stomach in knots. Something she'd recognized sometime after her mother's coercion. Thinking about it made her throat close in on itself, so Raegna focused on bringing her horse into line with the others, ready to depart.

Gittan and Thekla set off beside her, with Bai and Asmund behind them. The rest of the army trailed them, slinking through the trees and clambering up and down Sorelle's growing hills. The women talked among each other, but every so often, one or two congregated around Bai, right behind Raegna's horse.

"Good morning, Bai," a plucky young woman chimed in behind her. "You did well sparring Thekla this morning."

"Thank you, Gunilla," Bai said in a faint voice.

"You know what would truly put her on her ass is a tug of that ax beard under her ankle," she told him. "It might sound tricky, but Thekla's tricky too."

"Thekla is too skilled to give an opening like that," Bai admitted. "And even if she wasn't, I don't think you should give me advice when she's right in front of us."

"The old bat can't hear," Gunilla spat.

"The old bat is only thirty and six," Thekla grunted on the other side of Gittan. "And she can hear you. Nothing drowns out that shrill voice."

"Still older than twenty and two," Gunilla countered.

Raegna craned one ear toward Bai's voice—light with laughter. "Thank you, Gunilla. I'll keep it in mind."

A shadow sulked on the hill below them, beyond the thinning trees. All amusement dissipated within the army as every head turned to the blemish among the flourishing fall colors. Raegna's shoulders fell as something throbbed behind her heart. The blackened houses were as she and Bai had left them. Silence weighed heavily over the rooftops, save for the birdsong in the forest. The torn temple did not hold the ashes of the dead. The wind would have taken them by now.

Raegna almost gave Bai a look, but decided against it. Surely his face was the same as hers, blank to save themselves from the grief.

"Gaea above," Gittan breathed. "You lifted this, Shield-Priestess?"

Raegna nodded. "With help."

"Hearing the tales is one thing," Gittan said. "Seeing it is another. I'll send word that we've seen Syden to Her Majesty and the Council tonight. Or rather, what's left of it."

Raegna hung her head, and the Commander motioned everyone to ride on. With their head start, they would reach Judr by sundown. There would be no wolf attacks to fear with a group so large.

A chilled wind bit at Raegna's cheeks when they reached the familiar gates and the foreboding watch towers.

The warriors in the towers gave each other orders as the army approached. Gittan had sent word of their arrival to Matriarch Ase after the High Council meeting, so there would be no surprise at the sight of the army. The gates opened and Gittan rode through with Raegna, Bai, and Asmund. Thekla and the warriors stayed beyond the village walls.

Judr was also as they left it, but progressing in recovery. Men hauled lumber and pulled beams up where their women instructed. Both woman and man hammered future walls in place. Children flitted about to help but stopped in their tracks when the four riders appeared. Judr's attention turned to them as a familiar warrior met Gittan on foot.

Jora set her shoulders back with her hand around her sword hilt. She remained the same, though furs ran under her armor and winter sleeves covered the lean muscles beneath umber skin. A black cap with furred hems covered her head and hugged her ears. Her eyes flitted to the Shield-Priestess and her men, but she kept her chin high and regarded Gittan. "Commanding Maiden. My Matriarch will see you in her house."

Gittan nodded and followed, with the others riding behind her.

Clad in a fur cloak and armor, Matriarch Ase stepped off her porch and strode to the Maiden as she dismounted. Thick, long black braids hung down the Matriarch's back. The two scars that cut through brown skin along her jawline stretched with her smile. "Commander Gittan. Welcome to Judr." Then Ase found Raegna dismounting. "Shield-Priestess. Welcome back."

"Hello, Matriarch. It is good to see you and Judr doing well. And you, Jora."

Jora smiled, deepening the wrinkles under her eyes. "Your presence gives us hope indeed, Shield-Priestess. Raegna."

"Please come in." Ase ushered them inside. "I only wish we could do better and help feed your army. We've barely managed enough harvest to get us through winter."

"There's no need," Gittan assured her. "We brought our provisions, but we are grateful for a place to rest."

"Granted." Matriarch Ase kept the door open for Gittan and Jora to enter first. Raegna glanced back to ensure her men followed and stopped short when she saw only Bai. He blinked at her and copied her gaze to Asmund, who was still with the horses.

Their gentle friend praised the beasts with back scratches. Raegna cleared her throat. "Asmund? Are you coming?"

He looked up at them and shook his head. "You don't need me to go over the plan. And—and I don't want to go in."

Raegna's heart sank. Too many memories lay beyond the door into the Matriarch's house. So many more must surround him—Judr was Asmund's home village. Raegna would rather have him along to buffer the tension between her and Bai, but she couldn't force him.

"We'll be back soon, then," she told him.

Matriarch Ase gathered them in a side room where tapestries of warrior sagas hung on the walls. Maps lay on an open table with quills in inkwells, books, and pawns. Bai fit in alongside Raegna, the space pushing them together so their shoulders brushed. Raegna clutched her breastplate collar to draw herself in. Ase met everyone's eyes and her brow arched at Bai, causing her to frown.

"You've ... brought a man," she murmured, looking Bai up and down. "And you've armed him."

Bai shifted his weight beside Raegna, but she didn't let herself move.

"He has every right to be here as we do," Gittan said. "He and the other man outside are a part of the plan to infiltrate Haven."

Ase looked at her. "Haven?"

"The base these invaders call home," Gittan explained. "We have a plan to eradicate them for good."

She retold the plan, but Raegna had known every detail since they'd left Vakkar Hold. Her eyes dared to linger over Bai's boots. Then the ax blade at his hip. So much at stake, especially if the secret within her was true.

"What if these men are found out and killed?" Ase asked. "What then?"

Raegna's grasp on her armor made the leather groan.

"We'll give them both a ram's horn, which they will blow only as a last resort to warn us it's time to lay siege," Gittan answered.

Ase leaned over the table, her palms pressed to a map of Sorelle. "And only the Queen knows you're here?"

Gittan nodded. "The High Council and the rest of the royal court do not. Should anyone find out you've harbored us after this, it would be treason against the High Council. But no one has to know we were here."

The Matriarch pondered it with her shoulders arched. She turned to Jora. "What say you?"

Jora straightened. "Treason would shun a Matriarch from the Harvest Union. Your reign is young. But we know Syden's fate is true, and if the Maiden and her army are successful, Galaenia is saved. You would have harbored heroes. Just not in the High Council's eyes."

"Perhaps they'll forget about it by the Union," Ase thought aloud. "What of the men?"

"The men?"

"I understand Commander Gittan's plan," Ase went on. "But I have my reservations about arming the men. It is against Judr's law for them to carry these blades. Perhaps they can be sent to this Haven without them. You're from a different generation than the rest of us, Jora. Surely you agree?"

Jora's eyes went to the floor before she studied Bai. "Matriarch, I believe there is no better man we can trust with a blade. If it pleases you, my wife and I can give them and the Shield-Priestess a place to stay for the night. The men can be supervised and outnumbered by the women in our household."

A small smile crept across Raegna's face. Bai's chest rose beside her.

Ase considered this with a nod. "Very well. Commander Gittan, I would join your battle myself, but my village needs me here. I will give you any warriors who volunteer to fight for Judr. Many of them will want to be a part of this."

"Of course, we would appreciate it," Gittan said. "Let them know we will leave to camp near the River Sachi before dawn. Then we'll cross the river to send the men in."

Tomorrow. Raegna bit the inside of her cheek. Tomorrow would be her last ensured day with Bai.

***

Jora led Raegna, Bai, and Asmund up the porch and into the healing house. She held the door as they filed in. "Healer, we have guests to tend on behalf of the Matriarch."

Raegna beamed as Banu turned from her work over the cauldron. Her tired eyes sparkled with the lift of her fleshy russet cheeks. "Gaea! Look at you all."

"It's so good to see you, Banu," Raegna said as they embraced. "So good to see you are well."

"Forget about us, girl." Banu held her at arm's length. "Shield-Priestess. They even gave you robes with that armor. Gaea, how far you've come." She turned her attention to the men. "All of you."

Bai gave a shrug. "Hello, Banu."

"Thank Sigmund, he's answered my prayers to keep you strong," Banu cooed as she hugged Bai. "My, what does your wife think of that ax?"

Raegna and Bai locked eyes for the first time in what felt like years. His gaze dropped first, and his lips parted to say something. Raegna leaned around them. "It's actually my Leaf Fall Gift to him. For the battle ahead."

"I'm surprised the warriors let him in with it," Banu commented. Then she faced Asmund. "And one for you, too."

Asmund nodded and accepted her tight hug, though he squirmed when she let him go. Jora stepped in, maneuvering around the reunion. "Let me finish supper for her. We can eat and recount your journey."

Banu guided them to the table and cleared off the books, vials, and candles. "How is Naleem?"

"Well," Raegna answered. "He's safe in Vakkar Hold. It would be dangerous to bring him along, and the Queen gave us all rooms and invited us to live in the palace as long as we like."

"The man deserves it all," Banu said. "What is Vakkar Hold like? What is the Queen like?"

Raegna told their story, trying to remember every detail of Vakkar Hold, Queen Kjerstin, Duchess Elmba, and even the High Council. Jora served bowls of roast beef stew as the tales flew over the table. Despite how much she spoke, Raegna downed her serving.

"Vakkar Hold is marvelous," she went on. "Especially during Leaf Fall Gift. But you must tell us how Judr is doing. We saw reconstruction on the way in. And Ase seems to fit the role of Matriarch fine."

Jora chewed on her bite. "She is a good Matriarch. The best Judr could hope for in times like this. Firm, courageous, and confident, yet humble when she needs to be. She came to me for counsel often in her first few weeks—"

"Jora trained her as a warrior when she was just a girl," Banu added. "So, of course, Ase gravitated to her mentorship."

"I find myself to be her right hand these days," Jora admitted with a shrug. "A woman can't let that go to her head, but I don't take it lightly. Whatever I can do to serve my village and my Matriarch."

Banu squeezed her wife's hand. "Many who were injured are on their way to recovery. Some are even helping rebuild Judr. Progress may be a little slow, but we will all be ourselves again one day."

"That's good to hear," Raegna said.

With dinner finished, they settled around the table, swapping more stories over warm tea and an apple crumble Banu had prepared. The windows darkened with the evening, and Jora lit candles around the house. Raegna listened to stories while playing with a sleeve. Evening meant tomorrow was fast approaching. Tomorrow, they would send Bai and Asmund into Haven.

In the later hours, Banu prepared the healing room beds for her guests and the three of them slept separately. Raegna and Bai had not spared another glance since Banu's comment about his ax, which he leaned against the bedframe before turning in. Asmund was silent as always, and Raegna slipped under the blanket with a churning stomach.

She might have slept with the exhaustion of travel hanging over her, but it was short-lived as she tossed beneath the blanket. In between faint dreams, bile rose in her throat and she lurched upright. She clamped her hand over her nose and mouth as she fled from the healing room and out of the house. In her sprint, she dashed past Banu fixing something over the table.

"What on Jorde—"

Bracing herself against the porch rails, Raegna heaved and her stomach contents spilled into a fresh patch of snow. The sickly remains of the roast soup soiled the white frost. Steam rose from it and her mouth before she vomited again.

In the weeks of travel, her Leaf Fall wish had come true. But couldn't Gaea omit to answer drunken prayers?

"No," she sobbed as her muscles trembled. "No, no, no, no, no ..."

"What in Gaea's name?" Banu exclaimed as the front door shut behind her. "Did you lose a perfectly good dinner on my porch?"

Raegna dropped to her knees, her muscles spasming, and wiped her mouth with her sleeve. Tears streamed down her face. The old healer knelt beside her and used her skirts to wipe Raegna clean as if she were a little girl.

"There now, we all do it," she soothed. "Nothing to be ashamed of. Jora must not have cooked it through. You're all right, girl."

This can't happen. Raegna leaned against the railing and let Banu dote over her. She wiped her tears away, though more came. "I'm sorry, Banu."

"No need, sweetling." The endearment cut through Raegna's heart and she choked on a sob. Banu tilted her head and tucked Raegna's hair behind an ear. "Did Jora fail my stew? I try to let her have more freedom in the kitchen. She likes to help. But she's more skilled with the sword."

The corners of Raegna's lips pulled back. She couldn't bring herself to tell Banu the truth. It was too soon anyway. "No. I think ... it's difficult to be here. To sleep in—"

Banu frowned and squeezed her shoulder. "I'm sorry I do not have better means for you."

"No, it's wonderful that you would take us in again." Raegna rubbed her eyes with the heels of her hands. "I just—"

"Say no more." Banu gave a dismissive wave and grunted as she stood. "Come on inside before you freeze. I've got something for you if you're still feeling sick."

Raegna took her hand and hauled herself up.

As the healer guided Raegna to the table and sat her down, Jora walked in from the bedroom, rubbing her eyes. "What's going on?"

Raegna turned from the warrior, tears still burning her eyes. Banu ushered her to the table. "Just nerves. I'm giving her nuzzle twigs."

Jora placed a steady hand on Raegna's shoulder. "There now. Worried about the battle ahead?"

Raegna dragged a breath. "Among other things."

"You're a capable warrior, Shield-Priestess," Jora went on, taking a place at the table. "I imagine that Commander of the Maidens taught you a thing or two. The men as well. You're all great forces to be reckoned with. Don't worry, your tears are not a weakness. Not to me."

Raegna nearly crumbled to dust in her chair, appreciating the encouragement they gave her. But she'd have to keep her secret. No one could keep her from the battle. That was a warrior's choice to make, no matter her condition. Many would think ill of her choice, but it was ultimately Raegna's to make.

Did she think ill of herself? She would venture so near Haven and risk this? Adabelle had already lost her life.

Raegna winced as Banu stepped in, giving her the stick of nuzzle twig. The dark-brown piece flaked on Raegna's fingers, and she used her back teeth to chew it. The stuff was familiar enough, having eaten much of it when Adabelle stirred within her. This time it was enough to ground her, and Raegna pondered what it would be like to stay behind while the others went to Haven.

She had to go.

Raegna had collected herself by the time the men woke up. As Bai sat down, he did a double-take after a sideways glance. His brow knitted. "Are you all right?"

Breakfast was served and Raegna focused on her plate. "It was just difficult to sleep in there. Adabelle ..."

A shadow swept over his eyes, and Bai looked away. "I'm sorry."

"It's not your fault," she assured, hoping he understood the truth behind her words.

Jora and Banu proudly walked them to Judr's gates to meet Gittan and the army. Banu offered Raegna a second cloak as they walked out the door. Though she hesitated, Raegna took it and draped it over her shoulders. She recalled the last time the healer had given her and Bai cloaks to attend the horrific crescent moon ritual Matriarch Viona had invited them to.

Gittan made sure the three of them made it to their horses and gave Banu a warm greeting. "It's good to see the healer that harbored these heroes. You've done well for them."

"As a reward, you'll bring them back to me safe, Commander," Banu said. "An honor to meet you as well."

Each of them bid the healer and warrior goodbye. Raegna swung into her saddle, with Bai on his horse beside her. He ought to know, shouldn't he? What would Bai do?

Beg her to stay. Turn from her. She had done him wrong and had gotten what she'd wanted. Did she deserve to turn to him? Would she listen if he told her to stay behind? Haven would fall. Raegna would see that it did.

I pray you are fated to live, little one. But I must do this.

Chapter 22

Bai

A RAVEN CALLED OVERHEAD, but Bai paid it no heed. He pulled his cloak tighter and cursed the cold. Fall was quickly turning into winter—the worst season, in his opinion. That morning, the frigid air scraped his skin. Snow patches scattered the forest path, making him squirm at the prospect of blizzards and windchills.

Bai's earliest memory was running through the snow outside his home. His father watched from the porch as he tripped over his stubby legs and fell face-first into the ground. Looking back on it, he must have been merely three, rising out of the snow to give an unrelenting wail.

From then on, his father had always made an effort—genuine or teasing—to warm Bai's cheeks with his hands and blow on his nose, even when he pulled away as he got older. The memory of that warmth brought some comfort, despite everything else that weighed on him.

Haven would fall, if he died bringing it down. Nerves rattled him as the army traveled through the woods and approached River Sachi, but he rallied. Bai trained his gaze on Raegna ahead of him, studying how she held herself in the saddle.

Something had happened during the night, or maybe this morning. Something between her and Banu. All day, Raegna had failed to mask her despair. Bai had seen it in the way she'd sat at breakfast, curling on herself. And then in her eyes, when he'd dared to examine closer—still red and a little swollen.

It could have been memories of Adabelle. He'd found it difficult to sleep in that dreadful room, too. But it wasn't grief she hid from him. Even now, as she rode on her mare, she swayed differently.

The river made itself known, the rushing water echoing through the trees. It would run through winter, icy and unforgiving. Gittan stopped her horse and turned to Thekla.

"Have them prepare camp," she said. "Only the men and I will go from here."

"What?" Raegna snapped.

Bai let himself steal a look at her. She didn't notice as she stared at the Commander with wide eyes.

Gittan scolded her. "You heard right. This is part of the plan, and you're a warrior now. You'll set up camp with the others, and this is as far as you'll go."

Maybe Raegna wanted to be closer and see Haven for herself. Bai inclined his head. "You can take them by surprise when the time is right."

She didn't look at him. "Can I please see them off with you?"

"We'll be too close to the base, and we'll need stealth, which isn't something I've had time to train you in." Gittan dismounted. "If you wish to bid them farewell, you can. We'll travel on foot, boys."

They both swung out of their saddles while Raegna hesitated. Bai tilted his head up at her while she gripped the saddle horn, knuckles stretching her gloves. Her mind wandered somewhere else, somewhere that frightened her. What was wrong?

"Raegna," he murmured.

It was enough to snap her out of it, and she peered down at his boots. Bai gave her his hand, but she didn't take it, and steadily dismounted instead. When she landed on the ground, she lost and regained her balance before bracing herself against her mare. Even Asmund gave her a look of concern. So it wasn't just in Bai's head.

Raegna straightened. "Asmund. You're much braver than you know. I don't say it to be kind, I say it because it is true. Understand?"

Taken aback, he nodded and dipped his head as he always did. Raegna stepped forward and lifted his chin to meet his eyes. "Iida would be proud of you."

Asmund bit the inside of his cheek and gave another nod. Raegna brought him into a hug and held him tight when he returned it. Maybe that was what bothered her. Had she been that worried about sending them into Haven?

Bai wondered what sort of goodbye he would receive as she turned from Asmund. Raegna's eyes bore into his, the look of them enough to send him stumbling back, but Bai kept his balance. She was so different these days, wearing leather armor over maroon priestess robes, wielding that sword and knowing how to use it.

Snowflakes appeared, one of them drifting between them. "Bai."

He waited. All this time, he didn't think about the fact that these could be their last moments. He didn't plan on dying, but if the battle came, he would do anything to avenge Adabelle. She knew that.

Breathy steam escaped Raegna's mouth when she opened it, decided against something, and struggled with it. Her fingers quaked before she pressed them against her stomach.

"Be safe."

A smile spread across his face. Of course, she could only manage that, but he wouldn't want anything more.

"You too," he said. Then he remembered. Bai pulled his new wedding band off his finger and handed it to her. "They shouldn't suspect I still honor a woman."

Raegna took it in her palm, fingers closing around it.

Bai waited for his hug, but she didn't move an inch. Raegna stayed put until Gittan ordered them to follow her. Bai took in Raegna's image to keep in his mind for as long as he could. Chestnut strands escaped the half-braid behind her head and floated on the breeze. With her head lowered, her eyelids hid the rich brown irises he had grown fond of. It took everything within him not to reach out and touch her flushed cheek just once. If he told his past self there would come a day he'd be truly reluctant to leave her, he wouldn't have believed it.

Gittan led them over a hill and traveled through the woods. At its crest, Bai looked over his shoulder and found Raegna still standing there, watching them go and fidgeting with her gloves. If anything happened to him, he would never see her again. The thought brought a sharp pain to the back of his throat, but Bai wouldn't change course for anything. It meant avenging Adabelle and all their friends. It meant the possibility of a safer world for Raegna, for she was more likely to survive on the other side of Haven's walls.

You never have to be afraid.

He gave her a reassuring smile. This time, she forced a smile back, her lips pressing together. Bai stalled for long enough, dragging his feet to follow Gittan, his hand resting on the ax Raegna had gifted him.

The woods carried an eerie silence that pulled Bai's nerves taut. Gittan continued silently over the snow while Bai and Asmund traced her footsteps. Harnessing the focus he'd trained for, Bai drew a stinging breath of cold air, only to have it stolen from him.

Standing between the barren trees, a tall, broad-shouldered man had appeared out of nowhere. He donned a long white tunic with a black cloak and a wolf's hide over his shoulders. Shaggy black hair blew with the breeze, and his onyx eyes fixed on Bai through the woods.

Bai gaped at him and the firm expression on his pale white face flaked with gray stubble. The hint of a smile pulled at his lips. When Bai finally blinked, the man was gone again.

"Hey!" Gittan hissed from ahead. "What are you *doing*? Let's go!"

The raven cawed overhead twice more, and Bai shivered before he picked up the pace. The River Sachi sprayed cold water on them when they found a safe place to cross.

"Naleem spoke of a bridge," Gittan whispered. "But I don't think we would find it even if we had time."

Her words didn't soak into Bai quite like the cold had. He shivered under his furs. As they drew closer to a destination they weren't exactly sure how to find, the woods grew thicker. No trails appeared before them, and the overgrowth caught on their thick clothes.

Finally, Gittan stopped and dropped to one knee. Bai and Asmund did the same.

"This is where you two will continue without me," she whispered. "They must believe you've been fending for yourselves out here, so make them. You both have your stories straight?"

They nodded. Before Syden had been attacked, they'd been on a hunting trip. When they'd returned, they'd found their village destroyed. The point was to feign that they knew—or at least suspected—it was the Haven men, but were otherwise oblivious.

Gittan handed them both their ram horns. "Again, these are a last resort. Blow only if necessary. We cannot risk revealing ourselves, but should they harm you, torture you for information, you'll give it to them and call for us. We'll be prepared and come as soon as we can."

They each took one and Asmund stuffed his in a pack at his belt. Bai tied his beside his ax. Then they both exchanged a glance, acknowledging where the other's was. Bai also noted Asmund's ax.

"You both must promise you'll be careful and keep your heads low." Gittan's eyes were on Bai before they flitted to Asmund. "You'll fight—and fight hard when you need to."

"Promise," the two of them said together.

"Good. Keep heading south or southwest," she instructed. "If you hear the ocean in the distance near the cliffs, you've gone way too far—head back north."

"Thank you, Gittan," Bai spoke up. "For everything you've done. Thank you."

Asmund nodded in agreement.

The Commander took a deep breath. "I'd order you to come back safe, but that doesn't always work. You are both incredible men, no matter what anyone says. Now go."

They both rose—Bai leading the way—and left Gittan in the brush. All stealth and quiet didn't matter once they made distance from her. They had to appear as if they wandered through the woods. Bai pulled his ax from his belt and loosely held it in his hand, swinging the haft.

Asmund kept a pace behind him. He stumbled now and then. Though Bai would like to believe it was also a part of his act, he might have tripped on his own. Bai slowed down to match a lazy walk beside him. "Hard to believe we're this far south, that the cliffs may be just ahead of us."

"Why would they put their base close to the cliffs?" Asmund asked.

Bai shrugged. "No one can attack from all around, I suppose. No one needs to be this far out, and there are no villages. I've never needed to cross the river for anything, have you?"

Asmund shook his head. "My father never did when we went fishing, either."

"Mine too. So it's a fine place to hide."

"Naleem didn't mention the ocean at all," Asmund said. "He couldn't hear it, so they can't be very far. Gittan said every village lies along the two Rivers for fresh water. They would too."

Bai raised an impressed eyebrow at him. "You don't talk, but you sure do listen. That'll be good here."

"Ha," Asmund huffed before he slammed into something hard and fell back. Bai stopped in his tracks as the forest ahead of them wobbled and thick branches shook, leaves piling at their feet.

Asmund rubbed his nose. "Ow ..."

"Are you all right?"

"Uh-huh."

Bai stared up at the hoard of branches and brambles above them. They all clustered in a structure that matched the rest of the forest. "What in Helved is this?"

Asmund struggled to his feet. "Naleem said there was a door. The whole base is hidden by walls made of the trees. There should be a door."

Placing his hands on the branches, Bai pushed against them and shook the solid obstruction. More leaves fluttered around him. He shook it harder.

"What are you—" Asmund started.

"We're two oblivious hunters stumbling upon this," Bai said. "I'm acting the part."

Attempting to mask his worry, Asmund looked up to the top of the wall as it shook. Bai finally ceased when he became breathless. When nothing happened, he frowned and knocked a fist against the wood.

"What other walls made of trees could there be?" he growled. "It's daylight. They should have seen that."

Asmund ran his hand along a thick branch, following it down the wall. He applied pressure, and a few spots gave under his touch. Bai trailed behind him and shook the branches some more.

"Would you stop?" Asmund whispered at him.

Bai raised his brow, surprised the mouse was giving an order. "What? It'll catch their attention."

"But if we can find a weak point ... or maybe the strongest point."

The branches trembled without Bai meaning them to. A crash sounded that reverberated down the wall. Voices picked up, along with footfalls. Bai and Asmund exchanged a look before creeping toward the commanding shouts—deep and male.

Bai held his ax tighter but assumed no battle stance. When they rounded the bend, the men came into view. Asmund faltered at the sight of them: scraggly men covered in skins and wool tunics, worn leather boots crunching over the forest debris. Some of their hair dangled in ringlets, others kept theirs shaved or half-shaved, others braided. All of them grew long beards and menacing eyes peered over them.

"There!" one shouted and pointed at Bai and Asmund. "That's what it is! Not a bear!"

"Take them," another ordered.

Bai and Asmund gave each other another glance as the men dashed toward them. The act had to be kept up. *Run.*

They turned on their heels and took off through the snow.

They didn't make it far before Asmund slipped and fell. Bai halted and whirled, helping him to his feet before swinging his ax when the men got too close.

Bai shouted and knocked against his new opponent's ax. The man, a few inches shorter than him, countered his blows and brought him to his knees, but Bai let him. However, he feared he miscalculated when the man raised his blade and moved to swing down on his head.

"*NO!*" Asmund yelled. But a different voice stopped the man.

"I said take them, don't kill them! Fan almighty."

A skinny, lanky man wearing a simple vest over his bare chest, despite the cold, sneered at them as he approached. He wrinkled his long nose and flashed yellow teeth. "Never seen you two in camp before. What are you doin' out here?"

Bai's opponent lowered his ax and stepped away, never taking his eyes off him. Bai rose from his knees, standing before Asmund. "We—we've been out here for the last two seasons. Um, is this Judr?"

The lanky man erupted with manic laughter. The others joined in, though without so much bravado. Bai shrank back. *This one is insane.*

As quickly as he'd begun laughing, the man stopped and furrowed his brow at Bai, his jaw falling open. "Your eyes."

Bai blinked. Then he gripped his ax when the man marched right up to him, standing so close their noses nearly touched. The stench of his sour breath left Bai stifling a gag. The man giggled and clapped his hands together.

"This one has eyes like our lord Fan!" he exclaimed. "A sign from the Gods! Come, we must bring them inside. Bring them to the Council!"

Yes. For once, Bai didn't have to curse his most despised feature. His opponent took him roughly by the arm and dragged him forward. Bai gave a tug to show resistance, but otherwise let the men take him where they pleased.

He glanced back at Asmund, who trembled between the men that pulled him along. His terrified eyes never left Bai, his jaw clenched. Bai would have made an encouraging smile, but couldn't let the other men be swayed. *Don't lose your courage. You were doing so well. Don't let them frighten you.*

They turned the corner and passed through the forest wall. Bai's jaw dropped.

***

After everything he had heard about Haven, Bai wasn't sure exactly what to expect. Fiery hearths surrounded by wild men, a dark and looming great house, and Fan rituals performed on every corner. What his new captors pushed him through instead was an organized camp full of warriors, workers like blacksmiths, and farm hands—every one of them bustling about to fulfill their tasks.

Every one of them a man.

Women were trapped somewhere among them in some old shack Naleem had spoken of, but none walked the dirt paths. A barn stood off to the west, the red roof towering over the various tents. Their captors shoved them toward the great house where a large elk skull hung above the porch. Snow lay on the roof and decorated the skull's antlers.

The strange, lanky man strode ahead and up the porch steps while the others followed, pulling Bai and Asmund. Inside, rows of long tables filled the hall. Only one was occupied by a dozen men, who donned fur cloaks against the morning chill. Each of them looked at their visitors, but Bai recognized the two that sat at the head of the table. His teeth ached when they gnashed, and his muscles became stone.

It took every fiber of his being not to glower at Thenalious, who sat back in his chair, looking rather bored until his gaze fell on his new captives. The red-haired beast sat beside him, the one Naleem said was called Reynold. Sweat beaded down Bai's back as they stopped at the table.

Thenalious raised an eyebrow and did not refuse Bai's hard glare. His hazel eyes sparked with interest. "What's this you've brought us, Wyn?"

"Sorry I could not come to meet you all sooner," Wyn said. "On my way here, the men saw the wall shaking and thought another grizzly was trying to break in." He stepped closer to Bai and slapped his shoulder. "I've caught the bear."

A faint smirk pulled at Thenalious' lips. "Quite the bear."

Bai did not return the sentiment. In the back of his mind, Gittan screamed at him to hold his temper, keep calm, and stand his ground. Anticipate the opponent's next move. However, Bai's last encounter with this man replayed over the Commander's instructions. Bai's hand twitched above his ax.

"He has eyes like Fan himself, my lord," Wyn added. "To find him scratching at our door before Fan's Eye has to be a gift from the gods."

All of the councilmen studied Bai. Thenalious' features were curved with amusement. He rose from his chair, and all of them stood at once. Reynold growled at having his breakfast disturbed, but got to his feet and watched Thenalious round the table to view Bai close up.

"Is that what you are?" Thenalious rested his hands behind his back. "A gift from Fan?"

Bai said nothing. In his periphery, Asmund quaked between his captors.

Thenalious' eyes narrowed. "How did you find this place, then? Travelers have not visited us in many years. Neither did they leave alive."

Bai took a long breath, harnessing his anger before he forced the words forth. "We went hunting for a few days and returned to Syden to find it burned to the ground. We've spent the last two seasons in the woods, searching for Judr, but without a map or a woman to guide us, we've done nothing but survive and wander. We stumbled upon your ... wall."

Thenalious stepped back, his face lighting up as if he won a card game. "Two whole seasons. That's quite a feat, considering Sorelle's wilderness. You must have felt so lost."

He paced between the other men for a few strides. They all made a path for him, moving to the side like trained dogs. Bai's eyes followed him back and forth.

"So lost, in fact," Thenalious went on, "that you must have forgotten that you lived in Judr, for I believe I've met you before, *Grizzly*."

Asmund shook harder on the other side of them. Bai held Thenalious' gaze as they stood nose-to-nose.

"Fan's eyes indeed," Thenalious whispered. "I remember them pleading for a daughter's life."

A raging heat surged through Bai's veins, but he remained still.

Thenalious turned away from him. "Kill them both."

Wyn staggered. "My lord? We haven't received a sign from the gods in some time, and this coming Eye—"

"I don't care if he sprouts antlers," Thenalious snarled. "He's lying, and survived the last raid. Kill them both or I'll do it myself and include you."

"We both survived Judr," Bai barked, "but we've left that village. The women there are cruel and unjust. They would sacrifice our brothers and our sons to Gaea, and that is not the life we wish to live."

Every head turned to Thenalious, who looked over his shoulder at Bai. "Is that so?"

Might as well give him some truth. "The Matriarch was untrustworthy and not fit to rule a village. You found me in a healer's house recovering from wounds and a punishment I didn't deserve. The scars are still there—a flogging for being poisoned and taken advantage of, only for the wench to cry wolf against me."

Thenalious tilted his head. "But you would still defend a simple girl's life?"

Bai glowered. "The woman I've been bound to kept her from me, and then you took her for good. She is still my blood and heart, and I ought to rip your lungs from your body for what you've done to her."

Reynold threw his chair backward as he lunged, gripping a knife in his fist. The other councilmen clattered and clanged as they raised their weapons. Thenalious lifted a hand, and they all fell to a silent halt.

His voice came low and soft. "What's stopping you?"

"Unfortunately," Bai started, "you are keeping this place alive. This is a sanctuary, right? I'd rather fight for the cause here."

Thenalious laughed. "You wish to kill me, yet you also wish to fight alongside me."

"It's not all that conflicting when I tell you I fight for myself and against tyranny," Bai told him. "Not for anyone else."

"And you wouldn't attempt to kill me or any of my men in the meantime?"

This time, Bai allowed himself to smirk. "I make no promises."

Thenalious' face morphed with amusement. He glanced past Bai, studying Asmund. "Who is he to you?"

Asmund's fear did not help the situation. How could he be added to the mix of the story? "A friend. We've spent years in the fields together. After your raid, he had no one else to turn to."

Thenalious let his gaze linger on Asmund, the cat eyeing the mouse. Bai bristled. "Will you still kill us, then?"

"... If you wish to fight, there are trials we enforce to instate new warriors," Thenalious explained. "Unless Wyn deems you more worthy of another position, we could begin initiation."

Wyn, baffled, looked between Bai and Thenalious. "My lord. Of course, this man may be a capable warrior, if you wish. But, with respect, I would question how they found Haven."

"As would I," Reynold rumbled over the table. Other councilmen grunted in agreement.

Thenalious gave a playful shrug. "Must have tracked us, I suspect. It took them two seasons to find us. They're not very good at tracking. I want to see if this grizzly lasts through the trials. If he doesn't, he's dead, anyway."

No one said anything to that. They only shifted their weight. Bai straightened, wondering exactly what this trial would entail.

Thenalious pinned him with a stare. "If you die at any point, your *friend* will die as well. He doesn't seem like the fighting type. Otherwise, Wyn will find a place for him among us. What's your initial idea for him, Wyn?"

The skinny man took Asmund's chin in his hand. Asmund stifled a yelp, and Wyn shoved him back.

"The caregiver might benefit from extra help," Wyn reported. "This one's too timid to disobey like the last ones."

Yes. Hadwin was a caregiver, if he was still alive. Everything lined up perfectly. All Bai had to do was pass this trial. "When do we begin?"

In all his years, Bai had never seen someone feign giddiness as Thenalious did. His hazel eyes told everything despite his graceful stature, with a blaze as bright as the fires he inflicted on Syden. Bai would always judge those eyes.

"The day is young," Thenalious said. "We could gather the men and begin now."

Within the hour, a horn blared across the camp, which every man in Haven answered to. The congregation fit in front of the great house where Thenalious stood on the porch, Reynold to one side of him and Bai on the other. The rest of the councilmen stood before the gathering, Asmund's captors holding him beside them.

Bai looked out over the sea of eyes and gnarled features. Most of the men were his age or older, not many appearing younger than nineteen. Those who might be scattered and ducked behind the others. Each of them peered at him as he stood beside their leader.

Thenalious raised a hand to silence them. "Here is the bear many of you were worried about this morning. A commoner who seems to have favored our way of life and sought us out as the first of us did long ago. He offers himself as a warrior among us, but we have certain qualifications, don't we?"

The men cheered and shouted, lifting weapons into the air. However, the councilmen before them shifted uneasily, not all of them pleased to see this through. Reynold became rigid on the other side of Thenalious and would not look Bai's way.

Thenalious turned to Bai. His voice carried so everyone could hear. "Your first trial is to face every warrior in attendance today. You are not to kill them, but they will try to kill you."

"Afraid I'll single-handedly destroy your army?" Bai allowed himself to say.

An amused huff left Thenalious' nose while Reynold stifled a growl. Thenalious pushed Bai forward, and he took the porch steps to the frigid ground. "Who will fight the grizzly first?"

Volunteers cheered, and a few stepped forward. Between half a dozen of them, a man with a long gray beard and a shaved head went forth, pounding his ax against his shield.

Bai squared his shoulders and pulled his ax from his belt. He assumed his stance that he'd copied a hundred times over at Vakkar Hold and on the road, and waited.

The man shouted as he swung his ax. Bai countered, hooked and twisted, wrenching the man's ax from his hand. The crowd went silent, mouths agape. Bai hid his satisfaction and, as his opponent stared at his empty hand, moved to splinter the shield. He drove the man's legs out from under him with his foot.

With a yelp, the man fell back, the wind knocked out of his lungs. Bai raised his blade and swung down, acting as if he would hack the man's head off. Instead, he stopped just above his neck. The man gulped with the blade's edge hovering over his throat.

Bai retracted and offered the ax haft to pull the man up. The man spat off to the side and got to his feet. Bai waited for the next one, but now, each volunteer approached with caution.

The next man hefted a sword and shield. Bai glared at him and waited. When this one lunged, attempting to shove him with his shield, Bai spun and dragged his ax across the man's ankle. His balance taken, his foot snagged by the ax beard, the man shouted and fell forward, landing on his shield. The edge of Bai's ax landed just above the nape of his opponent's neck before he retreated again.

One after another, each volunteer battled and was defeated. Many toppled to the ground with ease, some jumped when Bai lunged, and a couple went running when he glared. Others proved themselves more lethal, especially when Haven ran out of lower-ranking volunteers and each councilman stepped forward.

Bai received a nick to the shoulder from one when he tripped up and an ax blade tore through his sleeve. Wyn gave him a blow to the head with his shield, but Bai took him down when he grew too confident, giggling madly only to fall on his ass. Another grazed his ribcage with a sword. Bai had turned on his heels to avoid the edge, but the blade was sharp enough to tear through fabric and slice skin. Nevertheless, each councilman was defeated as well.

Finally, Reynold towered over him.

The beast flexed when he lifted his heavy battle ax, and Bai waited. Reynold swung down, and Bai countered. Without shields to deflect any blow, the two ravaged and let their axes clash. Reynold pushed forward, and Bai let him before ducking around and attempting to catch him from behind. Despite his size, Reynold moved just as quickly. His blade came up from behind him and bit into Bai's thigh.

Bai screamed and caught himself before he could drop. The crowd cheered for his defeat. Gritting his teeth, Bai straightened and limped on his wounded leg. Blood seeped and stained his pants, the warmth of it snaking down his calf between skin and wool. His breathing labored, rising in steam as he stared the beast down, waiting.

The crowd urged Reynold to take him down, but the beast stood back, watching for Bai's next move. Bai pushed forward and acted as if he would swipe at Reynold's shoulder. The beast brought his ax up to deflect. Bai kicked his bad leg forward with all his might and cried out when he tripped Reynold backward.

Reynold quickly regained his balance. Bai struck his ax head against the beast's chest and knocked him down. He swung the ax to hover it over the beast's chest, which heaved for air. The blade quaked inches above Reynold, but Bai stood back.

The battle over, he limped and turned to Thenalious. Though his face remained as stern as stone, Thenalious' eyes gleamed. Reynold stood and might have slain Bai on the spot if Thenalious didn't intervene.

"Wyn, have this grizzly chained before the house," he ordered. "He is not to be fed or watered until I say so. The only warmth he'll have is the clothes on his back."

"With pleasure, my lord," Wyn said, still pouting from his loss, and snapped his fingers.

Bai staggered as several men snatched him, tearing his ax out of his hand. Within minutes, they placed iron around his wrists and chained him to a stake in the hard ground like a dog. The chain only allowed him to kneel. Bai shuddered with the pain from his wounds and the tight twist between his shoulder blades. He scowled at the other men, who laughed as they returned to their business.

Thenalious watched him before Reynold rejoined him and went off with the other councilmen. They dragged Asmund inside, shoving him behind the great house door. At least he would be safe so long as Bai survived. Asmund could make sure Hadwin was still alive. Bai focused on stanching the blood pouring from the gash in his thigh, recalling the battle healing Gittan had taught them. He worried that the combat would be the easiest part of the trial, and the worst was yet to come.

Chapter 23

Hadwin

A NY FANTASIZED DREAM OF escape never crossed Hadwin's mind again. Hopelessness took over between visits from Drengr and lying in bed, feeling sorry for himself and his nephew. If it weren't for Cadoc, he would have prayed for Gaea to take him away, no matter whether he would be lifted or not. Drengr wouldn't allow it.

The old warlock allowed Hadwin to rise once he'd recovered, his arm in a sling. Oberon had to return to his councilman duties, and Hadwin resumed his job as a caregiver. The boys greeted him with excited cries and open arms, clinging to their beloved caregiver before he winced and they jumped back.

"I'm sorry, little ones," Hadwin grunted. "I'm still a bit tender."

"What happened?" one of the younger boys whimpered.

Of course, he couldn't tell them outright. "I just got hurt. But I'm getting better. Come, let's get downstairs for your breakfast while it's still hot."

The boys slunk about to get ready, stealing curious glances at him. He must have looked grisly to them. Not only did his arm remain in the sling, but a red scar striped the bridge of his nose where Thenalious had almost taken both his eyes. Dark circles hung under his eyelids from the lack of sleep, despite being in bed for weeks. The stitches on his thigh, shoulder, and hip were covered by clothing, which the children wouldn't detect.

Cadoc and Audun stayed at Hadwin's side, being ever-helpful with the toddlers and babes. Hadwin needed all the help he could get, and he praised them for each task they carried out.

When it came time to take Else to her mother, Oberon showed up like clockwork. Hadwin bristled. "The women don't trust you. I can do it. Why must you go?"

"You're a fool if you think you can walk that distance just yet," Oberon scolded him. "And it's best that you don't make your presence in that shack known for some time, don't you think?"

Only then did Hadwin remember Thenalious' threats, which he'd fought for so long to erase. Any child Maura might produce would be killed no matter its gender. Weeks had passed since the beginning of fall. She would show by now, wouldn't she?

If Maura were with child, wouldn't she have told him before all this ever happened? Unless her silence was to ensure he kept his distance from the women and not encourage the suspicion that they'd all plotted against Haven together.

Thus, Oberon took Else to her mother and returned rather quickly after every visit. He also routinely checked the nursery. Hadwin suspected it was because of a desire to visit his sons. Then he realized it was an effort to monitor him—the unruly caregiver—and be sure he never left his post.

"I plan on taking the boys outside today," Hadwin told him at breakfast when he sat with Gael and Vihn.

Oberon shook his head. "Can't today. I don't have the time."

"Why does it depend on you? I said I would—"

"You're not taking them outside," Oberon said. "You'll keep them in the nursery, and they can play there."

"Why exactly?"

"Because you are to be kept inside."

Hadwin frowned. "Is this Thenalious' idea?"

"No, it's my idea. You're my responsibility now, and anything stupid you do will be on my head, too. You're staying inside."

"So you'd trap me and coddle me like a child?"

"Only because you've snuck around and broken rules like a child," Oberon snarled. "You're staying and watching over them inside. It'll be too cold for them in time, anyway. Besides, you're still in no condition to exert yourself."

Hadwin bit his tongue and swallowed his anger. Nothing good would come from arguing, and judging by the sharp edge of his voice, Oberon wouldn't budge.

Hadwin remained indoors, and if the boys ever played outside, Oberon would make time to watch over them, but those days were few and far between.

Even when the other boys scampered over the porch and raced about Haven's streets, Cadoc stayed with his uncle. Hadwin's heart sank to see him that way. It couldn't be healthy for him to look on as the others played, only to linger beside Hadwin, wounded and caged.

When shouts began outside the great house after the snow fell, Hadwin ignored them and continued his routine, waking the boys for breakfast. All morning, blades clashed and cries echoed. The older boys scarfed their breakfast to watch the commotion from the windows, but Hadwin told them to wait until the younger ones finished.

Whatever went on outside, he wanted no part of it. It had to be some new form of proving each other's strength, some new Fan ritual Oberon hadn't warned him about.

By early afternoon, the shouting had ceased, and the boys jumped and ran about the nursery since Oberon was too busy to take them out again. At least Hadwin thought so until a knock came at the door, and it opened.

Oberon and Wyn stood at the threshold with a young man Hadwin had never seen before. His mouse-brown hair was cut below his ears, light-brown stubble speckled his fawn-toned cheeks and chin, and his blue eyes darted about the nursery before finding the floor.

Wyn cackled as he shoved the stranger forward. "Caregiver, this is your new assistant. Teach him well, and should he forget his place, let any of us know. We will be rid of him like the others. Is that clear?"

Hadwin bowed his head. "Yes, lord."

"Good. Have at it then."

Wyn strode down the hallway, but Oberon entered the nursery and shut the door behind him. Gael and Vihn raced past the stranger to meet their father at once. Oberon pulled them close, but kept a rigid gaze on the new caregiver.

Hadwin frowned at his hostility. "What is it?"

"Wyn forgot to mention he's a survivor of the last raid," Oberon growled. "He and another one have been looking for us ever since, apparently." His eyes settled on the new caregiver. "I'm here to tell you I don't trust either of you for one moment."

Hadwin studied the stranger, noting how he trembled, and not because of the cold. "If you don't trust him, why is he here?"

"Thenalious. I haven't seen him this love-struck since your brother. Forgive me, but it's horrible. And the damned cock just won single combat with every able warrior in camp, including all of us and Reynold. How does a common man know how to fight like *that*?"

The stranger's eyes flitted across the floor, but he didn't dare look up. Hadwin imagined the question was for him, but he seemed too terrified to know that. This new information didn't settle well with Hadwin, either. A couple of men had tracked Haven down, and one had defeated every man within it?

"Where is the other man?" Hadwin asked.

"Chained in front of the house," Oberon snapped. "Something Thenalious planned for him. He talks about trials for warriors, but there are none. If you're able, you fight, and if you don't fight, you die. I *hate* it when he lets his cock control him, and he's always griping at us because we prefer women."

Hadwin let him vent and looked over the stranger more. Deadly quiet for such a man. Even his teeth didn't chatter as he shook. "What's your name?"

"... Asmund," the stranger murmured, his voice deep as mountain caves and not quite befitting his quaking frame.

"Asmund. I'm Hadwin."

Asmund finally raised his chin, and his trembling ceased. He blinked at Hadwin. "You're ..."

Hadwin raised an eyebrow. "Is there something wrong?"

Asmund shook his head and let his gaze fall to the floor again. Oberon snorted and rounded on him, leaving Gael and Vihn behind. "I'll have my eyes on you and your *friend* out there, got it? If you so much as spit the wrong way, I'll kill you both. I don't care what Thenalious does."

"Oberon," Hadwin warned as Asmund shook harder. "Honestly, he doesn't look like he would hurt a fly."

Oberon wrinkled his nose. "Gael and Vihn are coming with me today, and they will sleep in my chamber."

Hadwin rolled his eyes.

"Really, Papa?" Gael asked, beaming.

With another snort, Oberon turned and herded his two sons out the door, slamming it shut behind him. Once he was gone, Asmund relaxed a little and allowed himself to investigate the room. Blue eyes roamed over the beds and walls and glanced at the cradles in their corner.

Hadwin gave him an encouraging smile. "He's not all bad. He's actually the kindest out of all of them, if you can believe it. Now what's this about coming from the last raid and finding Haven?"

Asmund fixed his gaze on him but said nothing, though Hadwin waited. Why would two men seek out the ones who'd destroyed their home and families—to join their ranks? Hadwin agreed it was suspicious.

"Well, you don't have to talk now. But I would like to hear your story, eventually. In the meantime, are you good with children?"

Chapter 24

Raegna

Though Raegna had helped set up camp countless times along the journey to Sorelle, never before had it been this exhausting. She did her best, unfolding the canvas of the tents and tying ropes to keep them aloft once stakes were hammered into the ground. Unloading supplies winded her, and she had to settle on a crate to catch her breath.

Thekla came to her aid when she noticed. "What is it, Shield-Priestess?"

"Nothing. I'm fine. Just needed a rest, is all." Raegna got to her feet and hefted the crate to its new location. Her chest tightened as she scolded herself, making breathing a chore. If her mother were here and knew what she was putting herself through, she'd drag her by her ear to the nearest cot to have her rest. Jaleesa was incessant during her first pregnancy when the signs had made themselves known.

"We're not risking this, Raegna," she'd told her and had her do minimal tasks. "That could be a daughter waiting to meet you, and we'll not risk anything for house chores."

If only her mother were alive to witness her risking a daughter for all this. If only Bai were here, and if he knew, what would he do?

Raegna should have told him before they left, as she'd meant to. The words wouldn't come out, and she couldn't ruin this for him. But she should have told him. There was no telling if he would make it out alive.

No. He will. He must.

When camp had been made, Raegna withdrew from the others and allowed herself to sit. She imagined one of them might know her secret just by looking at her. Some had a way of knowing, even Maidens and rugged mercenaries.

Playing with Bai's ring over her belly, Raegna leaned back and watched the bare trees dance as a frigid wind ran through them. The cold nipped at her face, the only flesh exposed to the elements. Banu's house would have been more pleasant. Warm with a fire and a hot meal. The ride back wouldn't be difficult or long.

But Raegna had to see Haven fall. She had to know that Bai was safe. If he were, and if she could see him again, she would rather tell him outright. Maybe that would urge him to be more careful and come back alive.

They could begin anew if he did. Ride back to Vakkar Hold and learn to tolerate each other again, perhaps even care for each other. Rest easy in the palace with all danger gone and raise a second child in peace without a chasm between them. Without walls and fortresses held against each other.

"Shield-Priestess." The Commander's voice tore through her thoughts like a knife through fabric.

Raegna jumped and peered up at her, fingers curled over the ring. "Oh. Hello."

"What is it?" Gittan asked gently. "Worried about your man?"

Raegna's lips pressed together, and she held Gittan's gaze. A fist closed at the base of her throat, and it kept her words down. *You could say that.*

Gittan gave her an encouraging smile. "There now. You've seen him fight. He's a capable man. Both of them are."

Raegna gulped. "I know."

"Is this because I wouldn't let you see them off? You know why I had to, and you got to say your goodbyes. They'll come back."

"I appreciate you trying to make me feel better."

"It's all right," Gittan said. "I know you're worried sick. Tell you what, tonight when we listen for a report, you can come with. We're staking out rather close to what we believe is the perimeter and sending signals to see if either of them can hear. Is that all right?"

"Tonight?" The wilderness would be treacherously frigid, but to know if the men were all right ...

"Yes. So you'll have to bundle up. We'll have no fire, not even torchlight. You think you can handle it?"

You'll not risk a daughter for this. If she dressed warmly enough, everything should be fine. Gittan wouldn't let her freeze either. "Yes. I can handle it. Thank you, Gittan."

"Just try to learn how to walk soundlessly, Shield-Priestess."

Raegna practiced until evening, when they ate a ration of bread and cheese before embarking into the forest at nightfall.

The black shadows of the trees stretched all around them—the branches, like claws, reaching out to snag them. Gittan gathered Raegna and two other warriors to sneak through the brush and find a good spot from which to send signals. Raegna used their tracks and stepped where they'd stepped to deafen her footfalls. They'd made a considerable distance from their camp before Gittan halted them, and the four hid within a thicket.

The two warriors brought parchment, a quill, and a small inkwell. They lay on their stomachs with their utensils. Raegna sat on her folded legs beside them, making sure the foliage covered her figure even if the pitch-black night should conceal her well enough.

Gittan knelt before them and scanned the darkness before she cupped her hands and brought them to her mouth.

A low, chirp-like whistle echoed from her through the trees, imitating an owl. What kind of owl Raegna wasn't sure, but if she heard it out in the forest, she wouldn't know the difference between the bird and Gittan. The Commander dropped her hands and waited.

Several moments passed, but nothing answered. Gittan brought her hands up again and repeated the hoot. Raegna cocked an ear to see if she could pick up anything, but the forest held nothing but the constant blow of wind that shook more leaves to the ground.

Gittan continued the hooting for minutes that stretched out to a half-hour by Raegna's guess. When the calls remained unanswered, Raegna's heart drummed, and she shuddered.

"Do we need to get closer?" she whispered. "Maybe they can't hear us?"

"This is as close as I dare go without making ourselves known," Gittan whispered back. "We might stumble upon the place ourselves if we go further. This is farther than I took them when I sent them off."

Raegna wrapped her arms around herself to stop shivering. If they didn't answer, what were they to do then? What could have happened to them? Did the Haven men not trust them at once, and ... No—she couldn't bear it.

"Gittan."

Another distant hoot broke through the silence. Two short hoots echoed through the trees, and Raegna's heart lifted.

"Asmund," Gittan whispered. "It's Asmund."

"How do you know?"

"He said so, and his calls are a little shaky. Now hush."

The hoots passed back and forth in various patterns as they communicated. Anyone would mistake them for a couple of owls finding each other in the dark. Gittan paused now and then to listen, think of a message, and then answer back. The warriors listened as well, jotting down notes from Asmund's calls. Raegna tried to see them on the parchment, but the night covered their handwriting.

Finally, Gittan sat back and sighed. She gave another call, and when none came, she nodded to herself and turned to Raegna.

"They're all right."

"That's it?" Raegna whispered. "Why is only Asmund calling back? Is Bai there too?"

Gittan shook her head. "Bai is ... compromised at the moment."

"Compromised? What does that mean?"

"He's still alive, Shield-Priestess," the Commander hissed at her. "Let's go. I'm cold, and I'll explain everything back at camp."

The trek to camp proved to be more difficult as Raegna tossed all the possibilities over in her head. The hooting reverberated in her skull along with her anxieties until they reached the warmth of Gittan's tent, where others came to hear the news of their men.

The Commander laid the parchment out on the table that sat in the middle of her giant tent. The table had a map of Galaenia carved into it, and strategic pawns stood in Sorelle, one marking their camp. She placed a pawn just below it in the middle of the stubby peninsula before the southern cliffs met the ocean.

"Haven should be there," she told everyone, "according to Asmund, and I cannot deny that had to be where his calls came from. We sit closer than I wanted us to, but we couldn't have known."

"What did he say?" Thekla asked.

"They are both safe, and he has found Naleem's brother and son," Gittan said. "They're alive and well. Asmund has gained a position to remain beside them and protect them if necessary."

"What of Bai?" Raegna urged. "You said he was in danger."

"I *said* he was *compromised*. It was hard for Asmund to explain with these simple codes, but Bai is serving as a good distraction while Asmund can keep a low profile and find out what we need to know. Your husband is safe and has defended himself. The details are unknown."

Raegna fought back tears. She refused to weep in front of all these women. Was he truly safe, or were these words meant to reassure her? What could they be doing to him that he needed to defend himself? Raegna worried so much, she thought she might lose her supper.

She lost it the next morning, retching a short distance from her tent. Bread and cheese would not bode well, and next time, she would remember. Trembling, when she stood and turned, she found Gittan standing before her.

The Commander settled her hands on her hips, her eyes narrowed. "Thekla told me she has seen you taking more breaks than ever before. You've always been such a determined warrior. Now you're vomiting. I'd like you to tell me what's going on, Shield-Priestess."

"It's nothing." Raegna moved to push past her. "Last night's food just didn't settle well. I'm fine."

Gittan snorted. "If you are ill, I'll send you back to your healer. If it can spread, I don't need it in my camp."

"It won't. I'm fine."

"Unless, of course, you aren't ill."

"You're right," Raegna said. "I am not."

"You'll tell me what the matter is now, Shield-Priestess," Gittan snapped at her, making her jump. "That is an order. Just because I am a Maiden does not mean I am dumb to these conditions."

Raegna's neck flushed. "I don't know what you mean."

"For Gaea's sake. Are you with child or not?"

Gritting her teeth, Raegna held her ground, though her world swayed. Bile rose in her throat like she might vomit again.

Gittan's brow straightened, and her eyes widened. "That's why you're nagging about Bai. I don't think I've ever heard you fuss about him. Not like this."

"Wouldn't you do the same if it were Naleem?"

Gittan jolted and opened her gloved palms. "Keep your voice down! I'm still a Maiden to the women here, and if anyone—Never mind. Besides, we would be stupid to bring Naleem and put him back in there. Your husband is perfectly capable of handling himself."

"But what if he snaps and says something stupid like he always does?" Raegna whimpered. "What if they don't trust him, or they recognize him and decide to kill him? What am I supposed to do then? Raise his child on my own? I cannot do that!"

When the floodgates could not be held anymore, Raegna brought her hands to her mouth and muffled a sob. Gittan stepped forward.

"I'm sorry. I hadn't thought of it that way."

Raegna's shoulders ached, and heat prickled along her cheeks against the cold. "I didn't tell him. He doesn't deserve this or me. I won't go back when I'm this close."

Gittan's head quirked, her eyes roaming over Raegna. "You're still fighting."

"I plan to."

The Maiden opened her mouth, closed it, and inhaled. "Very well. Everything remains the same then. We'll reach the men with signals in a few days."

Raegna nodded. "Thank you."

CHAPTER 25

BAI

"Now, my Bai." His father placed two hot cups of cider and a plate of cinnamon biscuits before the fireplace. "Let's make sure you're warm. I know how much you hate the cold."

"Papa!" a much younger Bai squealed when his father cupped his face in his hands and blew on his nose. He had to have been eight years old. Winter was blowing in the night of Leaf Fall Gift. Bai's mother had left to help the Matriarch on her journey to Stadt for the Harvest Union. It had to be the best Leaf Fall of Bai's life. He and his father had the house to themselves.

His father pulled him close with a wool blanket around them. "There now. I won't let you freeze. I love you so very much, my Bai."

In his memories, Bai snuggled up to his father, warmed by the fire in front of them and the cider in his belly. He focused his mind there, away from the bitter camp where the chill bit at every exposed patch of skin.

The iron cuffs chafed his wrists, which were already dry from the cold air. Old blood crusted the wound where Wyn had bashed his shield against his head. His body ached, but his chest, ribs, and the graze on his side hurt worst of all. Then there was the gash in his thigh, which he stanched with part of his cloak torn for a makeshift bandage. Banu wouldn't be very impressed.

Instead of being there in the cold and in pain, Bai let his mind wander to other places. When that warm night by the fire with his father ended, he searched his memory for something else. Fall and winter had always been cruel when they were stuck at home with his mother. She was likely to lose her patience and lash out at a moment's notice. Even Raegna's company in the past seemed more inviting.

In those days, Bai didn't have to fear his wife striking him, but he always kept his distance and watched her from the corner of his eye while she cared for Adabelle. Just last winter, the three of them took shelter from the icy winds in that little house.

"Can Papa sit with us, Mama?" Adabelle had asked as she plopped before the fireplace, a blanket already draped over her small shoulders.

Raegna faltered as she carried a platter of treats and cider to her. "We're all fine where we are, Adabelle."

Bai gave his daughter a reassuring grin behind Raegna's back. He didn't dare speak in her presence. Likewise, he didn't dare to be so close to Raegna even to fulfill Adabelle's wishes. Instead, he looked on from the table and ate the nut bread his wife allowed him for the occasion. Raegna brought Adabelle close and kissed her head before she filled the night with stories and giggles.

Bai bit his lip as tears threatened him. He would give anything to see them together again. If only he could.

Then Gittan's calls came over the wall, and he perked to attention. They'd practiced those calls throughout their journey, learning the various codes and each pitch of the hooting that mimicked owls. Gittan said it was some old way of communication before the Dark Days and before the Maidens. It might not have even been Galaenian, but it worked.

He thought of calling back, and his chains rattled as he tried to put his hands to his lips. The restraints weren't long enough, but perhaps it was for the best. What would the men think of him hooting into the night? It would be up to Asmund.

But he was kept in the great house. Would he hear Gittan's calls at all? If he didn't, what would the women do without an answer?

Asmund called back, the hooting much closer. Bai struggled to keep up with the conversation between them, picking up bits and pieces. What he could understand was everything he already knew. Gittan asked questions about their welfare, then about Hadwin and Cadoc when Asmund reported them. Bai had questions of his own. Was everything going according to plan? How could he push these men in the right direction to let their guard down and benefit the army outside?

How was Raegna faring?

The way she'd hesitated and forced a thin goodbye still stirred in his mind. If only he could return to her and tell her he was all right. Mostly.

In the morning, Bai woke, and the sun rays warmed him. Chained before the great house, he had curled up for warmth overnight with his cloak wrapped as tightly around him as he could make it. He raised his head and examined his surroundings.

The Haven men paid him no mind as they busied themselves with their work. Animals brayed across camp. Metal rang from the black-smith's tent. Smoke from fires rose into the air, and the sizzling smell of breakfast came from all directions. Bai's stomach rumbled.

However, he wouldn't get a morsel. Thenalious had made that clear enough. Bai glanced over his shoulder at the great house and looked away when the councilmen emerged. The porch steps thudded and creaked as each man plodded down and scattered about the camp. One with umber skin and black hair and a beard glowered at him while two little boys trailed behind him.

Only the councilmen had sons, Naleem said. As far as Bai understood, the sons stayed with their caregivers, so why did this man allow his sons to follow him through camp?

Then a pair of familiar boots stopped before him, and Bai glared up. Thenalious stood over him, grinning and chomping into a bright red apple.

"Hungry, Grizzly?" he teased.

Bai wrinkled his nose as Thenalious took another bite. He tossed the apple so it landed in front of them, just out of reach of Bai's chains. Though Bai pretended the apple was nothing of interest, his stomach caved and growled in disagreement.

"I'll feed you when I think you deserve it," Thenalious said and started away. "That is, if you live that long."

Once he disappeared into camp, Bai eyed the apple and strategized how he might take it. When he looked about to be sure no one was watching, he thought to stretch a leg and kick it back toward him. Then he chastised himself. He refused to eat Thenalious' scraps and refused to give in to this trial.

It wouldn't have mattered, anyway. Reynold walked by and kicked the apple farther away with his stride.

The day dragged with the sounds of Haven. Bai thought he might witness the councilmen's sons play in the snow, but they were kept inside. Throughout the day, he never spotted Asmund or Hadwin or any other familiar faces from Syden as he might have hoped. Hundreds of men walked past him, but none gave him a second thought.

Dinner rolled around, and a horn blared. The horde of men migrated around him and filed through the front doors of the great house. Meat cooked, and the rich smell wafted through the open doors. Bai set his jaw and ignored it.

Night fell, and the cold wrapped its claws around him once more. Not that the day had been much less crisp, but the gnawing hunger served as an easy distraction. Tonight, hunger and cold joined, and even Bai's memories couldn't comfort him as they had the night before. His stomach ached for biscuits, cider, and nut bread. Even Raegna's burnt, stale nut bread and watery stew, and overcooked roast beef ...

"Bai."

The familiar deep voice broke through the night, and Bai straightened. Asmund's shadow came into view before he could make out his shape and features. He knelt and huddled before him.

"Asmund," Bai whispered, "what are you doing out here? You need to get back inside."

He thought he hadn't heard him, but Asmund pulled a bundle from his tunic and set it in the snow. "I brought you something."

Once he unwrapped it, he revealed the scraps from dinner he must have saved. Some bird leg, a slice of beef, salted root, and onions. Bai's mouth watered, but he winced and shook his head.

"Thank you, but I can't. You need to go back."

Asmund frowned and nudged the bundle closer.

Bai sighed. "You're going to get us killed if they see you out here. Don't you think they would notice this?"

Without a word, Asmund slowly blinked at him, waiting.

Bai pushed the bundle back. "Thank you, but I can't. Now go back to Hadwin and keep an eye on him. See if you can get more information. You can't be seen out here."

"And you need to eat," Asmund insisted.

"Go back."

"Eat."

Bai growled. "The point of coming here was not to risk your life for me. Go back inside before someone finds us."

"You're not supposed to risk your life, either," Asmund growled back. "But here we are. *Eat*."

Glancing down at the bundle, Bai snorted a laugh. "The joke is on you. These chains don't go far enough for me to even lift a scrap to my mouth. So there. Go back."

Then, much to his astonishment, Asmund rolled his eyes and took the bird leg to Bai's lips. The faint smell of the spices and herbs lingered on the stale thing, but Bai pulled back.

"I'm not having Thenalious' table scraps," he hissed.

"These are *my* table scraps, stupid," Asmund snapped back. "Eat it."

"But then I've—I've cheated and given in."

Asmund pulled the leg away and settled back. "What if they starve you to death? Or what if you freeze?"

"I haven't yet. And I don't think that's Thenalious' intention exactly. Do you?"

Hesitating, Asmund let his eyes drop to the snow, lost in thought for only a moment. "One of the councilmen is close to Hadwin. He said he had never seen Thenalious this ... love-struck since ... since Naleem."

Bai's brow furrowed. "What does that mean?"

"I think … I think Naleem knows so much about this place for a reason. I think Thenalious may have something planned for you. But I don't think he'll let you die out here."

Bai's mind raced, but he swallowed the nerves that raked at his chest. He feigned confidence, flipping loose hair over his forehead. "There. You see?"

Asmund looked at him then. "You won't even try a bite, will you?"

"I'll not risk keeping you out here or them finding out in the morning that someone helped me," Bai said.

After wrestling within himself, Asmund snatched up the bundle and rose to his feet. "Don't die, then."

Silent as the mouse he was, Asmund snuck back toward the great house. Bai listened for his steps or for the front doors to open and shut. Only the sounds of the night greeted him, then the rumble of his stomach. His heart ached when he found himself alone again.

The third day came and went. On the third night, Bai thought he might just die. Ice snaked down his scarred back, the frost air ripping at his dry skin so harshly, he couldn't bury his face in his arms to escape it. Instead of growling or just aching, his stomach cramped and caved.

Then two caws resounded over the camp. Bai wondered how many birds Gittan could mimic before he recalled the raven that had swooped over him as he'd entered Haven—and the man that had stood in the forest.

He raised his head, allowing the cold to bite at his face again. Through the void that swallowed Haven and the forest, there was no bird, but the calls echoed overhead. A pair of feet appeared before him, and Bai jumped, disturbing the fresh snow around him.

Dressed in a gray cloak over white garb, black wolf hide draped over his shoulders, the man from the forest towered over him. His black eyes rested on Bai.

Bai couldn't help but stare back. "You. You're—"

The man gave him a warm smile and knelt in front of him. Bai sat in place as the man cupped his cheek.

"Be strong, my son," he said, his voice as low as Asmund's, "in all things, not just Haven."

Bai struggled to find the words to inquire what exactly he meant. Then the man leaned forward and kissed his brow. Heat rushed through Bai's veins and the cold could not touch him. The man's hand fell away from his cheek, picking his chin up with a thumb and index finger instead. Having tilted Bai's head back, the man was gone. Nothing but pitch-black surrounded him.

The raven's calls persisted over the trees.

Bai must have fallen asleep after that, for he woke to the sounds of camp and the yank of his chains. Wyn knelt over him with a key to unlock the cuffs at his wrists. Two other men dug the chain pin out of the ground. A crowd gathered around him, but no one mattered except for Thenalious, who waited with his sword in hand. Bai glowered at him.

"Good morning, Grizzly. Sorry to wake you from a short-lived hibernation, but the rest of your trial awaits. It seems you've survived so far."

Bai wobbled to his feet. Pain shot up his thigh and hip when he stepped on his bad leg, but he kept a hard stare on Thenalious. Though the leader of Haven masked a playful grin, Reynold stood behind him with his lip curled.

"It also happens I am the last man to defeat," Thenalious went on. "The same rules apply. You cannot kill me, but it is my job to kill you since the cold couldn't. Bring his ax."

A man returned Bai's ax to him, driving the blade into the ground. He pulled it up and closed a fist around the haft. Everything within him raged to swipe the blade's edge across Thenalious' smug face, to hack him into bits in front of all his men. But he had to keep up the game, had to draw attention away from Asmund and the army of women outside the camp.

Though his fury festered, Bai promised himself he would have his chance. A raven's call echoed from a distant tree, stretching through the forest and fading over the camp.

Thenalious stepped forward and all the men looked on in silent anticipation. Circling like a wolf, Thenalious twirled his sword twice in his hand. Bai had faced real wolves before, and he wasn't nearly as terrifying.

Thenalious lunged for a blow to Bai's chest, which was parried by the ax, hooked around the blade. Bai attempted to rip the sword hilt from Thenalious' grasp, but metal rang when the sword broke free. Thenalious drove forward and Bai leaped away, only to land on his bad leg.

He stumbled and fell, catching himself with one arm. Thenalious stood over him and readied to plow his blade into him. Bai shouted and swung his ax up, twisting to miss the blow. Thenalious rammed his boot into Bai's side and knocked the wind from his lungs. A wave of pain crashed over him.

Without giving him time to recover, Thenalious meant to drive the sword into Bai's chest. Instead of parrying the sword with another ax swing, Bai reached with the ax head, hooked the beard around

Thenalious' calf, and pulled. The leader of Haven yelped and flew backward to land flat on his back. Leaves and snow piles crunched beneath him.

Bai snarled at the pain in his leg, which bled again, as he forced himself up and launched his ax down over Thenalious' head. The crowd gasped, but the blade cut through the soil inches beyond him.

Teeth bared, Bai snarled and dragged the blade through the dirt, drawing it closer to Thenalious' shoulder. If only it struck true.

Much to his disappointment, Thenalious grinned and chuckled. "Very well. You can stay. You're my warrior now."

***

Bai scarfed chicken and bread, wincing at the needle and thread that lanced through his skin. He had spent most of the day in Haven's healer tent with an old, gnarled man with long silver hair and a gray beard. Thenalious called him Drengr and ordered him to give Bai the utmost care. The same he would give a councilman. Bai would have been fighting the furious urge to take Thenalious out if he wasn't so fascinated by Drengr and his skills.

Drengr treated Bai's wounds with precision, tending to the gash in his leg. Bai repressed a growl as the old man stitched his skin into place, but refused to show Thenalious any weakness as he stood at the mouth of the tent. His lip curled as he finished his meal, his caving stomach finally appeased.

Thenalious leaned with his shoulder against the tent post, watching with his thumbs hooked on his belt. "You're very lucky to have survived. Anyone else would have bled to death or frozen in the night."

"Too lucky." Drengr slid his fingertips down Bai's face from forehead to chin. "There is magic in this boy. Sigmund's presence is strong. Stronger than Fan's during the Eye."

Bai's heart skipped a beat. Did he know what had happened last night? Even Bai tried to convince himself it was just a dream.

"Thank Sigmund, then," Thenalious commented. "Thank both the gods."

"I suggest a celebration for this boy, my lord," the healer went on, "and a proper sacrifice to the gods. Fan's Eye is upon us, and we ought to show him our appreciation and joy. Then pray for a warm winter."

"It will be," Thenalious said, not taking his eyes off Bai. "Let me know when you are finished with him. I will discuss a celebration with the Council."

And finally, he left Bai alone. Drengr took Bai's chin in his gnarled fingers, examining his face.

"In all my years, I have not seen eyes such as these. Not on a human being."

Bai yanked away. "When can I serve the camp?"

"You're in no condition to fight," Drengr scolded. "Raids will not begin again until summer. For now, you will rest. Seems that Thenalious has a mind to take good care of you so you can heal."

That was what worried Bai. Thenalious' interest in him had been keen from the moment he'd stepped foot into the great house—despite the trials. Asmund had said something about him being *love-struck.*

Love-struck for Naleem. And now for Bai. What happened here last summer that had Naleem quaking when they'd all left Judr together? Gentle, strong Naleem. What had they done to him?

Bai rested while Drengr sent word his treatment was complete. While Bai waited, his thoughts turned to Raegna and the others just outside the camp.

The image of her standing in the woods and watching him leave had been stamped into his mind when he'd stolen another look at her over his shoulder. He'd counted three days in Haven, but his departure felt like seasons ago. Raegna seemed to be another world away, camping with mercenaries and Maidens just outside the walls. What could she be doing on the other side? Was she thinking of him?

"Ready, Grizzly?"

Bai refrained from a groan as he turned to Thenalious from his cot. The leader of Haven smirked and offered his hand. Bai stared at it, deciding. All of this was some sort of personal game Thenalious played. He could see it in his eyes. Though Bai would truly rather slit the man's wrists, he clasped one instead and hauled himself up. Dropping it, he found his balance on one leg.

Thenalious nodded toward Haven's streets and Bai followed him out. "Let's get you into something better than the drab of a common man."

Outside, in one of the larger tents, several men worked leather into whatever Haven needed. They fitted Bai into his own armor and boots made of thick hides. Bai picked a belt where his ax could cling to his hip. A shepherd with a tent posted closer to the barn provided a wool tunic and a new pair of pants.

"Much better," Thenalious commented with a satisfied smile. He led him back into camp. "You can roam the place as you wish, though as a warrior, you do have a post to keep. We'll decide on that tonight over dinner."

"Wherever you'll have me," Bai said.

Though the muscles in his leg wrenched in agony, Bai limped beside Thenalious throughout camp. He held on to every word Thenalious had to say about the place. Every detail would be crucial to the mission.

The other men gave them a wide berth and gifted Bai with bitter glares. He passed them with his nose wrinkled. Thenalious briefed him on the barn on the west side of the camp where the livestock lived. Bai leaned against a horse pen to catch his breath and lift the weight off his leg.

Thenalious studied him with roaming eyes. "Should we retire to the house? I want you to know it as well as the rest of us. If it were up to me, your post would be there."

You offered Naleem a place in your house, too. "Why not?"

Thenalious smiled. "You'll have to prove yourself to the others before we give you that post."

"You're the leader here, aren't you?" Bai challenged as they turned for the great house. "What you say should go."

"I try to respect the wishes of my men when necessary," Thenalious admitted.

All of the men? Or Reynold? Surely, Reynold and the other councilmen shared a collective distrust for Bai, defeated sore losers like the rest of the lower men in Haven. At least Thenalious wasn't a complete dictator—only when it suited him.

The great house opened into the dining hall, where servant boys cleaned tables and set up empty platters and goblets. The table setting nearly surpassed that of Vakkar Hold's, though it had a far more common and rustic atmosphere. A tapestry of Fan and one of Sigmund hung from the rafters, and Bai frowned.

"Sigmund doesn't look like that," he noted.

Thenalious turned to him and then the tapestry. "That's a depiction from an ancient text our priests dug up years ago. It might not serve the righteous scriptures of Gaea well, but—"

"He's taller, with more bulk," Bai interrupted. "You ought to check a more realistic depiction."

He strode past him with nothing else to say. Thenalious didn't respond.

During the great house tour, Bai saw the kitchens, the downstairs rooms with some storage, and several little studies where the councilmen could work in peace. In one of those rooms, a councilman with his two sons looked up when the door opened. The boys drew on parchment before him while he pored over reports—until he was interrupted.

"Oberon," Thenalious greeted. "Are the caregivers overworked?"

The man blinked, his gaze flitting to Bai. "Um. Not to my knowledge, lord. Hadwin has managed well enough on his own."

Hadwin. Bai controlled his expression as his heart leaped into his throat.

"Why do you feel the need to allow your sons down here?" Thenalious said, his eyes narrowing. "Toting them around camp is one thing."

"I don't mind. They're not a bother."

"That's not what I asked."

Bai watched Oberon's head dip ever so slightly. "I'm concerned for their well-being. The new caregiver, this new warrior—frankly, I don't trust either of them."

Thenalious rolled his eyes. "There were less qualified caregivers watching over them before. I find it difficult to believe you would trust a caregiver who would sneak about the house and stick his cock where it doesn't belong more than one who has yet to prove himself. The boys belong in the nursery for their protection."

Oberon bowed his head. "Yes, lord."

"Return them there before dinner," Thenalious said. "Bai has proved himself a finer warrior than all of you combined. You better get used to it."

With that, Thenalious left him to get on with his work. Bai glanced back at Oberon while he fumed, then fell in line behind Thenalious. Oberon had to be the councilman Asmund had said was close to Hadwin—and Bai would keep their alliance in mind.

Chapter 26

Raegna

Bai flashed behind Raegna's eyes, wielding his ax or writhing beneath her. Gold eyes beheld her with such focus, reflecting firelight from candles, campfires, or horrific blazes. As she tossed in her sleep, he fell to his knees with his back to her. Bright red blood streamed from fresh gashes as the whip cracked. Raegna pulled against invisible hands to reach him. *Don't hurt him.*

"Mama!"

All thought of Bai vanished. Raegna stood in the woods among towering bare trees. The fall leaves were long gone. Cold crawled under her cloak, armor, and clothes. Snowflakes drifted to collect over the earth. Raegna whirled where the voice echoed, pivoting in circles to find her. "Adabelle!"

"*Mama!*" Her voice came from the middle of the forest clearing. Adabelle wept in that man's grasp. The same man Raegna faced in Judr in the wagon.

Thenalious held a fistful of Adabelle's blonde hair. He pressed a knife to the girl's throat, his eyes boring into Raegna with a slate glint. Raegna bared her teeth and unsheathed her sword. "Release her. Now!"

"You couldn't save her before." His voice drawled and filled the silence between the snowflakes. "What makes you think you can now?"

Adabelle screamed when he cut. Raegna's heart plummeted as she lunged. "*Ada!*"

Thenalious dropped the girl's body and braced for Raegna's attack. Her sword disappeared as she swung. He caught her wrist and drove his knife under her belly. Raegna's scream lodged in her throat as the blade's pressure sank into her womb.

"Your husband is next."

Raegna woke, paralyzed on her cot. The tent canvas flapped with a slight breeze. Warrior voices hummed outside with the birdsong. Raegna forced herself to inhale, though her lungs were steel. She pressed a hand over her belly. Still intact. Despite her breaths, tears sprang to her eyes. Raegna sniffled and sat up, shaking off the nightmare.

She kept a hand over the sword hilt at her belt as she walked about the camp. After a breakfast of jerky and soup, she withdrew to the outer trees. Steam rose from her lips when she exhaled, her gaze fixed in Haven's direction. Bai was somewhere through the forest—Gaea willing, alive. Raegna's fingers grazed her stomach where the babe would be.

Going back to Judr was an option. She would be safe with Banu and Jora, awaiting the mercenary army's return and praying Bai would be among them. If he did return, he would know and be glad she'd turned back. If he didn't, he would never know. Not until Gaea told him—and only if he was lifted.

If Raegna didn't stay, what was she meant to do? Wait and pray. She'd come too far to turn back. This babe wasn't so far along, and she could fight with Gittan or Thekla if they insisted. It might not come to a fight for some time—or at all. A siege was only necessary if the men blew their horns. Otherwise, the warriors waited in camp for a plan. How long would that take?

Raegna wasn't meant to wait far beyond camp or a shield wall. Going back wouldn't suit her.

"Shield-Priestess."

Thekla's voice startled Raegna out of a trance. She straightened to attention and turned to the woman clad in leather armor with silver beads decorating her braided hair. Though shadows clung to her eyes, Thekla returned Raegna's gaze with concern. "Are you all right?"

Raegna pitched her shoulders back. "Never better."

The woman frowned, unconvinced. "You looked as if you were recalling a painful memory. I'm sure there are too many of those on this journey."

"You'd be right." Raegna sighed.

"But there are better memories on their way," Thekla added. "Gittan told me your news. Congratulations."

Six years ago, when Raegna announced her first pregnancy, many women in Syden came to say the same thing. Back then, she'd squirmed, but had offered a grateful smile to each of them. Now, in a war camp surrounded by pine and hard, frozen ground, Raegna's heart flipped between excitement and fear.

"Thank you," she forced herself to say as she had in those old days.

"If there is anything you need, let me know," Thekla said. "Before my daughter was born, my first mornings were a lot like yours. Spent bent over a bucket."

Raegna's brow raised. "You have a daughter?"

Thekla smiled and leaned against the trunk of a tree. "Kaja. She's nearly fifteen now. She typically travels with me, but on this journey, I made her stay in Stadt."

"Fifteen."

Thekla shrugged with her arms folded. "I had her when I was young. Some bastard found me in the alleys of Hafelle, and I had no family to protect me, so what did he have to lose?"

Raegna's heart sank. "I'm sorry."

"No, I'm sorry, Shield-Priestess. I've overshared. We all have bad memories to recall. But despite it all, Kaja is my joy, and I've found a sort of freedom in her."

"I know what you mean," Raegna murmured.

"But I'm no inexperienced Maiden," Thekla proclaimed with a smirk. "If there is anything you need, anything at all, you just tell me."

"I appreciate that. But I should be all right, this isn't my first babe. Though there might be something else you could help me with."

Thekla tilted her head, her smile warm against the cold air. "What did you have in mind?"

Raegna's lips pressed into a line. "I hate being a sitting duck. Every day, Bai and Asmund may need our help and we don't know it. I only wish there was a way to ensure they're safe and give them more allies within the wolf's den."

The warrior frowned. "Gittan made her calls. They're doing well."

"As far as we know," Raegna said. "And for now. No, for that night. What if something new has happened? What if they're already dead before they could blow a horn?"

Thekla shifted her weight. "You're an optimistic one."

"Realistic. I can't wait for another round of owl calls. I have to do something."

"I'm not sure what we can do." Thekla settled her hands on her hips above blade hilts. "We can't simply go in and check on them."

Raegna scanned the ground. "No. Not as women."

Thekla's brow furrowed. "You're joking."

"We could." Raegna studied the warrior and her slender frame. High cheekbones and a sharp jaw housed a hard face. Deep, dark-brown eyes stared back at Raegna with fiery disbelief. Raegna's mouth quirked. "Keep our heads low. Our hair back."

"No."

"You know the calls," Raegna said without heed. "We could be another set of eyes. If Bai and Asmund have their trust, we could just mill among them."

"There's no *milling* among them," Thekla protested. "They'll discover us."

"They may already have discovered the men." Raegna straightened. "Gaea forbid, but what if the mission has already failed, and we're just waiting for the next evening to reach them? We could be a second plan. We can understand more about Haven and report to Gittan. The mission would have something to fall back on."

"You—Ugh, you're insane. You're with child."

"I'll decide what I do about that," Raegna told her. "I'll do it. You can stay here and tell Gittan, or you can have my back."

Because, frankly, Raegna knew she could use the support of a more experienced warrior. Thekla must have known it, too. Her jaw set, and she ran a hand over her face. "Sachi, help me. *Fine.* But I'm in charge of disguises. I've had my fair share of pretending to be a tramp, and I've convinced many people before. Let's hope these Haven men are just as drunk."

***

Raegna expected backlash from Gittan, and her eyes flashed as if she might give it, but as Thekla explained how they could support Bai and Asmund and add spies and another hold on Haven, Gittan recoiled. In her massive tent, they stood over the map of Sorelle with Haven marked by a red pawn. Gittan studied it with narrowed eyes as Thekla went on, though the map couldn't be registering in her mind.

When Thekla finished, Gittan sighed and looked at Raegna. The disbelief disappeared. Her expression was stony, and she gazed into Raegna's very core. "You want to help them."

Raegna held her ground. "I can't stay."

A small smile pulled at Gittan's lips. Her eyes softened. "If I didn't know about everything you've done for your village, I would call you crazy. Shield-Priestess. Very well. Just the two of you. Any more and we will be found out. Do what you must. You know as much about the place as I do, based on Asmund's report."

"We might do better to filter in around the wall," Thekla said. "We can't make a scene of ourselves as the men did. We can't draw attention. We would just need to—"

"Mill among them," Raegna teased.

Thekla gave her a sideways glance with a crooked smile. "Yes. We could still have our weapons."

"Find an occupation and always look busy," Gittan told them. "Naleem said every man has a purpose within those walls, and those who laze about are not tolerated. You'll stay close to each other. Find our men, report at nightfall."

Thekla nodded. "Time to make men of ourselves, Shield-Priestess. Ready to see things on the other side?"

Ready for anything.

They went through Bai and Asmund's clothes, packed for the journey from Stadt. Raegna could smell Bai on the shirt she held, folded in one arm. A sharp smoky scent and sweet like the treats he gobbled on Leaf Fall. She smiled and gripped the fabric before Thekla instructed her on how to transform into a man.

They bound their breasts with leather, and the constriction made Raegna ache. Carrying a babe made it far from ideal, but she would endure the faint pain to make her breasts disappear. Bai's scent was overwhelming as she slipped his shirt over her head and a tunic on top. She cinched his pants over her belly and added more winter socks to fill a man's boots. The layers helped against the cold. A wide, thick belt strapped around her waist. When she stood, Raegna set her shoulders back, slipping Bai's ring into a pocket beneath the armor.

Everything was tucked in—she was shorter than Bai. But just by the feeling the clothes gave her, by glancing down at them, she could nearly be a man. Thekla could as well—in Asmund's clothes, adjusted from his slight bulk to her thinner build. Raegna smiled at her as the warrior studied their attire.

"This will do," Thekla affirmed. "Just one more thing."

They braided their hair as close to their heads as they could. Some Haven men wore theirs long, but Raegna's and Thekla's would surely reveal them. When one couldn't reach so far behind her head, the other helped pin the locks in place. Winter caps covered their heads, and then Raegna squared her shoulders. "I'm fooling even myself."

Thekla smirked. "It's a performance. I like it now and again."

Raegna watched the way she walked, her feet falling in a different stride as she retrieved their weapons to add to their disguise. A stronger stride with a disregard for others. No, not for others, but for their thoughts.

In the woods, a raven called over the trees, and Raegna practiced stealth behind Thekla. Her sword clung to her back, and the hilt tapped her cap. Each deep breath rose as steam and soaked in the rising sun's glow. Thekla navigated based on Gittan's map, and sometimes she would stop to reroute and follow the woods. Raegna could do nothing but try to keep quiet.

"Tents," Thekla whispered so softly her voice could have been a falling leaf. Raegna followed her gaze. The sunlight touched tent arches, and Raegna blinked at them, her heart lurching. The tents weren't their own, and they were so close.

Smoke rose in several places. Movement shifted between close-quartered tents, and in the distance, a red barn peeked over them. Male voices grumbled, and Raegna's stomach dropped. Was this really her great idea?

"What if they recognize us?" she whispered.

"Second thoughts?" Thekla asked. "Don't speak. Don't look them in the eye. Stay close. Strut. Head down. I'll talk. All right?"

Don't speak. Head down. Strut. Essentially, act like Asmund. Let Thekla be Bai. Their clothes may have been misplaced, but Raegna nodded, recalling every movement of her timid friend.

Raegna followed Thekla into Haven, and her fists trembled. *Deep breath.*

The tents hovered over them as Thekla trailed the gravel paths blemished by snow piles. Raegna kept her head down, tracking Thekla's heels and Haven in her periphery. The men remained in their tents, bent over weapons or food, and grumbling to each other. Raegna allowed a peek between tent flaps when she could, but flushed when these grisly beasts rose to dress, exposed themselves, or—in one tent—intercoursed.

Raegna swallowed hard and kept wide eyes on Thekla's stride. They could do what they wanted, but Raegna prayed for the decency to close the tent to the rest of the world. But much like Thekla, the men who walked the paths did so without regard for others or their thoughts. A couple sneered at Thekla and Raegna, but did nothing. Each look sent Raegna into a fleeting panic, but each man moved on, and she remained near Thekla.

Was this how Asmund truly existed? Afraid of others with his head down. It contradicted everything Raegna was taught. Head up, chin level, eyes forward. A woman of privilege and renown. Nothing to fear. Her security was in the mass of women who would come to her aid.

Asmund had nothing and no one. Bai had nothing and no one.

Did Bai feel the same as this?

Other men would not come to his aid. They had not spoken up when he was flogged. Neither had the women. Only Raegna had found the courage to cry out. Because Bai couldn't.

They won't listen. He'd sobbed it when she'd knelt before him in Turid's house.

"Boys." The harsh grunt came a few feet away and jolted Raegna to the bone. She stared at a wiry man who stomped up to them. He was a frightening, spindly creature with only a vest to cover his chest from the cold. A few brown hairs floated above his head as he stopped before Thekla. "Where are you off to?"

Thekla looked him in the eye with her chin down. Her voice came lower than Raegna thought possible with a breathy husk. "Looking for work. We've finished this morning's chores."

Raegna fought to keep her head down, wanting to see the man's face should he not believe the disguises.

He hardly hesitated. "Thenalious wants a feast for his new warrior. Go to the kitchens and ask for work."

Thenalious. Raegna's fear burned into fury. Her teeth clamped down, and her nose wrinkled.

"Yes, sir," Thekla said, starting for the great house with a glance at the landscape. Raegna turned to follow her, but her chest tightened at the sound of the man's voice.

"Fine swords you boys got for yourselves."

Raegna's throat bobbed, but Thekla straightened. "Thank you. Got them off a couple of dumb broads and held onto them since. We're grateful for Haven's opportunities—we don't get outside, so we'll value these gifts."

Raegna breathed and nodded, tapping her pommel behind her head.

The man smiled and cackled. "Good boys. What are your names? I'm not sure I've met either of you."

"Thekr," Thekla answered immediately.

Only one name brewed in Raegna's memory. Her voice cracked, but she spoke to imitate Bai. "Felik."

"Well done, Thekr and Felik." The man waved them off. "On your way, then. You can show your gratitude by serving your lord."

"Of course." Finally, they were free of him. Thekla guided Raegna toward the great house that loomed over the camp, towering with two stories. Raegna dragged a sigh and studied the elk skull on the arch, releasing nerves in a shudder. Much like Asmund.

"I thought you would choose something like Raegna," Thekla muttered. "Felik?"

"It's my father's name," Raegna explained, a small pain puncturing her sternum. "He was lifted when I was little."

Thekla offered a small smile. "He protects you even now."

Raegna had not thought of him in a long time. Her mother had such a presence …

Did he cower as she did? As Bai and Asmund did? Her danger would be immeasurable if she revealed herself in a place that served men. No one would listen when she cried out, and she would only have herself, maybe Thekla. There were women trapped somewhere here, but they could not come to her aid for fear of the monsters that surrounded them.

Raegna braced against a slam of pain as if a shield rammed into her chest. She was the monster to Bai. She, her mother, and all others. The men in Haven were her monsters. Only if she remained quiet and complacent, low and out of the way, would she be safe.

You never have to be afraid. Bai wasn't her monster. Despite the guilt that ran through her for their Leaf Fall night, Raegna refused to be his monster any longer.

Don't be afraid. I'm here.

CHAPTER 27

HADWIN

ASMUND WAS NOT AS good with children as Hadwin had hoped. The boys seemed to sense this before he did, running and jumping about their new caregiver to test his limits. Asmund shrank away until his back reached the wall. Most of the boys ignored him then, chasing each other while others frowned in disappointment that Asmund wouldn't play along.

Hadwin pulled him to the cradles. "Don't mind them. They can be bullies. Here, will you keep Else occupied while I take care of the others?"

He trusted him to hold the tiny girl. Not many could mess up holding a babe. Asmund went rigid, grasping Else so she lay lopsided. Hadwin stopped and raised an eyebrow at them. Asmund gave him a desperate stare while Else gazed between the two of them, with her large, brown eyes blinking.

"On second thought," Hadwin said, scooping Else, "the boys aren't so bad when you get used to them."

He instructed Asmund to watch over them with a few simple rules in mind: put an end to roughhousing, bed-jumping, bullying, and anything else that might put their lives in danger. Thus, Asmund leaned against the windowsill and watched them play. For the rest of the day, he didn't do much else.

Hadwin had thought of sending him to the old barn to take Else to her mother, despite how uncomfortable he appeared around the toddlers and babes. But Oberon arrived on schedule to take her instead. On every visit, he glowered at Asmund, who cowered under his gaze.

Over dinner, every question Hadwin could think of for him swirled through his mind. How did he and this mysterious friend of his find Haven? How did this friend know how to battle with weapons like the more seasoned men in camp? Which village did they come from? Why did they leave?

Why come to Haven of their own free will?

Asmund obliviously ate dinner alongside the boys while Hadwin puzzled. For being lost in the woods, he had a rather average appetite, nibbling on cheese and carefully picking bones out of the fish.

Hadwin showed him how to put the boys to bed and how some of the younger ones preferred to be tucked in. They protested they would rather have Hadwin do the job. The babes needed to be rocked to sleep, and Hadwin placed Kili, the oldest toddler, in Asmund's arms.

"Just hold him like this," Hadwin instructed. "Rock back and forth. You were a child once, yes? You at least know how this is done."

Steadily rocking, unsure of himself, Asmund made no other movement. Kili wriggled before the motion lulled him.

Hadwin sighed. "I suppose you didn't have children before, did you?"

Asmund's blue eyes fixed on him before falling to the floor.

"I didn't have any either," Hadwin pointed out. "I lived with my brother and his wife, and they had many children. Cadoc, here, is my nephew. We're all that's left."

Asmund looked up once more. "My—my wife was killed. She was going to have a babe."

Hadwin winced at the twist between his lungs. "I'm sorry. Truly, I am. I never should have said anything."

"You didn't know."

"Still. Here, let's put these little ones to bed. I'll show you where we sleep."

He offered him the second bed in the caregiver's room, the bed he'd claimed when Naleem was still there. Asmund plopped down onto it, running a hand along the blanket. Hadwin settled Cadoc down before curling up beside him.

"I'll wake you up early to start again," he told Asmund across the room. "Goodnight."

Asmund nodded and turned in. Hadwin closed his eyes and slowed his breaths to feign sleep, though his mind whirled.

Sometime in the middle of the night, he drifted off to an owl's hooting, but he stirred when Asmund's frame squeaked as he slipped out of bed.

The floorboards creaked as he reached the door, but Hadwin did not open his eyes. Every fiber in his body urged him to sit up and ask just where Asmund thought he was going. But he might be on his way to relieve himself or find water. Something harmless. Still, even those simple nightly routines could raise the councilmen's suspicions.

Asmund shut the door behind him with a quiet click. When he returned several minutes later, Hadwin paid the little venture no mind.

When the great house slowly came to life at the break of dawn, Hadwin forced Asmund out of bed, and the new caregiver continued the day with drooping eyes, a little unnerved, though not as timid as he'd been initially.

Oberon appeared for Else, glowering as usual with Gael and Vihn at his side. Asmund ducked away from him and put his attention on the rest of the boys instead. Though caution prickled Hadwin's skin, he assured himself Asmund had every right to be nervous around Oberon.

Attempting to offer Else to him, Hadwin paused when Oberon nodded to the door. "I'll speak with you alone."

Hadwin sighed and followed him into the hall. *Alone* was a debatable word choice since Gael and Vihn waited for their father to proceed with their new routine, and Else cooed in Hadwin's arms.

"You've spent the night with him," Oberon stated. "What do you think?"

"Of him?" Hadwin shrugged. "He's shy, and I'm not sure why they wanted him to be a caregiver. He's never taken care of children before."

"Neither have previous caregivers. What else?"

Hadwin rolled his eyes. "He's not the fighting kind like this friend you've talked about. He mentioned a wife who was pregnant, but she was killed. I assume during a raid."

Hadwin thought about mentioning his leaving last night, but decided against it. The venture could have been completely innocent, but Oberon might lose his mind over it.

"Is that all?" the councilman urged.

"Well, yes," Hadwin quipped. "I think he's just another broken man who's found his way to Haven. Who *chose* to stay for some reason."

"Exactly. That hasn't happened since—Well, I was one of the last, and I was barely sixteen. And someone found me. They used to recruit us."

Haven's history had never crossed Hadwin's mind before, nor would it usually pique his interest. Imagining men and boys being recruited to live under this tyranny in the woods was more difficult to believe than the camp itself. "And these two newcomers weren't recruited. They found this place on their own."

"So they say." Oberon took Else from him. "The second one is still alive, chained outside the house. Sigmund willing, he'll starve or freeze to death."

The second man might have been the one to keep a sharp eye on, not Asmund. Though how this timid mouse could have traveled with this mysterious beast, Hadwin didn't know. He wouldn't bother to make such a fuss about Asmund's every move, no matter how much Oberon might insist on it.

That was until dinner, when they ate alongside the rest of the boys. He tried to be nonchalant about it, but Asmund snuck portions of his dinner under the table as if he were feeding a dog. None of Haven's dogs were in the dining hall, so Hadwin raised an eyebrow at him.

"You will eat again," he reassured him. "If nothing else, they give us three square meals. You won't go hungry."

Asmund blinked incredulously at him before saying, "I get hungry at night."

"Oh." *Is that why you left last night?* But Hadwin couldn't bring himself to say it out loud, not when the plan had been to fake sleep. Just another simple reason for Asmund's leave.

Until he left again, even though his midnight snack was in the caregiver's room. Hadwin peeked through a slitted eyelid in the dark, but could barely make out Asmund's figure creeping across the floor and then leaving to shut the door behind him. He returned much quicker than he had the night before, flustered and growling under his breath.

Strange.

If Oberon demanded another report, Hadwin wondered what he would give him. Asmund didn't seem to be a threat to the boys, but that didn't mean he couldn't be in the long run.

The next morning, Hadwin tossed the idea around in his head, but Oberon did not pull him aside.

Asmund supervised the boys, sitting on the windowsill and allowing his legs to kick out. Despite Hadwin's scrutinous watch, the day went on without a hitch, though Hadwin prepared to catch Asmund in another nightly leave.

In their bedroom, Hadwin kept Cadoc close as he made their bed ready for the night. Asmund sat on the edge of his bed to make himself comfortable when a knock came at the door. Dread filled Hadwin to the brim. Only councilmen knocked on this door, and Oberon was too busy caring for his sons as of late. It opened without a welcome.

Hadwin's shoulders tensed when Thenalious walked in, confident and smug as ever, with his head high and a smirk within his short, black beard. Cadoc scurried behind his uncle, and Hadwin hardly felt him bump against his arm and back. The man beside Thenalious made Hadwin's heart seize.

Bai?

Bai stood at the threshold, gold eyes lighting on Hadwin before he resumed a neutral face again. His sharp cheeks and brow held scratches and bruises. A bandage was wrapped around his head, flattening shaggy blond locks above his ears. He balanced on one leg, holding the other up. Dressed in a Haven warrior's leathers over a thick winter tunic, pants, and boots, an ax hung at his hip.

Hadwin clamped his mouth shut to keep from gaping in front of Thenalious. If the leader of Haven noticed his shock at all, he didn't show it. In his panic, Hadwin studied Thenalious and recognized the casual stance, with his shoulders relaxed and his chin high. He gave Bai a wry smile and gestured to the room. "I promised your friend would be safe."

Bai's attention flicked to Asmund. "You're well?"

Asmund nodded, looking from beneath his brow at him, to Thenalious, and back.

"He's been a fine caregiver while you were away," Thenalious assured. "This is their room. It's best to keep them near the boys. We treat them well so long as they remain in line and know their place is beside our sons." He looked at Hadwin. "Right, caregiver?"

Hadwin's stomach twisted. As much as he wanted to steal another glance at Bai, he inclined his head. "Yes, lord."

Thenalious hummed with a smirk on his face and turned to Bai. "We'll see if I can allow you with your caregiver *friend* on occasion. You both have yet to earn our trust."

"Of course." Bai pivoted to follow him out of the room but looked over his shoulder at Hadwin and Asmund with an encouraging smile before the door shut behind him.

Hadwin's heart drummed in his throat, and his world tilted. He sat on the edge of his bed, so Cadoc had to crawl out of his way. Bai was in Haven. But Bai was dead in Syden. There'd been no way of knowing. Hadwin had just assumed—because Bai had never appeared in the captive line to be taken to Haven—that he must have fought and died for his daughter and wife. How had he survived? How had he gotten in? Why did he get in? How did—

Hadwin's gaze fixed on Asmund across the room, and the timid caregiver jerked. His shoulders curled, and he dipped his head.

"How do you know Bai?" Hadwin asked slowly, his voice rumbling deep within his chest.

Asmund gripped the bedsheets. "I—I met him ... well, his wife, in Judr."

Hadwin's eyes narrowed. "In Judr? How did they get to Judr? They're both of Syden. They would have burned with it."

Asmund shrugged, shaking his head, and whispered, "He and Raegna came to Judr to tell us what happened. Our Matriarch didn't listen. My wife was the Matriarch's sister, and she befriended Raegna. I didn't know Bai then. We fled the attack, and she helped us, but went back to him and their daughter. That's when ... when I lost my wife."

She was lost to the raid, then. Though Hadwin's heart paused to ache for him, he couldn't help how his mind whirled. "Bai and Raegna survived in Judr, too?"

Asmund nodded. "Raegna lifted my wife and—my son. She's a priestess because she lifted Syden."

She lifted Syden. A breath fled from Hadwin's lips. Pinar was in Heimelle. She was there with her daughters to greet Dakarai. Tears gathered beneath his eyes, and they stalled Asmund's story. He studied Hadwin with his brow upturned. "It's all right."

Hadwin blinked to keep the tears from rolling down his cheeks. "I'm sorry. I thought ... I thought my family was in—We didn't know if they would ever be lifted."

Then his chest throbbed. Naleem couldn't have been lifted wherever Thenalious had taken him. Hadwin shut his eyes and bit his lip hard as Asmund went on.

"No apologies," he murmured. "She lifted the entire village. In Judr, she brought me to the healer's house where she and Bai stayed. I ... I met Naleem."

Hadwin's eyes snapped open, blurred with burning tears that seared them against the open air. His throat closed as he choked out. "What?"

Asmund forced a small smile. "I met Naleem at the healer's house. Raegna saved him during the attack on Judr."

Naleem is alive. Hadwin's mouth hung open. "Naleem?"

"Yes. He's all right. We all traveled to Stadt to take the new Matriarch's message of the attacks to Vakkar Hold. Raegna, Bai, Naleem, and me. The Duchess found us on the road. She took us to the Queen, and we told the whole court what happened. But even they and the High Council wouldn't hear us. But the Council allowed a few Maidens to investigate and speak to Judr's Matriarch."

The words seeped into Hadwin, but he couldn't fathom them at once. "Where is Naleem?"

Asmund's head bobbed, and his small smile remained. "In Vakkar Hold. He stayed behind for the winter. We want to bring you both back to him."

Naleem is alive. A broken sob escaped his throat, and Hadwin gritted his teeth, holding himself rigid. Cadoc curled beside him, still too terrified of Thenalious' intrusion, but he pressed his chin to Hadwin's shoulder. "Uncle Hadwin?"

Hadwin wrapped an arm around him and pulled him close. It took a few breaths to collect himself, bracing against the pulsing pain beneath his heart. *Naleem is alive.*

"If the Council sent Maidens," he started, his voice ragged, "why are you and Bai here?"

Asmund glanced at the floor. "There are Maidens outside the walls. Maidens and warriors paid for by the Queen. We disobeyed the Council's order and came here to bring Haven down. End this."

Hadwin shook his head as his core opened in a silent, triumphant scream. Yes! "But how?"

"We're figuring that out," Asmund said. "Anything you can tell me, I can report back to the warriors. We're here to help."

Thank Sigmund. Thank Sachi and Gaea. Hadwin trembled as another round of sobs built within him. "This doesn't feel real."

"It is," Asmund assured. "But we have to act as if nothing is happening. Bai has Thenalious distracted, and that's good. We'll see if Haven has weaknesses and do something from there."

"I've been watching them for so long." Hadwin wiped tears away with the back of his hand. "They—they could be taken by night. They are so confident in themselves; there are guards, but they are lazy. I've heard once they sleep at their posts, but I'm not sure how true that is. Maybe Bai can see for sure. And there are woods behind the camp that have no walls—"

Asmund raised a hand. "It's all right. Maybe Bai can look into that."

Hadwin chuckled and shut his eyes to gather his thoughts. Naleem was alive and in Vakkar Hold. The thought was enough to make him weep. Poor Cadoc didn't need him losing his control, and neither did Asmund. Neither did Bai. Hadwin dried his eyes and set his shoulders back. "Thank you. Truly, thank you. I wish I could have spoken to Bai."

"It's all right. You might just."

Hadwin's skin crawled as he imagined Bai walking beside Thenalious, being shown the great house. Oberon's words tumbled through his head. *I've not seen him this love-struck since your brother.*

"We need to keep an eye on Bai," Hadwin blurted. "Thenalious favors men. That's not the problem, but he's dangerous. I think he wants Bai close, and he would hurt him if he wanted."

Asmund's eyes sharpened. A muscle popped above his jawline. "We'll tell Bai."

Every ugly glare Thenalious had made flashed behind Hadwin's eyes. So different from the cool, teasing friendliness he'd offered first. What he'd said he did to Naleem ... was it true? Naleem was alive. What had happened that allowed Naleem an escape?

Tears came again, and Hadwin choked on another cry.

Asmund shook his head. "It's all right."

"It's just ... This is too good to ... If Thenalious finds you out, he'll kill you both. He's Fan himself."

Asmund shifted his weight, and the bed creaked beneath him. "We'll be careful. Gaea willing, Bai will kill him first."

Gaea willing. Bai could end Thenalious, and Haven would be in ruins. Hadwin would be free with Cadoc and even Maura. The women and boys could find better lives far from these dark woods. Hadwin would see his brother again.

But it wasn't guaranteed yet. A raven's call echoed in Hadwin's memory, and his mission was still set.

Pretend.

Chapter 28

Bai

*H*ADWIN AND CADOC ARE *well. Asmund is with them.* Bai kept a blank face as Thenalious shut the caregiver's door behind them. Seeing Hadwin was enough to split Bai's chest in half. He was a face from another lifetime, and he stood just a few feet away, whole and alive. Naleem would be overjoyed, but there was still a long way to go before Hadwin and Cadoc reached Vakkar Hold.

Bai squared a look on Thenalious, who gave him an arched eyebrow. His skin crawled, and his stomach wrenched, but Bai had to keep the peace. *Be patient. Watch.*

"So you've seen your man." Thenalious pointed down the first hallway, going right. "Bedrooms go there and there." Then left. "Down this hallway are the rest. Mine is at the very end."

Bai looked to the end of the hallway, where a set of double doors stood with iron knobs. A dark presence hovered over the frames and down the wood panels that made Bai shudder despite himself. "Good to know."

A soft chuckle came from Thenalious' nose. "Dinner will be ready soon. Let's get something to eat. You ought to sit beside us."

Down the stairs, Bai huffed with each step but kept a pace behind Thenalious. He distracted himself from the stabbing in his bandaged leg by recalling Haven's layout. The place was simple enough, and the easiest point of attack might be from the back woods, but that would be for Gittan and the others to decide.

Bai's stride faltered, his thoughts floating to Raegna and what she could be doing. He held her in his mind, staring back at him through the snowfall. He hadn't exactly followed her wish on being safe, but he might still return to her in a few pieces. He just needed to stay near Thenalious, play this strange game of push and pull, and know Haven as well as he knew Syden. All while keeping Hadwin, Cadoc, and Asmund at arm's length.

"Keep up, Grizzly," Thenalious said over his shoulder, his voice lilting.

Bai's lip curled, and he inhaled. *Be patient. Watch.*

The dining hall filled with nearly every Haven man, draining Bai of any patience as he waded behind Thenalious through the mass. The men broke a path for their leader, but closed it before Bai. He had to shove and glare to earn the space, and it didn't take much for any of them to stand down. The ugly scowls were not enough to deter him. The hall was far different from Vakkar Hold's, full of shouts, booming laughter, scrounging over plates, and men downing goblets.

When Bai thought he might throw his ax into the next man who tried his patience and took up his path, a small boy knocked into his shoulder. Bai snarled and whirled on him. Two black, flashing eyes turned his muscles to stone.

Bai's breath caught in his throat. Raegna's face stared back at him with her mouth flat and her brow straight above those fierce eyes. She wasn't quite herself, dressed in the clothes he had left behind in Gittan's camp. Her sword hilt peeked over her shoulder, the same petaled pommel that came with them from Syden to Judr to Stadt. A furred cap covered her hair, so it seemed she had cut it.

As soon as he found her, she turned and pushed through the crowd in the opposite direction. Bai regained control of his limbs and traced her stride.

What have you done?

"Grizzly," Thenalious called over the noise. "Come along."

She couldn't be here. Bai turned for him and obeyed with his ribs tight. Why was she here? She couldn't be here. This wasn't part of the plan. She couldn't be here.

Bai still had to feign a cool nature while his mind ricocheted in his skull. He followed Thenalious to a long table full of councilmen. Each gave Bai a nasty look as he sat in the empty chair Thenalious offered beside him. Bai swallowed as he squeezed between Thenalious and Wyn. The food wafted its caramelized meats and sharp spices, begging Bai to obey his appetite. But his stomach floated at the thought of Raegna. He added a few things to his plate and scanned the horde of men for her.

Where are you? Why are you here?

"You must be hungry after all you've been through," Thenalious said.

Bai tore into a pheasant leg and gave him a sideways glance as he chewed. Thenalious chuckled.

Reynold set his mug of ale down with a hard thud. "Tell us about the time you spent in Sorelle's hills. Let alone how you learned to use that ax."

A line creased the bridge of Thenalious' nose. Bai shared a similar irritation. He was busy searching for Raegna, but his efforts would bring their attention to her. He had a game to play. Bai straightened and set a bare leg bone on his plate.

"Despite the loss of our people and our families," he started, "it was like an extended fishing trip. That's what we lived on, along with some rabbits and squirrels. Whatever we could get our hands on. It wasn't until the temperatures dropped that we figured we ought to search for better shelter. I suggested we find where the invaders went to lick their wounds after failing to take Judr."

While his men glowered and Reynold's nails dug into the tabletop, Thenalious gave Bai an unappreciative side-eye.

Bai gave a relaxed shrug. "Not that I blame any of you. What Matriarch Viona lacked in providing her people with a decent crop and economy she made up for in warriors and law. Though her people could go hungry, they could go hungry while being protected, blaming their problems on the presence of men to justify more warriors."

"That much is true," Thenalious muttered, swirling the ale in his goblet.

"The Matriarch wouldn't allow men to carry blades of any kind," Reynold added. "How is it you know how to wield that ax?"

"Special talent," Bai told him. "There were plenty of warriors to watch and learn from. I would practice on friends if we had the time."

"The same *friend* you brought with you?" Thenalious asked.

Several little memories of sparring with Asmund in the Maiden's hall spotted the backs of Bai's eyes. "Naturally."

"We could use a warrior's hold over the caregivers," Thenalious thought aloud. "We've had some trouble with our current nanny. All the more reason to bring you into the house. The more eyes on him, the fewer problems he is likely to cause."

What exactly had Hadwin been up to around this place? "The same caregiver who's been sneaking around and sticking his cock where he shouldn't?"

Oberon tensed on the other side of the table, but did not lift his gaze.

Thenalious nodded. "That timid friend of yours ought to slow him down. It wouldn't hurt to have you on his tail, too."

"My lord," Oberon spoke up, "I have the caregiver under control."

"And this bitch doesn't need to be inside these walls," Reynold growled.

Bai resisted a glower and focused on scooping a spoonful of roasted root into his mouth. He took the moment to look across the hall once more. *Where is she?*

"You have better duties to attend to than hauling bastard children to the cows on the other side of camp," Thenalious snarled at Oberon. Then he turned on Reynold. "Honestly, cowardice and jealousy never suited you."

Oberon lowered his head, and Reynold shot up from his seat, swiping his platter over the side of the table before skulking out of the dining hall. Bai hardly had time to give the tantrum a second thought. He had Raegna to find and a game to play. But if he could keep Reynold jealous and Oberon on edge, the councilmen could snap at each other's throats, and Haven would destroy itself. He retracted his gaze from the hall and took a swig of ale.

"I couldn't get in the way of the operations around here," Bai lied. "If there is a better post—"

"No, you'll guard the halls tonight," Thenalious ordered and drained his goblet. "Keep that caregiver in line while I keep my men in theirs."

Bai nodded, taking the win with a hidden smirk. He picked each table apart but couldn't find Raegna amid the great beasts. His dinner churned in his belly, and he sipped another sampling of ale.

Where are you?

Chapter 29

Raegna

"I saw Bai."

Thekla sat on a stump, hunched and sharpening her knife outside a tent for stray young men. But the two women kept their distance as the boys settled in for the night, talking among each other. They remained near the fire that still flickered for late-night goers. Thekla raised an eyebrow at Raegna with her back to the tent and the firelight flashing over her deep features. "I did too."

"He's with Thenalious," Raegna whispered.

Thekla sighed and straightened, steam rising from her mouth. "Sit down, Felik. There's no need to guard."

The name brought a warmth that fended off the frigid air. Raegna sat on the adjacent stump and stared at the fire. "Should we meet with him?"

"No." Thekla's knife scraped the wet stone with a soft shriek. "He's fine where he is."

"He's injured."

"He's on the mend. They're healing him."

"But if he's hurt, Asmund could be, too." Raegna leaned in her seat. "We ought to make sure they are all right."

"We ought to stay low," Thekla corrected. "Meeting with them would just draw attention to ourselves. We're doing well as it is. I think we could be here another day, maybe two, and sneak back out to tell Gittan what we've seen. Bai has their leader where we need him—looking the other way. Asmund said he found the brother and son. We need only to attack."

Raegna squirmed. "Bai saw me, too. He knows I'm here."

Thekla shrugged. "That's fine."

"We can tell him all this so we are on the same page," Raegna said. "He might be preoccupied with worry and can't focus. We can tell him to stay on the path and assure him we're here to help."

"I'm sure he's a clever man. He can figure it out himself."

Raegna huffed and wrapped her arms around herself. "He'll be beside himself. I saw the look on his face."

"Getting close to him would only ruin things."

"Not if we had a reason." Raegna envisioned Haven as she'd mapped it in their day's exploration. She stared at the dirt between her boots, laying the map out before her. "Perhaps I saw something in the woods that a warrior could help investigate. We could swap orders between us for the good of the camp. Maybe a change of guard."

"You're staying with me, Shield-Priestess," Thekla hissed.

"How did Gittan make those calls?" Raegna thought aloud. "Like this?"

She layered her hands into fists with a mouthpiece between her thumb knuckles. Raegna blew, making a hushed whistle between her palms.

Thekla pointed her knife at her over the fire. "Stop that! You'll attract attention."

Raegna unfurled her hands. "There must be some way to reach him."

"Not tonight," Thekla told her. "Tonight we will sleep in that tent and play man. Tomorrow, we keep up the charade and scout the place. Am I clear?"

Raegna shuffled her boots in the dirt before she hovered her hands above the fire. "Yes."

Thekla shook her head. "You are something, Shield-Priestess."

With one cot left in the tent, Thekla let Raegna have it to keep up playing man. Raegna wanted to give it up for her, but decided against it. Thekla had to believe she would rest comfortably and not break the agreement between them. But Raegna had to reach Bai somehow. It wouldn't be strange for a boy to be looking for a warrior such as Bai, would it? If assistance was requested for something in the barn, or a second look at an animal in the woods.

Raegna slipped from the cot and tiptoed from the tent, snores and mumbling dreams lifting around her. The cold air greeted her outside, and she took an icy breath before she ventured down the dark paths. Voices rumbled along the way, and fires still glowed outside tents. How could any of them get things done without sleep?

Though playing man had meant keeping her head down, Raegna leveled her sight on the path ahead. She made a quiet hoot between her hands to encourage herself. When an unfamiliar noise echoed from a tent or a dog barked at her, her heart skipped a beat. A wandering cat leaped from a tent arch, and she jumped, holding a scream with a sharp gasp. The furry creature didn't give her a passing glance as it dashed off.

"Spooked, boy?" a deep voice asked from behind her.

Raegna turned and regretted it. Two men lumbered at a slow pace toward her. They were shadows within the darkness and the faint firelight throughout the camp. A chill ran down her spine, and not from the cold. *Keep your mouth shut.*

They were much bigger than her, with broad chests and shoulders, and one was heavier with a wide belly and stalky legs. Those were the only details Raegna could make out before she reached for her sword. Her fingers grazed it, and the men stopped.

"You are spooked," the same one said. He was the one with a triangle torso, his shoulders tapering down to a thin waist and hips. He rolled the thick shoulders with toned arms that reached for an ax at his belt and outstretched a hand to her. "Don't worry. We're all brothers."

Raegna made her voice as low as she could while she quaked. "Stay back."

"I'd hate to take that sword from you." The two men split to circle her. "You know what happens to you little ones who explore at night. Come on. No fight, and we'll give you something worthwhile when it's over."

Raegna's fingers tightened around the hilt, and the blade grated the scabbard before footsteps approached behind her. A familiar frame stepped between her and the men. Blond hair absorbed what little light there was, and an ax glinted with a far thinner edge than the stranger's.

Bai snarled with his fist around the ax haft. "Get back."

The men halted, and curled lips revealed teeth. "Back off. We saw him first."

"And we'll be the last thing you see if you don't go." Bai stood his ground and pulled the ax from his belt. "Get back or I sharpen my blade with your skulls."

The men scoffed and grumbled insults, but shuffled off. Raegna released a breath and cracked a smile when Bai turned. It disappeared when she took in his scowl. He reached her in a stride and took her arm. "Don't speak. Not yet."

Raegna wrestled against his hold, irritated and unsettled by the nerves that coursed over her skin at his touch. Though he acted rough, his fingers merely grazed her sleeve. He led her through the dark, keeping a distance from the great house and dodging fires. Raegna stumbled to keep up with his long gait despite his limping, and cursed under her breath. "Slow down."

"A little farther." Bai took them through the trees just outside of camp before he whirled her to face him.

Raegna shoved his light grasp away. "Enough of that!"

Bai glared at her. "What are you *doing*?"

"Don't talk to me like that!" she snapped. "I'm here to help you. I believe I'm owed a thank you."

Bai broke in a hushed chuckle. "Is that what you would call this? Helping? Raegna, what possessed you to do this? We have everything under control. Now you would sabotage the whole thing by stealing my clothes?"

"This isn't sabotage. Gittan, Thekla, and I agreed to this. I was worried they would find you out. If you were discovered, then we would still prevail. Now that I've found you, you can keep that devil occupied. Asmund can guard Hadwin, and Thekla and I can report back to Gittan the right moment to strike."

"You're insane, Raegna," Bai hissed. "You'll get caught. They *hate* women. If they find you—"

"They won't." Raegna's scarred palm opened to him. "I'll be all right."

"Yes, maybe if you don't wander the place like a lost puppy," Bai countered. "You could have been caught just now! They would have—and if I hadn't—"

"They didn't, and you did. Even if you hadn't shown up, I could fight. Gittan trained me too."

Bai's teeth gnashed, and he turned from her, catching himself on his bad leg. "*Gaea*, Raegna."

The tension fizzled between them, and she looked him over. So far from any light, he was darker than the shadows of the other men. He was the darkness, shaking in place as he breathed through his anger. His breath was like smoke against the trees. Did she dare to make matters worse now that she finally had him in front of her?

"You secured yourself among them?" she asked.

Bai clicked his tongue. "Yes. Thenalious and I have ourselves right where we want each other. There's something he must think he can get from me. He knows who I am to an extent. He ... he remembers Ada."

Raegna's heart molded into steel, driving through her chest with its weight. "I hope he does."

Gold irises caught hers, glowing against the snow patches beneath the trees. "He'll remember you."

"I hope that, too."

Bai held her gaze before he sighed. "Maybe it is a good idea to have the extra help. But you can't stay long. You have to stay out of the way."

"Thekla wants to leave within a day or two," Raegna assured. "Haven is simple enough to bring something back to Gittan. We can strike before you and Asmund are hurt."

"We'll be fine."

"I don't trust Thenalious. He wouldn't look away from you like a cat and a mouse."

Bai huffed. "Well, this mouse is very aware of the cat. And he needs to get back to his hole soon."

Don't go yet. "Bai. I need to say something."

He looked at her, and Raegna froze over as if she had become one of the trees, ready to collect icicles through the winter. "Bai, I—I'm sorry for what happened at Leaf Fall. It shouldn't have."

Gold irises sharpened. "What happened?"

Raegna's lips parted, her head swimming at the genuine question that he posed. The steel around her heart melted, and the heat traveled up her throat. "You … You don't remember. Gaea, Bai, I—I'm so sorry."

He cocked his head. "Why are you sorry?"

Raegna choked. "Because I—I wasn't in my right mind, and I wanted to—We were talking about Ada, and I thought too far ahead. I asked and you asked and I remember we agreed, but Sachi, help me, if you don't remember—"

"We …" His mellowed tone halted her, and it dragged out as stiff as the ground beneath them. "Did we truly?"

Raegna bit her lip. "Yes. You don't remember at all."

"No. No, I don't. Did—did I hurt you?"

The sob caught Raegna off guard. "No. No, you didn't. You would never hurt me."

Silence passed between them that not even the wind broke. Raegna shook her head. "You're not upset?"

"Well, I don't remember." Bai dug into the dirt with a boot toe. "I … I don't really know what to think. So long as I didn't hurt you."

"No, you didn't. Ugh, it's fuzzy, but you didn't. I don't know exactly what happened. And I had hoped we—"

"You hoped we what?"

Raegna's gut folded. "I had hoped we weren't successful."

"Successful?"

He might drag her all the way back to Gittan if she told him. But Raegna had made it this far, and they could both be gone tomorrow. "I'm with child again."

Bai stared with his eyes wide. He staggered and caught himself on his bad leg. A rough gasp raced between his teeth, and Raegna stepped forward. "Bai."

"I'm fine," he growled, finding his balance. He turned on her, his gaze flicking to her belly. "Raegna, what are you thinking? You *can't* be here!"

"Hush. I'll do as I wish."

"You would put your babe's life at risk for this?" he went on. "After losing Adabelle? Maybe I didn't hurt you this time. Maybe I did, and you're saving my feelings. But after Ada, Raegna, you can't do this."

"What?" Tears lurched in Raegna's eyes with Adabelle's name on his tongue so frequent and quick. "No, Bai. You didn't do anything wrong. You never did anything wrong."

"What is it, then? Please, if you would rather have me out of the picture completely when this is all over, you can. I'll leave this time. I'm not bound to you anymore—you told me that. I'll leave or I'll die here. Just please go back somewhere safe."

"Hush." Raegna clamped her hands under his jawline and held him in place. He froze like a stone beneath her touch, and his fists unclenched at his sides, his fingers straight. Raegna's heart raced, but she held him. "I promise you did not hurt me. You never hurt me, Bai."

Bai's lip quivered, and the gold shone beneath tears. "But ... but I woke up and you hated me like you did. Like you do."

"No," Raegna wept. "I don't hate you, Bai." She blinked as her body jolted at the words. "No, I don't hate you. I don't hate you, and you didn't do anything wrong. You never did anything wrong, all right?"

Bai sniffled, and his hands hovered in the air, as if unsure if he should touch her. "All right."

Raegna grasped his arms instead, clenching his sleeves. "I'm not risking the babe because of that, either. I just want to see the end of this. I want a world for this child where these monsters don't exist. Don't you?"

His fingertips grazed her elbows, so light she wouldn't notice if not for the muscles that moved under her touch. "Yes, I do."

Her grip tightened. "I just wanted to apologize for what I've done. Should we die tomorrow or any of these days—I couldn't ... I shouldn't have left us like I did. And maybe, now that you know, you can practice more caution to live to see this babe?"

Bai sniffled harder, and his voice sloshed. "Well, that's not exactly guaranteed for either of us, Raegna."

"I know. It would just be good if we could make it back to Vakkar Hold, and this babe could have you and love you like Ada did. When this is all over."

The idea seemed like a world away. Somewhere lost in the stars and unreachable. Raegna's chest ached at the prospect of it, and more tears streamed down her face. Bai shut his eyes tight, his own spilling over his cheeks and dripping off his chin. He heaved a sigh. "Raegna."

Bai leaned toward her, gravity pulling them close, and Raegna obeyed it. The stars could fall around them, and she wouldn't notice with him so close. The familiar sweet smoke scent filled her nose, and she was in Syden's lush green hills as if nothing had happened. Raegna braced against his faint hold and took him in as near as her body would allow.

You would never hurt me. I never have to be afraid of you.

"Bai." His name was on her breath as their brows touched. The tips of their noses met, and Raegna held him there. Stars fell behind her eyelids, and she hardly cared. There was no telling how long they'd stood there before she ground her brow to his, nose tips brushing, and she pulled away. Her heart cleaved in half. "We need to go."

Bai shuddered when they dropped each other's arms. "I'm walking you back."

Raegna nodded with a helpless smile. "Very well."

CHAPTER 30

BAI

RAEGNA SHUFFLED HER FEET back to the tent. Bai memorized the path, should he need to reach her again. At least he knew where she was, his mind churning like waves after a sea storm. He watched her stop at the tent, and her chest rose and fell as she turned to him.

Bai couldn't help but steal another glance at her belly, bound by the wide belt he'd left behind in Gittan's camp. Nothing had changed about Raegna except the clothes, yet everything had. The waves in his mind brewed with foam and crashed against his skull to conjure the idea that their babe grew within her. Another babe, but in Haven.

A harsh pulse lanced down his sternum like lightning over the seas. Bai met Raegna's eyes through the dark, silently begging her to go. Find safety back with Gittan and the others. Go back to Judr. The determination in her hardened stare wouldn't budge, and he knew her plan was set. There was no getting her out of it. Raegna gave him an encouraging smile.

The corners of Bai's lips pulled back to copy it. "You be safe."

Her smile went lopsided. "You too."

With that, she disappeared into the tent, and Bai forced himself back to the great house. He stumbled on his bad leg, wincing.

With a muddled head, he crept through the dining hall and sat to rest and make sense of things. He rubbed his face with an aggravated groan.

Raegna couldn't be pregnant. Why on Jorde would Gaea allow that to happen now? Why hadn't she said anything earlier? Of course, she had to have been terrified of another child forced on her.

No. She'd told him nothing had happened, that he'd done nothing. But then what had happened that night? Nothing that would lead to anything remotely romantic. That wasn't the way between them. And yet ...

His head throbbed, and Bai rested it in his hands to cover any remaining light in the hall, his elbows on his knees. He would be a father again if all went well. If Raegna could be kept safe. Why would she put herself in this much danger if she knew? Haven could be destroyed if she were there or not. He could easily tell her how it went. But she was too stubborn for that, even if it risked the babe.

Bai growled and shook his head. He would have to walk this off, turn it over in his head before losing himself in worry. All focus had to be fixed on Thenalious and Haven. Everything else would have to wait.

Climbing up the stairs put a pain in his leg that numbed the ache in his heart. Bai thought to check in on Asmund and Hadwin, acting like he was guarding. Rolling his shoulders to shake off the edge of his anxiety, he turned the corner at the top of the stairwell and came to a halt. His heart drummed against his chest.

Thenalious had Asmund pinned to the wall, one hand clamped under his chin and the other going up his inner thigh. His lips pressed against Asmund's ear as he whispered something Bai could not hear from a distance.

Heat surged through Bai's veins. *"Thenalious."*

The leader of Haven didn't even startle. He simply turned to look at Bai, unmoved.

"Leave him be," Bai snarled.

A chuckle emitted from Thenalious' throat, and his hand moved from Asmund's thigh to his hip. "Like a Maiden in shining armor."

Then he slipped away from Asmund, who seemed stuck to the wall, managing quiet, short breaths. Thenalious sauntered down the opposite hall, gifting Bai a wry smile.

"I told you to watch the caregivers," he said. "Fortunately, we could have a discussion, but *don't* let it happen again."

Glaring as Thenalious disappeared down the hallway, Bai waited for the bedroom door to open and shut before approaching Asmund.

"Are you all right?" Bai asked, searching his face.

Asmund kept his head down and turned away from him. His hands balled into tight fists at his sides, and he gave a faint, unconvincing nod.

"Did he hurt you?" Bai urged.

In the torchlight of the hallway, with tears glittering the rims of his eyes, Asmund shook his head. "No."

Doubtful, Bai took a step back to give him space. "What were you doing out here? I told you to stay with Hadwin and stay low. These men will kill you if you give them the chance. We aren't training in Stadt anymore. You have to keep your head down."

Asmund's trembling wasn't out of fear as he spun for the caregiver's door. "You weren't here, and I was worried. But it doesn't matter anymore."

With that, the door shut behind him, and Bai stood in the hallway alone.

***

Whatever Thenalious might have done sent Bai's blood ablaze. Asmund hadn't even looked at him, which didn't say much—he usually kept his eyes down. But this fear he emoted differently. He'd slammed a door shut in Bai's face.

Tirelessly thinking of Raegna's well-being and worried about Asmund, Bai stood guard before the caregiver's quarters to rest his aching leg. He glared at the double doors at the other end of the hall. There had to be a way to pin Thenalious down. There had to be something that left him immobile, terrified. If Bai could find out what it was, perhaps he could give him a taste of his own wrath, and someone else could take on Haven.

As Bai wrestled with it, a pleasured moan rose behind the double doors, and he straightened. Then another sounded, and another. Bai's nose wrinkled, recognizing the voice to be Thenalious', accompanied by the creaking of wood and then a growling moan that belonged to Reynold.

The last thing Bai wanted to do was listen to their bed-play, though when they were finished, would they find themselves at ease enough to spill secrets? At least some bits of information he could use?

Bai reluctantly paced up and down the hallway, keeping his footsteps light even with his limp, and waited. Unfortunately, the closer he crept to their door, the more details he could hear amid their endeavor.

Reynold's growls became softer but fervent. "Are you thinking of that blond bitch you like so much?"

Bai nearly missed a step, bile burning the back of his throat as his stomach twisted.

"No," Thenalious answered breathlessly, a chuckle leaving his lips. "Did you want me to?"

As the bed squeaked and Thenalious yelped, Bai hastened his pace. He reached the caregiver's quarters again, then rounded back down the hall. Their tones lowered, and Bai listened hard.

"I venture and take others," Thenalious breathed. "But I only think of you."

If that gave Reynold any pause, it wasn't apparent from outside the doors. Bai listened with his jaw clenched.

"I was never there with them," Thenalious went on, groaning between words. "Not when you were there, not when I could see your eyes. We were by the river again. Just us."

"No cursed warlocks," Reynold grunted. "No stupid nannies. No blond warriors?"

"Not when there's you. It's only you."

"And only you."

Halfway down the hallway, Bai grimaced at the final sounds of their pleasure, glad at least it was finally over—and perhaps more important things would be discussed. He took his time when he neared the double doors, treading lightly.

"What will you do with him?" Reynold grumbled. "You could make the new caregiver squeal if you weren't interrupted."

Thenalious sighed. "I certainly could. I imagine I could get him alone or hold either one of them down to make the other talk. Bai is strong, and though that little rat seems frightened of his own shadow, he has a bite to him."

He was trying to get information from Asmund. From both of them. It seemed Asmund wouldn't let him have it, even before Bai had intervened.

"If you wanted to fuck him, and I know you do," Reynold said, "it might take three of us, but I think we could. The rat would only need one or both of us."

"No, the men can pick him off. I don't care. There would need to be three or maybe even four of us against Bai, but I'm not sure if I want it handled that way." Another exasperated sigh left him. "I can't decide."

A few smacking kisses were exchanged before Reynold spoke. "I think we should just kill him and be done with it."

"No, I want to know *exactly* why they're here and why they survived long enough since the last raid in the woods. Why only now did they come to us?"

"The longer he lives, the more time he has to make trouble," Reynold argued.

"The more time you have to be jealous," Thenalious teased.

"I'm not jealous," Reynold growled. "By all means, have them both, make them squeal, and then kill them. I'm just tired of that bitch's smug face and those ugly eyes."

"Fan's eyes," Thenalious added. "Wyn was right about that. Almost like coins. They're a lot clearer when he's not weeping over a stupid brat."

Bai's hands rolled into fists at his sides, one of them tightening around the ax haft on his belt.

"We'll need a plan for them soon," Reynold urged. "I suggest we don't keep them here long. We killed his child, and he wants to join us? He has other motives."

"You're right. I'll come up with something today. Now, I don't want to talk about either of them anymore. Come here."

More kisses resounded, and Bai gave up on them, heading back to the caregiver's door only to endure more sounds of their lovemaking.

Bai and Asmund would need to be careful. Looking back, Bai wondered whether the trials had been a true attempt to kill him. Did Thenalious want him dead—or alive? Asmund's life wasn't their biggest priority. But it seemed Bai's was.

That night, Bai caught a few hours of sleep, leaning against the caregiver's door. He woke to the sounds of the entire house rising for the day—voices grumbling and doors opening—and got to his feet. The councilmen flooded from their bedrooms and headed downstairs. Reynold growled when he passed, his rust-colored hair tossed about.

Thenalious glided across the floor behind him and stopped before Bai. "If the caregiver still has to visit the cow pen, you will accompany him. Oberon's duties do not include swaddling babes or watching his sons."

Bai nodded. "Of course."

Thenalious' stare lingered on him before he smirked and followed the others downstairs. Bai's nose wrinkled once he disappeared, and he remained at his post before the caregiver's door.

The sun rose a little higher before Hadwin, Cadoc, and Asmund emerged from their room, and Hadwin halted at the sight of Bai. He looked like Hadwin from Syden so long ago, though hardened like he was forged over fire and steel. His brown eyes were dazed and distant above a wide, red scar that stretched over the bridge of his nose. What had happened here?

Bai's eyes drooped, though he attempted a kind smile. "Good morning. I'm supposed to escort you across camp for a babe, I believe."

Hadwin studied him with his brow knitted. "What?"

What could be going through his mind? He'd looked like a gaping fish when Bai first found him. They couldn't do anything about each other then, with Thenalious so close. Bai could barely do anything for him now. "I've heard there is a babe who needs to be taken to their mother on the other side of Haven. Oberon is indisposed, so I have to escort you."

Hadwin blinked, seeming to gather all that information before he nodded. "All right. Come on."

Bai stood outside the nursery but glimpsed the rows of tiny beds and the shuffling sounds of the young ones waking. Thenalious hadn't bothered adding the nursery's interior to Haven's tour. Seeing children so young struck a chord, and Bai tilted his head. How could children truly be here in a place like this?

"Hadwin," a few of them murmured, still on the edge of sleep.

"Good morning, little ones." Hadwin had turned a corner and spoke out of sight. "Asmund is going to watch you while I take Else. I want you all dressed by the time I get back. Can you do that for me?"

A chorus of sleepy, small voices echoed through the room, making Bai's mouth quirk. "Yes, Hadwin."

"Good boys." Hadwin returned with a babe cradled in his arms. Cadoc scampered behind him, but Hadwin stopped before Bai and turned to the boy. "Stay here with Asmund, nephew."

Cadoc faltered, glancing between his uncle and Bai.

Hadwin knelt before him, balancing on a knee and keeping the babe on one arm while he brushed Cadoc's hair back. "I don't want you near the barn anymore. You can stay here with Asmund and play with Audun, all right? I promise I'll be right back."

Silent terror lived within the little boy's gray eyes, and even Bai could crumble at the sight. The poor thing didn't understand. Naleem would be bereft to see him like this. Bai gave them space with a step back. "I'll watch over your uncle for you."

Cadoc fiddled with his fingers, staring between his feet before he nodded. Hadwin kissed his forehead and guided him back into the nursery. "I'll be right back. I love you."

Bai braced the pain that constricted his chest before Hadwin shut the nursery door and adjusted the babe in his grasp. "Let's go, then."

Steam rose from their mouths as they trekked outside. The sun just peeked over the trees, washing the sky in faded blues and yellows. Bai limped behind Hadwin at a decent pace, despite his injury. The other men bustled through the tents, and he hoped to find Raegna, but came up with nothing. He glanced at the babe tucked under blanket layers. Raegna would have to keep another babe warm next winter, and the thought made Bai's throat close.

He turned his attention to Hadwin. "You're quiet."

Hadwin drew a shuddering breath. "Is Naleem truly alive?"

"Yes. Asmund told you, then?"

"Everything," Hadwin whispered. "I'm trying to act normal."

Bai gave an amused huff. "You're doing well."

"I thought you were gone," Hadwin went on. "I thought you would have fought back in Syden. I just assumed they killed you like the others."

"Shh." Bai gave passersby a sideways glance and let his ax blade glint in the sunlight. "No, Raegna and I made it out."

"I know that now." Hadwin walked over a dip in the ground without tripping. Even as he stared ahead, he knew the path. "And Naleem is truly in Vakkar Hold?"

"Yes, truly," Bai assured. "He's safe and waiting for you."

An exhausted sigh made Hadwin's shoulders bob. "All right."

They crested a hill and looked down upon a sad horse barn that leaned to one side. Bai frowned at the rickety thing as he and Hadwin descended toward it. "The women are here?"

"Yes." Hadwin stopped a few feet away and turned to him. "I know you're supposed to watch me, but these women don't like strange men. So, could you wait out here?"

Bai nodded. "I don't blame them."

A scream split through the frigid air that made both of them jump. The babe whimpered as Hadwin whirled toward the barn. Another cry tore through the rotting wood boards that made Bai's racing heart leap into his throat. Outside, he knew such a scream well and balked at the sound, his skin crawling.

"No." Hadwin shoved the babe into Bai's arms before he could think. Bai staggered and nearly dropped the infant in his surprise. Adabelle's face flashed in his mind as he gathered the babe closer. Hadwin dashed for the door and shoved it open.

No, this can't happen. Nothing else can go wrong. "Hadwin! Hadwin, wait!"

One cry turned into many after Hadwin disappeared inside the barn. Bai hesitated until the sounds of a struggle came alongside a repeated bashing.

Summoning the rest of his courage, Bai held Else tight and dove into the barn. His mouth fell open with a sharp gasp.

The thin, ghastly women weren't his biggest concern as they all pressed themselves against any wall within their reach. Like his, their wide eyes trained on Hadwin, who had a knee digging into Reynold's chest. Reynold lay flat on his back—while Hadwin used a splintered board to rain blow after blow upon his face. Old wood shards and rusted nails ripped into Reynold's skull, blood spraying with each slamming motion.

Else whimpered. Startled, Bai and the women could only watch while Hadwin roared, raising the board in the air to crash down again. Reynold lay long dead.

Hadwin's rage faded, and the blows slowed. Blood splattered across his hands and face, and he dropped the board off to the side, breathing hard through gritted teeth.

"No, Hadwin, no," a young woman wailed near him. Her blonde hair tangled in different directions, and bruises appeared around her neck. The hem of her tattered skirt had been rolled up to her thighs.

"They'll kill you, Hadwin," she sobbed hysterically. "They'll kill you, Hadwin. No!"

Without hesitation, he took her in his arms, smearing Reynold's blood over her shoulders as she cried into his chest. Bai and the others came back to themselves. Each of the women dragged their attention to Bai, likely waiting for him to sound the alarm. Bai struggled to find his voice.

"Hadwin, you have to get out of here."

The young woman folded herself into him, and Hadwin fixed his eyes on the hay-strewn floor. "I'm not leaving her."

"If you don't, they'll kill you," Bai urged. "She'll be fine, but you have to go."

A honey-haired woman leaned closer to Hadwin. "Listen to him. Go take Else and get yourself cleaned up. We'll think of something."

"It doesn't matter," Hadwin growled. "I don't care what they do. I'm the only one who comes here, and if they think you all did it—"

"I'll take the blame for it," Bai blurted. "I'll say I did it, but you have to go."

"I'm not leaving."

"What about Naleem? He's waiting for you, and we told him we would bring you back. She'll be fine. I'll protect her. You need to get out of here."

At the sound of Naleem's name, every woman turned and eyed Bai warily. Of course, they all knew him. Naleem had explained that. But Bai hadn't realized how well they'd known him—or what he'd meant to them.

Then the woman in Hadwin's arms lifted her head, tears streaming down her face. "Go. If anything happened to you, I couldn't bear it."

"Maura—"

"I'll be all right," she stammered. "We'll find another way. Just please go."

Hadwin hesitated before embracing her, pressing his forehead against hers before standing on wobbly legs. Though his hands were bloody, he took Else from Bai and held her tight.

"She'll be all right. You can come back later," the honey-haired woman assured him through a broken voice. "Go out the back. There should be a creek past the brush. Clean up there."

Without meeting anyone's eyes, Hadwin nodded and snuck through a space in the back wall. Observing the bloodied wood board and the gap, Bai concluded where Hadwin had retrieved his weapon. They listened to his footsteps fade outside the old barn—and he was gone.

The young woman, Maura, released a sob, and Honey-Hair took her into her arms this time. A few others inched forward to comfort her. A woman with dark-brown skin stared at Bai through narrowed eyes.

"Who are you?" she said.

Bai couldn't pull away from the sight of Reynold with his face crushed and bleeding. "My name is Bai. I'm a friend of Hadwin and Naleem. That's all I can tell you."

"You mentioned Naleem as if he were still alive," she challenged.

"That's all I can tell you. I won't leave you until Thenalious or any of his men come looking for Reynold." He knelt and picked up the wood board, collecting blood on his hands. "There's no way we can hide the body."

"Maybe if we had more time," the woman said. "They'll surely kill you. You would sacrifice yourself for Hadwin? For all of us?"

Every one of their eyes turned to him while they awaited his answer. Bai stepped back from the body, tossing the wood board to one side. "Hadwin is my friend, and none of you deserve this fate. I'll handle Thenalious and the others."

With that, they waited in the cold of the old barn. Bai fought the urge to pace, so as not to worry the women. Maura continued to weep in her friend's arms while the others held their breath—for hours. Reynold's blood soiled the hay and frozen floorboards, and his once prominent brow caved above the rest of his disfigured face.

Bai didn't believe Hadwin would have had that within him. Some feeling for this woman must have driven him. Thenalious had spoken of the caregiver growing too close to the captured women. Maura had his heart, and how ironic for Gaea to present him with his first love in a place like Haven. But the Goddess had a funny way of weaving lives and events together.

Voices rose over the campgrounds, and Bai braced for the barn to be searched. It wasn't long before boots thundered over the hill and up to the door. Bai stood his ground while the women either shrank back or squared their shoulders.

The first to throw the door open was Wyn, his crazed eyes roaming over the barn's interior. He studied Bai, then spotted Reynold's body just behind him, and his brow lifted. "Fan ..."

Thenalious' voice approached from behind. "If that stupid bastard is in there again, I swear to Fan, I'll—"

He stopped dead past Wyn as his eyes fell on the body. Bai fought back a gulp, preparing for a fight, but looked on warily as Thenalious' face transformed from irritation to complete shock and fear.

A scream of anguish erupted from his throat, and he propelled himself past Bai, skidding over the blood and hay to reach the body. The women jumped back, but Thenalious bent over Reynold's body, holding his head in his hands. "Rey! Rey, love ..."

He sobbed into the body with every eye on him. Bai pulled his stare away to find Wyn glaring at him, his thin lip curled.

Instead of paying him any mind, Bai looked back down at Thenalious, who had his forehead pressed to Reynold's chest. No remorse filled his heart, then, recalling how he wept for Adabelle, how broken Naleem returned from Haven, how changed Hadwin had become, how frightened Asmund was in the hallway last night ...

And how Raegna sobbed at the loss of her daughter.

When he came back to himself, Bai met Thenalious' eyes as he raised his head, full of fury, with teeth bared. "*You.*"

"He was hurting her," Bai started.

"You wretched, rotten bitch," Thenalious snarled as he rose to his feet. "You killed him. Is that what you fucking wanted?"

"I heard screaming and found him over her," Bai countered. "You can't keep them here and do this to them."

"I should have killed you like he told me to. I should have slaughtered you along with your hideous little shit of a brat!"

Bai gritted his teeth. "Yes, you should have."

Raising his ax, he made a swipe toward Thenalious, who dodged the blow. Several women shrieked when Thenalious retrieved the sword from his belt and countered Bai's next attack. Metal rang when the blades collided. The two men tore into each other in a fury of movements. Bai continuously caught and deflected Thenalious' sword and attempted to rip the hilt from his hands.

Meanwhile, Gittan's teachings emerged from the back of his thoughts. *Check your rage. Control it.*

But all Bai's hatred boiled over, and he shouted as he knocked Thenalious' blade to the side and swiped to make a blow. Thenalious dodged and teetered back to fall on one knee, the ax blade whistling past his throat. He recovered and threw a punch with the sword hilt into Bai's wounded leg.

Pain reverberated through Bai's entire body. He released a scream and stumbled. Thenalious caught him and rammed his knee between Bai's eyes. The pain that sliced through his skull outdid that of his leg, and darkness took over.

Chapter 31

Hadwin

As soon as he slipped through the gap in the old barn's wall, holding Else tight, Hadwin came back to himself. The frigid morning air did not touch him, for his veins were coated with icicles. He stumbled between the trees, his periphery blurred into tunnel vision.

Else wept in his arms, and he turned his attention to her. All this time, he'd cradled her in his bloodied hands. He would have to keep her quiet. "Hush. Hush, Else."

Coming upon the creek Talia had told him about, Hadwin crashed onto his knees, and Else shrieked. Though his muscles spasmed from the adrenaline that ran through his body, Hadwin did his best to rock her gently. "Hush, everything's all right. Hush."

The blood on his hands made it difficult to calm even himself—her own father's blood. He'd killed him. Reynold was dead.

Hadwin sat back and forced himself to take deep breaths, panting from running. He continued to rock back and forth and focused on the burbling creek, soothing himself and Else. "Hush. Hush."

The babe resorted to faint whimpers, and Hadwin settled her on the ground with shaking hands. He washed the blood away. Crimson droplets stretched up his arms and dotted his shirt, but maybe he could change that when he reached the great house. He would have to move quickly. Asmund and the boys waited alone, and what would happen when Thenalious found the body in the barn?

Bai would take the blame. No one would think of the caregiver's part in the incident. But then what? What would Thenalious do to Bai? Hadwin's stomach twisted in knots at the possibilities. His last friend from Syden had willingly given himself to protect him—Hadwin couldn't leave him be. But what more could he do?

Stay put. Keep your head down. That was what Bai would want him to do. For Naleem. If he truly was alive in Vakkar Hold, he would want the same. Though Bai would need help. There would be no mercy for him when Thenalious found Reynold dead.

Once most of the blood was gone and Hadwin's hands went numb from the cold, he lifted Else and pulled her close. "We have to get back. Maybe Asmund will know what to do."

Hadwin reached the great house from the rear, avoiding any unwanted attention from the camp. Else curled into his chest to protect herself from the cold. She would surely be hungry for the day, but they could not return to her mother until this mess was sorted out.

The great house burst with edged voices droning about the missing councilman. Every available man on the Council was searching for him, ordered to report back to Thenalious. He had been gone longer than expected.

Please, Gaea, just let him spare Bai. Hadwin prayed on his way up the stairs and ducked into the nursery, panting again.

Instead of finding the nursery in order, as he'd hoped, Hadwin gasped at the sight of Oberon towering over Asmund and the young man pressing himself against the wall. The boys cowered on the other side of the room. Gael and Vihn attempted to bring their father's attention to them. "Papa! Papa, stop."

"Oberon," Hadwin snapped.

The councilman whirled on him, his eyes flashing. "Where in Helved have you been?"

"I—I had to take Else to her mother," he stammered, but took a breath to steady himself. "Obviously. What are you doing?"

"Reynold's missing," Oberon answered. "And I'll bet this pipsqueak and his friend have everything to do with it."

Asmund shook his head fervently and looked away from Oberon. His gaze fell on Hadwin in a silent plea, but changed when his brow furrowed and his eyes focused. "Where's Bai?"

Hadwin gulped. "He's ... I don't know."

Asmund shrank back with his hands balled into fists. Oberon lifted from him and turned toward Hadwin. "He's right. Thenalious' new love interest was supposed to escort you to the barn and back. Where is he?"

Hadwin glared at him. "You know you can trust me. Anything I do, I do to protect the children and the women."

Oberon bared his teeth. "Where is he, caregiver? What happened? Where is Reynold?"

"Not in front of the boys, Oberon. Please."

"What. Happened."

On the other side of the room, Asmund straightened and craned to listen. The boys shuddered in a huddle, and the oldest ones watched intently. Hadwin dared not glance at Ugo or Audun. Reynold was cruel, but he was their father, and Hadwin had taken him out of this world. They didn't need the details.

"I found Reynold attacking Maura," Hadwin explained rigidly. "He's gone. And I did it."

Oberon took a step back, his lips parting. The boys were all silent, perhaps unable to grasp the extent of his words.

"Bai stayed behind to take the blame," Hadwin choked out. "The women told me to leave too. So I did."

The councilman's eyes dashed about Hadwin's person, more than likely picking up on the drops of blood that stained his shirt.

Asmund strode forward. "Where is Bai?"

Hadwin shook his head. "I don't know. Still in the barn. He insisted on staying."

"Thenalious is going to slaughter him." Oberon glanced at Asmund. "And you too. He and Reynold have been inseparable since they were young. I can't believe you. That you of all people—"

"He assaulted Maura and has done countless other things," Hadwin snarled. "Bai is still there."

"Has Thenalious found out yet?" Asmund blurted.

"I don't know."

"We would know." Oberon turned on Asmund. "You will do nothing about it."

"Leave him be, Oberon," Hadwin snapped. "This isn't his fault. He's done nothing wrong."

"When Thenalious finds that bastard over Reynold's body, he'll want both of them dead. I might as well hold him in the meantime."

"Oberon, no, they're just trying to help." Hadwin shut his mouth as soon as the words came forth. Asmund's eyes widened on him, but the councilman turned back to him.

"Help? With what?"

"I ... I don't know. They're just—"

"I think you do know, caregiver." Oberon crept forward. "You told me I can trust you. Then trust me—that this place and, above all, my children come first. If you or anyone else mean to harm them, I *will* send you to Helved. I don't care."

He stood over Hadwin, who slammed backward into the door. "Oberon, please. They're not here to hurt the boys. They want to save them and the women. They want to save all of us."

"Save us? How? They're just two idiots that don't know the true strength of Haven and were stupid to think they could do anything but make Thenalious' cock rise."

"I don't know. They wouldn't tell me," Hadwin lied. "But I promise, they are not our enemy. You know who is. They're just trying to help."

Oberon's eyes narrowed. "I believe they wouldn't tell you. Either something is going on, or they're tricking you. It doesn't matter." He spun and grabbed Asmund by the arm. "You're coming with me."

"Oberon!" Hadwin thought he might strike the new caregiver. Instead, Asmund threw a fist into Oberon's gut. With the air knocked out of him, Oberon doubled over, and Asmund ran his knee into his nose. Then Oberon dropped.

"Papa!" Gael and Vihn screamed in unison.

Hadwin gaped and stood back, never having seen any of the councilmen crumble so easily. Then he looked at Asmund, who'd always been so timid ...

Though he faltered a bit, Asmund squared his shoulders. "How far is the barn?"

"You shouldn't have done that."

"I don't care. How far is the barn?"

"It's on the other side of camp." Hadwin placed Else in her crib and knelt before Oberon to turn him over. Blood streamed from his nostrils, and the bridge of his nose began to swell and bruise. "I can't believe you did that."

"If he wakes up, he won't hurt you, will he?" Asmund said. It was more an observation than a question.

"He won't be happy," Hadwin admitted.

"But he would protect you and the boys if you were alone."

"Yes." Hadwin looked up at him. "But you can't go out there. He's right. Thenalious will kill you both. This is all my fault. Bai just wouldn't let me take it."

"Stay here," Asmund instructed and stepped around them toward the door. "If anything happens, know we are here to help. We're not tricking you."

"I know. I just hope I didn't completely ruin whatever you had planned."

"No. Maybe you've just sped it up."

Chapter 32

Raegna

Raegna dreamed of Syden that night. She and Bai shared their bed with Adabelle between them, and the world was whole. Haven didn't exist until a rough hand shook her shoulder.

"Felik."

Papa. Raegna opened her eyes and groaned. A dizzying whirlpool of nausea spun within her.

Thekla knelt before her cot but leaned back. "Don't puke on me."

"Hm." Raegna pushed herself up and wrestled with her innards. Thekla stood and filled her vision, standing rather close. "What are—"

The warrior's voice dropped to a whisper. "Saving you a few sights not fit for a lady. These bastards would make a priestess blush."

Raegna swallowed, her brow knitted, before familiar soft groans stretched across the tent. It did make a priestess blush. She dropped her eyes to her boots, and that took care of the nausea and the men. Thekla chuckled and offered her a hand. "Come on. Eyes down."

Outside, sunlight brimmed over the trees. Fresh air greeted them with a cold sting, but Raegna drank it in. "That tent is disgusting."

"Well, it's full of men." Thekla pulled her tunic and hat closer to her. "Even the worst brothels are cleaner than that pigsty."

Raegna glanced at the charred wood that sat within the fire pit. Had she and Thekla truly been sitting before it just last night? After finding Bai and holding him, it seemed as if another world had passed. Another time. Were they even still on the same path, or had Gaea pulled down the stars around them? Rearranged them the moment Raegna and Bai had shared words?

Swaying, Raegna pressed her hand to her stomach, then to her mouth, before she fled to retch behind the tent. A few men walked past her. As she heaved, they laughed. "Too much ale, boy?"

You could say that. Raegna coughed up the last before she rose and wiped her mouth with her sleeve. She gave them a look as they passed, but these men only laughed more.

"Keep it to one drinking horn tonight, little one."

They sauntered off as Thekla joined her. "You all right?"

"Why does Gaea torment us with so much while they get to pull their cocks every morning and snore like bears every night?" Raegna grumbled.

"Ha, I've met many a woman who could also snore like a bear."

"At least we don't make disgusting fools of ourselves."

Thekla looked to the sky in thought. "I've also met many a woman who played with her womanhood every morning. And I helped."

Heat spread through Raegna's face, and she drew a cool breath. "Not all women."

"Not every man. Just most every one of them here."

As if on cue, every one of them raised their voices across camp. Raegna and Thekla looked up to the growing shouts that trembled through the tents. "Murderer! Kill him!"

The crowd appeared in a gap on the path with Thenalious in the lead. Raegna's blood seared, and she glared as he passed, gliding as if the stones and gravel could not touch him. He kept his sight ahead. Even from a distance, Raegna recognized the hideous look on his face with his lip curled and his nose wrinkled like a snarling dog.

Behind him, two men carried another with his arms over their shoulders. Raegna's breath caught in her throat as she jolted.

Bai.

His head hung, blond hair covering his face. His feet dragged over the gravel, and he was limp in their grasp. Raegna's chest pulsed with an ache as Judr flashed behind her eyes. But Bai was awake and fighting against the warriors' holds then. What had Thenalious done to him?

Without caution, Raegna fled for him, and Thekla's voice called behind her. A flood of men followed Thenalious, closing the space between him, Bai, and Raegna. She joined them, shoving for a place to get closer. A hand wrapped around hers, and she whirled, ready to throw a fist into whoever would touch her.

Thekla raised her palm before she could. The men swarmed them and knocked into them with grunted curses. Raegna and Thekla ignored them.

"You can't," Thekla panted. "Don't barge into this."

"They'll kill him."

"They'll surely kill you too," Thekla argued. "We can stay close, but do nothing."

"What if they hurt him?" Raegna snapped. "Someone needs to blow a horn. Only he and Asmund have one. Asmund is—He's in the great house. We can get him."

Thekla's eyes darted over Raegna's face as the men dissipated past them. "All right. You go find him. I'll watch your man."

"But—"

"Go find him. Don't get killed." Thekla released her and nudged her toward the great house. "If they mean to kill Bai, I'll make a plan. Go now."

If she waited around, Bai would surely be dead. Thekla was a more skilled warrior, but not before a horde of warrior men. She was clever enough ...

Raegna growled under her breath and ran for the great house. The icy wind nipped at her face and ears. Her boots thudded on the hard ground. More men walked past her to see the commotion, hardly giving her a glance. They were more interested in a possible slaughter.

What had Bai done to get into that mess? What did Thenalious mean to do? Had he seen them last night? All stars would have been tainted with his presence. But there was no one but them in the pitch darkness. Raegna gritted her teeth. It didn't matter now. She had to find Asmund, get the horn, and sound the alarm.

The great house mocked her with its looming elk skull and its wicked antlers. Raegna's throat closed as she pounded up the stairs, gasping for air. She hauled one of the double doors open, and it gave as someone pushed out. Raegna stared into a face she thought she might never see again.

"Asmund."

Asmund froze before her and blinked hard. "Priestess?"

"Yes, it's me." Raegna stepped aside to let him through. "They have Bai. Where is your horn?"

Without hesitation, he yanked it from the tie on his belt beneath his shirt. "Hadwin killed Thenalious' man. Bai took the blame. They'll kill him."

Raegna's stomach somersaulted. "Call for Gittan and the others. It'll take time before they can gather and get here. We'll go help Bai."

Asmund nodded and brought the horn to his lips. The shrill blast rang through Raegna's skull, and she winced. It split the air and spread over Haven. He let it linger, and it traveled over the tents within the trees. Would it be enough? Would Gittan hear it?

Asmund gasped when he stopped. "Another?"

"Maybe." Raegna started down the steps. "One more and we'll help Bai."

Another blast carried overhead as she bolted from the great house. Her heartbeat was in the back of her mouth with the swelling of tears. *Please, Gaea. Not Bai. Please, All-Mother. Not Bai.*

Chapter 33

Bai

A SHARP, HIGH-PITCHED HORN echoed in the darkness. Bai's consciousness stirred, and he listened to the second call.

Cold water splashed Bai's face, and pain seized him in place. His eyes snapped open, and the bright yellow sunrise blurred his vision. A fist rammed into his stomach as soon as he grasped his bearings. His body hung by his wrists as he gagged and gasped for air.

"You're about to wish you were never born, Grizzly," Thenalious growled through the temporary darkness.

Bai forced his eyes open again and took in his new situation. He hung from the ceiling of some shack on the outskirts of Haven. Several animal carcasses hung alongside him, including a skinned boar and a stag with its belly torn open, freshly gutted. The rancid stench crawled into Bai's nose, and steam rose from its empty body.

Before him, hundreds of Haven men looked on with anticipation. Several of them chatted and took bets among each other. How long would Thenalious' new victim last? Meanwhile, others—mostly the councilmen—bore witness with more stoic expressions. In front of them, Thenalious glared, eyes burning with fury.

"I've been wanting a new bearskin." He circled to Bai's back. "You're a little smaller than the last. But you'll do."

Bai's heart stopped and started. His wrists were numb as he jolted and rattled the iron hook and wood boards that held him up. He fought to keep his composure, looking for a chance of escape. Even if he did get free he was surrounded.

A man with a thick brown beard and bloodied apron over his large gut stepped out from the little shack behind Bai. "My lord, I have all the tools ready for you. Whatever you wish. I know you like to skin your own kills."

The hushed sound of a blade gliding across leather emitted from Thenalious' direction, but Bai could not see him. "You know me well, Eluf. It's just too bad. The last time I saw this grizzly in Judr, his back was cut up. That would ruin the hide."

Bai shuddered. "Thenalious—"

"You will shut up."

A blade snaked up Bai's shirt, tearing it off. The edge grazed his skin, and Bai stifled a yelp. His shirt hung from the sleeves over his biceps, and Thenalious circled back to face him.

"You are in no position to speak," he growled. "There is nothing you can do that will get you out of this. For what you did, you're going to suffer. Whatever those wenches in Judr did to you, I'll do far worse. You might think you've known pain, but you haven't."

The blade ripped through the front half of Bai's shirt, and Thenalious used precise movements. The edge did not touch Bai's skin this time, but the flat of the blade brushed like ice over him until Thenalious tossed the shredded shirt aside. The cold wind wrapped itself around Bai's body and raked through him, sharper than any knife.

"Unless, of course," Thenalious started, "you're going to tell me exactly why you appeared out of nowhere and chose to be one of us. Even the most reluctant house-husbands are not turned so quickly. You have a motive."

"I couldn't live in Judr anymore," Bai told him. "I had to leave."

Thenalious rested the point of the blade at the base of Bai's belly. "Yet I destroyed your family. I've slit your precious brat's throat, and you would crawl to me and my men peacefully?"

Adabelle's terrified face filled Bai's thoughts, but he shoved it away. "There was nothing for me there."

The knife pricked Bai's skin. Thenalious didn't allow it to go deep, but he practiced a steady cut upward. Bai gritted his teeth.

"The more you lie, the more I cut," Thenalious whispered. "Tell me why you're here."

Blood dripped from where the cut striped from the bottom of his abdomen and up. Thenalious stopped the blade just below his ribs. It wouldn't go any deeper. Bai snarled at the pain. He truly meant to skin him alive.

"I ... I couldn't stay."

"You are pathetic." The knife stretched up and tore under his skin. Bai growled on a scream when it reached the center of his chest. "Tell me everything."

Baring his teeth, Bai snapped. "You're a worthless pile of shit and I pray you burn in Helved for all the lives you've ruined."

Thenalious smirked. "We can go together."

The blade ran from Bai's breast to the base of his neck. Small creeks of blood streamed down his body and dripped onto the ground.

"Tell me everything you know," Thenalious persisted.

Bai spat into his face, whimpering when the movement nearly drove the knife right through him. Thenalious closed his eyes and wiped the saliva away.

"I ought to sink this blade into your thick skull," he threatened, eyes burning. "But that would be a waste of hide. You will tell me what you know. We can go all day."

"Bai!" A voice tore through the crowd that made Bai's stomach drop.

A few men side-stepped as Raegna pushed through the crowd. She unsheathed her sword over her back. Asmund trailed her, hefting his ax and staring Thenalious down. Bai gaped as Thenalious turned from him with his head tilted.

"Perfect. Both of your boys have come to rescue you. I heard you found a second one."

"Let him go!" Asmund snarled, but Raegna lunged forward. All at once, every councilman surrounded them and clashed their blades. Bai growled as he fought to free himself, his blood rushing in his ears and dripping in splatters down his torso.

Raegna could not be here.

In the blur of action, the councilmen had Raegna and Asmund with their hands behind their backs. The gathered men cheered with their blades high overhead. Thenalious flipped the knife and skulked toward them.

"No!" The rafter creaked with Bai's strength. "Thenalious, you don't need them!"

Wyn and another councilman held Asmund in place as Thenalious approached them. Instead of quaking in fear, Asmund threw his weight, but the men held him firm. With the two men gripping her, Raegna bared her teeth, black eyes flashing. Thenalious pressed the knife to Asmund's cheek, and he froze in place, breathing hard.

"This one I can understand." Thenalious let his voice carry. "Such a pretty face. Could you not leave Judr without him, is that it?"

"He hasn't done anything," Bai gasped out. "It's me you want. I killed Reynold. It's me you want."

"You've no right to say his name!" Thenalious roared at him. "I will have your skin drawn up on our gate. But this one can go free if you tell me why you're here."

"Please, he has nothing to do with this."

"Now, I know that's a lie." Thenalious swiped the knife down and cut Asmund's face open from cheekbone to jawline. Asmund yelped, but continued to fight back. Thenalious placed the knife edge on his left eyebrow. "I'll take his pretty eyes next, Grizzly."

"Thenalious!"

He angled the blade to cut deep. Blood trickled down Asmund's temple. "I guess I'll carve his face out like a gourd, then."

"Leave him alone!" Raegna shouted. She lowered her voice, but it wasn't quite enough.

Thenalious twitched as he turned his attention to her. A new light glinted in his eyes. He sliced the knife past Asmund's brow and went to her. Bai thrashed and his torso stung. The hook groaned in the rafter, and the rope held his prickling wrists.

"You like this one, Grizzly?" Thenalious called over his shoulder. "There's something about him. I can't place the knife on it."

He tucked the knife beneath Raegna's cap. Bai's voice ripped his throat. *"Don't!"*

The cap flipped backward onto the hard ground. Raegna gnashed her teeth as she glared at him. The men shuffled, and the councilmen who held her shifted, studying her braids. Thenalious remained as still as the trees, his sight fixed on her. He put the knife behind her head, and Bai yelled when he cut.

Raegna's braids fell apart. Thenalious yanked at one and unwove it so chestnut locks tumbled above one shoulder, the other half braided behind her neck. A stunned whisper traveled through the crowd, and even the men holding Asmund jumped. Thenalious was solid, tilting his head to the other side.

"Don't!" Bai shouted. "Don't hurt her!"

Thenalious snatched Raegna's jaw in his hand, and she cried out. Her white skin gave with his nails digging into her cheeks. "I remember you. Rotten cunt."

A raven called over the tents as Bai swung from the hook. "Don't touch her!"

"Or what, Grizzly?" Thenalious pulled Raegna from her captors and pinned her arm behind her back. Raegna yelped and winced before he brought the knife to her throat. "You think you can save her instead?"

Tears sprang to Bai's eyes. A deeper pain tore into his sternum as if the bone split. A sob came out as a growl through his curled lip, and his muscles strained. "Don't hurt her."

The knife's edge pressed under her chin. "Tell me where she came from and I'll make it quick."

"Burn in Helved, you fucking monster," Raegna snarled through her teeth.

Thenalious pushed the knife up, and Raegna threw her head back, her hair hanging over his arm. Her neck lay open for the knife to cut. Blood splattered in Bai's memory, and he trembled. *Don't.*

"Every man will take his turn with her, Grizzly," Thenalious yelled with his teeth flashing. "Everyone will take her, and then Pretty Blue there. You will watch it all before I kill them both."

A horn called from the same direction as the raven. Battle cries reverberated between the trees, and hooves thundered like a distant avalanche. Bai writhed and pricked his ears. The excitement in the crowd dwindled as the sounds grew. Women's shouts carried through the woods behind Haven.

Thenalious cocked his head toward the woods. His keen gaze lost its fire, swimming with uncertainty as the hazel irises flickered.

"It's over." Raegna bent, ramming an elbow into Thenalious' side, using their weight to sweep him onto the ground. The knife was in her hand, and his dumbfounded men stared at their stoic leader sprawled over the mud and snow.

Raegna retrieved her sword from the ground and pointed it at his chest. "If you knew what was good for you, you would stand down now."

Thenalious' brow arched, and he glowered from beneath it. "Kill them all!"

Bai could only watch as Asmund twisted, and Wyn brought a blade to his side. Raegna raised her sword to swipe, and Thenalious pushed to his feet. Those at the front of the crowd surged forward while the others whirled to the stampeding warriors of Galaenia.

CHAPTER 34

RAEGNA

THENALIOUS LUNGED, AND RAEGNA swiped. He dove beneath her. Raegna dodged to the side and swung with a shout. A scuffle scraped the dirt behind her, and Asmund yelled, "Raegna!"

In her periphery, Asmund dashed past her. Steel flashed, and she whirled to face the men who had him. They brandished blades. Raegna parried them while Asmund crashed into Thenalious, sending him back to the ground. The thin, crazed man screeched when Raegna battled him and his ax with ease. Her sword made a red stripe through his shirt, and he dropped. She didn't have time to catch her breath before the second man towered over her.

He gagged, blood spattering his chin, and fell. Thekla stood behind him and hauled her sword from his back. Raegna couldn't thank her then. Thekla spun to the next opponent, and Raegna turned.

Asmund had Thenalious on the ground, his hands wrapped around the snake's neck. Thenalious choked and rammed a knee into Asmund's gut. He flipped Asmund off and scrambled in the opposite direction. Raegna lurched to pursue, but Asmund's deep tone halted her. "Let him go."

Her lips parted, but she followed his gaze to Bai. If it weren't for the chaos of battle around them, Raegna might have given under the anvil that was her shame. Bai took on more pain, and she could do nothing to stop it. The wicked cut down his body sent an invisible gash down hers.

Tears streamed down Bai's face at their approach. His once fierce expression fell to relieved despair. "Raegna."

"Hang on," she told him.

Asmund cut the rope. Men were on them at once. Raegna faced them, bracing against their strength and finding her openings. Asmund and Bai snatched axes from other bodies, or perhaps the butcher's shed, and they joined her in a fury. The three mowed down their enemies with enough space to witness the battle in a flash.

The Haven men seemed shaken, if not furious. Their place of refuge would be taken from them. Galaenian warriors screamed with blood-thirsty swords. Shields slammed and broke. Horses and riders flew over tents. Arrows pelted their ranks, and the warriors and their horses fell.

Raegna shook her head. The Galaenian warriors had some hold on the fighting, but other lives dwelled within the camp. Not all men fought. Some hid among the tents and structures, which would soon be torn down. Innocents trapped in Haven.

A gasp left her throat. "Hadwin."

Bai and Asmund exchanged a swift look with her, and the three bolted for the great house. They circled the central battle, a mess of screams and blood. Straggling Haven men met them head-on, but Bai tore them down in the lead. Raegna and Asmund countered those who tried to flank them. Some men on their path ignored them, fleeing the camp with the clothes on their backs and the weapons at their belts. Bai made a swipe at one, cursing under his breath. If they lived, Raegna would tell Gittan and the others to search for deserters.

Pain struck Raegna's thigh, and she shrieked. The sensation lanced through her hip. She made it another few strides before she stopped and stared at the arrow in her leg. Others struck the ground around her.

"Raegna!" Bai was at her side with her arm over his shoulder. Asmund snatched a shield from a fallen man and held it behind them.

Bai carried Raegna up the porch steps to the great house. She clawed his shoulder at the pain she anticipated, but her adrenaline dulled it. At the great house doors, Bai yanked the handle and pulled one open. He ducked Raegna inside, and Asmund slipped in behind them. The two men slammed the door shut.

Raegna clenched her jaw and hobbled to a long table in the dining hall. Kitchen boys shuffled down the halls to hide, and she paid them no mind. Bai and Asmund turned to her as she sat and gripped the arrow shaft. "Raegna—"

She ripped the arrow out and screamed through her teeth. Blood soaked her pant leg as she pressed a palm against the wound. "Where is Hadwin?"

The men blinked before Bai spoke first. "Upstairs."

"Fucking stairs," Raegna cursed. "Go ahead and make sure he and Cadoc are safe."

Bai nudged Asmund. "We'll be behind you."

Asmund nodded and dashed for the hall. Bai sat beside Raegna and snagged her sleeve. He tore the fabric with a harsh grunt and flexed arms. Raegna held on to the bench seat while he tied the fabric around her wound, over her pants.

"You were stupid out there," Bai grumbled.

Raegna chewed her lip. "We had to distract them long enough to give Gittan and the others a head start. It worked. There's no arguing about it now."

"He would have killed you." Bai cinched the fabric tight, making her hiss. "I cannot believe you, Raegna."

"Well, you know how it is." She panted while her leg throbbed. "There was no one to knock me unconscious and prevent me from being a righteous fool, right?"

Bai snorted. "Is there any convincing you to hide somewhere here while we protect Hadwin?"

Raegna shook her head and flinched as she rose. "Seven years of marriage and you'd think you would learn."

"You're injured," Bai argued as he followed her to the stairs.

Fucking stairs. Her knuckles turned white around her sword hilt as she climbed. "You're not exactly the picture of health yourself."

They reached the top, and Bai led them down the left hall. "I'm also not with child."

"Details," Raegna muttered, though the disregard squeezed her chest.

They stopped before the second door in the hall. Bai threw it open to be greeted with the swipe of a sword. He jumped back and stood between the door and Raegna.

A man with umber skin and black hair and beard glared at them, waiting for an attack. Raegna's eyes widened at Asmund strewn across the floor, groaning as he lifted his head. He blindly searched for his ax, which lay just inches away from him. A group of a dozen young boys cowered in a corner of the room, crying and whimpering. Before them stood Hadwin—a far more hardened and scarred version of him, but Hadwin—alive and well.

"Oberon!" Hadwin shouted at the man. "Stop this now!"

"We're not here to hurt them," Bai assured.

"Like Fan, you aren't!" Oberon snarled.

"Please." Raegna lowered her sword. "We mean them no harm. Our mission is to return them and the women to safety in Stadt. We want innocent lives to be spared."

Oberon sized her up, his mouth clamped tight and his nose wrinkled.

"Listen to them," Hadwin pleaded. "They wouldn't hurt the boys. They're my friends. They just want to help."

Holding his sword high, Oberon hesitated, staring Bai and Raegna down. Meanwhile, Asmund got to one knee and leaned against the frame of a child's bed. Alongside the boys, a few babes wailed in fear, which tore at Raegna's heart. They were all too close to this battle, to the bloodshed that echoed through the window.

Finally, Oberon relaxed. Keeping a watchful eye, he stepped to the side. Bai and Raegna slipped into the nursery.

Raegna knelt before Asmund. "Are you all right, my friend?"

He nodded, a bruise forming across his forehead. "I deserved that."

They all turned to Hadwin, who busied himself with comforting each of the boys. Bai looked them over before giving his attention to Hadwin. "Are you all right?"

"Fine," Hadwin managed with a frigid sigh. "I'm just glad you're alive. Raegna. Good to see you again."

Raegna nodded to him, quite over the surreality of her life so far. "You too."

"How do you all expect to help the boys with that mess going on out there?" Oberon demanded through their greetings.

"We'll protect them here until the battle is over," Raegna explained. "Then we'll wait for instruction."

"You're so sure you're going to win," Oberon sneered.

"If we do, they and their mothers can be given a second chance in Stadt," Raegna told him, "or wherever they wish to live."

Oberon grunted.

"Farah could take care of them," Hadwin interjected. "Perhaps you can too."

Whoever Farah was. Despite the encouraging words, Oberon kept his frown and stood off to the side. "If anything happens to them, I will kill you all."

"We believe it," Bai assured him.

"Why not kill them now?" a voice growled from the door. Every head turned, and every heart sank to find Thenalious looming at the threshold of the nursery.

An agonizing pain rose in Raegna's core. Thenalious stood at the threshold, his face soaked in dark red blood. Dull, yellowish eyes peered through the dull crimson. His shirt, covered with a leather armored vest, was splashed with red. The thick fluid dripped from his sword and onto the wood floor. He heaved for breath and held his left arm at a strange angle. He must have been wounded, but there was so much blood on him, it was hard to tell what was his and what was not.

Raegna tensed, swallowing the nerves that scratched under her skin.

Thenalious stalked forward. "Come on then, Oberon. Let's bring these bastards down. Including your caregiver. We'll find you a new one."

Raegna and Asmund got to their feet, and Bai lifted his ax, the three blocking the path toward Hadwin and the children. But Oberon stepped in front of Thenalious, halting him in his tracks.

"Thenalious, they're protecting the boys," he said. "There's no one here to fight."

"Is that so?" Thenalious took a step forward. Fat red drops fell to the floor. "That's very thoughtful of them, isn't it? I wonder what they could possibly be protecting the little ones from."

"Thenalious," Oberon started again. "Even if we lose Haven, or if we surrender, the boys would be safe and could grow up with decent lives. Reynold's sons can live good lives."

Thenalious' eyes flashed. "That is *not* your decision to make. That is not what we wanted for any of them, and you know it. Now, help me slaughter this lot before I consider you a traitor!"

Oberon stood his ground. "This isn't what I wanted for my sons. Not this."

"You should have thought of that before you made them, you whore-son."

Thenalious raised his sword, and Oberon parried his blow. Twisting, Thenalious shoved him away and jabbed the hilt into his nose. Oberon shouted and made another blow, but being dazed, he left an opening even Raegna could see from across the room. Her breath caught in her throat as Thenalious pushed his sword through Oberon's chest.

The boys screamed, a couple of them wailing, "Papa!"

"Oberon!" Hadwin shouted along with them.

Thenalious pulled the blade from Oberon's body, and he fell to the floor, gagging on the blood that spilled from his mouth. Before Thenalious could turn on the three who protected the children and their caregiver, Asmund lunged forward. Raegna took a step, but Bai placed his ax in front of her before joining their friend.

Asmund swung his ax at Thenalious, who quickly countered it. Metal rang against metal, and the two spun about each other until Thenalious' sword ran through Asmund's side. He screamed and fell as the blade ripped away from him.

"Asmund!" Raegna shouted and went to his aid.

Without another beat, Bai swiped his ax wherever the blade could taste flesh. Thenalious blocked and dodged, laughing hysterically.

"I wouldn't hold back, Grizzly. The trial is over. We can both try to kill each other now."

Raegna fussed over Asmund, tearing off the fabric of her other sleeve to stanch the blood rising in his wound. "Hang on, Asmund. You'll be all right."

"Help ... Oberon." He replaced the hand she had pressed against his wound with his own.

Raegna looked past Bai and Thenalious and her eyes fell on Oberon, who spat up blood in the middle of the floor. She squeezed Asmund's shoulder and went to the man's side. Instead of using her shirt, she ripped a blanket off the top of a child's bed and pressed it into Oberon's wound.

"It's all right," she assured him. "Everything will be all right."

Then Hadwin was beside her. He put his hand over hers in Oberon's blood. "I'll take care of him and Asmund. You need to help Bai."

"The children—"

"Thenalious won't hurt them, not for anything," Hadwin told her. "You and Bai can beat him together."

Raegna looked up as Bai crashed through the cradles that sat in one corner. Wood splintered from the force of his weight. Thenalious raised his sword again, pointing it down at him.

Raegna got to her feet and charged at Thenalious. Her sword grazed his shoulder, and she rammed him into the door frame where she fumbled from her velocity. Thenalious grunted and growled as his eyes locked on her.

"You little cunt."

Raegna turned on her heel and pounded down the hallway with lopsided strides. The puncture in her leg stretched painfully beneath its makeshift bandage. Thenalious took the bait and raced after her.

Bai cried out, "Raegna!"

The hallway spiraled around her as she searched for a way out. Heart drumming in her head, Raegna turned to the closest door and wrenched it open. A bedroom lay before her, but most importantly, a window. Thenalious' footsteps thudded behind her. She slammed the door and wobbled across the room.

At the window, Raegna broke the glass with her sword hilt and brushed away the shards from the edges. She climbed out, careful of her bad leg.

Her stomach dropped at the sheer height of two stories. The battle raged below her, with scattered fires burning tents and a distant barn. Screams stretched across the camp, and weapons clashed against each other to spill blood. With her hair whipping about her, Raegna recalled her days climbing trees to scale the house.

Thenalious reached her, shouting as he tried to snatch her leg. Raegna yelped and climbed. Scrambling over the rafters, she found her balance on the wooden roof. There didn't seem to be an easy exit from that standing point. The mellow daylight was no comfort, and a raven swooped across the boards. Raegna scanned the space the bird traveled but found only the roof edges.

Raegna tiptoed across the beams for a simpler way to climb back down. From the corner of her eye, she spotted Thenalious, who'd conquered the roof and stood grinning at her.

"Nowhere to go now, eh?" he teased. "I thought women were supposed to be as brave and strong as us. Yet here you are, running away."

Raegna gritted her teeth and faced him. Her heart pulsed behind her mouth. "And I thought Haven would be harder to find. Yet here we are, burning it to the ground."

Thenalious chuckled before his eyes lit up. "I thought you looked familiar. The rotten cunt that cut me in Judr. Let's get this over with. I'll kill you, and we can part ways from there."

"Thenalious!" Bai's voice cried over the sound of the battle below. The two of them turned to find him hauling himself over the roof, using his ax embedded in the wood. His gold irises blazed, reflecting the sun's rays. "Touch her and you lose your throat!"

"Fan alive, Grizzly." Thenalious gave an irritated sigh. "You truly don't know how to give up. I thought you didn't favor women."

"No more games," Bai snarled and ripped the ax from the roof. "Leave her and fight me."

Thenalious laughed. "Better yet, I never thought you'd choose such a fat cow for a wife. But you didn't choose. Just shows how badly your mother wanted to get rid of you. Any village cunt would do."

Bai lunged and swung his ax for a killing blow. Thenalious dodged, stepping out of the way. Stretching his sword out, he attempted to cut Bai, who hooked his ax around the blade instead.

Panting, Raegna dropped to one knee. The pain in her thigh stretched down her leg, and blood dampened her pants. She bit her lip and watched the two men fight. Where could she place herself to help?

Bai wouldn't be able to withstand the battle forever. Something kept Thenalious going despite all odds. Though Bai had his fury, it might not be enough. Raegna stood and rushed toward them.

Shouting, she moved to strike Thenalious from behind. He turned and countered her sword, shoving her back. Raegna yelped and caught herself. Before Thenalious could do anything more, Bai swung his ax as he turned, grazing the blade edge across Thenalious' shoulders.

Crying out, Thenalious turned on Bai and attacked in a fury of blows. In better conditions, Bai would have no problem parrying every last one of them. But he staggered with each clash of Thenalious' sword.

Raegna got to her feet, preparing herself for another assault from behind, then Thenalious twisted Bai's ax from his hand.

The ax clattered and tipped off the roof. Raegna's breath caught in her throat as Bai stumbled. Thenalious threw a punch with the hilt of his sword into the side of Bai's face. Bai would have dropped had Thenalious not wrapped his hand around his throat and pulled him up.

"Stop!" Raegna couldn't move. If she did, Thenalious would surely kill Bai. "Stop, please! Don't hurt him!"

"Hm, there's something oddly familiar about this," Thenalious hummed. "What happened last time? Oh, yes."

The sword snaked through Bai's right side like he was made of nothing. He jerked and cried out through gritted teeth.

"*Bai!*" Raegna screamed.

Thenalious discarded him. Bai dropped and rolled, but caught hold of the roof. Teeth bared as his face strained to keep from falling over the edge, one hand clawing the wood and the other pressed to his new wound. If Thenalious knew, he didn't care. He turned on Raegna, and her leg gave out from under her.

"Funny, he spoke of you as if there was no love between you," Thenalious purred. "Yet you mourn for him, as I'm sure you mourned your little brat."

Raegna's fist wrapped around her sword's hilt as her sobs racked her.

"It's a wonder you haven't killed me yet," he went on, "or at least taken the task more seriously than this. Especially since I am the one who slit her throat. Aren't you such a strong, brave, and *cunning* woman?"

Adabelle. Raegna's heart clogged her airway.

"The little blonde one your husband fought to protect. Pretty thing she was, but not with her throat open. That cut wasn't even the best part. Do you want to know what the best part was, *m'lady*?"

Raegna's body shook as tears spilled over her eyelids. She could breathe again, but her lungs screeched at the dry, cold air. She glared into Thenalious' blood-framed eyes.

A wicked grin crossed his face. "The best part was the sound of your adoring husband's mourning wail. Just as helpless and worthless as your little girl's life."

Releasing a scream, Raegna shot up and raised her sword to drive it through his heart. Thenalious threw it off course, and the two clashed with each other. Raegna rammed the blade at his waist. Thenalious curved to avoid the bite, but the edge grazed him, leaving a bloodied tear in his shirt.

Thenalious roared and struck her again, but Raegna parried and shoved him. Bai grunted and rolled onto his back behind Thenalious' feet. Raegna drove him close to Bai, but Thenalious kicked and took one of her feet from her, forcing her backward. She cried out and fell flat on her back, her head smacking the roof. Darkness edged her vision, but she fought through it, staring up at him.

Thenalious stood over her and raised his blade above her chest. "Join the rest of your precious little family, woman."

Raegna took a deep breath, bracing for the pain as she used her bad leg to hook a foot around Thenalious' ankle. He wobbled but fell back despite his efforts. As he did, Raegna wrenched them both sideways and sliced her sword up into his shoulder.

Thenalious shouted, and she pushed him back with the rest of her strength, driving the blade through his back. He snatched her collar, and she flew forward with him, both of them tilting over Bai and the roof edge.

"Raegna!" Beneath them, Bai lunged and wrapped his arms around her. His motion forced her back, his shoulder under her chest. Thenalious' grip slipped from her shirt. Raegna lost hold of her hilt.

Her sword remained in Thenalious' shoulder as he disappeared over the roof. Raegna gaped before she and Bai landed in a heap over each other. Bai's arms still wrapped around her waist; Raegna's fingers bunched in his hair. They panted, eyes wide on each other. The only thing that snapped Raegna from her trance was Bai's paling face.

"Bai." Raegna released him and sat up. Blood streamed down his side, adding to the horrific cut down his torso. She clamped her hand over the gash. Her heart sank with her palm into the wound. "You idiot. Now look at you."

Bai stared up at the pale blue sky, his gold eyes dulling. "Raegna ... Did we ... did he fall?"

"Shut up. Don't talk. We have to get you down from here."

"Raegna."

"What did I just say?" Raegna's bloodied fingers fumbled over her tunic as she wrenched it and the undershirt over her head. Kneeling over him with only the binding around her breasts to combat the cold air, she wadded the tunic and stuffed his wound. The undershirt could serve him soon. "Save your breath. I need to get you down from here."

Bai grunted and drew shaking breaths. "Raegna."

"Gaea, you're insufferable," she growled. "Can you not shut up for one moment? Even with your life at stake? Do as I say for once in your life."

A short huff emitted from his lips. "Yes, wife."

Raegna studied the roof and the edge, her leg pulsing and blood ruining her pants at the thigh. She couldn't carry him. Couldn't even be a crutch for him. Not on the climb down.

When she glanced at his face, Raegna gasped at how white he was. How his eyelids lowered. "Bai. Stay awake. You must stay awake."

"Ada. We did ... we did it. For Ada."

Tears sprang to Raegna's eyes, and her throat closed as she searched for a way off the roof. "Gaea, forgive my selfishness. I'll not let you see her yet."

"Raegna."

When she peeked at him, his eyes were closed.

She gritted her teeth and patted his cheek. "Bai. Stay awake, Bai. Stay awake."

Was his chest even moving? With trembling hands, Raegna rested a palm at its base. His skin against hers was an odd feeling, especially with blood in between. If he was breathing, it was light. "Bai. Bai, you must wake up."

What would jolt him awake? Raegna crawled closer and winced as she raised him onto her lap. One hand remained on his gash, and the other cradled his head. "Bai. Please wake up. You have to wake up. You can't leave."

She watched his face, waiting for the crooked smirk and the gold eyes. All his sharp features remained still, his face turned toward her arm. "Bai, please. You can't go. I can't lose—I can't lose you, too."

When he didn't move, a sob escaped her throat, and she pressed her forehead to his. "Please, Bai. Don't leave. Don't leave me, Bai."

"Shield-Priestess."

Tears rolled down Raegna's cheeks as she looked over her shoulder. Thekla grunted as she reached the roof and swung a leg over. Before she could get another word out, Raegna choked on a cry. "Get a healer. Please, he needs a healer."

Thekla crouched over them and assessed Bai's wound. With deft hands, she worked, removing Raegna's blood-soaked shirt and pulling vials and bandages from the pouches at her hip. She cleaned the wound with whatever the vials contained and dressed it. "Never go into a battle without a healer's kit." Then she nodded to Raegna's undershirt. "Put something on, Shield-Priestess. You're shivering."

Was it the cold or losing Bai? Raegna trembled as she put the undershirt back on. Snowflakes drifted between them, and Thekla's breath steamed as she wrapped a bandage around Bai's waist with Raegna to prop him up. "That'll do for now. Wait here, and we'll see if we can't lower you both down."

"Thekla—"

"It'll be all right." The warrior was already climbing from the roof. "Keep him stable and talk to him. I'll get help."

She was gone as quickly as she'd arrived. Raegna might have wondered how she knew to check the roof, but her attention turned back to Bai. Cradling him, she waited and watched his chest rise slowly. A raven called twice overhead as Raegna leaned over him.

"Stay. Please stay."

CHAPTER 35

BAI

Between consciousness and darkness, Bai remembered lying beside Raegna and not much else. Nothing existed but the darkness until pain stabbed his side. Bai woke to Raegna kneeling beside his cot and a healer on the other side. Thekla held him down at the shoulders. "Steady, man."

"Bai." Raegna's eyes lit up. "Thank Gaea."

Her voice came wavering and worn. Bai looked up at her. Wisps of hair floated out of her braids. Smudges of grime and blood spotted her bronze-tinted skin. Her dark-brown eyes were soft, her brow upturned as she gave a faint smile of assurance.

Beside Thekla, a healer focused on his side, running a needle through him to mend his wound. Bai cursed when the pain wedged through him with the needle's point. Thekla kept him pinned, and he drove his attention to their surroundings.

Tent canvas covered the large space where a few other warriors lay on cots, tended by their friends or healers. Another woman carried a friend in, aiding her like a crutch. Bai winced at another stab, and with his sharp breath, his entire torso stung. The length from chest to belly had a long cut from nearly being skinned alive.

"Thenalious," Bai growled.

Raegna's eyes shifted from brown to black. "In custody."

Then Bai frowned. "Custody? Didn't you push him off the roof? After you ran him through?"

"Fan is hard to kill," Thekla grunted. "Rest assured, the fall disabled him, and though we all wanted the Shield-Priestess' sword to remain within him, Gittan begrudgingly had a healer treat the wound under supervision. She thought it best that the man meet his punishment in Stadt."

Bai's jaw clenched, and the needle didn't matter anymore. "Maybe I'll just kill him on the way."

"Not when Gittan has him under guard." When the healer finished, Thekla rose and nudged his shoulder. "I promise he can't hurt anyone with so many of us and no use of his legs."

She rose and went to help someone else. The healer, a middle-aged woman with black hair edged with gray, stood over Bai and looked at him sternly. "Try not to move too much. Shield-Priestess, if he complains about pain, he'll have to suffer. There isn't enough fern to save everyone. I prefer to give it to those who need it most."

With that, the healer left them. Bai snorted. "Lovely, isn't she?"

Raegna smiled. "Men often complain when they are ailed. But you're no such man."

"I've been worse," Bai admitted. "Where are the others?"

Raegna squirmed before she answered. "I've seen Gittan. She was helping the children and Hadwin out of the great house. I assume they are treating Asmund. I hope. I've been here with you."

"I'm all right now if you want to see for yourself." The worry in her eyes was too much as it was.

Raegna shook her head. "No. I couldn't leave you here."

"Sure you could. Just stand up and let your feet take you."

Her smile returned. "I too got stitched up." She reached down and picked up a wooden crutch, twisting it in her hand. "But I'll heal. Standing up and walking should be minimal for a while."

She placed the crutch back beneath her and straightened with her hands in her lap. Bai took her in without meaning to. Such a long way she had come from reluctant wife to Shield-Priestess. It seemed like a lifetime ago he'd returned home to her glare over her shoulder before the fireplace. Now she watched over him with worry and a gentle uncertainty, as if she wasn't sure how to tend to him—or if she should. He had seen that look on her face when she cared for Adabelle. The very need to mother him brimming within, but fear holding her back.

Before Bai could say anything, Raegna broke the silence between them. "I almost lost you. I'm not sure I could leave you here even if I were able."

The words were simple and would be beautiful if things were different between them. If they were completely different people. "I'm all right."

Raegna gazed at the floor before glancing back at him. "Well. Just do not frighten me like that again. I forbid it."

Bai grinned. "Yes, wife."

***

Wherever they kept Thenalious, he was out of sight as Gittan intended. The army surrounded him while a few of her best warriors guarded him up close. Spare those he harmed the visage of a monster.

Better spare the monster from me. Bai leaned against the wall inside a wagon while supplies piled around him. Knowing the snake was nearby and breathing sent Bai's blood boiling. His bristling ceased when Raegna appeared, limping with her crutch, around the back of the wagon.

With a couple warriors behind her, Raegna grunted as she propped her good leg on the wagon edge. The other warriors hoisted her, and Bai offered his hand. Once she'd gained her balance, Raegna took it and hauled in beside him. After a few labored breaths, she thanked the warriors, who continued to pack.

"Nearly time," she told him.

"Thank Gaea."

Asmund stepped around the corner, wincing as he held his side. Bai marveled at him, covered in cuts and bruises and still climbing into the wagon himself. "There you are. Look who was brash and stupid now."

"Still you," Asmund grunted as he rested on the other side of Raegna.

"Are you all right, my friend?" she asked.

"I will be, priestess."

Children's voices rose in the wagon beside theirs. A babe's cry echoed through the trees as one of the mothers tried to hush them. It took two wagons to fit the women and one for the children. The reunion between mothers and children had not been what most expected, but knowing the circumstances, Bai couldn't blame them. Only two women chose the children's wagon. Hadwin joined them, his tawny head above most of his company. Maura curled at his side, and Cadoc's dark hair was just visible over the wagon walls.

Bai's heart sank. "We'll have to check in on him."

Raegna followed his gaze. "Hadwin? Yes. I can't imagine what's going through his mind now."

Watching his friend, Bai recalled the evening before Syden was attacked, walking home after a day in the fields with Hadwin, as always. They were two completely different men then. Men who couldn't have known where fate or Gaea would take them. Steeling himself, Bai slipped off the wagon and hobbled toward Hadwin's, ignoring Raegna's soft call after him.

Bai rounded to Hadwin and tapped his shoulder. He and Maura glanced back at him, and Hadwin rearranged himself to view Bai better. He gave a faint smile with tired, puffy eyes that glistened. "Hello."

"Hello." Bai leaned against the wagon and lifted his bad leg. "I wanted to check in. Haven't spoken to you properly since ... well, this morning."

Hadwin blinked. "Was it only?"

Bai nodded. "I know we have a long way until we reach Stadt. When we get there, you'll want to spend time with Naleem. But I wondered if I could ask you something."

Hadwin's brow raised, stretching the scar along the bridge of his nose.

"Do you still want to go fishing?" Bai asked. "Vakkar Hold has some good ponds. I'd love to show you."

Hadwin's brown eyes darted all over Bai's face before they halted in understanding. Biting his lip, Hadwin drew a wavering breath. "Yes. Of course. But not everyone we expected will come."

Bai knocked on the wagon before he turned. "Don't worry. They will."

Getting back in his seat was harder than the first time. Raegna gave him her hand and pulled him in. She leaned closer when he settled. "What did you say?"

"Before all this, we planned a fishing day," Bai answered. "When we get back, we'll worry about it more. I'm sure you can come if you would like."

Raegna's mouth quirked. "Maybe. In the spring. Here."

She lifted his wrist and produced his ring from a shirt pocket. Bai let out an amused huff and held his hand steady as she fitted the ring on his finger. Raegna dropped his hand as quickly as she had plucked it. "Don't lose that. It's expensive."

Bai smirked. "Yes, wife."

Commands echoed over the riders and wagons before theirs lurched forward. The wheels churned over hard ground, and the party proceeded in a line. Haven shrank behind them, mostly ash and blackened tents. The great house and barn remained for the forest to consume. Warriors collected all the bodies they could find to lift so Gaea could see to their fate. Others scouted ahead in search of deserters.

"They won't hurt anyone again," Bai murmured.

Raegna nodded and placed her fingers over his on the wagon floor. With his gaze fixed on the place they'd fought so hard to destroy, Bai turned his palm up so his fingertips met hers. Raegna retracted to clasp her hand around his.

Epilogue

Raegna

B Y WINTER, STADT FINALLY came into view. That morning, heavy snowfall fluttered overhead, and a few voices lifted at the head of the party. Raegna raised her gaze.

The silhouette of the stone walls encircling the city's rooftops could be seen through the snow. Several relieved breaths lifted as steam into the air. Raegna sighed and pulled the layers of furs around her shoulders and belly, which had grown a little during their journey. She glanced at Bai, who rode beside her, his shoulders much broader with the coat and furs that covered him.

Bai returned her look, gifting her a smirk with tired gold eyes. Upon their return to the palace, they would enjoy many things, but a real bed might be the most exciting. Thinking of that, Raegna smiled back.

Most of the army had disappeared along the road. Mercenaries who had the Queen's coin in their purses took off with or without goodbyes. Only Thekla and a few others remained to see the survivors of Haven safely behind the walls of Stadt. They took shifts guarding the cage that contained Thenalious—shackled and unkempt. Though they kept him a distance from the party, Raegna refused to let his presence loom and plague her thoughts.

Everyone else either rode horseback or were gathered in the back of a wagon. Asmund steered his horse behind Bai and Raegna for most of the journey. Hadwin rode with Cadoc in front of him and Maura beside them. Gittan took the lead with the few Maidens, but often visited among the party to check on everyone's well-being, especially that of Haven's survivors.

The once captive women and children huddled between two different wagons, along with the injured who hadn't been left with Banu and Jora in Judr.

With a thick blanket of snow on the ground and more coming down, Udstodt had become a silent husk of a town just before the city gates. Stadt still bustled with other riders, wagons, and carriages that had to make a path for the large group. Many eyes stared at the iron cage that took up the rear and the motionless form within it.

Gittan moved through the square, and Vakkar Hold's gates opened to her. She raised a hand to the royal warriors in the tower above. Raegna's heart quickened as the doors slowly pulled back to reveal the courtyard beyond. A beautiful wintry landscape had crystallized in the time they'd been gone. The cobblestones had all but disappeared under the glittering powder, which would be trampled by the horses within a few hours.

The group entered just as courtiers trickled out from the palace doors, shoving on coats and cloaks. Raegna and the others kept their eyes out for one in particular who would stand out from the rest as not a born nobleman.

Naleem came out to the courtyard just ahead of King Jerrick and his grooms, stopping dead at the edge of the snow. Raegna's heart broke that he couldn't see his family right away—he might think they had not survived, locking eyes with Gittan and expecting her to deliver the sad news.

But there was no way he could imagine that for a moment longer, not when Cadoc's shrill voice disturbed the calm snow. "*Papa!*"

Cadoc leaped down from the saddle, landing in the powder below. He took off toward his father as fast as his little legs could carry him. "Papa, Papa, Papa!"

A sob left Raegna's throat, and she chewed her lip to keep it from quivering. Naleem broke into a sprint toward him. The two met halfway as Naleem scooped Cadoc up, falling to his knees in the snow. He held him tight. From a distance, his weeping and Cadoc's resounded through the drifting snowflakes.

Hadwin slipped from his horse and ran to them. Wrapping them both in a hug, he pressed his forehead to Naleem's, and the two brothers held each other there. Naleem only pulled away to cover Cadoc's face in a million kisses.

Raegna dismounted with Bai and Asmund and stood alongside the others to watch the family reunite. Joy bloomed through her chest, knowing Pinar was watching from Heimelle. The last of her family had survived and could live happily again. Her last child could be safe from any harm within the walls of Vakkar Hold.

Raegna caved within, and a pressure pushed behind her throat as she wished Adabelle could have had the same fate.

Weary, she leaned against Bai, who took her in with an arm over her shoulder, draping her in his cloak and furs. Such a gesture would have been unthinkable just two seasons ago, but Raegna welcomed it as it stabilized her and reminded her she was not the only one who wanted to embrace her lost child again. Though Adabelle was surely with them—just as Pinar was—watching her parents fight and draw close to each other.

The iron cage creaked along the ground on the other side of the courtyard, past the reunion. Raegna frowned as she spotted Thenalious glowering through the bars, a ghost of his former self. Though she prayed Naleem would not see him, his gaze lifted and followed the cage. He gripped his son and brother tighter. Fortunately, Gittan dismounted and stepped forth, tearing Naleem's attention from the cage.

The Commander smiled down at them as Naleem stared back up at her.

"I've made you a promise, haven't I?" she said.

"You have," he said, his voice shaking. "Thank you. All of you, thank you."

Turning her head closer to Bai to hide her tears, Raegna nodded with the others. Gittan moved to help the two brothers to their feet. "Come. Let's get this little one close to a fire. Let's get *all* of these little ones warm inside."

Naleem held Cadoc and carried him to the palace. Hadwin stuck close with Maura behind him. One by one, the women and their sons piled out of the wagons. Asmund went to help the warriors and Maidens with the supplies, leaving Bai and Raegna behind.

Bai squeezed her shoulder under his cloak. "That means you too, you softy."

Raegna brushed tears from her eyes. "I don't know what you mean."

He nodded toward her belly and guided her forward. "*This* little one needs a warm fire. You need to rest. You and I both."

"Hm. Yes, husband."

Galaenian Glossary

A-B

Abela – Royal secretary in Vakkar Hold.

Adabelle – Raegna and Bai's daughter.

Ailbhe (ALE-beh) – Sachi and Sigmund's first daughter.

Alv (AHlv) – Matriarch of Syden.

Ase (AH-seh) – Matriarch of Judr.

Asmund – Iida's husband.

Audin (AH-din) – Reynold's son.

Awevi (AH-wehv-ee) – A large country across the sea with desert, grasslands, and jungles. Home to Awevi people.

Bai (BYE) – Raegna's husband.

Banu (BAH-noo) – Healer of Judr.

C-E

Cadoc – Pinar and Naleem's youngest son.

Dagfinn – Lady Abela's companion.

Dakarai (DAH-kah-rye) – Pinar and Naleem's oldest son.

Drengr (DRAIN-ger) – Haven's healer.

Edric – Duchess Elmba and Duke Ioan's eldest son, Signi and Vig's brother.

Elmba – Duchess of Galaenia, Ioan's wife.

Else (EHl-seh) – Talia's daughter.

Eluf (AE-loof) – Haven's butcher.

Estrid (EH-stread) – Pinar and Naleem's oldest daughter.

F-G

Fan — The Evil One and overlord of Helved.

Farah – A Haven captive.

Felik – Raegna's father, Jaleesa's husband.

Femke (FEHm-keh) – Viona's second sister.

Fritjof (Frit-yoff) – A farmer in Haven.

Fotr (FOH-ter) – A Haven boy.

Gaea (GAY-ah) – The high goddess or All-Mother, creator of Jorde.

Gael (GAYl) – Oberon's son.

Galaenia (GAH-lay-nee-ah) – The country of the four realms: Ostern, Sorelle, Vesten, and Norden.

Gittan (GEE-tahn) – Commander of the Maidens.

Gunilla (GOO-nilla) – A sell-sword.

H-I

Hadwin – Naleem's brother.

Heimelle (HIE-mehl) – The paradise afterlife, heaven.

Helved (HEHl-vehd) – The underworld.

Hilde (Hil-deh) – Elmba's carriage driver.

Hol Rekke (HOHL REH-keh) – A village in Norden.

Iida (EE-dah) – Viona's youngest sister, Asmund's wife.

Inge (EEN-geh) – Councilwoman in Galaenia's High Council.

Ioan (EE-oh-an) – Duke of Galaenia, Elmba's husband.

J-K

Jaleesa (YAH-lee-sah) – Raegna's mother.

Jerrick (YEHR-ick) – King of Galaenia, Kjerstin's husband.

Jora (YOH-rah) – Warrior of Judr.

Jorde (YOHr-deh) – The world, the planet.

Judr (YOO-der) – A village in Sorelle, east of Syden.

Kaja (KAH-jah) – Thekla's daughter.

Kaliq (KAH-leek) – A country across the sea, north of Awevi, with deserts and forests.

Kili (Kee-lee) – A Haven boy.

Kjerstin (KYEHR-stihn) – Queen of Galaenia, Jerrick's wife.

Kunto (KOON-toh) – Awevi Ambassador.

Laefold (LAY-fold) – Homeland to Galaenian ancestors, left behind after an ice age and famine.

M-O

Maura (MAHR-ah) – A Haven captive.

Mork Skov – The dark mountain, believed to be Fan's domain.

Nalani (NAH-lah-nea) – Pinar and Naleem's youngest daughter.

Naleem – Hadwin's brother. Pinar's husband.

Norden – Galaenia's northern realm.

Oberon (OH-behr-ohn) – Councilman of Haven.

Olena (OH-lay-nah) – Raegna's servant.

Ostern (OH-stern) – Galaenia's eastern realm.

P-R

Palungt (PAH-lung-t) – A large country across the sea, north east of Kaliq, with great mountain ranges, jungles, and forests.

Pinar (PEA-nahr) – Naleem's wife.

Raegna (RAYg-nah) – Shield-Priestess, Bai's wife.

Reynold – Councilman of Haven.

S

Sachi (SAH-ckea) – Daughter of Gaea, Mother and goddess of women.

Sassa – Former Queen of Galaenia, Kjerstin's mother.

Sigmund – A god, Sachi's husband.

Signi (SEEG-nee) – Duchess Elmba and Duke Ioan's second twin daughter, Vig's twin.

Sorelle – The southern realm of Galaenia.

Stadt (Sh-tAH-dt) – The capital of Galaenia.

Surlied (SOOr-leed) – A village in Ostern, north-east of Judr.

Syden (SUU-dehn) – A village in Sorelle, west of Judr.

T-U

Talia – A Haven captive.

Thenalious (THEH-nah-lee-us) – The Leader of Haven.

Thekla – Rogue sell-sword.

Turid (TOO-read) – Woman of Judr, works for Matriarch Viona.

Udstodt (OO-sh-tahdt) – Impoverished village outside Stadt's walls.

Ugo (OO-goh) – Reynold's son.

V-Z

Vakkar Hold (VAH-kahr Hold) – The royal palace.

Vera – Elma's lady.

Vesten – Galaenia's western realm.

Vig (Veeg) – Duchess Elmba and Duke Ioan's first twin daughter, Signi's twin.

Vihn – Oberon's son.

Vildr (VIL-der) – Savage, a derogatory term for the Wa'Ni.

Viona (VEA-oh-nah) – Former Matriarch of Judr.

Wa'Ni (WAH-nee) – One People, Galaenian natives.

Wyn (Win or WUUn) – Councilman of Haven.

ACKNOWLEDGEMENTS

My family and friends deserve a special thanks for believing in me and celebrating *The Maiden's Husband* release. Without your encouragement, I don't know how well or quickly *Haven's Warrior* would have published. Especially my brother, Joe, who endures my story and idea dumps. You've helped clear things up as well as any beta reader and continue to do so with future books.

Thank you so much to my beta readers, even those who weren't mentioned. The time you took to read means everything and your feedback is priceless. Jade Nioma, Zaylynn Flynn, Megan Turner, and Hannah Greer are all such busy authors and humans. I am so grateful for the time you spent with the story and characters.

My editors are the best anyone could ask for. Thank you Samantha for your immeasurable knack for story and characters, and your teachings through the sensitivity read that has helped me grow as an author and a human. Claire, you're an amazing editor with your keen eye and speedy communication. All authors deserve your devotion and thorough work. Pamela, thank you for taking me on and also being so communicative and helpful through the proofread process.

A lot of changes happened in the publication of this book, and still it sped through the process like it was nothing. With that, I want to also thank myself for sticking to it and grinding out my dream. Wherever life takes me or *The Matriarch Chronicles*, I know this is meant to happen and roadblocks are only temporary. Keep following your heart and trust it!

Thank you, Reader.

Thank you for spending time with Raegna, Bai, and the gang! We hope you enjoyed their tale so far, and would greatly appreciate your review if you feel so inclined to leave one on your favorite platform like Goodreads or Amazon.

Explore Galaenia on my newsletter with prequel e-books, coloring pages, and updates!
https://morganrchristensen.wixsite.com/author

You can also find me on social media!
Tiktok: @morganchristensen_author
Instagram: @morgan_christensen_author

CREDITS

The Matriarch Chronicles: Haven's Warrior **was created and written by**

Morgan Christensen

Beta Read by

Jade Nioma, Author of *The Frayed Threads Series*

Zaylann Flynn and Megan Turner, Authors of *To Be Damned: Arawn's Realm*

Hannah Greer, Short Story Author

Development Edit and Sensitivity Read by

Samantha Kassè

Copy and Line Edit by

Claire Cronshaw, Cherry Edits

Proofread by

PS Livingstone

Map of Galaenia by

Alyssa Hurlbert

Cover Art by
MiblArt

Software and Tools
Novelpad, Microsoft Word, Atticus, Adobe Acrobat

Morgan Christensen began writing *The Matriarch Chronicles* in high school, discovering a passion for gritty legends filled with rigid emotions and bloody swords.

In the heat of Arizona, she can be found bingeing shows like *The Last Kingdom* and *Vikings* while snuggling her cat, Freyja. By day, she works as an office admin to stock her bookshelves and plan her next visit to the Renaissance Fair.